A born and bred Yorkshireman with a love of country, history and architecture, Simon spends most of his rare free time travelling around ancient sites, writing, researching the ancient world and reading voraciously.

Following an arcane and eclectic career path that wound through everything from sheep to Microsoft networks and from paint to car sales, Simon wrote Marius' Mules. Now, with in excess of twenty novels under his belt, Simon writes full time. He lives with his wife and children and a menagerie of animals in rural North Yorkshire.

COMMODUS

SIMON TURNEY

ORION

First published in Great Britain in 2019 by Orion Books,
an imprint of The Orion Publishing Group Ltd
Carmelite House, 50 Victoria Embankment
London EC4Y 0DZ

An Hachette UK company

1 3 5 7 9 10 8 6 4 2

A CIP catalogue record for this book is
available from the British Library.

ISBN (Hardback) 978 1 4746 0736 0
ISBN (Export Trade Paperback) 978 1 4746 0737 7
ISBN (Ebook) 978 1 4746 0739 1

Typeset by Input Data Services Ltd, Somerset

Printed and bound in Great Britain by Clays Ltd, Elcograf S.p.A.

MIX
Paper from
responsible sources
FSC® C104740

www.orionbooks.co.uk

To the memory of my grandfather, Doug, who introduced
me to Roman history at the age of six with the line:
'Agricola . . . first cousin of Coca-Cola.'

DAMNATIO MEMORIAE

Upon the death of an emperor, it became practice for the senate to confer apotheosis upon his name, granting him divine status and a cult of his own. If the emperor had been despised, however, the senate could choose the precise opposite and vilify rather than deify him – damnatio memoriae *(a modern term) would occur. Without hesitation or ceremony, the emperor's name was erased from all public inscriptions (a process known as* abolitio nominis*), his image would be scratched from frescoes, his statues smashed. Sometimes even coins bearing his image would be defaced. The damned emperor was not only denied an ascent to heaven, but wiped from history. Such was the fate of the wicked, the unpopular or the unfortunate.*

A medallion struck in the reign of Commodus, 192AD, showing on the reverse the figure of Hercules, clutching his club and the body of the Nemean lion.

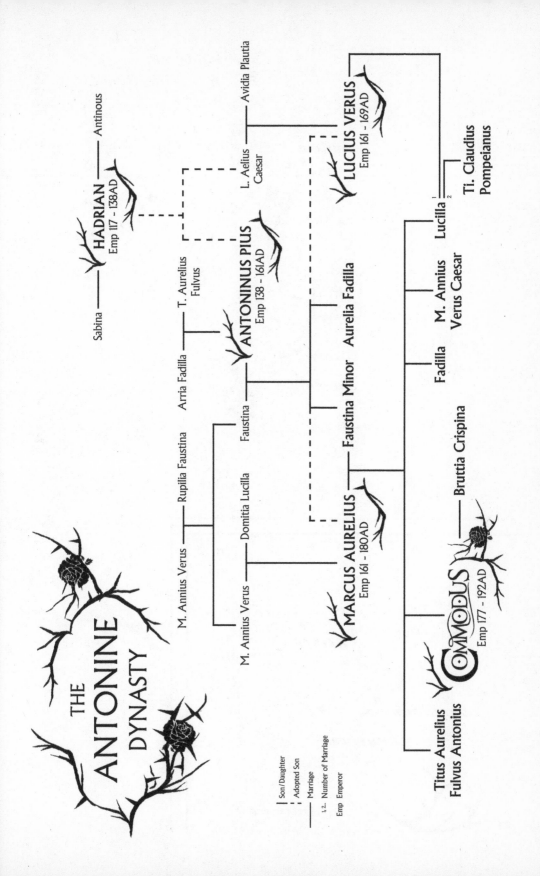

THE ANTONINE DYNASTY

Sabina —— **HADRIAN** —— Antinous
Emp 117 – 138AD

Arria Fadilla —— T. Aurelius Fulvus

ANTONINUS PIUS
Emp 138 – 161AD

M. Annius Verus —— Rupilia Faustina

Faustina

Domitia Lucilla —— M. Annius Verus

M. Annius Verus

MARCUS AURELIUS
Emp 161 – 180AD

Faustina Minor

Aurelia Fadilla

L. Aelius Caesar —— Avidia Plautia

LUCIUS VERUS
Emp 161 – 169AD

Lucilla
Ti. Claudius Pompeianus

Fadilla

M. Annius Verus Caesar

Bruttia Crispina

COMMODUS
Emp 177 – 192AD

Titus Aurelius Fulvus Antonius

Key:
—— Son/Daughter
- - - Adopted Son
| Marriage
₁,₂ Number of Marriage
Emp Emperor

GAUL

Vindobona
Carnuntum

DACIA

Aquileia
Tergeste

Sirmium

MOESIA

Pisae

I T A L I A

ILLYRICUM

Serdica

THR

SARDINIA

Capri

Surrentum

Heracleum

AFRICA

Athens

Centum
Cellae

Via Cassia

R. Tiber

Tibur

Villa of Verus

ROME

Praeneste

Ostia

Quintilii Villa

Laurentium

Via Appia

Lanuvium

GOWER

Antium

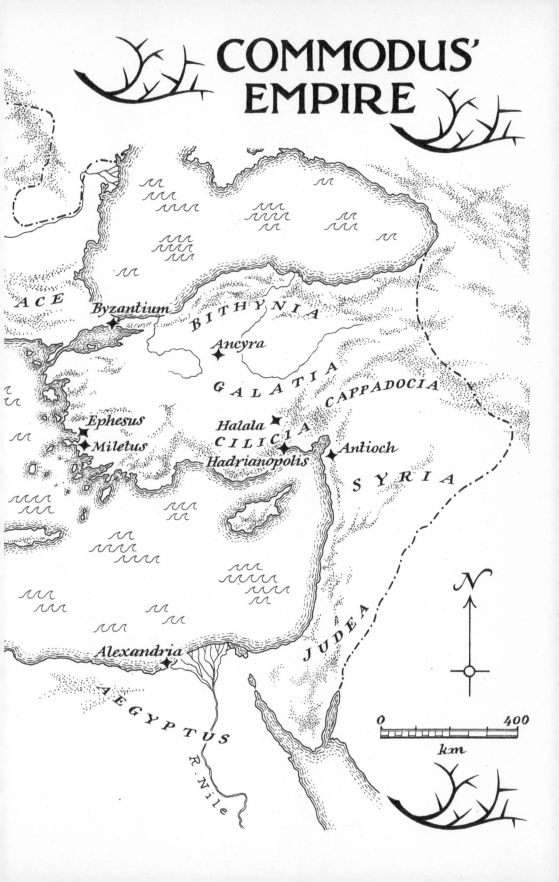

*I*t begins with a rush of water; terrifying and murderous. It also ends with a rush of water. A choking, deadly torrent, cloying and dreadful. In my life I witnessed a fire that tore through the dry houses of Rome, destroying all we held dear and leaving an age of death and ash. I survived a plague that made husks of strong men, ravaged the army more than any barbarian horde, and robbed Rome of its beating heart: its people. But, for me, nothing matches those killing waves at both beginning and end.

I am Marcia, daughter of Marcia Aurelia Sabinianus, freedwoman seamstress of the emperor Lucius Verus.

I was a bad Christian.

I would have been a great empress.

Rome, the Palatine, AD 193

*L*ucius, my dearest man, I beg leave of you now. I have known you for so many years, and you, despite our closeness in many ways, both kind and cruel, have never really known me. That we might be together has only ever been a fiction based upon mutual survival, for you know that in my heart I only ever loved one man, and despite your goodness, it was never you.

Our world has collapsed through our own devices and the chaos to which we gave birth comes to consume us. You know my faith as I know yours. I must away to my confession with a priest and pursue some kind of absolution for all that I have done, and you must seek peace in your own way before they come for us. Please consider this tale my confession to you, and my explanation for how we come to this dreadful place.

I pray that my leaving you will save you the blade's edge. You were the best of us, and you do not deserve what is coming.

Dearest heart, go peacefully into the next world and pray that I can still be saved.

Marcia

PART ONE

BORN TO THE PURPLE

'Never while I live, shall you slay these sons of Heracles'

– Euripides: Heracles, trans. Coleridge, 1938

I

FALLING INTO THE GRAVE

Rome, AD 162

I was having a nightmare, though I cannot for the life of me remember remotely what it was about. I lay wrapped in my blankets on the upper floor of our house in the Velabrum when it all began.

I was just four years old, though my mother thought me beyond my years already. It was the year of the consuls Rusticus and Plautius in the reign of the new glorious emperors Marcus Aurelius and Lucius Verus. It was spring, a strangely warm and sultry night despite days of storms over the nearby hills.

The Velabrum – my home – is a shallow valley between Rome's greatest hills, the Capitoline and the Palatine, stretching from the forum to the river. In times past it had been a swamp, liable to flooding, but then the *cloaca maxima*, the great sewer of Rome, was built to drain the area. The cloaca runs beneath the Velabrum, its route defined by the valley's course. But this was still not enough to prevent flooding and disaster and so, under the lunatic Nero, the ground level had been raised. Now, only the heaviest of floods would cross the bank.

In a region where most other buildings were wooden *insulae* reaching seven storeys towards the clouds, filled with the crying poor, beggars and thieves, our house was a small oasis of quality. A brick residence only two storeys high, level with the structures below the palace on the slopes of the Palatine. I remember it well, though that was the last year we lived there, for that spring the banks could not contain great Father Tiber.

A crash cut through the shroud of Morpheus and forced me to the waking world. My room was as dark as it ever got, for even in the middle of the night torches and lamps keep the shadows at bay in much of the city.

I sat up sharply, shivering, confused. For a moment I could not work out whether the noise had been part of my dream or from somewhere in the true world, but a second crash clarified the issue. It sounded as though the world was collapsing into Hades below and I stood, shaking. I thought there was silence then, but it was a trick of the senses. The crashes had been so loud they had driven out all other sound for precious moments. Then it came flooding back in. Screams, bellows, thunderous rumbles and bangs. I could tell the lights in the Velabrum were going out as the shade of gold leaching through the tatty window hangings grew weaker.

Slowly, with infinite trepidation, as though by delaying my investigation I could hold back events, I padded across the cold tiles to my window. I know. Tatty curtains and cold tiles. It sounds so poor now, but back then we were considered lucky – wealthy, even – for the emperor paid for our house and a small stipend allowed us to furnish it. I approached the window, and the noise outside crescendoed as the glow dimmed further. There was a roaring like that of some great, titanic subterranean lion. I flinched as I reached the curtains, hardly daring to touch them for fear of what lay behind.

I pulled them aside and stared into the vaults of Tartarus.

A great wave was washing along the Velabrum from the direction of the river. Even by what light remained, which was not much, I could see the flotsam borne by the crest of the wave. Not the remains of some broken vessel, though, but of homes and shops; splintered wood and chunks of plaster that had been swept along. Only the stronger buildings were surviving the crashing wave and the hungry waters it brought, and only the torches and lamps on the upper floors of those buildings continued to burn and illuminate the horror.

I watched in shock as the heavy stone covers over the drains down into the cloaca maxima were thrown into the air as though they were made of terracotta by a torrent of water that was simply too vast to be contained by the ancient watercourse.

Screams came from the men and women, children and grey-hairs who were caught up by the wave, until they were dashed against walls or pulled down beneath the churning water. The living struggled and splashed, the dead bobbed and eddied, carried here from parts of the city upstream. I took everything in within mere heartbeats.

Horror. Destruction. A fluid grave that claimed more lives with each passing moment. The spell of shock shattered at the sound of my name. Mother. She burst through the door into my room, wild-eyed and dishevelled, her short-sleeved woollen tunic unbelted and askew.

'Marcia, come. Hurry.'

Cold and unemotional as always, but I needed no further bidding. Mother's word was law, her will iron, had been ever since her husband passed, or so people said. I had never known Marcus Aurelius Sabinianus Euhodius, my father, though his reputation still carried weight among those who had the slight-est concern for freedfolk. Hurriedly straightening her hair, as though to be seen in such a state even during the midst of a disaster might somehow lower her standing, Mother dashed back out of the room into the dim stairway and descended. I paused at the top, watching her hurrying down, hastily knotting the belt around her waist. Down seemed like a bad idea. Down: towards the churning waters that so terrified me. But Mother was already there and lighting a lamp. By its golden glow I saw that the water had not begun to consume the chamber in ear-nest. Not yet, at least.

I hurried down and my heart rose into my throat. Water was already rushing beneath the door from the shop out front, and I could see it pouring over the windowsills beneath the bottom edge of the shutters, which were held fast with iron bars. An ominous creak made me realise the horrible truth. The door and the twin window shutters were all that was holding back the flood. The waters were even now pressing against the shutters, threatening to burst them. If the bars gave way, this room would fill like a bath in moments.

I stood rooted to the spot in panic. Why were we here? We were trapped downstairs, waiting until the water came in and stole our breath.

Then I realised in astonishment why we were here. Mother was rooting through the chests and racks in her little workshop, which doubled as our living area. In her arms she was gathering neatly folded garments of linen and wool and even silk, some threaded with gold, some dyed purple. Garments fit for a king. Fit for an emperor. Garments *belonging* to an emperor.

'Hurry, girl. Take these.'

She thrust an armful of tunics at me and I took them, still in disbelief that we were rescuing her work in the face of impending doom.

'Mama . . .'

'Go upstairs. I will follow.'

I watched her for a moment, still frozen there.

'God will preserve us. Go, child.'

I ran. Leaving my mother in that makeshift cistern, I ran up the stairs, hugging those priceless garments to my chest as though they contained all my mother's love.

At the top I stood, heaving in breaths, watching the empty patch of the workshop visible from the top of the stairs in that golden glow. There was no sign of Mother, though occasionally her shadow moved into view, distorted by the rising waters that had consumed the floor. There was half a foot of lapping filth down there now, but I knew how much dangerous water was being held back from the room by just thin layers of wood and iron bars.

I stood clutching those precious bundles, willing Mother to hurry. Then there was an ominous creak, a splintering and a crash. The flood filled the ground floor of the house in an instant, a surging torrent of foaming darkness battering the walls and rushing up the staircase towards me. I felt my heart pounding, my eyes wide with shock.

Mother . . . I couldn't see her.

Perhaps I should have turned and run; the water was rising towards my rooted feet so fast. But my mother was not there. The waters surged and churned, rising and consuming all, and Mother was gone.

I couldn't leave her . . .

Suddenly a sodden bundle of clothes broke the surface of the water, a hand clutching each side. Step by step, Mother gradually appeared on the staircase, her face fixed on the vital imperial garments she was trying to keep above the filthy flood.

I nearly dropped my own burden to throw my arms around my dripping mother but had no such chance; she bustled past me, urging me on.

'I wish we lived in one of the tall insulae,' I said in wavering tones, eyeing the water already rolling out onto the landing.

'No, you do not, Marcia,' Mother replied, and I turned to follow her gaze. Through her bedroom window we had a clear view of one of the neighbouring wooden apartment blocks leaning further and further out towards the Capitol, its foundations undermined by the floodwater. It seemed to reach an impossible angle, where only God was keeping it erect, and then it fell. I realised, as I listened to the almighty crash, and the screams, that it was one of those blocks falling that had dragged me from sleep in the first place. I watched figures dropping from the upper floors as it fell, perhaps thrown clear, perhaps leaping in the hope that the water would break their fall. They were doomed. The doomed, falling into the grave.

'Pray, Marcia. Pray for deliverance.'

Mother placed her pile of garments on top of a chest and dropped to her knees, hands clasped to her breast, invoking the blessed Saviour to come to our aid. I was four: I believed what I was told to believe. And yet even then, despite having been raised in the faith of our Lord the resurrected Christ by my mother, in the face of all this I found that my faith was simply not strong enough. God would surely be of little use when faced with what I had witnessed outside. Still, driven by faith in my mother as much as faith in the Lord, I added my garments to her pile, dropped to my knees and pleaded.

Perhaps God spoke to Mother then, though I heard only screams and watery destruction, for she suddenly snapped out of her prayer, eyes full of purpose, and pointed to the rickety wooden ladder at the back of the landing.

'The roof, Marcia.'

The water level was at the upper floor already and ankle-deep, and I needed little urging. I rose, unclasped my hands and followed her to the ladder.

'I will go first,' she said. I watched in astonishment as she gathered a pile of the garments and began to struggle up the rungs with one hand, clinging to her livelihood with the other. With a little effort she unbolted the wooden hatch at the top and clambered out onto the roof. I saw her struggle with her footing for a moment, and worried that she would fall. But then she steadied herself, placed her precious burden on the tiles and made sure it was secure, then motioned for me to climb. I did so, my own pile of garments forgotten. I clambered up the rungs and flopped out onto the roof, exhausted. Mother wasted no time in descending to retrieve my abandoned cargo.

The pitch of the roof was low, just enough to allow rainwater to gather in the runnel and drop into the barrel below, which was now, ironically, under several feet of water. Like other houses of this height, a hatch had been built into the roof to allow access, for the impoverished inhabitants of the towering insulae to each side had a habit of discarding their waste from high windows without care for whose roof it might coat. A broom stood close to the ladder for sweeping unmentionable mess from the tiles.

She re-emerged with the rest of the garments, muttering her thanks to Heaven for having been preserved from the floodwater with the best of her stock relatively intact. I was a touch sceptical. We may have escaped the rippling cistern of our ground floor, but we were now trapped on a roof. My gaze took in the full extent of the disaster around us. Perhaps half the towering insulae in our street had gone, turned to sediment and kindling in the churning waters below. It would have been impossible to tell where the usual course of the river was but for the circular roof of the Temple of Hercules Victor just protruding from the surface, which I knew to stand close to the riverbank. Each street was now a river in itself. Lights continued to burn in the high places, but the low-lying regions were lost, just a world of screams and shouts.

'Woman!'

We turned. It was odd and perhaps even arrogant that we both assumed the voice to be aimed at us, but somehow it seemed naturally to be the case, for every other voice in Rome was raised in a scream while this one was deep, authoritative and, above all, calm.

A man stood upon the roof of the small bathhouse that nestled into the lower slope of the Palatine hill just behind our house. He was clad in the uniform of the urban cohorts, the branch of the military whose role was suppression of crime and preservation of public safety. Even as I realised that his uniform was dry, and that he must therefore have come from higher ground, I saw others of his unit clambering onto the roof

13

behind him. Though the water had reached the upper floor of our house, parts of the bath complex still touched dry land thanks to the slope of the great hill.

'Are you Marcia Aurelia Sabinianus?' the man shouted.

My mother, her brow furrowed, nodded. Then, realising the man probably couldn't see her nodding, she cleared her throat and responded, 'I am she.'

'We are here to rescue you. Are you injured?'

I stared in surprise. A party of the urban cohorts had come through all this for *my mother*?

'No. I am fine.'

'The emperor wishes you brought to the palace.'

The *emperor?* The emperor, in the midst of all this chaos, had thought to preserve my mother?

'How do we escape?' Mother asked, staring at the water all around.

'Here.'

Four of the men were now skittering carefully across the tiles carrying a plank towards us. I realised then where they had come from. The far wall of the baths was being renovated. We'd heard the workmen at their task for several days, their scaffolding enclosing one end of the complex as they hammered and shouted and sang. The men of the cohort had climbed the scaffolding and brought a plank across the roof. I had not realised how close we were to the bathhouse until I saw them slide the timber out and slip it into place across the narrow street. It only just reached. One heavy shake would likely send it and anything on it down into the roiling waters below, but somehow the dangers seemed unimportant. The plank represented unexpected hope amid disaster.

'Come across. We'll anchor it as best we can from this end, but come slowly and carefully and hold tight as you go.'

'My daughter goes first,' Mother said with an air of command.

'All right. Come on.'

Mother gestured for me to cross. Heart pounding, skin prickling with nerves at the danger all around, I slid slowly down the roof towards the plank and grabbed tight to the tiles as I neared the edge. I rose to my feet and clambered onto the end of the shaky board. I began to cross.

'Hands and knees, girl,' the soldier bellowed. 'Hands and knees.'

Though I was fairly sure I could cross safely enough on foot, I did as I was told and dropped to my knees, crawling slowly along the plank. It wobbled and bowed precariously even under my negligible weight. If I can identify three moments that are responsible for my lifelong fear of water, they are looking out of my window at the Tiber rushing towards me, fearing Mother pulled down into the depths, and staring at the boiling currents below that plank. I was shaking like a leaf as I reached the far end and was lifted bodily to safety by muscular, hairy, tattooed arms. The men of the urban cohorts held me safe as Mother took her turn. She gathered up the huge pile of garments and placed them on the plank, least important at the bottom, and began to edge them forward.

'Leave the clothes!' the Guard officer shouted in disbelief.

'These are the emperor's tunics. Only he can give that command.'

And so, my mother edged slowly forward across the plank, nudging the pile carefully ahead of her with each shuffling movement. When she lost control for a moment and the top tunic of deep aquamarine and silver thread fluttered down into the water, her cry of anguish was akin to any of the screams of loss that night. Indeed, she fought so hard to regain control of the pile of clothes that she almost fell herself.

A few heartbeats later she was across. With the staunch support of the men of the cohort, we crossed the roof and began to clamber down the scaffolding ladders. One of the soldiers tried to take my mother's burden, but she would not relinquish her precious clothing even to him and hugged it jealously to her all the way across and down that nerve-wracking escape. I had never felt more grateful than when we stood on the solid ground of the Palatine slope, not far above the level of the floodwaters. Following Mother's example and earning us both black looks of disapproval from the soldiers all the way up the steps of the Scalae Caci, I prayed to God on high for the safety and peace of the city and its inhabitants.

We were led past the temples of the Great Mother, of Victory, of Apollo Palatinus, and into the sprawling complex of the imperial palace. As we passed each of those three great pagan shrines, Mother made the sign of the cross and gave them a wide berth, as though their idolatry could somehow infect her. For my part, I was always more than a little fascinated with the gods of our fellow Romans and the ways they kept. They seemed to me, for all their oddness, exotic and enticing. I could never have said as much to Mother, mind, or I would have spent my life in penance.

Finally, we were shown into the palace itself and escorted by the eight men of the urban cohorts past pairs of Praetorian guardsmen and through corridors of rich marble and bright paint, lorded over by busts of great men both past and present. Busts that I reached out and brushed my fingers across the base of whenever Mother's eyes were not upon me. I suppose for most plebs it would have been a thing of astonishment to see such gilded luxury. I, of course, had been in the palace as often as any senator or general, attending to the apparel-based needs of the emperor, yet I still felt awed by the imperial grandeur. At the end of one corridor, my trailing fingers found an unstable plinth, and the bust of some ancient dignitary rocked gently. Mother said nothing. She did not need to. Her glare carried more warning than any words and I kept my arms by my sides from then on.

Eventually we reached a wide chamber painted with images of fantastic creatures and *trompe l'œil* that made it appear as though we were standing in some grand park overlooking a lake of swans. We were motioned to silence as we entered, and instantly I understood why.

The two emperors stood over a desk spread with a map of the city, accompanied by men in togas and men in armour. Two senior officers, almost certainly the Praetorian prefect and the commander of the urban cohorts, several men of high public office, even a priest.

The great Marcus Aurelius, successor of Divine Antoninus and Emperor of Rome now for over a year, was involved in deep, muttered debate with one of the politicians, while my mother's master, the co-emperor and adoptive brother of Aurelius, was busily haranguing the Praetorian prefect.

'I want him found and brought here to answer to me, personally,' Lucius Verus snapped.

Aurelius turned, drawn from his low conversation by the shout, his intelligent grey eyes filled with worry.

'Who?'

'Statius Priscus,' Verus replied. 'That fool.'

Aurelius nodded his understanding and turned back to his own conversation, leaving Lucius Verus to snap at the officer. 'It is Priscus' responsibility to monitor the river and waterworks and to be aware of any issues. A good *curator alvei Tiberis* should know everything, right down to how many fish there are in the river. He should certainly damn well know when there's a flood coming that's big enough to drown a city!'

'Majesty, we have checked the curator's house and the major-domo says he is at his villa on the slope of Mount Lepinus near Norba.'

'*What?*'

'Apparently there was some drainage issue he needed to attend to.'

17

The emperor's face passed through a number of expressions before settling into a deep, purpling anger.

'Have him sent for with all haste and we shall see how humorous he thinks the irony of attending to his estate's drainage while the city slowly drowns in his absence. Hot irons might await.'

The emperor Aurelius, never a man to miss a thing, cast a warning glance at his brother. Verus subsided under that wise gaze. 'Send for him,' the elder brother amended, 'but when the crisis is over. For now, we need to concentrate all our efforts on making sure the dry regions remain secure. The waters could rise still, and whole regions remain at risk. Have every man available barricading the streets –' he reached over the map and jabbed repeatedly with his finger '– here, here, here and here.'

Lucius Verus turned, his temper cooled, and his gaze fell upon us, standing unobtrusive and quiet in the corner of the room. 'Marcia? Good, they found you in time. I hear horror stories of what is happening in the Velabrum. No matter how many times we institute building codes, landlords cut corners and the result is invariably disaster. At least you are not hurt, nor your charming daughter.'

Mother bowed respectfully, which proved to be difficult with an armful of folded clothes. Verus realised then what she was holding.

'Jove above and all his bolts of thunder, tell me you did not risk life and limb to bring me my tunics?'

My mother had the grace to look a little sheepish, but Verus chuckled with genuine fondness. His hair and beard gleamed gold in the lamplight and his face creased naturally into a smile. 'Marcia, you are a marvel.' He gestured to the officer beside us. 'Libo, I want these ladies taken care of.' He winked at my mother before addressing the officer once more. 'I go to war with Parthia within the month, and it does not do for an emperor to face the King of Kings in drab apparel.' He chuckled again.

'Quarter them with the boys for now, until we can settle more permanent arrangements.'

And that was our dismissal. We were escorted from the imperial presence, but even that brief moment had given me an insight into the world of the emperors. These were no Neronian fools or Tiberian tyrants. These men were the best of *Romanitas*, leading their people and caring for the city as the *patres patriae* – the fathers of Rome. Despite everything we had endured and witnessed that night, I left sure that Rome was in good hands.

I lost track of our route through the palace. We had been many times before to attend upon Verus, but often in the same areas: either the public halls or his private apartments. The part of the palace to which we were now led, with windows that looked out upon the great Circus Maximus, was reserved for the imperial family and important guests and relations. Somewhere along the line, the soldiers passed us off to a palace functionary who escorted us the rest of the way, full of his own self-importance and without thought to ask my mother whether he could help her with her burden as the soldiers had done.

Our journey's end turned out to be a room painted with exotic wildlife, lit low with oil lamps. Two babes lay in beds that cost more than our entire household. Both were blond, with curly hair, and both, despite the lateness of the hour, were awake. One was crying while the other examined the cot's headboard with an air of fascination. I know now that they were both less than a year old at the time. A nurse with a ruddy complexion and the figure of a well-fed matron was busy trying to settle the crying child.

'This,' announced our escort, 'is Hestia. She will take care of you for now. When I have had rooms made ready, I will send for you.'

I could see my mother's eyes narrow at being spoken to in

this manner by a slave, no matter how powerful that slave might think he was. Hestia turned to us and I liked her immediately. Her face radiated sympathy and friendliness. She opened her mouth to speak but, as she did so, another door swung open without warning and a woman entered. I recognised the empress Faustina. Hers was a face I had seen in the palace from time to time, though I had never been personally involved with her. She was tall and elegant, even as heavily pregnant as she clearly was now. She carried her unborn child with her arms beneath the bump supporting some of the weight, and her face reflected her discomfort. My mother said later that she thought that, after bearing twelve children, the empress should be more at ease than she was.

'Hestia, would you kindly keep the boys quiet?' the empress snapped. 'I find it difficult enough drifting to sleep in perfect quiet, let alone with Lucius howling like that.'

'That is Titus, Majesty,' Hestia said with a smile.

'Whichever,' snorted the empress, 'kindly keep him from howling like some monster from Aenean legend.' She turned and noticed us for the first time. 'You, you're Verus' woman, yes?' Mother bowed her confirmation. 'Good,' the empress added. 'Your girl looks quiet and sensible. Let her look after them.'

And with that, the empress Faustina spun and departed, the door clunking shut behind her.

'Don't mind her,' Hestia said indulgently once the empress was out of earshot. 'She's actually very nice, but this pregnancy tests her and makes her waspish.'

Mother smiled and put down her pile of garments. 'These are the empress' twins?' she asked, peering at the two boys.

'They are,' nodded Hestia, and my eyes widened at the realisation. I was in the presence of the twin sons of Marcus Aurelius, heirs to the empire. Titus Aurelius Fulvus and Lucius Aurelius Commodus. Titus Fulvus, then, was the one wailing and noisy,

20

while Lucius Commodus was the one playing with the carving. Presumably both boys had been calmly asleep earlier, but the noise outside was loud even from here as the city panicked and died, ravaged by Father Tiber.

I took a hesitant step towards the beds, glancing across at the nurse, but I had no need to fear. I had been commanded by the empress, after all. Hestia gave me a nod and a flash of her smile, and I crossed to the beds. As I reached the foot and stood between them, the strangest thing happened. Both children turned to look at me and the hair at the nape of my neck rose, my skin turning to gooseflesh. Fulvus stopped crying in an instant and peered at me as though inspecting the very soul of which I was made. Commodus looked deep into my eyes, gave a strange little giggle, and then wet himself.

Hestia laughed. 'They like you. I rarely see them so calm, even with the empress. *Particularly* with the empress,' she corrected conspiratorially, with a sly glance flicked at the door.

I smiled and brushed off the strange encounter, but something in my soul seemed to have clicked into place.

I was in the house of the emperors, and there I would stay.

II

INTELLIGENCE AND PRECOCIOUSNESS

Rome, AD 164

I turned seven in the autumn of the year of the consuls Macrinus and Celsus, with no fuss, and a tunic of fine green cotton and a grey braided belt made by my mother for a gift, which complemented my dark hair and olive skin. It had been common for the emperor, or more likely one of his lackeys, to give Mother and I gifts on our birthdays, being his freedwomen, but the glorious Lucius Verus was no longer in Rome to do so.

The emperor had gone east with the legions to deal with that ageless enemy, Parthia, and his absence left us without a patron, at risk from the less scrupulous powers of the court. In the month the jovial and attentive Verus had stayed in Rome following that dreadful flood, I had been introduced to his ice-white, haughty betrothed, Lucilla, the cold and humourless daughter of Marcus Aurelius and so now niece and wife-to-be at once to Verus, and had found her to be unfriendly, ambitious, and as bitter as an artichoke. I would say it was because she did not like Christians, which clearly she did not, but since her snobbery and snide attitude seemed to be aimed at the world as a whole I did not feel particularly victimised. All I knew was that the prospect of acquiring the empress Lucilla as a mistress was not an encouraging one. When Verus took her east with him, we were not the only figures in the court to heave a sigh of relief. He left her partway, at Ephesus, safely out of reach of the war but close enough for marriage when she reached the appropriate age in a few short months. Despite her absence, the loss of our patron left a bitter taste.

The senior emperor, Marcus Aurelius, remained in Rome, where he became embroiled in a legal dispute over the will of his aunt Vibia Matidia. He argued his case as ably as any of the great advocates, yet it was taking its toll on the great man in private, making him look weary and wan as he trod the halls of the Palatine.

My life had changed utterly following the flood. At the behest of the emperor, Mother and I had been given apartments in the palace close to those of the imperial family and, despite Verus' absence, my mother received many lucrative commissions from other members of the imperial family, including the emperor himself. And while Mother worked her magic, I was enrolled with tutors. It was a little strange for me, since I was essentially dropped into the imperial children's educational path at their level, which, bearing in mind the difference in our ages – the twins were now three and I was seven – felt like a waste of time. Looking back, it was, in truth, far from unusual. The two emperors had, after all, been educated together, their age gap sufficient that Aurelius had been a man in the eyes of Rome while Verus still bore the *bulla* of childhood. The lessons were basic at first. Wooden blocks bearing letters to assemble words, brightly painted abacuses. Simple learning. The tutors seemed to feel that my sex made me somehow lesser than the boys and, as such, that I would work well at their level. I will admit to having no command of letters until I began at the palace, but I understood numbers, and knew a great deal for my age. I was bright, and a quick learner. So, might I add, were Fulvus and Commodus, though they were given to bouts of foolishness, especially Commodus.

Their intelligence, and mine, was made evident when the

tutor, who had been assigned for a full four months to teach us basic numeracy, reported to the emperor after just two that we had learned his entire syllabus. This was despite the fact that almost any time the man bent over my work with his back turned to them, Commodus would nudge Fulvus and the pair would disappear into the next room to hide or wrestle. I longed to join them, and might have been welcome, but it had been made abundantly clear to me by Mother that my place was to be deferential and behave myself, for I was only the daughter of a freedwoman, after all. So, every time they disappeared and the tutor turned back to address his class, he would find only me sitting there, looking forlorn and, naturally, a little guilty.

The boys would be chided for their impish behaviour, but all that did was encourage them to do it more often. Little planning appeared to be involved in their games, each seeming almost instinctively to know what the other twin was thinking.

Despite their close sibling bond, though, I had quickly come to see the differences between them. Fulvus was slightly less robust than his brother, with a perpetual look of faraway thoughtfulness and an insatiable desire to investigate and learn things. When he was not being taught basic counting – Lord, but I was bored with counting to ten, I had been counting to a hundred for years – Fulvus would find something that interested him and take it apart to see what was inside. Commodus was every bit as bright, but he was not so applied. He seemed bored by his lessons, despite natural ability, preferring to be moving and laughing, always active and testing himself physically.

More than once I found the pair of them playing some frightening game that would have horrified their parents: waddling along a wall-top, or taking turns jumping across an open grate. Once or twice I was present at the inception of such larks, and it always seemed to be Commodus that urged Fulvus on, daring him to ever more worrying heights.

Being around those boys made me happy in a way I had

never experienced before coming to the palace. And, oddly, my being held back in line with their education, when added to their intelligence and precociousness, somewhat evened the ground between us, despite the age gap.

The world moved on, with news arriving from Verus' campaigns in the east periodically. It seemed that he was thoroughly chastising the Parthians, and the tales of his deeds were exciting to us children, relayed like heroic stories of old. I remember hearing the name Panthea on more than one occasion, though the conversations always drifted to silence as we children appeared. I knew nothing of it at the time, but Verus had, apparently, taken a beautiful and exotic mistress in Antioch, while his brittle and unpleasant betrothed waited and fumed in Ephesus.

Life changed notably on one day that winter as Saturnalia approached. It was the first step on the stairs down to Hades. The empress Faustina was closeted away in her rooms with her new baby boy, Annius, who, at only a year and a half, was too young for tutors and too young to play with his brothers. Our lessons were done for the day and we left the library where we had been trapped into learning our vowels with a dusty, dry old man who seemed slightly less animated than the marble busts that watched over our lessons. The world was a crisp white. Not snow, sadly, for children of any age wish eternally for snow. No, this was that hard white that leaves a million glittering diamonds on the surface of the stones and makes every step a treacherous one. I had been granted some warm, fleece-lined shoes that had previously belonged to another child of the palace, and I was grateful for them as we passed the vast banquet hall and emerged into the chilly air of the Flavian Peristyle. The fountain in the great octagonal pool was not working, and hadn't been for the past week. A pipe somewhere had been ruined by the cold, according to a slave I asked, and the flow had stopped until investigations and repairs had been carried out. Consequently, the pool was now little more than an eight-sided sheet of ice, contained by low walls.

Fulvus, Commodus and I spent a few entertaining moments on the ice, skittering this way and that, sliding and laughing guiltily, knowing that we would be for it when one of the adults found us. But, with just a little testing, we had decided that the ice was thick enough to cast aside all worries. Likely it was solid right down to the base, for it was only a foot deep. Still, this being a garden frequented by many, we decided to move on and find our entertainment elsewhere, especially as slaves and functionaries began to wander around the edge beneath the colonnades.

We spent some time playing hide and find among the small rooms and colonnades at the western edge of the palace, where the windows overlooked that great forbidding temple of Apollo. On my third turn as the finder, I located Fulvus easily enough – a blond head badly concealed among shaped miniature laurel bushes – but it took us so long then to find Commodus that I had become quite frantic by the time I heard his familiar giggle echoing up from an open doorway. Fighting my fear of the dark stairs beyond, remembering that awful night of the flood and the terror that my mother had drowned, I gingerly descended to find Commodus alone at the foot of the steps in some dank chamber.

'Too slow, Em,' he giggled, using the shortened name the boys had saddled me with. 'I win. Your turn!'

I argued against it. After that nightmare stair into damp darkness, I really didn't want to play on, but Commodus was insistent. Returning once more into the cold light with relief, I reluctantly agreed, and hurried off to find a hiding place. And it was there that I first discovered magic.

Fulvus and Commodus were scurrying through the various halls and rooms, calling my name and laughing, shouting to one another and drawing very disapproving looks from a dozen slaves whose station forbade them from chastising young princes. I had found what I thought to be an excellent hiding place. I didn't even know what the room was for, it was little more than a cubbyhole beside a doorway. I hunched down in the darkness, making myself small and unobtrusive, and that is why the girl never noticed me. She was a kitchen slave, judging by the aroma she carried with her. She moved furtively, which immediately piqued my interest, and I watched with fascination as she checked to make sure she was not being observed. She then dropped to her knees in the doorway and rummaged in a woollen pouch at her belt before producing something oddly shaped, a small roll of something black, pinned through the middle with a nail. She began muttering in little more than a whisper and it irked me that I couldn't quite make out what she was saying, but I did hear a name: Hekate. She then lifted a small iron grille in the floor and dropped the strange item down into the gloom.

I was rapt. Hekate was a name I was vaguely aware of, in that Mother had reeled it off among many others in a long list of demons we were to loathe and shun as followers of the true faith. The slave continued to kneel for a moment, murmuring, then replaced the grille.

'What was that?' I asked from the shadows. The slave girl leapt to her feet with a shriek, eyes wide, searching the shadows. Feeling a little guilty for the fright I'd given her, I emerged from the gloom. I was clearly no slave, but my clothes also marked me out as low-born, and her shoulders slumped as she relaxed a little.

'You gave me a turn there, Mistress,' she said.

'What was it?' I repeated. 'And who's Hekate? Is he a demon?'

She gave me a baffled look, as though I had asked her what yellow smells like. Finally, she looked this way and that conspiratorially, and hunched over again. 'I cursed a man. A bad man.

27

A man who will end me if I don't deal with him first.'

'You cursed him?' I had no idea what it meant, but it was clearly something forbidden even to pagans, and I was positive that my mother would be horrified at the notion.

'I asked that his skin slough off and he die an agonising death.'

'And this Hekate can do that? He *must* be a demon.'

'Hekate is a god*dess*, Mistress. The dark lady of Achaea. And I hope she can. I really do. Cretheus deserves nothing less than Tartarus.'

Just then I heard the boys approaching, laughing and calling my name. The scream had probably drawn them. The slave gave me a desperate, hopeful look. She could not just leave. I was a freedwoman and she a slave, and she could not go until dismissed. I took pity on her and waved her away, wishing I'd had time to quiz her more on the subject. I made a mental note of the name Hekate and planned to investigate further. If only I could read more than a few basic sentences, perhaps I could have used the library. I would have to be careful with my questions, for there was a very good chance that a word in the wrong ear would land me in trouble with Mother, or the slave in trouble with her masters.

Commodus and Fulvus found me easily, then, for I had little time to hide away again. We played twice more, then moved on. Outside the grand dining hall, flanking it on both sides, are beautiful nymphaea, elegant and architecturally magnificent shrines to the nymphs of the Palatine water supplies. They are oval basins perhaps twenty paces long and three feet deep, with a central core of brick and marble sporting delicate statues of the nymphs, a constant flow of water between them. This place was clearly fed by a different pipe from the fountain in the garden, for the water gushed clear and fast, splashing into the basin only to flow away beneath the ground, probably washing along that curse the slave had dropped in the doorway.

The nymphaeum is surrounded by a colonnade and, while the buildings around it rise two and three storeys, the narrow sacred space is open to the air and freezing cold. One end of the nymphaeum pool was iced over, the water from the fountain slopping down onto the ice, and the two boys immediately hurried over to it. I adopted the manner of a disapproving matron as they grabbed sticks from somewhere – I have never known from where boys acquire sticks to play with, but they seem to be able to do it at will, even indoors – and started to poke the ice with them, giggling.

I left them to it, my own attention once more on the slave girl, her strange, rolled-up curse and her Greek goddess of magic. I worked through everyone I knew well in the palace, discarding each name in turn as unwise to approach on the subject, and was beginning to become exasperated when my attention was pulled back to the present by a shout of alarm. I looked around and could see only Commodus. He was waving his stick, white-faced and wild-eyed and shouting incoherently.

I ran over and, as I did so, my heart caught in my throat as my eyes fell upon the shape of Fulvus thrashing in panic beneath the frozen surface of the pool. The foolish boy had fallen into the pool somehow and been pushed under the edge of the ice by the current. The water would be colder than I could imagine. Commodus was wailing, pointing at his brother, and I realised with a start that I was watching this dreadful tableau and doing nothing about it.

Taking a breath and fighting my dread of water, I vaulted over the lip of the basin where the water wasn't yet frozen and tried to grab Fulvus. He was still awake under the water, eyes wide and face almost blue. Somehow, he had slid further under the ice and I couldn't grasp him firmly enough to pull him out, my young fingers swiftly becoming almost unusably cold and his limbs hard to grasp. I began to hammer at the ice, hoping to break through, though achieving little more than splintering

29

thin shards from it and cutting myself on the sharp edges, my hands running with blood. I was too weak, and I was freezing, and there was little chance of me freeing Fulvus in time.

As I smashed at the ice, suddenly another figure was there with me. He was a slave in a ragged grey tunic, a little older than the boys, a little younger than I, yet his strength was surprising as he cracked and smashed the ice, bringing his whole body weight to bear. In moments, he reached Fulvus and hauled him clear as I climbed out, shivering. The prince's eyes were closed, and he had become still as the slave boy laid him carefully on the ground. His skin was blue-grey, and I felt a rising panic. Was he dead?

I held my hand above his mouth and nose and felt nothing.

'Hit his chest,' the slave boy said, urgently.

'What?'

'That's what they do with drownings. I've seen it. They hit the chest. Like this.'

And the slave began to pound rhythmically on Fulvus' chest. I stared in shock. Surely he was going to *break* the prince, not save him. The constant wailing of Commodus, who I knew instinctively had dared his brother to cross the ice and started this whole mess, blared out like a fanfare across the courtyard and was already bringing others, footsteps slapping across marble as they approached.

Fulvus awoke suddenly, a torrent of icy water bursting from his mouth as he rolled onto his side, and the slave, panting, stood back. The prince coughed and choked, shuddering and hugging himself as Commodus continued to wail, regardless of this change.

'Blankets,' I shouted. 'He needs to be warm. Blankets!' Despite the freezing air, and in a moment of what I can only call unexpected heroism, the slave pulled off his ragged tunic and wrapped it around the ice-cold prince, hugging him tight while he himself shuddered in the cold.

Adults were there a moment later, grabbing the prince and taking him away, with not a word for the slave who'd saved his life and who now stood naked, shivering and unnoticed. Commodus followed them, howling like a lost wolf cub, batting away all attempts to mollify him, the guilt at having almost killed his twin all-consuming.

And then, suddenly, I was almost alone.

Almost . . .

I turned to find the slave boy watching me curiously. He had disconcerting grey eyes, so pale that I could barely make out where they met the white, the pupils black pinholes. His face was swarthier even than mine, betraying an eastern origin, and he was narrow and reedy for all the strength he had displayed at the pool. But it was nothing physical about him that touched me, even those peculiar eyes. It was something indefinable about the way he stood, the way he looked at me. It made me uneasy, like watching a caged predator. He might be just a slave, but there was something about him, and I spotted it the first moment I set my eyes on him. Just as something had connected inside me at the sight of young Commodus, so a similar thing happened with the slave. He was handsome in an odd way, and he had proved his value by saving Fulvus even at the expense of his own well-being. Yet I couldn't find it in me to thank him.

His name was Cleander, and I shuddered as he walked away.

Night came and with it tension in the palace. Something was wrong with Fulvus. He yet lived, and was breathing once more, but his colour remained inhuman, and he did nothing but shiver and stare. I saw him twice that evening. Everyone was so busy that no one gave any thought to shooing away a palace child who happened to be in the room. Besides, everyone was so used to seeing me with the princes that finding me with Commodus near Fulvus' sickbed was no surprise. The emperor shuffled

31

aside all his work and worries that night to sit with his son, and Faustina, her face drawn and anxious, joined him.

When I retired to bed, I needed no urging from Mother to say my prayers. I knelt willingly, eagerly even, and asked God with every fragment of my soul to make Fulvus well again.

My relationship with the Lord did not improve. The next day, Fulvus had not recovered. New physicians were sent for from across the city. The best to be had, whether they be Roman, Jewish, Greek or even Aegyptian. They all said the same thing. He had not only technically drowned but had also suffered due to an extreme change of temperature. That he had been warmed and yet still not reacted as expected was not a good sign. The physicians would attend on him, but they recommended that the emperor and empress implore the gods, make appropriate sacrifices and, if at all possible, visit an important sanctuary of Aesculapius to seek his aid.

There being little chance of reaching a major cult centre of the healing god, the emperor and his entire entourage visited the sanctuary on the Tiber island that day, giving lavish offerings and seeking counsel and aid. I remained in the palace, of course. I was nowhere near important enough to be involved in such a visit. In the absence of Commodus, who I presumed was with his mother and father on the island, I stayed out of Fulvus' room, though I rarely strayed far from it. That afternoon I had been in the corridor outside and had moved to the end, where a wide window gave bright light, far enough away from the two Praetorian guards on the prince's door not to draw their attention, and I dropped to my knees and began to pray. Perhaps the Lord had not heard me last night due to all the noise and commotion in the palace?

I was so surprised at what happened next that I failed entirely to react. There I was on my knees, imploring God to save Fulvus, and suddenly I was shoved sharply sideways. I fell to the floor in shock and sprawled, wondering what was happening.

As my rolling eyes settled on a figure in the window's silvery light, they narrowed. The shape of Cleander the slave stood there with a haughty expression, lip curled and strange grey eyes unreadable.

'So this is *your* fault,' he said in quiet tones. I could think of no real response to such a ludicrous accusation, and simply stared at him. He pointed at me. 'You and your stupid Judean cult. I saved him, but you're killing him. The prince would be up and eating now if you sacrificed to the gods like a proper Roman.'

I was dumbfounded. A *proper* Roman? My mother had been brought from Greece, yes, but I had been born in the city to a freedwoman. I was a plebeian, but I was as Roman as they came. Cleander, on the other hand, had been brought over from Phrygia where they worship stranger gods than ever rose in Rome. A proper Roman? I hissed back at him. 'I ask God to *save* Fulvus.'

'Your god has no power here. And what do you sacrifice to him anyway? Words? Where's your incense? Where's the wine? The coin?'

I rose, anger beginning to get the best of me. It was the first time I can remember being truly furious. I was raised to be passive and understanding. To try and always resolve without conflict. But I tell you, had I a rock in my hand at that moment, I might well have stoved in his head.

'I'm supposed to turn my other cheek to you, ignore your violence and forgive you. And because I want to be a good Christian, I'll do that. I'll forgive you. But only this once.'

He made to push me again, but perhaps something in my expression stopped him. Certainly, he stepped back. I was a freedwoman of the emperor Lucius Verus, and he was a slave. I had allowed him to get away with pushing me over in anger, but I had warned him not to do so again. For my part, I meant every word. I would punch him in the eye if he tried again. For his part, I suspect he thought I meant I would report his behaviour to the major-domo, which would have seen him beaten at the very least. Whatever the case, he walked away. As he reached the door, he paused and turned.

'In the old days, they used to burn your sort.'

And then he was gone. I seethed, shaking, promising myself that one day I would settle that score. I received my second shock in a short space as Commodus emerged from the shadows near another door, confusion creasing his young, innocent face.

'What's a Criss-chen?' he asked, stumbling a little over the unfamiliar word.

Hmm. I thought lessons would be cancelled today, what with Fulvus bedridden, but it seemed I was to teach instead. I thought long and hard on the question as he watched me with those intelligent, searching eyes.

'We believe in only one God. He is the creator of all things and the world is made according to His plan.' I shrugged, trotting out the words I'd heard so many times. 'There's more to it, but that's the main thing.'

'Which god?'

I frowned in turn now. Mother had never actually named him. He was just God. My silence seemed to decide the boy, and he smiled.

'It'll be Jupiter. Or Saturn. No, Jupiter. Father's a god, you know?'

This was difficult territory. I was seven years old and no master theologian, but even I could see the narrow, difficult avenues *this* conversation was heading down. I tried to change the subject a little. 'It's the same god as the Jews have. Or so Mother says. I'm not sure how that is, but apparently it is.'

'When I grow up, *I'm* going to be a god,' Commodus said with a strange faraway look in his eye. 'Like Father, but not the same one. He's him. I'll be Hercules. I *like* Hercules.'

And suddenly he was off again. In his head, he was now the

34

Greek hero, completing trials and slaying foes. My theological crisis had been averted by the attention span of a three-year-old, and I could only thank him for that. But suddenly his eyes darkened again.

'Wish I was Aesculapius. Then I'd make Fulvus better. When will he be well?'

Lord, but this was a day for difficult conversations. His parents had explained to him that his twin brother might never be well, and that they were praying and sacrificing in every way they could, yet to Commodus it was never a question of *if* Fulvus would get better. Just when.

The month passed and Saturnalia came and went, though celebrated in a rather subdued manner in the palace. It made little difference to me. Mother would not allow me to celebrate that pagan ritual anyway, though I would often sneak out to watch what I could, and once I even caught sight of the red-painted Lord of Misrule being released to cause havoc.

The slave Cleander put in increasing appearances over the winter, whenever the adults were not watching, and always welcomed by Commodus. While I did not like him, especially since his tirade against me, I could hardly deny how important he became to Commodus, distracting him from his worry with games and humour. I had not the heart to try and stop him.

Januarius came and there was a little visible improvement in Fulvus, hope restored with the new year. The emperor made sure to visit the Tiber island at least once in every market cycle and gave such gifts to the god as might buy a kingdom somewhere. The physicians, though, were cagey. When consulted, despite the apparent improvement, they still sucked their teeth and refused to commit to the belief that he was on the mend.

Physicians know their craft. Despite having gained colour and a little activity, Fulvus died before Aprilis.

The loss hit me hard. Very hard. I had spent two happy years playing and learning alongside that extraordinary little prince and he was as close to me as any brother. The emperor and empress went about the business of state and managed to fit in the appropriate mourning time and ceremonies. Fulvus was to be elevated among the gods despite his youth. Looking back, I realise now how badly Aurelius and Faustina took the death, and it is a credit to them both just how thoroughly they continued to rule and administer, giving way to grief only in private. I was to be allowed neither the time nor the room to grieve in myself, for Commodus was there, and with the increase in activity around the imperial family now, Cleander was unable to play his part in keeping the prince happy.

The empire mourned. The imperial family mourned. And me? I supported the surviving prince, trying to fill the role that Cleander had created over the past month. I have heard it said that there is a link between twins that does not exist between other siblings, or indeed any other people. I suspect that when such a link is broken something fails inside. Certainly, Commodus changed the day Fulvus died. Something came over him then, something that never left.

I spent months with Commodus, and our parents not only allowed it, but actively encouraged it. He was troubled, and I seemed to be the only thing he clung to. I know that he could easily pass a day in lessons or social activities as though nothing untoward had occurred, but then suddenly he would suffer in the evenings. His mood would plunge, and he would become dour and untalkative. Once, even, I found him pulling out clumps of his glorious golden hair, leaving raw skin in patches. I did not know what to do, other than try to calm him and brush his luscious curls so that they covered the worst of the damage. Then, one day in late summer, I decided that, since no one else seemed to know how to deal with the distraught and unpredictable prince and they were all content to leave me consoling him, I would have to find a way to heal him myself. I found him in his room, staring at the floor.

'Why didn't I die?' he asked without looking up as I entered the room. I gently clicked the door closed behind me.

'Why *should* you have?'

'Nikandros is teaching me about halves,' he answered, seemingly at a tangent, but I knew him well enough to wait for the connection. It came directly, and when it did, it floored me. 'I'm half a person, Em, and Fulvus is the other half. When a man loses an arm or a leg, he dies. I losed *half* of me. Why am I still alive?'

I nodded. That explained the hair tearing in some warped way. 'Maybe God still has a plan for you.'

He gave me a look that made me regret bringing my faith into the subject.

I sighed and tried again. 'You still have a future. *More* than a future. You're the son of the emperor. No emperor's had a son since the Flavians. You know what that means? It means you will be the next emperor. The first boy born to the purple in a hundred years. That has to mean something. Your father needs you. The empire needs you.' I smiled weakly.

He slumped back. 'I'm . . . broken. Don't know how to get better.'

I shivered. He was not yet four years of age, and such words from his mouth as would make a philosopher marvel.

'Then let's find out. Together.'

And we did. The next morning, I found him still moping in the dark. The sun was out, and bees hummed, almost as much as the reek of the streets in the heat. But I had an idea.

'Come on,' I said, grabbing him and leaving no room for argument. I took him to the old stadium on the eastern side of the palace. In truth, it had probably never been used as a stadium and had always been a garden, but during the reign of Hadrian part of the garden had been turned into a bestiary, containing some of the exotic creatures that wide-travelled emperor had seen in their native countries. Most of the beasts had long since perished and had never been replaced by successive emperors, but there was one creature there that I knew Commodus loved. The lion was known as Maximus, named for the assassin who had put an end to hated Domitian, and he had been here more years than anyone could remember, yet still seemed virile and powerful.

As we crossed the marble chipping path and passed between well-tended flower beds towards that cage, I knew I had done something right. I caught Commodus' eye and there was a sparkle there that had been lacking these past few months. I had kindled something. He approached the cage and nodded.

'Why do we follow a silly bird?'

I chuckled. 'The eagle of Rome. It is noble. Powerful. Ancient.'

'It's just a bird,' he replied. 'Put it in the cage with Maximus and see. Rome shouldn't be a bird. It should be a lion.'

And that started it. Over the next few days we visited anything that sparked interest in the young prince. The change was noted by the emperor and his empress, and my mother was astonished when a gift of a whole bag of silver coins appeared in our apartment. With the emperor's permission, and an escort of Praetorians, slaves, lackeys and freedmen, of course, we visited the supplier of beasts for the arena and secured the purchase of a number of new exhibits for the Palatine.

And with every new beast we caged, I watched the boy's smile widen.

III

THE ERRANT PRINCE

Rome, AD 166

Another year passed in the palace. The emperor Marcus Aurelius continued to rule from the city itself, leading processions and rites and presiding over important matters of state, attending meetings of the senate and the like. Commodus seemed to have recovered somewhat from the shock of Fulvus' death, thanks in no small part to my efforts, I believe, and, though I am loath to admit it, also the efforts of Cleander when access was possible. Still, sometimes I would catch him with a distant, forlorn look. His odd obsession with Hercules continued, and he could sometimes be found carrying a makeshift club and wearing an old piece of drapery resembling a lion pelt. The emperor seemed to find this endearing, and perhaps he approved of his son's interest in so great a hero, for on his fourth birthday, his father commissioned a statue that now stood in the palace, depicting young Commodus as a childhood Hercules, battling serpents. In my head, the serpents were beginning to bear a marked resemblance to Cleander.

I did have another, more welcome, helper in keeping the prince grounded and lively, though. While I was now eight and Commodus nearing five, little Annius had grown into himself at a lively three, with his next birthday rapidly approaching. He was every bit the lively scamp his older brother had been, and the two of them had begun to form a definite bond in the

39

absence of Fulvus. It was not the same sort of bond the twins had shared, of course, but there was a closeness which, added to my own connection with the prince, began to stitch together the open wound of Fulvus' passing.

I must admit to a little jealousy on my part. The closeness that was growing between the brothers impinged on the connection I had with Commodus, and I found that I preferred his attentions all to myself – not an attractive trait in a person, I know, and I suppressed it as best I could and concealed it beneath a warm smile. It was not Annius' fault I felt that way, and the positive influence he had on his brother was undeniable. Still, it was an insight into myself that I was not particularly proud of.

The palace on that morning of the Ides of Aprilis was in turmoil. Rome seemed to be a whirlwind of events, and its beating heart on the Palatine even more so. With the birthday of the young prince approaching, the palace was being made ready and slaves and freedmen rushed this way and that in an organisational flurry. My mother was working flat out, even though she had been given permission to bring in another seamstress to help spread the workload, for finery was required for the celebration, as well as other, perhaps even more important, events.

Lucius Verus was on the way home. Couriers had brought the news a matter of days ago. The emperor had been victorious over the dreaded Parthians, as we all knew he must be, and he was coming home. His legions had been settled and veterans were flooding back west ahead of their glorious master, who travelled slowly, in state, visiting every important town on the way. One of the great burdens of empire is to be omnipresent, but even with two emperors, it was difficult. I was less thrilled to realise that this meant the ice-cold Lucilla would be returning to Rome alongside her husband, but, apparently, as well as marrying while in Ephesus on campaign, she had given birth and was bringing home a new princess of the Antonine dynasty.

Perhaps the baby would keep her busy and away from us all. There was talk that the emperor would have a triumph, and certainly there would be celebrations across the city.

But every coin has two sides, and the coin of Verus' success bore a reverse face of misery. A shadow was already falling across Rome for, in advance of the glorious emperor, his veterans brought back more than victory. From somewhere in the east, they brought sickness. As yet, Rome seemed to be enduring, but there were tales from Asia and from Greece, and even from other parts of Italia, that towns were being ravaged by a plague brought from Parthia. Not for the first time was I glad that we lived on the Palatine with its lofty heights and spacious gardens, high above the narrow, reeking streets where the disease would take hold soon enough.

There were days now when the boys and I did not share lessons. Officially it was in order to vary the subject according to the student, such that Commodus was now learning sentence structure using the translated works of Hesiod, while I was given tuition in household matters, like sewing, and Annius was dragged through his numbers and letters to catch us up. I wanted to sit through Commodus' lessons instead, for I needed precious little instruction in sewing, and household management bored me, but in my paltry free time I had discovered a love of reading already, even stuffy, dry Cicero.

Thus it was that one day I was sitting on a marble bench beneath a colonnade, alone. I had been given a project to sew that I could have done with my eyes shut. My tutors seemed to forget that my mother was a seamstress, and that I had been watching her sew since before I could say my own name. Annius was off in some dreary room somewhere learning to count, and I knew Commodus was being walked through the basics of ancient sentences by Nautius Costa, a master of language and a funny-looking man who reminded me of a stork.

So, I sat, and I sewed, and all was peaceful despite the

41

organisational flurries of the palace. Occasionally a freedman or slave would pass the time of day with me, and I would respond pleasantly and go on with my work. And then, suddenly, Commodus emerged from a passageway with a gleam of mischief in his eye: the sort he used to have when running off with Fulvus. I paused in my task.

'What are you up to?'

The prince grinned at me and scurried over, checking the peristyle to confirm we were alone. 'Hesiod's boring. C'mon.'

He grabbed my arm and hurried off towards another corridor and, flustered, I followed on. We threw ourselves into the shady passageway and Commodus stopped, still grinning, and put a finger to his lips to keep me silent. We turned and looked back across the gardens in time to see the ungainly, avian figure of Nautius Costa emerge from that same archway as the prince had done. The old man stopped and looked this way and that, grumbling to himself. Honestly, with his gangly form, tendency to bend sharply, and the avian aspect to his nose and eyes, he was so stork-like that I would not have been surprised had he stood there on one leg. He called 'Highness?' and began to circle around the colonnade, peering into doorways. Commodus chuckled very quietly, then ran away along the shady corridor, flat sandals slapping softly on the marble.

I followed him and a short while later we emerged into another garden and paused for breath. 'You will get into so much trouble,' I reminded the prince, but young Commodus really did not care.

'Costa is boring. Rhetoric's boring. Come on.'

And we were off again. Two further corridors and we burst out into sunshine once more. I had no idea why we were taking the somewhat circuitous route that we were, but the reason became clear when Commodus shouted Cleander's name. Across the garden, the slave was sweeping a balustraded area.

'Highness?'

'Come on.'

And now we were all scurrying through the palace, a slave and a plebeian in the wake of a prince who was exhibiting far less decorum than either of us. As we ran, Commodus ahead, leading us to some as yet unannounced destination, Cleander and I shared a look. Empires have clashed with less force than that which passed between our gazes, yet both of us kept silent. Ours was a private hatred, we did not share it with the prince.

We arrived at the stadium soon after, and Commodus hurried off to the ornamental garden at one end. Half a dozen slaves were at work clipping hedges and weeding flower beds. Some poor unfortunate was sawing lumps from something dead and pushing it between the bars of Maximus' cage at the far end, snatching back his hand hurriedly as the ageing lion's powerful jaws closed on the food. But Commodus' purpose today was not in the menagerie. As Cleander and I stood on the path, the young prince ducked behind a neatly tended hedge and reappeared carrying two wooden swords, the sort that soldiers train with, though reduced in size to suit a child. Where he had acquired the weapons and how he had managed to keep them safely hidden from the myriad gardeners, I could not say, but he seemed immensely proud of himself as he stepped back out.

I swallowed, imagining the vast amount of trouble for which we were headed thanks to Commodus skipping out of his lessons to have fun. I half expected him to hand me one of the swords and was struck by an odd mix of relief and disappointment when he did not. Instead, he held out one, hilt first, to Cleander. The slave boy stared at the weapon as though it were a cobra, rearing back to strike. Slaves do not touch weapons unless they are given them to clean or handed one and pushed out onto the sands of the arena to bleed for the crowd. If he grasped that sword and someone important saw him, he would almost certainly lose his arm, if not his head.

Commodus grinned. 'Go on.'

43

Gingerly, as though it were coated with something vile, Cleander took the sword by the pommel between sweating fingers. He still stared in horror at it.

'This is dangerous,' I breathed.

'And fun.' Commodus grinned. 'Take it, Cleander. No one cares.'

Not strictly true, yet with only garden slaves in sight no one would gainsay the young prince, so we were relatively safe for now. 'What if someone comes?' I whispered.

'You're lookout,' he said and pointed to the arcades above. I sighed. Wonderful. Commodus played games that would get us all punished and it was my job to keep us from being seen. I found a bench close by from which I could see the two boys, but also the bulk of the palace and the various entrances that opened onto the stadium.

The boys stood facing one another on the grass. Commodus held his little sword with a surprisingly professional grip. Cleander was still clutching his as though it were trying to leach through his skin and poison him.

'Don't hurt each other,' I hissed. 'One bruise and the empress will know you've not been standing in a classroom.'

'You're the editor, Em,' Commodus grinned. 'You say when.'

I wanted nothing less than to give the word for the two boys to start clubbing and stabbing each other with bits of wood. I tried one last time. 'This is dangerous. You'll get hurt. Put them away.'

'I'll be editor, then,' Commodus said, throwing me a black look. He turned back to the slave. 'Go.'

Cleander did not move. Commodus watched him for a long moment, and then struck. I was surprised. The prince was not quite five years old yet, but still he struck with force and speed. The blunted wooden tip slammed into Cleander's upper arm and sent him spinning away with a yelp.

'Fight me,' Commodus said, excitedly. The slave struggled

back upright. There were tears in his eyes and I almost felt sorry for him. But I could not, for I knew he hated me. Cleander stood, gripping the sword, his bruised arm hanging limp. Commodus struck again. His second blow was a swipe that hit the already injured arm near the wrist. Cleander cried out again.

'Come *on*,' Commodus urged him, beginning to sound angry.

His third blow was stopped. Cleander's wooden sword clonked against the prince's weapon and pushed it aside. Commodus laughed, though the slave stared at the sword in his hand in horror, as though it had moved of its own volition.

The slave's sudden involvement just increased Commodus' desire to fight, and he swung again. This time Cleander deliberately placed the blade in the way, parrying the blow. Another strike. Another parry. I realised suddenly that I'd not been playing lookout at all but had been watching the energetic young prince and his slave fight. I dragged my attention from them and noted with dismay the array of slaves standing rigid, shocked and silent around the gardens, watching this diminutive display of prowess. There was little hope of the tale of this fight not circulating throughout the palace within the day. My watching for adults was largely moot. Still, my gaze raked the arcades and doorways. I was drawn to the fight once more by a cry of pain, and I glanced back to see Commodus clutching his leg with his free hand. Cleander was ashen-faced, looking back and forth between the weapon in his hand and the prince he'd hurt.

I hurried across, heart in my throat, but before I got there Commodus was standing straight again, weapon out ready. I could see the red mark and graze from the slave's blow and knew that it would soon blossom into an impressive bruise. While he might ordinarily have been able to explain such a mark away as accidental, it would be difficult not to connect it to the inevitable rumours that the prince had been sword fighting in the stadium garden.

The combat began again, and Commodus was relentless, his miniature sword swinging with little true skill but a great deal of intent, Cleander parrying desperately, unwilling to risk bruising the imperial flesh any further. I felt cold to the bone; this was wrong. And despite the chasm of animosity that lay between Cleander and I, truly I pitied him now, for Commodus' blood was up. He was enjoying himself entirely too much, and I had a feeling that the only way Cleander was going to get out of this without a broken limb was to actually hurt the prince. And if he did that, the lash awaited, almost certainly with a fatal conclusion. He was trapped in a fight he could neither win nor lose.

Curse me for a fool, but for the first, and only, time in my life, I came to Cleander's aid. I hurried across and stepped between the two of them, earning a look of narrow-eyed confusion from Commodus. I turned and tried to take the sword from Cleander's hand, my intention to end this mess and save him from punishment. To my amazement, the slave gave a low growl, clung on to the blade and heaved me aside.

I staggered and almost fell into the flower bed, and by the time I righted myself they were fighting again, Commodus laughing gleefully, Cleander doing little more than constantly pushing aside the prince's blows. It was pure chance that my gaze happened to wander up to the balcony of the level above in time to see the gangly figure of Nautius Costa emerge into the light.

'Trouble,' I hissed.

I was impressed. One moment Commodus was there, fighting and laughing carelessly. The next, there was no sign of him, just Cleander standing alone, staring at the wooden sword in his hand, still a little shocked. A shaking movement among the hedges betrayed Commodus' location to me as he scurried away to the arcade and safety. Cleander dropped the sword as though it burned his fingers.

Commodus was gone. The slaves around us, deprived of the

spectacle of a prince fighting a slave, had gone back to work on the gardens, and Costa, at the balustrade above, swept the grounds with his birdlike gaze and, seeing no sign of his student, stalked off elsewhere in search of the errant prince. Suddenly I was alone in that corner of the garden with Cleander. The slave, finally comfortable that he'd got away with it, turned to me.

'You'd better hope that the prince doesn't blame you for his bruise,' I said. 'You know word of this will get to the emperor.'

'I'm his friend,' Cleander spat back. 'He'll look after me.'

I bridled. This sneering jackal of a slave? A friend of princes? Somewhere inside I was rather worried that he was right, but I had already lost some of my closeness with Commodus to little Annius and I was damned if I was going to admit that Cleander had a share.

'You're a slave,' I said unpleasantly. 'You can never be his friend. At best you're a toy.'

I thought that had won the argument, especially given the colour of his face and the fact that he seemed to be lost for words. I turned my back on him, partially for the meaning of that very gesture, and partially so he couldn't see the smug grin I wore. That smile slid away instantly as the slave's next words thudded into my back like knives.

'You love him. You're *in love* with him.'

I stopped, frozen in place, shocked. It was a common jibe among playful children, of course, a sly mockery to put friends in their place, but the tone of his voice made this remark something different. It was said almost as an insult.

'But you're the daughter of a freedwoman. Your father was a slave. And he's a prince.'

Was he being serious? I shook it off and turned, narrow-eyed. 'You'd best keep your opinions to yourself, slave,' I snapped. 'I may be a pleb, but even that is more than you can ever hope to be.'

It was an equally childish jibe, but it felt good and it shut him up long enough for me to walk away. For the next few hours I sat somewhere secluded where nobody would find me and worked furiously on my sewing. Of *course* I loved Commodus, but like a brother, or a friend. To suggest anything more was clearly Cleander just trying to annoy me.

The days continued to pass, and Commodus was confined to his lessons, two slaves given the specific duty of keeping tabs on him so that such a thing could not occur again. He had blamed a trip on the steps for the purple welt on his leg, but no one was fooled. He was suddenly trapped in education and, as often as possible, the emperor himself sat his wayward son down and oversaw his education. Consequently, Annius and I spent our time working and learning too. Cleander and I avoided each other at all costs, taking wide and complex routes through the palace so as not to cross paths.

The mood on the Palatine became subdued, for the plague had struck Rome at last. Annius' birthday celebration passed, and though the imperial family and the entire court enjoyed feasts and plays and entertainers, the atmosphere remained tainted by the conditions all around us. Initially there were just a few cases of the poor coughing up blood and it was brushed over as a normal illness typical of the sort that bred in the squalid conditions of Rome's poorest areas. Soon, though, shopkeepers were closing their stores and public servants were choking and dying in the suburbs. The bodies of the dead began to be hauled to burial pits outside the walls by the cartload. Physicians were working flat out, earning huge amounts of coin from people who were clearly past saving and, though I did not yet know him, it was then that the great *medicus* Galen fled the city for his homeland in the east, escaping the worst of the plague-ridden streets. While the spacious, wealthy areas of the city remained as yet untouched, it was becoming hard not to feel worried and threatened by contagion so close to our doorstep.

I was more oblivious to the true horror of the disease than many, locked away as I was in the palace, safe among the rich. I knew what was happening, and the gloom of the Roman mood had settled on me, but I did not truly understand the threat until the day Verus returned.

A courier reached the city one afternoon with the news that the absent emperor was but two days from Rome. He had landed at Puteoli rather than Ostia in order to proceed in a stately procession up the Via Appia to Rome, drinking in the adulation of the cities on the way and indulging in wine and banquets at each stage. Once it was known that the emperor was approaching, men were set to watch for him, and when we heard he had reached Albanum, the palace became a blur of activity. The resident emperor had decided to march out to meet his brother at the city limits alongside the senators who traditionally welcomed heroes home by issuing forth to greet them.

Marcus Aurelius, divine emperor of Rome, was at the head of the column on his fine white mare, bedecked as though for war. He was quite a sight. Of course, I say he was at the head, but that is not quite true. A sizeable unit of Praetorians moved in front, clearing the path and securing the route for their emperor, others of the Guard moving out to the sides in a protective cordon, and behind them, the ever-present imperial lictors with their bundles of rods and axes stepped ahead of the emperor's horse in two lines.

Behind Aurelius, the empress Faustina was carried aloft in a litter of gleaming wood and gold, draped with white and purple that had likely come from my mother's hands. The curtains were drawn back enough for the crowds to catch tantalising glimpses, but not enough to give too clear a view. Faustina was far from shy and withdrawing, but streets crowded with plague-riddled beggars were not to her taste.

Then came the imperial children. Commodus and Annius

were in a biga driven by a dedicated charioteer, their only unmarried sister following on in a litter of her own. Whenever the column rounded a bend, and I could see far enough forward to catch that biga, I saw Commodus and Annius leaning precariously out over the side, laughing and pointing, daring one another to lean further and further until finally one of the Praetorians was forced to have sharp words with the princes, after which they remained out of view inside the vehicle. As if to separate the important ruling family from the rest of us, a small squad of the imperial horse guard came next, then the household with its servants, freedmen and slaves. At the rear came more Praetorians, keeping the column safe and simultaneously maintaining an eye on the slaves and lower-class attendees.

We descended the Clivus Palatinus in a flood of colour and grandeur to the clamour of the crowd. The people of Rome love spectacle and no mere threat of lingering, rotting death was going to put them off watching their emperor in all his pomp riding out to meet his brother. I, of course, shuffled along in the rear with that part of the procession that no one cared about, and it was on that one occasion that I realised two things. Firstly, that no one looked at the unimportant, and they were overlooked enough to be granted a certain freedom. Secondly, that I had no wish to be so overlooked and unimportant, no matter how much freedom it granted me. Oddly, that procession gave me a taste of what it must be like to be one of the imperial family.

The procession flowed down the hill and through the streets, heading south and past the end of the Circus Maximus. Turning there, we followed the Via Appia between the tombs of ancient heroes, once outside the city walls and now crammed between garden walls and city blocks, as far as the grand Temple of Mars and its sacred grove.

It was at the same time fabulous and harrowing, that journey. Travelling as part of the imperial procession and just being part of what the population adored gave me a glow, but it also opened my eyes to the reality of what was happening outside our gilded rooms and delicate surroundings. We passed one street in particular that shocked me. I had caught the heady, rich scent of garlands and bouquets and had presumed them to be something to do with our procession until a chance parting of the folk beside me allowed a clear view of that narrow alley. With revulsion, I saw the bodies of the poor lying in the gutters and the filth, white-faced and spattered with their own coughed-up blood, and I realised that strong flowers had been deliberately gathered near the scene to overpower the scent of death and decay.

Once I understood that, I realised I could also smell the putrefaction beneath the flora. Two miserable-looking men in long leather aprons with garlands of flowers slung beneath their chins moved about the street, picking up the dead and throwing them gracelessly into the cart. It was death on a grand scale, something I had never seen before. I wondered what the emperor thought as he watched his people dying while we travelled out to meet the man who'd unwittingly brought this pestilence back to Rome. Mother often voiced, in private whispers, her opinion that God was punishing Rome for its pagan ways.

The Temple of Mars was busy. Senators and the rich knights were there to welcome back the conquering hero. They moved to the sides in response to the arrival of the great Marcus Aurelius and we waited as functionaries moved along the lines, settling the less important into a pleasing array in the background. By dint of being smaller than the adults, I ended up at the front of my part of the crowd so I could see, behind only the imperial family and a few soldiers. I watched eagerly, eyes raking the hazy distance.

It did not take long. We had been waiting less than half an hour when the victorious column came into view, led not by soldiers protecting their master, but by golden Verus himself on his magnificent steed, heedless of any danger, drinking in the glory of his arrival. A modest man Verus was not, but a glorious one he certainly was.

Seemingly mere moments later, the emperors were reunited, Aurelius stepping his horse out to meet his brother and clasp hands with him warmly.

'Welcome back,' the resident emperor said simply, and Verus laughed.

'I bring you peace with Parthia and all I get is "*welcome back*"?'

The two men laughed then, and the crowd around them joined in, gradually subsiding to an expectant silence. 'Peace carries a high cost,' Aurelius said finally with a sigh. 'Rome suffers, brother. Parthia sent your men back with a last shot to the heart, it seems.'

Verus shrugged. 'Disease. It's always rife out east. It will soon end here. Parthian rot cannot survive in Rome, I am told, so we just wait it out.' I was, I admit, somewhat surprised by the emperor's blasé attitude, so different to the man I remembered on the night of the great flood, rushing around to avert the disaster for his people. Clearly Marcus Aurelius also disapproved, for something in his expression caught Verus, and the junior emperor was taken aback. 'Physicians will keep the city functioning until it passes,' the younger man added with another shrug.

Aurelius' expression remained dark. 'Word is that your men destroyed the Temple of Apollo in Seleucia. Some are saying it is his anger that brought the plague on us.'

An admonishment, rare between the loving brothers.

Verus frowned. '*Avidius Cassius'* men destroyed the temple. But we made reparations and enormous donatives to the god in response. Apollo is satisfied, so the priests say. This is not a divine punishment, Marcus, it is just an illness, like a winter cold or a bout of the flux. Winter will see it end. In the meantime, we should make sure to stay clear of it. I find it strange that you remain in the city.'

'There has been much to do.'

Verus rolled his eyes and leaned a little closer, his tone quiet enough not to carry to the bulk of the crowd, though I could just hear him, and I suspected from Aurelius' expression he considered it still far too loud. 'You do not have to mollycoddle your people so, brother. Let them do the work for you. That's what they're for. Retire to Tibur, or Praeneste or some other imperial estate until the worst passes. I have a mind to expand my family's villa on the Via Cassia outside the city. Far enough to be away from the rot, but close enough for my triumph, eh?'

'Triumph?'

I saw the confusion in Verus then. 'I am not to have a triumph?'

Aurelius sagged a little in his saddle. 'You deserve one, brother, I shall not deny, but with the dead filling the streets by the cartload I do not think one prudent at this time.'

Verus nodded, all energy again. 'Quite right. After winter, when the rot is dead and the streets are clear. That is the time. Come, we have much to discuss, and I should introduce you to your granddaughter.'

And with that the mood lifted once more and all was right for a shining moment. Our glorious, happy column combined and returned to the city.

IV

AN OASIS OF PEACE

Rome, AD 166–167

Much as the procession had been, the following months were a time of high and low points for me, though blessedly more of the former. As the daughter of Verus' favourite seamstress, I was dragged along at imperial whim, which in this case meant to relative safety and glorious abandonment in the countryside. The junior emperor had inherited a somewhat ancient villa on the Via Cassia a few miles north of Rome and, upon his return and the terrible visible reminders of the pestilence that his legions had brought to the capital, he made that rural sanctuary liveable and moved his court there immediately.

The more austere Marcus Aurelius was, I think, somewhat derisive of his brother's decision to abandon Rome for his own safety. He never openly said as much, yet he remained on the Palatine in the heart of the world's most afflicted city despite the danger. The disease had reached even the imperial palaces now – one of the Praetorians had fallen prey to it. Aurelius' constitution having never been the strongest, there was an undercurrent of worry among the more serious courtiers that Aurelius might succumb to the illness himself.

I look back fondly on my months at the Via Cassia villa. Life was a delight, an oasis of peace, and it was surprisingly easy to forget for a time the plight of the people just a few miles away, especially since Commodus was a habitual and long-term visitor to his uncle's haven, giving me a welcome distraction. Verus languished there, hunting anything larger than a mouse, watching gladiator pairs fight for his entertainment and riding a chariot around his estate as though he had not a care in the world. We passed the autumn and the winter entertained by a constant stream of expensive games, hunts, plays, performances and races, all paid for with spoils Verus had brought back from Parthia. Commodus was in a good mood, and with Cleander still serving at the palace back on the Palatine, his rotten influence had dissipated like a bad smell in a breeze.

The house was filled with playwrights, musicians, dancers and artists that Verus had brought back from the east, as well as freedmen from a variety of provinces and the few members of the senatorial elite with whom Verus could be bothered. Unlike Aurelius, Lucius Verus was not over concerned with maintaining the fiction that the emperor was in some way beholden to the senate: he preferred to fill his household with talented unknowns rather than noble wastrels. It was a trait in him that Commodus took note of early, for good or ill.

Throughout autumn those entertainments often passed me by. With the emperor's return and the presence of his wife and the baby princess, Mother was very busy once more, which meant that so was I. Here in the villa's isolation, Mother had no local seamstresses to call upon for aid, and so such tasks fell to me. I spent what little leisure time I had with Commodus and that time was good, for he was in his element at the villa, about the most content and positive I had seen him since the death of his twin. I only realised just how much the sojourn was affecting him on the kalends of November, when Mother's workload had once more grown light. I was invited by Commodus to the private matches held at the villa as our answer to the great Sullan games being celebrated in the plague-ridden city.

It was the first time I had seen gladiators at work. Not because of my age or standing, of course – plenty of girls younger and poorer than I had passed the time in arena seats – but I simply had never had the opportunity. Mother disapproved of the practice and believed that all Christians should do so. I was less settled in my faith, I think, and had always been intrigued by the *ludi* – the great, bloodthirsty games of Rome. Whatever Mother's opinion, though, she was not about to refuse the prince's offer, and so this time I attended, with numerous warnings from Mother still ringing in my ears:

'Do not revel in blood, for sin will eat deep into your heart if you let it.

Pride is a terrible sin. Do not feel glorious in the presence of the prince, for even happiness at his closeness could pave your way to hell.

Pray for the souls of those poor men who fight. Always. Never forget that they are men.

You are a striking girl and the court is full of lechers and debauchers. Stay still and try not to be noticed.'

It was the first time Mother had ever acknowledged my looks and in hindsight it probably did more harm than good to draw attention to them.

The villa's arena was a small affair in comparison to those in the cities. It was just an oval of sand with three rows of wooden seats, but it was comfortable, and well-provisioned tables of snacks and wine stood at intervals all around. Commodus brought me in and indicated the seat next to him, only a short distance from the emperor. Praetorians stood silent and watchful around the periphery. Had we been in public, my seat next to the prince would have been a high honour, though in a private arena traditional restrictions are not usually observed.

'*Secutor*,' Commodus whispered as the hubbub among the observers died away with a last chuckle from Verus at some humorous comment. I followed the prince's pointing finger and saw the gladiator emerging from the doorway onto the sandy arena floor. He was a heavy man, short and bulky with fat bulging out over the leather belt that topped his loincloth. His sword was gleaming in the autumn sunlight and the arm above it was encased in a thick linen sheath. His other arm held a shield like those of the legions, but his helmet was a thing from nightmare. Like a smooth, gleaming skull with only two dark eye sockets and a mouth slit for decoration. It made me shudder to look upon it.

'He's fat,' I whispered in surprise. 'I thought he'd be fit, like a soldier.'

Commodus chuckled with the confidence of a boy who had seen a hundred fights like this, but it was Lucius Verus, who had overheard, who leaned towards us and answered me.

'*Soldiers* have armour, child. Gladiators only have fat. Fat heals much quicker than muscle, and don't think for a moment the man's not fit just because he's fat. He's called secutor – the *chaser*. Watch now for the *retiarius*.'

I did so, feeling at once embarrassed and wondrous that the emperor himself had spoken to me. The net man appeared moments later, as the applause for the secutor began to die away, rising once more at the second man's arrival. This man was thinner than his opponent. Or perhaps that was just an illusion of the mind because of the lightness of his equipment, for all he bore was a net weighted down with lead balls around the edges, and a trident, his only armour a mere loincloth.

'Surely he's at a disadvantage?' I whispered. 'No shield? No helmet?'

Again, Commodus laughed, but this time it was he who answered. 'No. Watch, Em.'

At Verus' command, some unseen official gave the signal and the bout began. The secutor closed in slowly, shield held forth, ready to turn aside blows. The retiarius stood his ground – in this small arena there was not an awful lot of ground to stand – trident jutting forward. His left arm began to move in a strange, twirling pattern. The motion transferred down to the net, and it began to swing, slowly at first, but then picking up speed once it had sufficient momentum to overcome the weight of the lead balls. I suddenly realised that the net was more than an opportunity to snag an enemy – it was a weapon in itself, with those lead weights whirring through the air. The secutor knew it, too, for his advance slowed and the shield moved that tiniest bit closer to his flesh.

Lucius Verus, close by and clearly already enthralled, stood and shouted, 'A wager on the secutor. Any takers?'

I turned in surprise. I may not have spent time at the games, but I knew enough about imperial etiquette to know that even in close company like this it was unseemly for the emperor to make low wagers. Certainly, Marcus Aurelius would not have done so. But Verus' house was more relaxed, and a wiry man in a toga with a strangely equine face rose and opened his mouth to answer, but Commodus beat him to it.

'Me, uncle.'

The togate man threw the prince an obsequious, ingratiating look, and returned to his seat. Verus threw an approving nod to the boy beside me and for the first time, looking at the two of them, I could see the similarity between them. Not only physically, but in their personality and even in their relationships, too. Commodus and poor Fulvus, Verus and Marcus Aurelius. One golden and reckless. One thoughtful and quiet. So alike in so many ways. And at that moment I also realised that, over the months he spent at the Via Cassia villa, Commodus was changing. Every visit made him a little bit more like his uncle.

I was so busy contemplating the two that I missed the first clash. As the small crowd roared their excitement, my gaze snapped back to the arena to see the secutor staggering off to the side, adjusting the shield, which now had two long grooves carved across its painted face.

I watched. On one level, I was appalled at this show of barbarity, largely because Mother had spent nine years *training* me to be appalled at such things. On a deeper level, I was excited. And I thought that Verus had the right of it with his money on the secutor. He may have taken the first blow, but he was unwounded and clearly better equipped. He also knew what to do, for even as I weighed up his chances, he struck. His reeling had not been random – he had masked his preparations as a withdrawal from the blow, but in fact he had been moving to his opponent's trident side, away from the swinging net. Now, suddenly, he was running. I never saw him set off. One moment he was lurching as though confused, the next he was racing full pelt at his opponent. The retiarius, taken by surprise, could do nothing with his net and managed more by luck than judgement to get his trident in the way. But the secutor had planned for it. As the long weapon wavered at him and he closed, he turned his shield and took the three points on it at an angle, so that the weapon was pushed harmlessly aside. The heavy secutor hit the net man hard, throwing him backwards to the ground. I never saw the sword strike, so quick was he, but as he ran on and slowed, the retiarius struggled to his feet, nursing a vicious wound on his trident arm.

'You took a foolish bet,' I whispered to Commodus, realising that no figure had been named and wondering how much Verus was willing to fleece his nephew. Commodus simply shrugged with an odd look. He was still so young, but was so much his uncle's nephew. Although this was my first fight, Commodus had been watching them for years.

The retiarius was on his feet again. His trident had dipped, the points in the sand, and I realised the wound must be bad. He had not the muscle to lift the weapon. Instead, he began to whirl the net as the secutor, now confident, closed on him. I realised I was holding my breath and forced myself to breathe steadily. I had never known such excitement and anticipation. And the blood did not bother me at all. Mother would have been so disappointed in me.

The net swung. The secutor stomped forward. The retiarius let go.

I watched the weighted net fly through the air, cast with expert skill, and marvelled at the throw. The net took the secutor fully in the upper body. I heard the lead weights clacking together and bouncing off steel, leather, bone and flesh. I think it must have broken a rib or two from the way the secutor lurched and almost doubled over. But he was not entrapped as I had feared. The weird, frightening helmet was designed with purpose, I now realised, for it was so smooth that there was nothing for a net to catch on. Doubling over, the secutor shook and the net slithered off him to the floor. As he straightened I could see that he was in pain from the numerous contusions caused by the weights. But he was free and advancing once more. The retiarius had let go of his net, and his trident was still lowered, blood gushing down that arm. Verus would win the bet. I knew it.

I was sure.

The secutor came in for the winning blow, but suddenly the retiarius took a single step forward and the trident rose in the blink of an eye, showering sand all about. When the cloud settled and our view cleared, the two men were standing perfectly still. The secutor's arms were held out wide in surrender, for the triple points of the trident rested against the flesh of his throat. I'd wondered why the retiarius had not swapped the trident to his other hand, even if he was not so good with that one, and I think the secutor had been pondering the same question as he made his final disastrous move.

The audience erupted in a roar of approval, and I stared. Commodus had been right. He'd evaluated them straight out of the door and decided that the retiarius would win, and he'd been sure all along. He turned and smiled up at the emperor, who laughed.

'Always be prepared to sacrifice to achieve the end goal,'

Verus announced to the crowd, gesturing at Commodus. 'I am tutored now by my nephew, and bested by him too. Fortunately, I do not believe we set a value on the wager, and fortunately I have a copper *as* to hand.'

He flicked the tiny, almost worthless coin across at Commodus, who caught it with a grin.

'Don't spend it all at once, nephew.'

The games went on for the afternoon. I watched two more bouts with the prince, whose judgement was often shrewd, and who was careful to put a price on his next wager. I eventually left, not through offended religious values, but because my posterior had gone numb and I needed to move about.

The year rolled towards a close in the presence of Verus, who treated Commodus more like a son than a nephew, paying him considerably more attention than his own daughter, much to the irritation of the empress Lucilla, I might add. The young prince clung to excitement and glamour in the company of his uncle, idolising the charioteers and cheering the gladiators at every occasion, sometimes with me, sometimes not.

On occasions when he roared at the games but I was not present, I would spend my time avoiding Lucilla, and it was on one of those occasions that I met a man who would become central to everything crucial in my life. One of the freedmen the emperor Verus brought back from the east, and who had become his *ab epistulis* – his secretary – was an easterner called Eclectus. He was a quiet fellow; one might even say taciturn. He was unremarkable in almost every way, and yet there was something about him that made him stand out to me. Perhaps it was God's plan at work. At least, finding friends in unexpected places helped me while away my time.

Winter crawled by with frozen ponds and brittle branches, white frost settling on the world and chilling the city and its surroundings. I noted a downturn in Commodus' mood during that time and it took a while for me to realise that he would not go near, or even look at, the icy waters, for they brought back such painful memories of Fulvus. I had not realised, in fact, how optimistic and excitable he had become until the winter stripped it away again.

We never once returned to Rome throughout that time, though regular visitors would deliver important news. Marcus Aurelius remained in the city, healthy despite having been a martyr to illnesses and colds throughout his life, and continued to administer efficiently. Verus' court simply waited for the plague to run its course and fade. With his removal from the city to his rural villa to avoid the plague, and his seeming hedonism, I expected dismay from the populace. In fact, strangely, the legend of his Parthian victory continued to grow, and his exploits hunting wolves and bears on his estate became the talk of taverns. While Aurelius worked every hour the gods sent to ease his people's suffering, it was Verus the golden who won their hearts. Fickle as ever, the people of Rome. There were even mutterings that a triumph had been expected and never occurred. But such positive news was tempered with ill tidings too.

We listened to every report that came to us, hoping to hear that the icy conditions which had settled upon Rome had killed off the Parthian plague. It had not. Despite Verus' convictions that the disease would not survive the winter, it continued to kill many hundreds each day. New burial pits were being opened on the Esquiline to cope with the sheer volume of the dead. Moreover, despite the true origin of the pestilence, it was already being dubbed the 'Antonine Plague' after the imperial family who had brought it to the city.

We waited as the world thawed and spring came with its growth and fresh new warmth. The disease failed to disappear, and physicians worked flat out. Other news began to filter through to us with the approach of the warmer season. The tribes on the northern frontiers were stirring, causing trouble. Despite having so recently returned from war in the east, Verus began to mutter about the possibility of taking an army north in the summer, knowing that of the two emperors he was the one with the more robust nature, made for war and activity, and such duty would fall to him. Even with the pending likelihood of a new campaign, Verus made his decision. The triumph that had been put off because of the plague would go ahead in the spring, before the campaigning season began, whether the city had healed or not.

Word was sent to Marcus Aurelius, who consented to the event, and in a torrent of activity, a few days later the court moved from the rural villa back to the Palatine.

I was horrified as we passed through the Campus Martius and the northern regions of the city upon our return. What had once been a lively world of street sellers, citizens and slaves all shouting, laughing and making noise was now eerily quiet. People kept to their houses, fearing the pestilential air outside and contact with other humans. I saw dogs, cats, even chickens, that had been run through with a blade and burned in the belief that they carried the disease from door to door. A few places seemed to be thriving with activity, though. The bathhouses still seethed with customers, where those as yet untouched went to be clean and scrape away the dangerous grime of the city. The shops of the physicians displayed queues of pale, scrawny sufferers hacking up blood. Temples experienced a constant stream of people begging the gods and giving more than they could afford in an attempt to persuade the divine to strike down the disease.

It was a vision of Hell straight from the pious tales of my mother. I noted her making the sign of the crucified Christ as we passed each new horror. It was a subdued and dispirited column that finally reached the Palatine. The accompanying units of the Praetorian Guard left us and returned to their barracks once we were safely within the walls of the palace complex. Verus' household administrators immediately went about their duties, preparing the Palatine apartments and beginning work on the coming celebration. Those of us without pressing tasks remained with the emperor's entourage, standing in the *aula regia* as the great Marcus Aurelius burst through one of the rear doors, accompanied by his own following, and hurried over to his brother with a genuine smile.

'Lucius Verus, your absence has been a shadow over my soul.'

The younger emperor laughed and embraced the great man.

'I have missed you, Marcus. And there will be much to do in the coming days, but tell me first that you are truly well. I was appalled by what I saw as we travelled through the city.'

Aurelius frowned. 'The pestilence? This is the disease in *abeyance*, brother. You should have seen it a few months ago in the midwinter. The best physicians in Rome tell me it is now notably on the decline.'

Decline? I could not imagine how the scenes I had witnessed passing through Rome could have been any more distressing. Still, even the possibility that the worst was now over was a balm to the soul. I glanced at my mother, whose eyes were closed in silent prayer, and in one of my less pious moments I pondered on the possibility that all those myriad offerings given in the temples of Rome might have had something to do with it. Or was Verus right and the cold had killed it off, just more slowly than he had anticipated? Either way, I remained privately unconvinced that this was God's work.

My attention was diverted as Marcus Aurelius gave a throaty chuckle and beckoned to someone in the gathering. Commodus emerged with a grin and hurried over to his father, who swept him up in an embrace.

I smiled. All things seemed to be improving once more. Then I caught sight of Cleander among the functionaries at the rear of the room, and my spirits sank again.

'This sudden slew of mortality has me thinking,' Verus said finally, speaking to his brother. 'It is said that some of the more noble lines in the city are dying out. We cannot have the same happen with the imperial family. Remember how many dynasties have fallen through failure to prepare the succession.'

Aurelius frowned. 'I have sons. There is no need to adopt, as my childless forebears did. Commodus will be emperor after me. And your son after you.' He gave Verus a slightly uncomfortable, disapproving look. He did not like speaking of such private things in front of their retinues, though Verus had no such notions of propriety, and simply snorted.

'I have a daughter only,' he replied, 'and you have *two* sons, Marcus. But Rome has not had a boy born to the purple for a hundred years. People will be uncertain. Make it official. Make Commodus and Annius Caesars. Make them your heirs designate. Then, if the worst should happen with this rot in the streets, at least the succession will be smooth.'

'Jove, but you are an uplifting conversationalist, brother,' Aurelius said, stepping back and releasing his son from his grasp. 'Months I have not seen you and your first concern is what might happen when I become diseased and die?'

Verus rolled his eyes. 'It makes sense, and you know that. Do it, and they can ride with us in the triumph.'

'Us?'

Now Verus laughed. 'I may have gone east, but do you really think I once drew a blade and thrust it in the Parthian's black heart? No. I reviewed the troops, reorganised the lines and bases, then settled in at Antioch where I could deal with both my armies with equal ease. I mostly spent my time scribbling.'

'And drinking,' Aurelius noted wryly.

Verus laughed off the jibe. 'That too. We built a canal at the Orontes, brother, and found the most astounding thing: the bones of a Titan. Enormous, he was. A true giant. We tried to bring him home as a curiosity, but there was a mishap on the voyage and the bones were lost. Perhaps the gods do not approve of giants?' He chuckled. 'I digress from my purpose. My point was that not once did I draw blade from scabbard, yet I deserve a triumph for leading them. And so do you. It is your policy and mind and wisdom that put us on that victorious track. This is a triumph of the whole family. Of the empire entire, in fact. And the people of Rome need something to lift the spirits. Let them see the imperial family in glory, and we shall give largesse and hold games. We shall make Rome cheerful once more.'

Aurelius looked unconvinced. Whether it was the inherent danger of taking his young family through the pestilential streets unnecessarily, I do not know, but he was uncertain. Verus badgered him, though, until he relented and accepted the notion. I was too busy to listen, for while the emperors held their discussion, Commodus returned to the waiting group and found me.

'I will be emperor,' he grinned.

'Heir designate,' I corrected him, but with a warm smile.

'*Then* emperor,' he said over his shoulder as his father and uncle made to leave, and he reluctantly followed his beckoning mother while the palace staff sent the rest of us to our appropriate quarters.

We settled back into the palace and I was oddly lonely and listless in the days that followed. Everyone was busy on the Palatine in preparation for the coming triumph – everyone but me. With such a grand affair planned for the whole imperial family, the entire palace was aflutter. Mother acquired a second helper from somewhere and worked hard, even by guttering lamplight, to provide garments fit for such an occasion. There was no time for lessons, and the tutors were dismissed for a time, young Commodus and Annius instead being prepared for what would be expected of them. Consequently, since Mother once more had her professional assistants, I had no chores, no lessons, no family and no friends to occupy my time. I drifted around the palace like a ghost.

Occasionally in my wanderings I would come across the empress Lucilla, and hurriedly find something to do while she passed. Commodus' sister-and-aunt was tetchy at the best of times, but during our time at the villa she had become pregnant once more, and pregnancy did nothing to improve her moods. Indeed, she had been in a particularly foul temper since it had been decided that she would be the only member of the imperial family not to be part of the triumph, given the danger it could present to her unborn child.

Finally, the day of the triumph came around. The palace was in utter turmoil, or so it seemed to my nine-year-old eyes. In fact, given the administrative ability of the two emperors and the efficiency of the many freedmen upon whom they relied, I'm certain that everything was moving like a well-tended machine, but to a child it appeared chaotic.

I was finally useful, though. Mother had me running back and forth, fetching her work for various members of the imperial family and the extended court. She had even sewn a tunic for the prefect of the Praetorian Guard, which was a new honour. I dithered at the edge of the organised chaos, watching silently and respectfully as I waited for my next job.

At the centre of the room, the imperial family were gathering, and Aurelius' voice suddenly cut through the hubbub.

'Where is my son?'

Young Annius looked up at his father, but it was clear that he meant Commodus, for the young prince was the only member of the direct imperial family not present. Galeria, one of his older sisters, gestured back towards their private apartments. 'He was in his room when I last saw him, Father. He was shouting at someone and banging around.'

I felt a flutter in my chest. I had not seen him in many days now. Since returning to the city, he had been full of energy and excitement once more, and it was only with the sudden realisation that he had not been around that I remembered how swiftly he had sunk into gloom during those icy months at the villa.

'Go fetch him,' the empress waved at one of the slaves.

I turned to Mother, who was making last-moment adjustments to the hem of a *palla* for one of the girls, and cleared my throat. 'Mother?'

'I'm busy, Marcia. Go and find something to do.'

Gratefully, I nodded and backed from the room with a respectful, slow gait until I was in the corridor outside, where I turned and hurried off after the slave, my sandals slapping on the marble. I found the poor hapless lad at Commodus' door. He raised his hand nervously and knocked.

'Go away,' came a muffled shout from within. The slave dithered, hand still raised. He was caught in an unpleasant situation. To return to the empress without the prince would land him in deep trouble, but disobeying the heir-apparent to the empire was almost as unpleasant a notion. Had it been me, for I have ever been a practical woman, I would simply have disappeared into the palace and left the matter to itself, for I am well aware that nobody pays the slightest attention to slaves, and even ten heartbeats after the lad had left the room, Faustina would not have recognised him in a line-up. He was simply mobile furniture. But the slave remained, and dithered.

I hurried along the corridor towards them as the boy cleared his throat and called through the closed portal in a wavering voice, 'Highness, your father awaits you in the aula regia.'

I came to a breathless halt behind the slave just as the door was wrenched open from within. Commodus was an impressive sight. Closing in on his sixth birthday, he might still be a child, and he might have been hiding away in his room, but he was already dressed for the occasion, and *what* a panoply he wore.

His tunic, belt, boots and short cloak were all of the highest quality and threaded with gold, but clearly modelled after the military dress of a general. Oddly, despite his age, an image flashed into my mind of him on a battlefield, and he did not look out of place there. His hair was neatly coiffured in a far more ordered manner than was common for the active prince, and a wreath of gold nestled among the curls, almost lost against the similar colour of the hair. Only his face spoiled the image of a hero of old, for his skin was sallow and pale, his eyes rimmed with red. My heart skipped as I realised how tortured he looked.

The young prince glared at the slave, caught sight of me behind, then returned his attention to the boy.

'I'll come soon. Go away.'

The slave bowed and ran, leaving in the air a vapour of fear and gratitude that he could now legitimately return to the empress. Something made me aware that there was another person in the room beyond – just a vague shuffling sound, but I felt my spirits sink a little further, sure it would be the ever-present viper Cleander.

'Highness,' I began. From the outset, I had been one of very few privileged to be able to call the prince by name, and rarely used his title, but right now, dressed as he was, it felt appropriate.

'Come in,' he said, simply, and then withdrew into the gloom of his room.

I followed him, becoming more worried as I did so. His window was covered by thick drapes, blocking all the light from outside. The only illumination in the room came from one small oil lamp and the dying glow of a brazier – it more closely resembled a Stygian cave than a royal bedchamber. And it was warm in there, too. I had another notion that this was an echo of my mother's tales of Hell. I didn't like it. I wanted to throw open the curtains and let in cleansing light.

My eyes fell on the other occupant of the room and I was grateful to discover that it was not Cleander after all. The man was old, his long robe and leather bag indicative of a physician

– Lord knows, we saw enough of them those days to recognise one instantly. He was not the court physician, though. I turned to Commodus as he closed the door, plunging us into darkness once more.

'Are you all right?' I asked quietly.

'Can't sleep.'

I glanced across at the physician, who shrugged. In an accent of some eastern region, I guessed probably Judean, he said, 'I can find nothing wrong. Physically his Highness is hale and untroubled, barring a clear case of exhaustion. He is, in fact, in fine shape. Given the souls I am used to treating in the city these days, it is a relief to *find* such a healthy person.'

'Then what's stopping him sleeping?'

Commodus sloped over to his bed and dropped heavily onto it, gripping his knees and shaking his head. '*I am.*'

'What?'

He raised those red-rimmed eyes to me and I shivered at the flood of raw emotion that poured through them. 'I . . . I lie down and close my eyes, but all I see is . . .' He faltered, and I noted how tightly he gripped his knees. It must be hurting him. 'I'm Fulvus. I'm under the ice, drowning. And it only stops when I open my eyes. I get a few hours sometimes, but even then, I wake up frightened.'

And I had not been here to help him. Was this what he was like when I was not around? I dreaded to think of it, remembering the torn chunks of hair, the self-blame, and even the unwillingness to look at the frozen ponds of the villa. I hurried over to him. I wanted to hug him and tell him it was all right, but it wasn't, and no matter how close we were, a pleb did not embrace a prince, especially in front of a stranger. Moreover, his description of the scene in his head took me back to my own watery horror – the memory of that day of the great flood, which still chilled me.

'I fear he suffers from melancholia,' the physician said with a sigh.

'Melancholia?' I asked, unfamiliar with the term.

'An inclination to negative thoughts and innate sadness that is not of conscious choice,' the easterner explained. 'The noted medicus Aretaeus of Cappadocia has researched the subject more than anyone. He advocates bathing in a certain form of brine salt, though given the nature of the prince's night terrors, that may do more harm than good.'

'And it won't help right now,' Commodus said with sagging shoulders.

'I will enquire about the subject and see if I can uncover any more useful research,' the physician said.

'Do not speak of this outside this room,' I said to the man, then blinked as I realised that I, a low plebeian daughter of a freedwoman, had just issued an order to a man who was probably a full citizen, in the presence of a prince, and yet neither seemed to disapprove.

Indeed, the physician threw me a chastened look. 'I would never do such a thing.'

'Good,' Commodus said. 'Leave me.'

The physician bowed and withdrew, closing the door behind him. Oddly, it never occurred to me that Commodus might mean me too. I stood, biting my lip, wondering how best to approach the problem, beset alternately by unwelcome images of Fulvus under the ice and of that deadly surge crossing the city and felling buildings on the night of the flood.

I had found Commodus in similar states to this in the past, but those times we had been simply children at leisure, and I had been free to divert him with the menagerie and other activities. Now, his family awaited him in the imperial audience chamber, gradually growing more impatient, while the whole of Rome expected him in the streets. I had no time.

'You're not Fulvus,' I tried.

'I know, Em.'

I took a deep breath and looked at his dreams from another angle. 'You are not responsible for what happened to him.'

'I am.'

'No, you're not,' I said with some firmness. 'And nor am I. Nor was he. It was an unhappy accident, plain and simple. It could have been you. Had I been more playful that day, perhaps it might even have been me. But it was Fulvus. You cannot torture yourself for that.'

He said nothing, simply slumped back on the bed.

'And there is no time for this.'

I had no idea what it would do, but there was no time right then for gentleness. I strode over to the window and wrenched back the drapes, so that Rome's bright sunlight flooded into the room, driving back the gloom and destroying the shadows to which the unhappy young prince clung. He recoiled, slinking off into the darkest corner he could find. My directness might have been making him worse, of course, but I had little option. In mere moments the emperors would send someone else and demands would be made. I threw open the window. The air of Rome in spring is not as bad as it gets in the heat of summer, but it was still cloying and malodorous, though against the foetid heat of the room it felt balmy. The embers in the brazier flared with the sudden breeze, and I walked across to the room's centre, where I peered at Commodus. He was blinking and looked panicked.

'Come on,' I said, gently this time. I held out my hands, enticing him, urging him to stand. To my surprise he did so, and hurried straight over to me, throwing himself into my arms. I shivered for a moment, not sure how to react. Yet it felt right. He was shaking, and I realised with deepening concern that he was crying dry tears, all the moisture long since wrung from his red-rimmed eyes.

'Your father is waiting for you,' I said. 'All Rome is waiting to see their emperor's heir ride in triumph. The city is sick and poor, and they need this. And so do you.'

It took long moments, but finally I felt him nod in my embrace. I let go and he stepped back, wiping his face with the backs of his hands. 'I . . . I'm not sure I can do it, Em.'

'The prince who ran from his tutors and challenged a slave to a fight in the gardens could do it,' I said with a wry smile, and he smiled back. His whole face changed with that smile, the broken prince gone, *my* Commodus returned.

'Come on, then,' he said, and we left the chamber. As we passed one of his sister's rooms, a slave girl emerged, startled, and dropped to a knee in shock. Something occurred to me. I stopped, and called to Commodus to do the same. I had seen what the girl was carrying.

'What is it?' the prince asked, hurrying back.

'This is your sister's *cosmeta*,' I replied, gesturing to the girl with her pouches and boxes of makeup and rolls of brushes.

'So?'

I fixed him with a look. This was no time for gentle approaches. 'You look like a spirit freshly returned from Tartarus. I swear even if we applied white lead you could not get paler. You don't want your parents to worry, and the city to think you're ill.'

'You want me to wear my sister's makeup?' he asked incredulously.

'You want people to think you've caught the plague?' I turned to the girl, whose eyes were locked on the floor beneath her. 'The prince has not slept well. He is perfectly healthy, but tired. I want you to make him look well rested and healthy and then never speak of this again. Do you understand?'

The girl, maybe a year older than me, nodded hurriedly.

We were in the room perhaps two or three hundred heartbeats before the cosmeta stepped back and the prince rose. She

73

knew her business well. I crossed to Commodus and peered at him. Close up, the makeup was evident, but might not have been had I not been expecting to see it. Certainly, from any further away than a few feet he looked perfectly healthy. I grinned. 'Just right.'

He examined his face in her bronze mirror and blinked in surprise, then threw the girl a smile that was probably more than she'd ever had from his sister. As we emerged into the corridor once more, a functionary turned the corner ahead with a Praetorian at his shoulder.

'Highness, there you are. Your father is starting to grow impatient.'

Commodus simply nodded and we joined them, all of us returning to the aula regia. Once more entering the world of the imperial family, the prince was lost to me, pulled away by his mother and chastised for his tardiness. I saw him once throw me a long-suffering look as he was prepared and positioned with the rest of the family. Mother was busy adjusting the hang of her work on the Praetorian prefect, whose sneer annoyed me, and a wiry, horse-faced man in a toga, who I recognised as the one who'd risen at the games a few days earlier, stood with Marcus Aurelius. That man gestured at Commodus, sharing some smiled comment with the emperor, and then turned to me. I flinched as though struck. For someone as unimportant as I, being singled out by the powerful was rarely good. The man pointed at me and said something to Aurelius, who nodded and replied in quiet tones. I wished that the room was less busy and loud, for I'd have given gold coins to have heard the words that passed between them.

One thing I did know was that I did not like the way the man in the toga looked at me as the emperor returned his attention to other matters. As his eyes scoured me from my curls down to my bare ankles, I felt as though my outer layers had been peeled away like an onion. I did not understand the look, nor the discomfort it brought forth in me, until a snide, unpleasantly familiar voice close behind me made it perfectly clear.

'You'd best make a willing bed slave for that one.'

In an instant, Mother's words that day at Verus' villa flooded back in.

'You are a striking girl and the court is full of lechers and debauchers. Stay still and try not to be noticed.' God, was this what she had worried about? I did not turn. If I saw the look that I knew was on Cleander's face I might well have scratched it off him, and that would not be a good idea in the imperial presence.

'I'm not old enough to be married,' I said firmly.

'Who mentioned *marriage*?' he said nastily. 'That's Marcus Ummidius Quadratus, the consul. He wouldn't even marry his dog to someone like you, but he'll *screw* you.'

. . . the court is full of lechers and debauchers . . .

I spun now, angry. I had to force my arms down and restrain myself, keeping my tone low, given the company we were in. 'I could have you beaten for speaking to me like that.'

Cleander simply smiled again. 'Our good prince has already promised me my freedom as soon as he can arrange it. Don't think yourself safe behind your status forever. Remember that while the consul ruts on you at night.'

I turned away from him again. Looking at his face any longer would have resulted in a fight. Instead I focused on the imperial procession, which was now making ready to leave the room. My mother had completed her final ministrations and was stepping back. Commodus was looking at us, his expression troubled, questioning. Whatever Cleander did that I couldn't see seemed to settle the prince and he nodded as I felt space open up behind me with the departing figure of the obnoxious slave.

My mind furnished me with a timely memory of the slave girl pushing her lead curse tablet down into the drains to bring horrible ruin upon a man, and I found myself wondering where I might buy such a thing, before reminding myself that Mother would tear strips from me if she found out.

I would just have to hope that something nasty happened to Cleander.

And plan something myself, if it didn't.

V

A CLOAK OF GREY

Rome, autumn AD 168

Following the great and glorious triumph, there was a time of strange positivity. Though plague still ravaged the streets of Rome and the news from the north continued to be of concern, that grand event succeeded in lifting the worst of the pall from the city. Verus, unusually self-effacing, continued to promote his victory as one for the entire dynasty. Despite his protestations – possibly even *because* of them – Marcus Aurelius commissioned a grand triumphal arch to stand across the Via Appia at the point where we had met the victorious general upon his return.

I say *positivity*, but do not mistake that for *peace*. There was no peace to be had, for, as Verus had predicted, a campaign had been announced against the tribes from beyond the Danubius that were besetting our northern borders, and both emperors were to take part. Consequently, Rome became a hub for the transfer of troops and supplies: the Praetorian Guard were thrown into a frenzy of pre-campaign organisation; legionary cohorts came and went, camping outside the city before they moved on to various marshalling positions on the route north; and the Misenum fleet sent ship after ship in and out of the Navalia up the great River Tiber.

I think Commodus was disappointed. He had expected to travel with his father and the golden Verus, along with the court, but the joint emperors made the unusual decision to treat the campaign as a military exercise rather than an imperial expedition and did not take the entire court on tour with them, relying instead on a small *consilium* of senators, generals and knowledgeable freedmen. We children, the wives, and the endless support staff were all to remain in Rome.

At Verus' insistence, we accompanied his empress Lucilla and his *familia* to the villa outside the city once more, keeping us as clear of the pestilential urban sprawl as possible. It would have been a good time for me, had it not been for the company.

Though Cleander remained blessedly in Rome and out of earshot, Lucilla was a constant icy, bad-tempered presence and, despite the danger of courting rumour, she invited a number of the more important members of the senatorial class to attend her in an endless cycle of long-term visits. One such, who seemed to be ever-present, was that consul Quadratus, whose gaze continued to fall upon me with an unpleasant hunger. I was almost eleven now, close to marriageable age, and blossoming into an attractive young woman, or so Mother warned me again and again.

The senior empress Faustina, perhaps distancing herself from this procession of nobles, preferred to stay at Aurelius' favoured villa near Praeneste with her youngest son. Commodus, who remained close to Annius, felt keenly the absence of his younger brother, and while I sympathised, especially after losing Fulvus, I was grateful to be able, to some extent, to fill the gap left by the prince.

Commodus shone in those days. In the absence of his favourite uncle, the young prince slipped seamlessly into Verus' role as patron of sports and entertainment. The changes wrought by his stay with his uncle came to the fore, and he even began to have his hair styled like Verus, as close as possible with his young curls. Had he been able to grow a neck beard, I'm sure he would have.

The races began once more. Gladiator pairings fought for

our excitement. Plays were performed – though only the light-hearted ones with blundering slaves and kicked behinds, since he had no interest in the dour Greek tragedies. Music. Dance. Art. And Lucilla left him to it, not through a serious desire to please her brother, I think, but rather because she had no interest in such things and was busy constructing webs of patronage in the villa while Commodus kept the rest of us entertained.

The similarity between the prince and his uncle was as clear as ever. I spent much time now watching chariots or racehorses thundering around the circuit in the grounds, or half a dozen poorly armed Thracian criminals trying to take down an iron-clad *crupellarius* gladiator. Once, I went with Commodus to hunt a boar. I simply could not believe he was allowed such latitude, given the incredible dangers of such a pastime, though it turned out in the end, to the prince's disappointment, that he was only to observe and direct, and the few nobles and men of the Guard who were there to keep him safe were the only ones to face danger as the great hog burst from the undergrowth intent on goring flesh. One of the Guard died the next day of his horrible wounds even as the rest of us ate roast pork. Such is the world.

Mother periodically dragged me in to aid her once more in the absence of more suitable helpers, though I was almost full-grown now and, with the emperors away, her work was scarce.

The first news of the war's progress reached the villa one day while we were in the stands of the arena, less than a month after Commodus' seventh birthday. My gaze was torn from the Gaul, who was busy jabbing at an agile Aegyptian with his long spear, by an imperial courier, dusty from his ride. He approached the stands where Commodus and I sat together, stopping four seats away, and bowed deeply. Commodus, one eye still on the closing stages of the fight, beckoned to him. The half-dozen Praetorians standing cold and observant nearby moved closer without a sound, their attention focused on every movement of the man. The dusty rider stopped nearby and extended his hand, proffering a scroll bearing the imperial seal. I noted, from a quick glance, four more such scroll cases clonking together in his leather satchel. We were not his last port of call, and we had probably not been the first; that would have been the prince's older sister in the villa proper.

'Is it from your father?' I asked.

A number of senatorial nobles sitting nearby threw me a look of faint irritation. It clearly irked anyone of rank that I could address the prince almost as an equal despite my low birth, while they, the product of centuries of carefully arranged political marriages, were forced to address him as 'Highness'.

Commodus nodded, rubbing his thumb across the wax seal that bore the head of Minerva, a divine reflection of Aurelius himself – wisdom and war.

'Aren't you going to open it?'

Commodus frowned. 'Will the news change if I don't, Em? Because the *murmillo* might die while I read.'

We turned our attention back to the pairing. Sword against small shield, spear against large. A contest with no clear outcome to my mind, though the *hoplomachus* spear-man had clearly had the best of it so far. Both gladiators bore several small, bloody badges of courage, though.

I watched as the spear clonked off the shield and was turned aside. The murmillo, clad in bronze and padded linen with red streamers trailing from his limbs as he moved, capitalised on the failing and leapt forward, attempting to get his sword to somewhere critical. But the Gaul was fast. He danced back three paces as easily as if he'd been stepping forward, and as the heavy swordsman lunged, suddenly his target wasn't there. He fell gracelessly to the dust and the Gaul casually stepped close and dropped his spear point to rest on the murmillo's spine, just below his helmet's neck guard. The fallen man raised two fingers together in supplication, and the spear-man looked to Commodus.

Somewhere not far away, a gruff voice called, 'Highness, he should die. A clumsy attack.'

Commodus weighed this up for a moment, and then smiled.

'*Missio*,' he announced magnanimously, to a rumble of disappointment from the senators.

'Not a popular choice,' I murmured as the gladiators rose and bowed to the prince.

'He fought well. It was one mistake. A prime fighter is worth too much to kill for one fall.'

Nothing to do with mercy, just economy and expediency. I could hardly fail to notice that Commodus was growing, and with the increased maturity of his conversation came a corresponding increase in the wisdom behind it. His choice may not have been made out of mercy, but it would *feel* like it to the man given a reprieve. As the two men staggered from the arena and a slave entered, raking the spilled blood into the sand, the prince finished running his finger across the wax likeness of the goddess and snapped the seal, opening the leather case and unfurling the short scroll. He read it through, his face inscrutable, and I smiled to think that only a few short years ago I had watched him struggling to read the line *Cato's cat eats birds* in the schoolroom.

Finally, he rolled the scroll back up and tapped it on his knee. I waited patiently. We were friends, but to pry into the affairs of the imperial family without invitation was not done. Eventually, he leaned back with a sigh.

'Aquileia is destroyed,' he said simply. I frowned. I had heard of the city, of course. It was an important regional place with a distinguished history. It had been destroyed? 'A tribe called the Marcomanni from across the border,' he elucidated. 'They looted and burned the place. Father and Verus are based there now, rebuilding and fortifying it. He says they are having to chase around to find any sign of the tribe, who seem to have moved back north. It sounds as though there won't be much of a war. I expect they'll be home for the winter.'

'Your uncle will be champing at the bit to get to them, to win more victories for the empire.' I smiled. The glorious Verus was Rome's leading winner of military victories, and I knew Commodus idolised his uncle, so I was surprised when he gave a bored shrug.

'War's not a thing to prize, Em.'

I was somewhat nonplussed by his comment, given how we'd just watched two men thrusting deadly steel at one another for mere sport. Commodus must have seen my eyes flick to the bloodied sand, for he gave me an odd, wry smile. 'It's not the same.' I threw a confused look at him and he shrugged. 'War is different. It kills men by the thousand, and rarely solves anything. In ten years, for all Uncle's victory, we'll be watching Parthia rise again. All war does is hold back the tide for a bit. The only fighting that's really worth anything is what you see down there.' He pointed at the arena, where the last of the blood had been covered and the slave was slinking away. '*That*'s a contest of skill and bravery, and it's got a purpose. To entertain. Give me two talented gladiators over a sea of soldiers any day.'

More news came as winter edged closer, though none of it was drastic or exciting. In the north, the tribes continued to hover just out of the reach of the two emperors, who concentrated on organising the defences of Italia in the region, raising new legions – which was apparently a difficult proposition given how far the plague had depopulated the countryside – and securing promises of peace, tribute and good conduct from whatever chieftains they could corner. In a way, I suppose, it could be considered a victory in itself that no more Romans had to die on a barbarian blade that season, though enough were reportedly falling in camp from the ongoing pestilence.

As the cold winds and the rains came in, and the more rustic of the freedmen serving in the villa assured us that snow was in the wind, I found myself fighting my own war. Consul Quadratus, who was now nearing the end of his term, found every opportunity to corner me when I was alone.

He was polite, which was oddly more unpleasant than if he'd been openly lascivious, but he was overly tactile, and his gaze was hungry. In numerous encounters across the villa, Quadratus made a habit of touching me lightly, on the shoulders, the hips, the arms. He was there when I emerged from the baths, freshly dressed. He was there in the corridors and hallways, always with the look of a predator. His presence made me shiver, made my gorge rise. He never made a move on me beyond those gentle brushes of fingers, and I felt safe from true danger, for if any harm befell me, Commodus would have him pay for it, but he was always there, an ever-present threat for the future. I am surprised I did not rub off my skin in the baths given how long I spent in there trying to scrub away the memory of his touch.

Commodus assured me that he would never let me fall into the clutches of a man who I didn't want. It was comforting to hear, though I reminded myself that he may be a prince, but he was not even eight years old yet, and his opinion would likely be overridden by his elders.

I persevered, but my world was shaken at Saturnalia.

The emperors had not returned from their campaign as Commodus had predicted. Despite their inability to bring the troublesome tribes to battle, Aurelius and Verus opted to remain in winter quarters with the army, fearing the Marcomanni and their allies might capitalise on a winter withdrawal. Thus we suffered a somewhat subdued Saturnalia, with the patriarchs of the imperial family absent. Quadratus continued to cause me trouble, Lucilla was pricklier than ever with the ongoing absence of her husband, and Commodus had started, I think, to really miss his uncle, especially with the continuing absence of his little brother, Annius, who had remained in Praeneste with their mother and whom we had not seen for months.

On the second day of the festival we went to visit the *palaestra* where the wrestlers were training. They were to be part of the evening's entertainment, at the instigation of the young prince, and he wanted to be certain that they were prepared. I was worried. Commodus had been complaining of a sore throat for days, and the villa's attendant physician had prescribed a potent liquid to gargle with and insisted that he remain tucked up beneath blankets. Despite this, though he gargled with a rigid adherence to schedule, the young prince refused to spend Saturnalia in bed. I chided him gently for emerging onto the palaestra in just tunic, boots and short cloak, when there was still frost on the ground and the air carried a bitter cold that sank into the bones in mere moments. He brushed my concerns aside, though with little in the way of words, wincing whenever he swallowed.

The throat illness didn't worry me. I'd had something similar years earlier, and it had lasted but a matter of days. His unwillingness to look after himself was another thing entirely. He claimed that fresh air was better for his health than wallowing in bed all day, but I worried, for I trusted the physician. We watched the wrestlers, and I endured Commodus' rasped notes and comments on their various strengths and weaknesses, all the time wishing we were inside. One of the wrestlers, a hulking bruiser of a man, explained some of the more difficult moves to us, and bowed respectfully as Commodus thanked him. Finally, seemingly content with what we had seen, we turned and made our way back to the villa proper.

I was discussing one of my prime concerns with him as we walked.

'I cannot say that he is discourteous, as such . . .' Quadratus, of course.

'He hasn't insulted you? Harmed you?'

'No,' I replied, hurriedly. 'No insult or hurt. It's just a threat. Or maybe a promise. There is something odd about him. I mean, what Roman nobleman reaches thirty years without marriage?'

It *was* odd, and Commodus knew it. But Quadratus was a cousin of the prince's, carrying imperial blood, *and* he was a consul of Rome. He'd not done anything officially wrong, for all my concerns. Still, I didn't like him.

'Perhaps . . .' the prince began, and then his voice disappeared. I had taken another step or two, watching the icy ground beneath my feet, and I turned. Commodus was lying on the floor, gasping. I stared in surprise. My first thought was that he'd slipped on the ice, and I almost laughed automatically, but something was clearly not right. His face, which had been pale with his illness, was suddenly waxy and red, and he was gasping as though fighting for breath.

Before I could help him up, the Praetorians were there. Two of them had been following us at a discreet distance, as they always did with members of the imperial family, and now they were lifting him carefully. His eyes rolled, and I hurried along in front as they carried him, as fast as they could, into the villa. We put him in his room, and I was instantly dismissed by the soldiers, who took to his door on guard. I hovered in the vestibule outside, frantically pacing, worried to death.

That hook-nosed physician arrived quickly, with an entourage of slaves carrying his equipment. Various noblemen gathered in a group in one of the antechambers, concerned for the prince's health. Notable by their absence, to my mind at least, were Lucilla and Quadratus. No great concern for the prince from his sister or his cousin, though even the meanest senator staying at the villa hurried to his apartments.

I fretted as the physician disappeared inside. I waited, worried, impatient, and finally a slave called for me. The prince was calm now, stable and breathing, though the sweat on his brow was flowing like the Tiber, and he still had that waxy sheen. The physician pressed me for details of everything the prince had done, said or endured the past three days since his treatment had begun. I told him everything I could, which was virtually nothing of value, and then I was dismissed to the corridor again.

Two days passed in tense concern. Lucilla still made no appearance, though she very thoughtfully sent him a message that she would implore the gods on his behalf. *How generous*, I thought. Quadratus did visit once, though he spent more time pawing at me than showing concern for the prince. I almost snapped at the man to leave me alone, only just managing to keep a tight rein on my tongue. Commodus' tutors turned up occasionally, arguing among themselves as to the cause and nature of the illness. One of them seemed to have spread a rumour that the prince had somehow contracted the plague that afflicted the empire, and consequently his visitors tailed off to just a core of those most concerned. Even then, several of them would only visit him with a posy of dried flowers slung beneath their mouth and nose to ward off the deadly vapours of the plague.

He was not getting better. He regained a more conscious attitude periodically, though he was so weak and confused that he did little more than gasp and attend to whatever medication the physician prescribed. The medicus himself began to get that look of sleepless worry about the eyes. If the prince died, he had little doubt that the blame would land with him when the emperors returned.

Our deliverance arrived on the fourth day, when all hope for his recovery seemed lost. I was kneeling in the corridor outside, praying to God for His help, and somewhat impiously adding the odd plea to Aesculapius just in case, when the door of the antechamber suddenly burst open and a small party of men flooded in. The one in the lead wore a long tunic of pale green

86

and a cloak of grey. He sported an impressive curled beard and his eyes were everywhere, like a watchful hawk. He had with him several servants, carrying bags and satchels. One, I noted, was a roll of surgeon's tools. My heart fluttered at the sight. Behind him came the lady Annia Fundania Faustina, one of Marcus Aurelius' more favoured cousins. Both she and the new physician seemed focused and determined, and they were followed by half a dozen Praetorians.

'Stand aside,' the man in the long tunic said to the guards on the door as though he had the natural right to command Praetorians. The two soldiers dithered for only a moment, but the presence of the lady Fundania decided them and they swung open the door and stepped out of the way of this marching man. I risked much by simply slipping in among the man's entourage as they passed and found myself in the prince's chamber with them.

'Gods above and below,' the lady breathed as she caught sight of Commodus.

'Hot fever,' the physician said confidently as he approached the bed.

'Can you save him?'

I felt a chill run through me at the very notion he might not be able to, but my doubts were dissipated by the confidence of the physician. 'He is mis-prescribed. Some two-as halfwit thinks he knows what he's doing. Medici should only be allowed to practise if they're licensed. I've said as much before.'

I was all but knocked aside as the villa's resident physician arrived and pushed through the crowd in a mix of anger and panic. 'What is the meaning of this? My patient . . .' His voice tailed off as he reached the bedside and the man in the green tunic turned, one eyebrow rising. The man who'd been treating Commodus swallowed nervously. 'Galen?'

'The very same. What was your diagnosis? Inflammation of the tonsils, I hope?'

The man nodded, his face ashen. 'You went back to Perga-mon,' he said, weakly.

'Until I was summoned. The emperor apparently feels Rome needs my skills. He was clearly as shrewd as ever.' I stared. This was the famous Galen, who they said was the greatest physician since Hippocrates. My pulse thundered. Could the great man save my prince? 'I reached the city,' he said, 'and the good lady here told me of the prince's condition. I came with all haste.' He picked up the cup by the table, peering at it and giving it a sniff that made him recoil. 'What in the name of sacred Aesculapius are you giving him?'

'A standard concoction,' the other physician bridled.

'The salt content is far too high. And you have bird faeces in it?'

'Owl.'

'And?'

'Listen,' the villa's doctor said angrily, 'there is nothing in there that is not recognised as curative for infections of the throat.'

'But you need to be careful and sparing, you dolt. You do not simply shovel every ingredient that could help into a liquid and stir. The prince is fortunate indeed that you have not also poisoned him.'

'Now listen to me,' began the physician, but it took only a look from Galen and a nod from Annia Fundania, and the former court physician found himself unceremoniously ejected by the muscled hairy arms of two Praetorians. The room settled to silence once more as Galen bent over the patient and exam-ined him. He opened Commodus' mouth and peered down into the throat, tested his pulse and his temperature and stood back, satisfied.

'He will be fine. Get rid of this cup. Burn it, in fact. Find a new cup and fill it with slightly warmed water, containing only honey and essence of rose. It is all he needs. With it he will be fit in a day or two. I am somewhat sad to say that he would probably have been up and about by now had he been simply left alone for the illness to run its course. The cure prescribed by that idiot has done more to hurt the prince than the infection itself.'

That night I stayed beside his bed, the prince finally sitting up, looking perkier, with some of his colour returned already. Galen remained at the villa with the lady Fundania, though both were elsewhere at the time there came a knock at the door. Commodus took a last sip of the gentle medicine and placed the cup down, then smiled weakly at me and gestured for me to get the door. His voice was still painful and croaky, and he saved it where he could.

I opened it to find one of the villa's slaves holding a scroll case with the Minerva seal that labelled it as from the emperor's pen. Another update on the war, of course, as we'd received periodically during our stay. Still, it would help to take Commodus' mind off his discomfort. I thanked the slave, closed the door and passed the scroll to the prince. I lit two more oil lamps to make reading easier.

Commodus broke the seal, withdrew the scroll and unfurled it, his blinking, tired eyes devouring the spidery words as he worked through it. I glanced across and smiled just as his face paled and his jaw dropped. His fingers shaking, he let go of the bottom of the scroll, which instantly furled, and he dropped it to the bed, his eyes staring, lips moving soundlessly.

I stared in shock. 'What is it?'

Whether because of his painful throat, or because he could not bear to repeat the words he'd read, he gestured at the scroll, urging me to take it. Gingerly, I did so, peering at the small, spidery writing.

In a somewhat strangled and brief missive penned by the great Marcus Aurelius himself, we were informed that Lucius

Verus had succumbed to the plague on their return journey from the Danubius River. So virulent was his affliction that he never even made it back as far as Aquileia, passing from the world of men after a mere three days of agony.

My shocked, horrified eyes rose to the prince and I saw all hope and spirit drain from him.

First Fulvus, his twin. The other half of his soul.

Now Verus, his beloved uncle, after whom he had moulded himself.

Commodus' heart had taken a second blow.

VI

THE YEAR OF SORROWS

Rome, AD 169

The year of sorrows began with a soul-wrenching wait in subdued misery as the emperor and his entourage escorted the body of Lucius Verus back to us from the north. We received periodic updates on the procession's progress, so we knew when he came close to Rome. Lucilla, who I thought typically unfeeling considering her husband's unexpected death, took the reins and was all business, making what arrangements she could in advance of the body's arrival. The household was quiet and all affairs, bar that of funerary preparations, stopped. I was at a loss. Commodus retreated into his rooms, and no matter how persuasive I tried to be, I could not gain access to him, for he had given the Praetorian outside his door orders not to be disturbed.

I imagined all the things he would be doing, just as he had years ago, tearing out his hair, failing to sleep, sitting in the dark, and there was nothing I could do about it.

Sure enough, when Marcus Aurelius and his sombre column reached Rome with the embalmed remains of his brother, Commodus finally emerged from his chamber with pale, sallow skin and dark circles beneath the eyes. I tried to speak to him, to judge his state and see whether I could help, but there simply was not time. All was now preparation, and every-one was busy, including Commodus, and I myself was aiding

Mother in preparing all the garments required for the coming days.

Mother disapproved, quietly and in private, of the arrangements for the passing emperor. Her – *our* – faith is rooted in the belief that the dead will be judged, and those found worthy will ascend to Heaven. Despite the seeming positivity of such a belief, I had always found Mother, and those few other Christians we regularly came into contact with, to treat the world with a dour joylessness. She clearly felt that theatre performances, chariot races and the like were inappropriate ways to mark a death. And as for the fights in the arena in his name, the less said the better. But it is the way of Rome, if it is not *our* way, to mark the passage of the great in such a manner, and the people of the city remember Verus that way, which is reassuringly fitting.

We watched as Verus was rendered down to ash on a massive pyre in the Campus Martius, and the urn interred in the great mausoleum constructed by Hadrian across the river. Illustrious company awaited him: Hadrian himself, and Antoninus Pius and his empress. We then attended the various games and ceremonies in his honour as the senate declared Verus' divinity. It is perhaps a mark of the change we could expect with our patron's death that even Mother attended the fights, albeit with a sour, stony expression. Verus had understood and had been indulgent in allowing us our faith's tenets, but, with his passing, Lucilla would grant no such tolerances. No matter what our beliefs, we were to watch men shed blood for the gods and cheer them on. In my secret heart, I was grateful. I had discovered an unexpected appreciation of the sport back in the villa with my golden prince.

We moved back to the Palatine for the time of mourning, to be near the temples and the tomb and the various venues for events. Lucilla came too, obviously, though while the entire imperial family wore drab faces of grief, she was more concerned with putting her own house in order. The death of her husband had left Lucilla in a strangely uncertain position: she was the daughter of one emperor and had been the wife of another. From Aurelius she inherited the status of an imperial princess, which carried advantages I could never even dream of, but from her marriage to Verus, she had become an empress, which placed her above every woman in the empire, barring her mother. With Verus gone, though, and the succession settled on the shoulders of her brothers rather than her own children, that status appeared destined to shatter and fall away. I think I knew Lucilla well enough even then to realise that she had no time to mourn – she was busy building her webs to maintain her position in the empire's hierarchy.

On the fifth night of the funerary games I finally spoke to Commodus. The summons came unexpectedly, one of the many palace slaves sent to find me, and I was grateful it was not Cleander, who was back in circulation now that we had returned to Rome. I had seen the man a few times, but we had yet to speak, which was undoubtedly a good thing.

I found Commodus sitting on a chair in front of his private *lararium*, a small replica temple on a base containing the statues of the deities to whom he currently turned. Hercules was there, of course, as well as the more popular gods of Rome and a newly fashioned, bearded one that I think must have been his deified uncle. An odd parody of the ascent of Christ, it seemed to me.

The door closed behind me, and we were entombed in a dim room, lit by two small oil lamps.

'Are you . . . How are you faring?' I managed, not sure after all this time how to approach the subject.

'Badly,' was his simple reply. He was almost eight now, and yet there was a strange maturity to his manner that reminded me he was precocious and sharp, and no ordinary boy. Like the infant Hercules he so revered; a gifted child who strangled serpents and made a conscious choice to follow a path of virtue.

What would Hercules have been had *his* twin died while just a boy? I wondered suddenly.

'It is not good to suffer in solitude,' I managed.

He turned a look on me that suggested otherwise and indicated the small altar with a sweep of his hand. 'I think the gods send me messages. I have dreams. Nightmares. Each night is different. It's not Fulvus under the ice now. But it's always death. Always decay. Like the plague got into my head and sits there, hurting my mind. If the gods have a purpose, then these must be portents. Signs.'

I frowned. This was a new and, to my mind, dangerous line of thought.

'It is only natural to suffer such terrors. You had barely recovered from the loss of Fulvus when Verus was taken from you. A twin and favourite uncle wrenched away from you? Of *course* you dream of death, especially with what is going on outside. Rome suffers the pestilence from Parthia, and wars in the north threaten the world. I dream of such things on occasion, and those losses are nothing to me compared with what they are to you. But there is no plan to this. Your dreams are not signs.'

I tried to push down the repeated memory of my mother telling me that everything that happened was all part of the divine design. That notion was particularly unhelpful just now, echoing the pagan suggestions of the prince as it did.

'There is no portent in them,' I went on. 'All this is just what that physician a couple of years ago called "melancholia". You are not consciously sinking into sadness, but it pulls you down regardless. And the only way to beat it is to fight back. To drag yourself up into the light. I've seen you rise from these black moods before, remember.' *And on occasion slide into them from a state of euphoric delight, too*, I thought unhelpfully. 'I can help. I *will* help.'

He did not look convinced.

'I . . . sometimes I think what it might be like to die. I consider it. I . . . I don't know.'

Dangerous paths indeed. I shivered at the raw emotion behind those words.

'Don't give in to it,' I said, probably more urgently and pleadingly than was helpful.

'I think this is what happened to my grandfather,' he said in an odd voice. My brow creased again. I never knew his grandfather, and neither had he. The man had passed away long ago. Another shiver ran through me as the prince went on. 'He died young. And when I ask Father about him, he just gets a strange, sad look and refuses to speak about it. I think . . . I think he might have—'

I grasped his shoulders. I, a pleb, grabbed the shoulders of the empire's heir. If the Praetorian on the other side of the door had seen me do such a thing, I'm certain my life would have been forfeit. Still, I held him like that and locked his eyes with my own.

'I will not let anything like that happen to you. I will not let it. Do you understand?'

There was another heavy pause and then he nodded.

'Father says that when the games are done, we will move away again. To his Praeneste villa.'

I felt a lurch in my heart. I would not be able to follow him. I was bound through Mother to the empress Lucilla, and her villa was north of Rome.

As if reading my thoughts, he gave a sad smile. 'My sister will come with us to Praeneste. She stays close to Father now.'

I bet she did. Fearing the loss of her grand status, she would be endearing herself to him, I thought bitterly. But at least it meant that Mother and I would go too. I would be with him, and that drew from me a smile.

We talked for an hour then, he constantly bringing the subject back to his fears and the dreams that haunted him, me constantly steering him to bright notions and optimistic plans. When I left, finally, I think he was in better spirits. At least I did not fear he would take his life in the night, now. I found myself wondering, as I wandered, what so tied me to the prince that I automatically planned my life to be near him.

We moved out to Praeneste in the spring, and I felt relieved and grateful to be free of the ever-present atmosphere of a city crushed beneath the weight of disease. The imperial villa in that quiet, rustic region – one of several built by the illustrious Hadrian – sat among green fields and shady woodland below the hill of Praeneste itself, surrounded by considerable estates. It was larger even than the one of Verus' in which we had spent so much time, though the grounds here were not utilised in the same grand manner. While there was a small theatre that could double up for fights, there was no racecourse, and the resident emperor here had little interest in hunting through the estate.

Still, it was a rural idyll if ever I saw one. But my positivity was to be short-lived. Lucilla was a prickly presence even to begin with, but her moods plummeted to new depths early on. Her ongoing uncertainty over her status was swiftly cleared up when her father, barely allowing her an appropriate period of mourning, betrothed her to his favoured general, Pompeianus. The decision caused what I can only describe as a human explosion.

Upon receiving the command for her betrothal, she rose from her chair like a phoenix from the ashes, all fire and fury. 'This is *unacceptable*,' she snapped, directing her ire at the man who ruled the world, drawing wide-eyed shock from those family and close advisors present. The emperor turned a tired look on her but said nothing, and she had the temerity to jab a finger at her father. 'Pompeianus is *nothing*. A provincial soldier. I am an *empress*.'

As though speaking to a tantruming child, which, in a way, he was, Marcus Aurelius spoke levelly and quietly. 'You *were* an empress, Lucilla.' She bridled, and I prepared for the worst, but the emperor went on quietly. 'Pompeianus is a senator, a former consul, one of the most senior commanders of my army, and a clever, respectable man. You could use a little sensible, I think.'

Lucilla made a strange growling noise and stalked two steps forward, more leonine, now. 'Pompeianus is new money,' she sneered. 'A backwater farm boy whose father grew too big for his boots and made it to Rome. He is a rustic and low-born and wholly inappropriate. I will *not* accept this match. I am an empress and the ashes of my husband – *your brother* – are not yet cooled.'

Aurelius took two steps towards his daughter – *two* lions now, meeting in ire – and I actually thought for a moment he might strike her. Instead, he squared up to her, his expression cast in stone. He had always been a great emperor, wise and clever, but I had never seen him so forceful. That afternoon, he stared down his daughter and spoke in tones of steel and bronze that could have bested a legion.

'You are no empress. You are my daughter, who shows scant regard for the niceties of mourning, busily positioning herself among the great instead. It is you who have outgrown your boots, Lucilla, in believing that because I married you to my stepbrother you are my equal in some way. You are not. I rule Rome, and I alone, now. And when I die, my sons will rule. That is the way of it. You may keep your petty privileges: seats in the arena, positions at banquets and the like. You may keep a villa or two. But you will also keep your tongue tucked away inside that swelling head of yours and you will make a good wife for Pompeianus, who is a great man, if born of the *equites*, and who does not deserve to be saddled with a shrew. Now get out of my sight.'

It was impressive. Had it been me before the great man, I fear I would have shrivelled and perished on the spot, and I am no shrinking flower. Lucilla was made of even sterner stuff. She accepted her berating with cold silence, bowed her head respectfully, a hair's breadth short of insolence, and left. She would be remarried and no more an empress. But this would not be the last blow of that particular combat, for sure, and the following months at the villa were appalling in her presence. I avoided her as much as possible, but could not always do so.

The presence of his icy sister did little to raise Commodus' still flagging spirits, though the companionship of young Annius, so long absent but now returned, helped a great deal. Between my periodic ministrations and the youthful spirits of Annius, we began to lift Commodus from the misery of his uncle's passing.

A second unpleasantness was caused by an old enmity. Cleander came as part of the emperor's household. His access to Commodus and also to myself was extremely limited, since he was constantly beset by chores and tasks in this, a smaller complex than the city palace, but whenever opportunity allowed him close to either of us he continued his machinations, ingratiating himself to the prince and bathing me in snide remarks. Between Lucilla and Cleander, I spent every hour in the villa on the lookout for someone determined to ruin my day.

On one occasion, mind, when Commodus was again in good spirits and fine physical form, I was forced to acknowledge a certain value to Cleander's influence on the prince. Commodus and young Annius played a game in the grounds that had begun innocently as a series of simple physical competitions – seeing who could jump the furthest across the flower beds and the like. I had been half watching as I sewed a tunic for my mother, sitting on a marble bench. Had I paid more attention, I might have noticed the brothers, throughout their laughter, becoming more and more dangerous, daring one another to ever greater feats. It was only when I looked up to see them both tottering along a narrow balustrade over a sizeable drop that I realised what was happening and my heart lurched. I rose to try and interfere and, even as I came to my feet, saw Annius waver and begin to slip, toppling out towards the drop. I saw it all about to happen, and then suddenly Cleander was there, as he had been that ice-cold day to fish a prince from the deadly water, his hands reaching up and grabbing another brother of Commodus, preventing his fall.

I started running to join them, but on the way bumped into Mother, who had been looking for me. As she rattled her disapproval at me, my eyes continually flicked towards the tableau out in the gardens. Cleander had lifted Annius down and was now talking almost sternly to Commodus, then helped him too down to the ground.

I realised that, in an odd way, Cleander was the down to my up. While I was there to pull Commodus from the gloom of despair and lift him into the light, so Cleander seemed to be there when the prince pushed himself to excess, keeping control of the situation. Had he not been such a constant drain on my own spirits, I might have been able to find an odd appreciation for him, then.

And then there was my third trouble. Among the many courtiers who managed to secure an invitation to Praeneste and, rather unsettlingly, with the support of Lucilla, came the former consul Quadratus. Everywhere I went in the villa, when I wasn't being sneered at by Cleander or shouted at by Lucilla, I was being leered at by Quadratus and occasionally touched and caressed. Perhaps worse still was the fact that he had recently adopted a son who was around my age, and the son kept fixing me with the same hungry look as his father. I shuddered a lot.

Other than Commodus, my only ally and the only true relief I found was in the form of Eclectus. The former secretary of Lucius Verus had not passed to Lucilla but had instead been taken on by Aurelius himself, and become a man of some importance. And Eclectus liked me. It might purely have been born of the fact that we had both spent ample time in the icy, difficult presence of Lucilla, but more than once Eclectus interrupted difficult moments and saved me from trouble.

Throughout our time there, with the companionship of young Annius, I managed to work my little miracles with the prince. Commodus returned fully to the waking world once more. He was not quite the same, I believe. The loss of Fulvus had shaken him to his core, and he had recovered well but, compounded by the loss of Verus, he simply could not reach the heights of easy humour we had once shared. In fact, I think that, more than ever before, his sullener moments became counterpoint to peaks of idiotic spirit that often went too far. In high summer, an incident brought one matter to a head, much to my regret.

I had been in the gardens, hiding from Lucilla, who was once again on a rampage, and as I passed into the atrium at the villa's northern side, I stumbled into Quadratus' son. I rounded the corner and, walking directly into him, stumbled back, startled and embarrassed. I mumbled an apology, for I was a nobody, while he was the son of an important man. The next thing I knew, he was on me. We were alone in the place, which was a rarity in that busy villa, and I was in trouble.

His hands were suddenly on my shoulders, pushing me back. His leering mouth opened, and his tongue darted out, moistening his lips. I felt my breath forced from me as I hit the painted wall, and I almost fell.

'You're too pretty to be alone,' he said, his voice little more than a sickly whisper.

'Get off me,' I said, desperately. I dared not shout, oddly. Though he was attacking me, I was wise enough to the ways of the court and the social levels we moved in to know that any accusation I made would come down to his word against mine, and mine would count for nothing. Consequently, I knew I had to fight this battle here and on my own.

I pushed him away, but he was stronger than me and he came back with another shove, smashing me against the wall once more, this time delivering a painful crack to the back of my head. He was holding me now, forcing me to remain still as his tongue advanced on me. But I am not weak, and Christian charity and forgiveness go only so far. I brought my knee up into his groin. I was wearing a flowing tunic with plenty of give, and I hit him hard. I left him in the atrium, doubled over and whimpering as blood trickled down his lip from where he'd bitten deep into it. Just as I would not tell anyone what he had done, I knew he was bound in a similar manner, especially faced with admitting that a plebeian girl had bested him.

I ran through the corridors, ignoring demands that I slow and stop, and finally reached Commodus. For the first time in our lives, our common situation was reversed. I was shaking and fearful, and the young prince consoled me, and tried to talk me round. When he drew out of me something of what had happened, he was angry. I didn't tell him all of it, of course, just that Quadratus' son had shoved me. I once more voiced my fear over the former consul, and now of his son also. I was almost twelve, and only a year away from being promised to someone. I had to make sure it would not be him.

The next thing I knew, Commodus was leading me to his father. I had not needed to ask. The prince knew what needed doing. We were admitted to the imperial presence, and my spirits sank as I noted the familiar shape of Lucilla on another couch.

'My son?' the emperor said curiously.

'Father, I don't want Marcia to be Quadratus'. He wants her, but he's not good for her. Since Uncle is gone, could I be her patron now?'

It was not well put. He was still only eight and without the tongue of an orator, but it was said from the heart, and his father recognised that. I was on my knees behind the prince, respectful in the imperial presence, and I kept my gaze lowered, just enough to still see everything. I could see the emperor mulling it over, deciding what could be done, but all my hopes were dashed when Lucilla shook her head.

'No.'

'I'm not asking you, Lucilla,' Commodus replied. 'I'm asking Father.'

'But the girl is mine,' Lucilla snapped. 'Her and her mother. They were both part of my husband's household, clients of his, freed by his hand. And when his estate passed to me, I inherited all of his people, barring the one that Father took as a secretary. The seamstress and her daughter are mine, not yours. If her mother wishes to remain gainfully employed and not have all her debts and favours called in, then she and the girl will submit to my will.'

We were, of course, beholden. Our home had been destroyed in that flood, and even that had been paid for by Verus. Yes, my mother was a talented seamstress, but we owed so much to the family of the divine Verus that my mother and I could never hope to live without their patronage. I felt the world crumbling away beneath my feet, and Commodus, clearly desperate, turned to the emperor.

'Father?'

Marcus Aurelius shrugged. 'It *is* her estate, son. They are her women.' And I knew what was happening, here; what games were being played. The emperor had put down his foot with Lucilla, betrothing her against her will, and knew how badly it sat with her. He would not compound that decision by overruling her and meddling in her estate. Ever the wily ambassador, he had imposed his will upon her, now he must give concessions.

Lucilla's icy glare of triumph sickened me.

'You are almost of marriageable age, girl, yes?'

I nodded. 'Almost twelve, Majesty.'

'Quadratus cannot marry you. Look at you, just a raggy doll in a cheap tunic with slave's blood. But Quadratus is a cousin, an important man, and it is crucial to keep the senatorial class of Rome, family included, loyal and content. You will be Quadratus'. Not a wife, for he has no wish for a wife, but a mistress. A plaything. And you will accept it. You will enjoy it, or at least appear to do so, for Quadratus is a friend, and I shall hear if it is otherwise.'

I felt sick. Nauseous and with shaking legs, I bowed lower, accepting my fate. Mother and Father had been slaves before the great Verus freed them. I had grown up free and had never known the feel of slavery. Yet even as a freeborn pleb, I realised now I was enslaved by Lucilla and Quadratus. Commodus could do nothing to stop it, and the emperor *would* do nothing.

I spent the following month largely in hiding. When Commodus was available, he kept me busy and accompanied me, for even in the knowledge that I was practically his, Quadratus would do nothing in the prince's presence. The rest of the time, I tried to stay hidden and out of circulation. Occasionally I would meet Quadratus or his son, both of whom simply gave me a knowing glance, assuming that I would be theirs as soon as my age made it socially acceptable. Other times, I would meet Lucilla, who treated me like some unwanted rodent. And yet others, I would find myself in Cleander's presence, though he had stopped taunting and pushing me now. That I had been effectively sold into sexual slavery and was waiting only until I first endured my monthly cycle was a dream come true for him, and he revelled in my misery.

But the time of sorrows was not done with us yet.

The last timber on the funeral pyre of that year came during the night of a feast in late autumn. I forget what it was celebrating. I had no cause to be happy and simply sat with Mother at the periphery of events, for once less enthusiastic than she. Among the imperial family and the high nobles near them, the night was one of good-natured banter, and it peaked when the empress Faustina urged her younger son, Annius, to sing a song. Annius had a lovely voice, clear and perfect, and the boy, now almost seven, stood at the centre of the room and held out his hands. He began to sing, a popular melody of the time that I cannot for the life of me remember now.

When it started to go wrong, it was assumed to be some humorous childhood slip, and his parents and siblings, and all those present at the near tables, smiled and laughed. Annius had mispronounced something, and then his words slid to a halt, his brow folding in confusion. With a shrug, he began the refrain afresh, but this time, even the basic words came out as unintelligible noises. He seemed unable to speak, as though he had reverted to some foreign tongue.

Then he fell.

At that moment, we all knew something was wrong. The whole feast stopped instantly, and everyone rushed forward to be of aid if they could. I saw bits and pieces of it through the legs and between the bodies of other guests. Annius was on the floor, shaking, eyes rolling. On an impulse, I looked to the side, to Commodus. The emperor and the empress, the princesses and the nobles, were all intent on the suddenly fallen boy. No one was looking at Commodus.

No one but I.

And I saw it all flood back in.

The dreadful blackness of his moods after the passing of Fulvus, the despair and visions of death when Verus died. The dreams of decay and ruination that he believed had come from the gods in prescience, foretelling more pain. And he had been right. I should not, as a Christian, give credence to such ideas, but I find it impossible to deny. Commodus had thought his dreams of death to be omens sent by his gods. And that very notion seemed to be being played out. He was vindicated in the worst possible way.

And because I knew what had passed between us, I knew Annius would die.

It was an awful feeling, but I knew it with leaden certainty. And I believe Commodus knew it too.

The feast ended abruptly, and the young prince was carried to his room. The physician who was on hand in the villa announced that it was an affliction that struck the great and the glorious. Alexander had had it, he said. And Caesar. Now Annius of the Antonine dynasty. But, the man smiled, remember that Alexander and Caesar lived full lives with the affliction. It did not kill them, and it would not kill this prince.

I knew otherwise.

Perhaps even the emperor did not believe him, for the next morning the noted physician Galen arrived in Praeneste, having hurried hither from Rome at Aurelius' summons. The great medicus had been doing his best to heal the beleaguered city of its plague. Placed in charge by the emperor, he had instructed the *vigiles*, the authorities and the populace how best to minimise risk of contagion and how to deal with it when it arose. He was slowly bringing Rome under control. But now, with Annius' fall, he had ridden hard for Praeneste.

When he was escorted into the imperial apartment, the local doctor had no argument. Galen's reputation spoke for itself, and it was known how much the emperor valued him, after saving Commodus' life so recently.

'It is the falling sickness,' the local physician said confidently.

Galen flashed him a look. 'Tell me what happened. Precisely. Leave nothing out.'

And the physician did just that. Galen looked less and less

convinced as it went on, and finally gestured at the man. 'This is no more the falling sickness than it is diarrhoea. Go find me somewhere hygienic to work and have everything made ready. There will be surgery, I fear.'

The other man frowned, but did so without argument. In the presence of Galen and the emperor, he was hardly about to stand on his convictions. Galen hurried in to the prince, Aurelius at his heel.

'Surgery, you think?' the emperor said breathlessly. 'What is it?'

Galen bent over the bed. His hands went to the boy's neck, then up to his ears, around the back, behind them, and then, with a sigh of regret, he turned Annius' head. I peered out from beside Commodus, where I had a fairly clear view. I could see the lump even from this far back, which meant it must have been large and pronounced. I had known the prince was doomed. Now it seemed revealed how.

'It is a tumour, Majesty,' Galen said. 'I once saw a similar rapid progression in a man in Pergamon. There will have been signs earlier if only you had known to look for them. A little memory loss, perhaps. A fall here and there. Nausea.'

And thinking back over the past month, I realised those signs had always been there but had been dismissed as unimportant. That day on the high wall when he teetered and had been grabbed by Cleander, perhaps even that had been the work of this ill. He could have been saved, had we but known.

'Can you heal him?' the emperor asked. His voice was steady and calm, though his eyes were wide, frightened. He was maintaining his composure for the benefit of his wife and other children, but even I could read a state of near-panic beneath that veneer.

'I cannot say for certain, Majesty. Had I got to him a month ago, I would be inclined to say yes. Even days ago would have been better. But it is advanced, and the effects are critical. Even

106

if he lives, he may now be permanently affected. He might be blind, or unable to hear. He might have no balance. But all that is moot, Majesty, as I would give at best even wagers as to whether he will make it through surgery, let alone the night.'

'Do it, Galen,' the emperor said.

The physician went to work. The non-crucial guests departed politely, and the imperial family and their close associates remained in that wing of the villa, waiting nervously. As had so often happened throughout our youth, my proximity to Commodus secured my place among them. The prince and I sat for a while in the garden outside, discussing our fears where no adult could overhear. Neither of us held out the slightest hope for Annius' survival.

After some two hours, Galen emerged, covered with blood. Annius still breathed. The tumour was gone. The imperial family poured out their thanks and relief, but Galen held up a warning hand. He did not believe he had got to it in time. The surgery had been hard and bloody work, and he was far from convinced that Annius would last 'til dawn.

That night, Commodus prayed to Aesculapius for hours. He bade me join him, but I prayed instead to God, and we both beseeched the powers in our own way that Annius would make it.

God does not look favourably upon pagans, though. And Aesculapius is, in my mother's words, one of the Devil's many faces.

Annius died in the small hours of the morning, and with him went the last of the shining flames in Commodus' heart.

The year of sorrow had claimed another Antonine prince.

PART TWO

A YOUNG HERCULES

'Lo! he stands erect and laughs at the danger, and sweeping together the hostile forces he puts them in his lion skin'

– *Philostratus: Imagines*, trans. Fairbanks, 1931

VII

A GILDED CAGE

AD 170

Time rolled on after that horrible season in Praeneste, and I saw little of my prince in the ensuing months. With the loss of another son, the emperor threw every resource and every ounce of his spirit into Commodus, trying to help him grow strong and swift and keep him safe, preparing him for what was to come. Now nine years old, the prince was all but a man already. He had always been advanced and precocious, after all. And partially in an effort to keep the prince's mind off that last disastrous death, his father pushed him endlessly into preparations for rule. He was constantly at study; taught grammar and rhetoric, economics and administration.

On the rare occasions I saw him, my heart broke all over again. While his family could see only a son focused on his tasks and advancing with a stolid manner, I could see that his calm was but a shell. Inside, all was turmoil, still. He was paler than he should be, and he looked permanently tired, his eyes having acquired a quick, dancing, haunted aspect, as though perpetually seeing Fulvus, Verus and Annius out of the corner of his eye. His father did not know how to help him and assumed he would heal from this heartbreak in time. He was right, as it turned out, though the prince's journey back from Hades was torture. Commodus, ever a loving son, hid the worst of what he was going through from his parents and suffered alone.

I could not help.

After Annius' death, Lucilla made sure that Mother was sent back to the Palatine, and I was given to Quadratus like chattel the day my first period ended and I was fit to be with a man. My new master had a rich town house on the Caelian Hill and we settled in there for a time, a gilded cage for the former consul and his pretty new mistress.

I never liked Quadratus, and posterity bears out my feelings. My situation might have been a boon to some of my status, who would be willing to sell their womanhood for baubles and pretty flowers. For me, it was sexual slavery, pure and simple.

I had spent years now overhearing tales of the hair-raising carnal exploits of several rather forceful women of the Antonine court, though I had assumed them to be exaggerating. When Quadratus first came to me, he was full of lust and joy for the acquisition of his new plaything after so many months of desire. He entered my room like a conquering general seeking his prize and tore my clothes from me.

My every instinct was to scream and to fight. I was only just out of childhood and this animal who had cast such a shadow over me for so long seemed determined to ruin me. I cannot say why, but for some reason, instead of reacting with anger or panic, I simply stood, silent and still amid the tatters of my clothes. He seemed oddly taken aback, since his prey was not playing the game. With a grunt, he pushed me back, down onto the bed amid sheets of silk and linen that had cost more than my entire childhood home had been worth.

My first time was painful, I will not deny, but it was no more painful than the descriptions I have heard from other girls. In fact, it was less painful than I expected. And with my seeming compliance, he had not needed to grasp and pull and force, and my flesh escaped bruising. It did not last long, and when it was over, we lay amid the bloodstained sheets. His fingers sought my hair, entwining in the dark waves almost in a caress, almost lovingly. It felt like a successful thief caressing his ill-gotten wares. It was at once tender and sickening. If I'd not hated him before, I certainly did then. And yet, through the unpleasantness, it seemed that I had unwittingly tamed the beast.

I suspect the encounter, and Quadratus' reaction to it, surprised him as much as it did I, for he did not come to me again for many days, yet had mirrors and jewellery provided in my room, inviting me to sit on the balcony with him and drink wine. He acted, almost, the caring lover. I complied. I always complied. I never smiled, though, and the fact that he seemed to neither notice nor care says much about him.

I was slipping into a false sense of security, and when he came to me next, he did little to damage that notion. He came gently and treated me with seeming care, though even his touch made me sick.

At first, I had been wary, but, once I realised that there was nothing to fear from the act of congress, I realised something: I had an advantage. Quadratus wanted me, but he wanted me to take the lead sometimes, too. I began to relive some of the less outlandish stories I remembered from the women at court. Within a few months of arriving on the Caelian, I knew how I could control Quadratus. I still hated every moment, and my flesh crawled at the mere sound of his voice, but pushing through my fear and my hatred, I decided even early on that I would not be a victim, not while I had strength and will. It was then, I think, I realised that even as a concubine I could wield power. My body and spirit were two of the strongest weapons in my array.

His son was forbidden from touching me. I suspect that initially Quadratus might have been inclined to share his new plaything purely for the sinful fun of further degrading me, but the way things had changed between us, and the way I felt he now needed me rather than merely desiring me, drove him to keep me all for himself. From the first time Quadratus found his adoptive heir pawing at me in a corridor, the invective he used made me flinch. I belonged to Quadratus, and he would not have even his son interfere. In fact, the lad was quickly sent to serve out a military tribunate and I only saw him infrequently after that.

I had time and freedom unparalleled thus far in my span. Though Quadratus lusted after me and I was his, my status as a pleb was poor enough that the last thing he wanted was to parade me around in front of his noble friends and acquaintances, so I was spared too much exposure in public places. I was his creature – and occasionally he was mine now, had he but realised it – but he was surprisingly equitable. When he wanted me, he came to me, but most of the time he kept himself to himself and I found that I was able to live much of my life however I pleased, as long as I was in the house when he wanted me. I had access to more money than I had ever seen and was given licence to spend it, which I did, as though it gushed from a pipe. I had my own slaves and a more spacious apartment than I had ever lived in.

Some days I wondered whether this was how powerful women like Livia and Agrippina had secured their power in a world where their men were in theory omnipotent. Whatever the case, as I learned more and more about my body and about his, I gained ever more hold over the man who'd thought he would cage me. Directed to a certain market with an unsavoury reputation one morning, I managed to acquire a copy of Aristides' *Milesiaka*, which considerably enhanced my knowledge of private skills and filled my sexual armoury with an array of dangerous new weapons to use in cowing my master. I spent much of my free time reading, and secreting such a work among my books was no troublesome chore.

So I endured.

What I found *hard* to endure was the enforced distance between Commodus and myself. Since the age of four I had

114

lived in the prince's palaces and villas, learned with him, played with him, suffered heartbreak with him. And now he was forced to survive on his own, and I was stuck with Quadratus and his domus, and with a supply of books and ready cash to keep me sane.

Commodus and I were not the only ones to suffer in that season of crows, though. Lucilla entered bitterly into her marriage with Pompeianus, who seemed no more thrilled by the match than the former empress. Rome continued to suffer the plague, though through the work of Galen and other wise men the effects had been somewhat lessened. The emperor's good friend Avidius Cassius was forced to take military action in Aegyptus to put down a revolt there, and once more the barbarians of the north, given heart by the emperors' withdrawal from Aquileia, crossed the great river and massacred a Roman force near Carnuntum.

The spring after Annius' passing, the emperor announced, somewhat wearily, a new campaign in the north to put down the troublesome Marcomanni and their Germanic allies. The military was gathered, and the court prepared to move north. This time most of us would go, including the great general Pompeianus and his bitter wife, the emperor and empress, Commodus, and even Quadratus, who was granted a position in command, more through familial connection than talent, it turned out.

At the beginning of the month of Junius, on a warm, bright morning, Marcus Aurelius himself, with Commodus at his shoulder, passed through the city with the Guard and to the great temple of Bellona in the Campus Martius. There, accompanied by the sacred *fetiales*, he cast the bloodstained spear into the patch of ground that signified enemy territory and officially declared war on the Marcomanni.

So, by summer of the year of the Consulship of Clarus and Cornelius, one hundred and seventy years since Christ's coming, the court and everyone I cared about left Rome for Pannonia.

I was excited. Even though I was still to travel as Quadratus' mistress, among his entourage, I would be close to my prince. But more: I was to see the empire. Remember that I had spent most of my life in the city of Rome, and the furthest afield I had been was to Praeneste, perhaps twenty miles from the city as a bird flies. I had never seen mountains, or plains, or the sea.

While the legions moved across the Apenninus mountains and north, trudging along endless gravel roads like an iron caterpillar, the court instead travelled a few miles downriver to Ostia and took ship there. I had been excited at the prospect of the sea, but the reality was entirely different as we reached the great port of Rome and approached the grandest of the triremes that waited.

The ship looked so stable and calm at the dockside that my concerns abated for a while, though I felt a lurch in my stomach that almost rose into my mouth as I stepped onto the plank to board. The sight of the wine-dark sea rolling fifteen feet beneath me with only a board to take me to safety was all too familiar and I was dragged eight years back to that dreadful night crossing a plank to the bathhouse as Rome drowned.

Matters did not improve much when the sailors cast off and the ship pitched and bucked as it moved out into the current and the oarsmen began their work, falling into a rhythm to the piped music with a professional calm. In truth, it was one of the smoothest sailings in history, and certainly while we were still within Ostia's great Portus harbour, but to me it felt horrifying. While others stood at the rail and drank it in, I panicked that we would capsize and I would be pulled down to the choking, cold depths. Eclectus, ever thoughtful and seeing my distress even if he knew not the cause, drew me over to the rail and began to point out places of interest in the hope of pulling me from my fears. All I could do was stare at the boundless, infinite stretch of water that lay ahead or look down the side of the ship at the white, churning water. The rail was not for me. I made hasty excuses and moved back to the very centre of the ship, as far from the water as I could manage, where I shook.

That is not to say that I made a bad sailor. I was not ill like some of those on board, and the rolling of the deck beneath me did not unsettle me in itself. But the very sight of that much water made my courage shrivel inside and left me sweating out my fear. I tried to read to keep myself busy, but the motion of the ship made concentrating on the small text difficult in the extreme.

I did not enjoy the journey from Ostia up the coast to Pisae, so much so that even Quadratus' visits were less unbearable than usual, my disgust and loathing and fear focusing on him for a short while, rather than the endless deeps of the ocean. I was as relieved as I have ever been when we put in at Pisae at the end of our fourth day of travel.

From there we set our course north-east, across the narrower stretches of the mountains that form Italia's spine, making for Verona, which we reached on our seventeenth day.

The fascination of seeing new terrain, new cities, lofty mountains and low marsh was tempered somewhat by the conditions that were clearly visible throughout the empire as we travelled. Plague was not confined to Rome itself, and the effects had been equally dreadful in the provinces. We saw innumerable farms that had simply been deserted and fallen into ruin, overgrown, their owners dead and no one willing to take on the property for fear of lingering disease. Whole villages were empty places, inhabited only by shades. And as a consequence of the depopulation, food was becoming scarce. The people we *did* see were usually hungry and miserable, begging at the roadside. The recent wars had cost Rome dearly, too. Poverty was everywhere, manifested in each hollowed cheek and every dead eye.

Near Verona we converged with the bulk of the army that had been gathered to chastise the tribes, and I was astounded.

I had only ever seen the Praetorians and the men of the Urban Cohorts in Rome, uniformly equipped, neat and very traditional. My image of the armies of Rome was simply an expansion of the units with which I was familiar. The truth was far from that. The assembled mass was so varied and exotic, from African cavalry to Syrian archers, to Gallic cohorts, to Iberian slingers and Thracian spear-men. And, it transpired, there was even more unusual to be found in that mass if one only pried. The shortage of manpower following the plague had left the emperor and his generals in dire need of new sources of men. Consequently, there were units of sailors here, looking wholly uncomfortable armed like legionaries and on dry, immobile land. There was even a legion formed of *gladiators*. I half expected to find Commodus near them, given his fascination with the sport, but he was kept busy by his father and the imperial court. He was, after all, the heir to the throne and old enough now to witness battle, if not to actively participate.

The idea of Commodus in battle perturbed me. Not that I worried about his ability or courage, of course. He had ever been a boy ready for a fight or a match, and his strength was surprising even as a youngster, like his revered Hercules. No. I feared for him in battle for, unlike his father, I knew that he was still that lost and hollow shell of a boy, reeling after so much death and loss, a solid smile painted on his face for the court. I remembered his talk of bereavement and of what it would feel like to die. And I shivered at the thought of how easy it might be for him to find out in Pannonia.

In equal parts marvelling at the grandness of the empire and the army that moved through it and suffering great dismay at the condition in which much of the land lay, we moved north once more through the Carnic Alpes and on to Pannonia.

I began to learn fragments of military thinking and reasoning purely through proximity to the commanders during that time, and I expanded on that where I could with dips into the rather unfamiliar military texts that were available among the officers and their households. The emperor had thought to be engaged with the enemy before now. Reports had detailed attacks by the Marcomanni and allied tribes down almost as far as Aquileia once more. And everywhere we went, we found evidence that those attacks had occurred, yet no barbarians. It was always an aftermath, and usually long since suffered. They had been there and killed, stolen and burned, but they had gone and the populace was now rebuilding. The army began to send out scout units to locate any tribal warbands, and they returned each day after no contact with the enemy and with ever-increasing reports of destruction long since visited, though sometimes it was hard to tell whether it had been the Marcomanni who had ruined the region, or simply plague, hunger and poverty.

Whatever had occurred there, wherever we went we found no tribes awaiting us. By the time we reached Carnuntum, which had itself been badly battered during the conflict, the campaigning season was drawing to a close. The Marcomanni had clearly ravaged Pannonia and then crossed back into their own lands, safe and smug at their victory. And with a northern winter, which I was told could be harsh, there was no chance as yet to move on them and chastise them for fear of being caught far beyond the great river when the snows came.

Consequently, diplomatic parties were sent up- and down-river, seeking out the lesser tribes, securing peace and their loyalty, with an oath not to fall in with the Marcomanni in subsequent years. The emperor began planning to cross the river once the winter was past and to visit upon that murderous tribe everything they themselves had visited upon Rome. And while planning was the order of those cold, frosty days, the army set to work rebuilding and strengthening the fortress and the frontier it guarded.

I passed an odd winter in Carnuntum. Everything here was

very military, and I was unused to such things. Carnuntum was a provincial capital and a grand municipium, and the most important stop on the amber road that fed that precious stone to the empire, but despite that, every building looked like a barrack block. All was walls and spears and hard-looking men with equally hard-looking families. It was far from the quiet, peaceful world of Praeneste.

Quadratus visited me less and less often as he attempted to make up for a clear lack of military talent by being present and enthusiastic for the emperor at all times. Commodus was kept relatively busy, too. He was learning the craft of a general from his father and the great Pompeianus, and was involved with planning, training and the constant tasks of rule as often as he could be. Consequently, I spent a lot of time in the civilian areas of Carnuntum, which were far too military for my liking. I socialised with the officers' wives – the lesser ones, who were willing to be seen with a plebeian woman who was mistress to a former consul, anyway. I learned another lesson there: not to place my faith in the women of Rome's aristocracy. Each one has more than one face and would eat you alive if it suited them. But among the wives of senior centurions and non-patrician prefects, I found friends. Moreover, I gradually gathered together a cadre of humorous women who liked bawdy humour, enjoyed nothing more than poking quiet, irreverent fun at their menfolk, and whose related exploits sometimes shocked me, sometimes made my sides hurt with laughter, and sometimes gave me very useful ideas.

Without my books and those women, I might have gone mad in the northern winter.

I saw Commodus again, more often, as the snow began to fall on Carnuntum like a soft shroud. Once we were settled in and winter surrounded us, all planning done and all campaigning over until spring, the prince suddenly had free time. He was still occupied with his tutors, of course, but not all the time, and in a reflection of the old Commodus I knew on the Palatine, he would occasionally skip his lessons and seek amusement elsewhere.

We did not talk about what he had been through over the past year without me. He had suffered, though, and that was clear. He had lost weight and had acquired a seemingly permanent sallow complexion. Furthermore, he had not managed to pull himself out of his melancholia the way I would have managed, by inducing a joy in the things around him that lifted his spirits above the gloom. Instead, he had more or less ridden it out like a fever, nailing an expression of hardy competence to his face each day as he pushed the pain and the anguish deep down inside and contained it. And eventually, like a healing wound, he had begun a slow recovery, though like such a wound, it had left its own scar tissue.

All this he did not tell me directly, but I surmised it easily enough from his words. Slowly, over the winter, Commodus regained something of his old self, partially through the rekindling of our relationship. Indeed, there was something new there, now. Something stronger than before. I was now a woman, and he approaching manhood, and there had been a subtle shift in our attitudes. When I found myself alone I would reflect again and again on those words of Cleander's so long ago, accusing me of being in love with the prince. It had, I was sure, been but a childish jibe, yet now the truth of it was becoming harder and harder to ignore or refute. I was the mistress of an ex-consul, but it was growing clear to me in those cold days that I loved someone else. And though he never said it – *could* not say it – I felt certain that my feelings were matched in him. I could see the hard stares I was getting from Quadratus for spending so much time with the prince, but even my current master would not argue with the emperor's heir. Daily, I suppressed my emotions. No matter what we shared, I could never have Commodus and one day, probably

121

quite soon, I might have to distance myself from him, lest we both be hurt.

And so, the winter passed.

Spring saw a return to military activity and preparation. Enduring periodic visits from Quadratus and enjoying occasional ones from Commodus, I watched in fascination as everything unfolded. I was in an almost unique position as an observer. I was too low-born and unimportant to grant expensive and much-needed protection, and Quadratus was too busy to spend a great deal of time with me. Consequently, I had almost unparalleled access to everything that happened in the campaign.

I watched the first forays of soldiers crossing the great Danubius and searching the closer regions of Marcomannia, looking for trouble and setting up bridgeheads in advance of a full push. I watched them come back, nonplussed. They found little. By late spring the advance units had confirmed that Marcomannia was largely depopulated, and interrogations of those they found, in addition to a few well-placed threats to neighbouring tribes, revealed the reason. It transpired that the bulk of the Marcomanni from the nearer lands were south of the Danubius again. They had crossed the river early in the year, as soon as the snows melted, and begun a fresh spell of raiding before the army of Rome stirred and considered the campaign season open.

New units were raised from the sparse manpower of the region, and more forces arrived at the central Danubius, drawn from other frontiers to bolster the army. By early summer the military at Carnuntum had to be one of the largest forces ever assembled by Rome. I wondered why we remained at Carnuntum, gathering soldiers, while the enemy ravaged the lands behind us. But then even with access to military texts, I was no strategist, and Commodus was the one who explained it to me. Pannonia was already depleted and ruined. The further ravaging by the Marcomanni would not change things. But they were an army of raiders, and not an entire tribe on the move. They could not advance into the empire forever, and the lands beyond the Alpes were well defended and patrolled since the rebuilding of Aquileia. The tribes could not go far and could not do too much damage. And, critically, they would have to go home, which meant crossing the river into the north once more. Thus, the emperor and his generals had sent out scouts who kept tabs on the enemy and their movements and location, while we secured the support of other tribes, destroyed untenable crossing points and observed and fortified the ones that needed to remain in use. The Marcomanni would not try to cross at Carnuntum, but somewhere nearby, likely the very place they had crossed in the winter before the army was ready. I realised what was happening. The Marcomanni in their greed for further loot thought they had been clever and slipped past Rome. What they had done was trap themselves south of the river with a huge Roman force.

Battle was joined in late summer. The tribes, feeling that they had taken all they could and that it was time to return to Marcomannia, made their way north, unaware that Roman scouts watched their every move and that riders hurtled back and forth between the advancing tribes and the waiting legions of Rome.

Women have no place on the battlefield. Our wars are fought in the domus and the bedchamber, whatever certain infamous barbarian queens might think. Yet I saw this battle with my own eyes. The servants and slaves of the generals were kept close, and so with Quadratus' household I stood on the bench of a carriage on the hillside and watched the whole thing. My view was uninterrupted, and I could see Quadratus, Commodus, Pompeianus, the emperor himself and numerous other leading lights of Rome on another high point nearby.

What followed was the most awful thing I had ever witnessed.

The Marcomanni, laughing and victorious, ambled north, itching to be home with their ill-gotten gains. I didn't see the opening moves as the Roman heavy cavalry appeared behind the tribe: cataphracts armoured from scalp to toe and with long, heavy lances, their horses similarly clad in iron, auxiliary cavalry from Gaul, Numidian riders, Mauretanian horse, Greek cavalry, even a few units of unorthodox, Parthian-style mounted archers. They came from the south where they had been in hiding and fell upon the rear of the Marcomanni. The effect must have been awful, though their job had not been to kill, but to drive the enemy north. This they did with ease. The Marcomanni, taken by surprise, panicked. What had been a happy journey home had suddenly become a descent into Tartarus.

The first I saw of the enemy was as the tribe hoved into view across a low saddle to the south, desperately making for the crossing of the Danubius that lay a quarter of a mile behind me, guarded by heavily armoured Praetorian units. The Marcomanni were hungry, swift, believing they were outrunning their deadly pursuers and would make it to the crossing.

That was the moment that I realised why Rome ruled the world and why even the great Parthian King of Kings had agreed to peace. Rome's army is unbeatable; even beset by plague and famine, staffed by sailors and gladiators and all manner of combatants, no force could hope to overcome them.

The Marcomanni flooded onto the flat ground south of the river, eager and hopeful – an optimism that was dashed in a heartbeat. The gleaming serried ranks of Rome awaited them, blocking the way to the bridge, thousand upon thousand, men from all over the empire, each dedicated solely and simply to ending the Marcomanni, who had troubled the empire for decades. The huge mass of tribesmen, some on foot, a lucky few on horseback, slowed at the realisation of their peril, but the nightmare for them had only just begun. The Marcomanni force was large enough that the rear ranks were entirely unaware of what waited for them, and were being driven on by deadly cavalry, pushing into those who had drawn up at the sight of the legions.

All turned to chaos.

The tribes north of the Danubius seem to have little in the way of tactical command, unlike our armies. Where in such a situation a Roman general would already have been planning their response and sending out orders to musicians to relay, the Marcomanni simply responded if not individually, then in small regional groupings. Some bore the hope of breaking through to the river and rushed at the waiting Roman force. Others preferred their chances against the cavalry and turned into their own, fighting a way back to the waiting horsemen. More still broke off east or west in the hope of fleeing the field along the near bank of the river. That was when the generals Pompeianus and Pertinax closed the trap, swinging the two wings of the army around at speed to enfold the enemy in an iron embrace.

The Marcomanni dithered and panicked. Some fought. Some tried to run. Others simply dropped their weapons and called for their leaders to seek terms. No terms were to be given, though.

Artillery began to loose with dull thuds as thousands of arrows slithered through the blue sky from the archers on the periphery of the field. It was slaughter. A butcher's shop on a grand scale. Those who knelt and beseeched were riddled with dark shafts as often as those who bellowed defiantly. The Marcomanni had utterly slaughtered a Roman army near here two years ago, and Rome never forgets a debt owed.

I watched that battle – that mass murder – and not once did I close my eyes or turn my head from the scything of metal into flesh or the screams of agony from men transfixed. I watched, and I hardened myself to it, for these men deserved no less than they received. Yet I also felt sick at what I saw, and I was minded of Commodus' words that day at his uncle's villa: 'War is different. It kills men by the thousand, and rarely solves anything.'

I watched to the end. It lasted but an hour in all, and the Roman officers were merciless. I gather from later conversations that they tore through the surrendering barbarians in the last stages, seeking their king, wanting him alive to kneel before the emperor, but it seemed that this Ballomar was not part of the army. The king who had led them to sack Aquileia and to defeat the legions at Carnuntum was still somewhere in his tribal lands in the north.

I finally turned away when it was over, the plain by the river a grim tableau of death and decay, twisted bodies issuing sound-less screams from open mouths below wide, terrified eyes, pila and spears standing proud of the bodies like a forest of branch-less trees. The metallic stink of blood was almost lost beneath the rank odour of opened bowels that sat upon the land like a miasma. Crows hopped from still warm body to still warm body, gorging on succulent flesh. Other scavenging animals moved around the areas with the least movement to deter them, and the Roman camp followers were already sawing off fingers to claim prized rings or lifting bodies up to remove expensive torcs from necks. It was quite the most appalling sight imagina-ble, and after that, Hell holds no fears for me, for God cannot inflict upon us any torment worse than that we can visit upon each other.

Prisoners taken and sold to the numerous slavers that fol-lowed the column in hope were fewer than any man would expect from such a conflict, while the mass burnings of the bodies turned the air black for days. The Danubius stank of cooking pork for the rest of my time there, for once that sickly-sweet smell lodges in the nostrils it is there to stay.

The return to Carnuntum was a lively and grand thing, the officers satisfied, slapping each other on the back and antic-ipating who would receive awards and recognition for their part in the victory. The soldiers, already enriched from looting the dead on the field, heedless that much of that wealth had so

126

recently been looted in turn from the Roman provinces, were in high spirits. I was not. I knew that the Marcomanni deserved what happened to them, and I was content to watch two men of skill attempt to best one another in the arena, but I would hope never again to witness the horror I had seen by the Danubius.

I was saved the rest of the campaign. The emperor, determined to chastise King Ballomar for his actions, led his armies north of the river in the following days and spent the rest of the season in Marcomannia. The great generals went with him, and so did Commodus and Quadratus. I was left with the courtiers and the families in Carnuntum. I felt a panic when the season closed and there was no sign of their return, though missives confirmed that the entire army would remain beyond the river, settled into winter quarters among the enemy, while ambassadors secured alliances with other neighbouring tribes.

Winter in Carnuntum is cold and dismal, worse than the worst Roman winter by far, and I spent much of that time tucked up in warm rooms reading and drinking expensive wine that came along supply lines from the south. As part of one of the most senior officers' households and with access to seemingly unlimited funds, I lived more comfortably than most that winter, and as mistress of a household with an absent master I used Quadratus' house and his money to entertain my friends among the lesser officers' wives, all of whom were in the same boat, with their menfolk away. I wrote missives to Mother on occasion, when I had anything to say, anyway. She might not be able to read them, but I sent them anyway, sure that a palace functionary would read them to her. And I prayed to God that Commodus had a good winter. I had promised myself never again to be apart from him when he needed me, but events kept us separated during this last great push of the campaign.

I need not have worried. Not about his sinking into melancholia, anyway.

Time rolled on with regular news of victory after victory, and the army of Marcus Aurelius returned to Carnuntum before the summer faded. Ballomar had been found and had surrendered. He had begged for clemency for himself and his people and, while the emperor was noted for his mercy and understanding, even he would not see the Marcomanni reasoned with. I rushed to the gates of the city when the column approached, along with the rest of the populace. I watched the glorious emperor with his Praetorians and his senior officers, riding for the gate as the army began to disperse behind them, seeking their own camps in the locale.

It took me long moments to spot Commodus. I had been looking for my prince in his rich tunic, perhaps wrapped in a cloak against the northern breezes. What I found was a ten-year-old Caesar riding alongside his father, armoured as a great Roman commander, purple cloak draped over his horse's rear, golden hair shaggier than ever. And as he approached the gate with a smile of satisfaction that mirrored his father's, I saw something startling. The prince had something dangling from his saddle horn, bouncing from the flank and from his knee occasionally, and I realised with rising bile that it was a human head. That of Ballomar, King of the Marcomanni. The empire's revenge was complete.

I wanted nothing more in the ensuing days than to spend time with Commodus, but still, that was not to be. For one thing, Quadratus had returned and, though he had sated himself from time to time in some indulgent way on campaign, he had missed the ministrations of his mistress. Once more I was a concubine – a plaything for the sickness of Quadratus, who revelled in his 'military glory'. For another, Commodus was something of a celebrity, kept busy at all times. It seems he had deported himself during the campaign with every bit of the vigour and glory to which his uncle Verus had been wont. It had been he the emperor had given the final say over Ballomar, and it had been Commodus who ordered his head be taken. He had led units and directed some of the action. He was being lauded by Pompeianus as a man who held great potential as a general.

So it went on as things settled upon their return: I played mistress to Quadratus and Commodus drank in the adulation of his peers, and rarely did we meet, never in private.

The festival in October that is known as the Ides of Hercules – no coincidence there, I am certain – came around and was celebrated by the emperor and his heir. We were far from the Circus Maximus, where the October Horse was busily being sacrificed to Mars, but the emperor mirrored the sacrifice in Carnuntum. I could imagine my mother back in Rome, hiding away from such pagan blasphemy and praying by rote. I am made of different stock, and I simply cast up an apology to the Lord in advance and then enjoyed the festivities. The world in which we live is too complex to survive with such rigid thinking as my mother's, and I was not the pliant girl I had once been.

Commodus and his father were honoured at the festival. Sufficient senators were with the court to confer titles upon the imperial personages, and both father and son were granted the title 'Germanicus' for their definitive victories. I watched Commodus receiving his honours as the poor horse busily bled dry nearby, and my heart soared to see him becoming the man I had always imagined he would be.

I could not speak to him that night, for his attendance at all times was expected, and Quadratus needed me, anyway. But the next day, when all was quiet once more and the festival over, finally the prince came to my rooms. Quadratus was busy ingratiating himself with the emperor, and I was alone when Commodus came, his Praetorian escort waiting patiently outside my door, out of earshot.

As he stood in my room and the door was closed behind him, I realised I had seen at the feast only what he wanted me to see, what he had wanted everyone to see. Now, close up, I noted a certain hollowness about the prince's eyes. He was not suffering as he so often did – I had seen it often enough to recognise the symptoms, after all – but still he wore a mask of contentment that no one else seemed to notice.

'What is it?' I asked. I wanted nothing more than to hug him, but I had not seen him for a year. He had left a troubled prince and had returned a victorious general. It was hard to reconcile. For him as well, apparently.

'What do you mean?'

I frowned. 'You are not as happy as you make them all think. I can see it in your eyes. Your mask slips from time to time.'

He gave me a weak smile. 'There may come a time when I regret you being able to see into my heart, Marcia.' Something about that sentence chilled me, but I overrode it as he sighed and stretched. 'It seems I am good at war.'

'All of Rome is aware of that, now,' I smiled.

'My father berated me for becoming *too* involved. "A commander does not actively draw a blade and take part in war," he told me. I reminded him of Caesar, of Tiberius, of Vespasian and others. Men who had done just that. Once upon a time to lead Rome was to fight. Still, I fought, and I led. I strategised and gave orders. I was every bit as much a general as Pertinax or your . . . or Quadratus. *Better* than he, for Quadratus is no soldier. I am, it seems, made for war.'

I felt cold at that notion and opened my mouth to reply, but he waved me to silence and sagged. 'No, that is the problem, Marcia. I am made for war, but I simply do not want to be. War is not a thing to be wished or sought. It is every bit as much a disease as the Parthian plague, ravaging our people and killing indiscriminately. I do not like war. Father intends to continue his campaign next year, to press on against other tribes in the region and make the Danubius secure for all time. As though war could ever settle a border permanently. I do not want to fight on, Marcia. The Iazyges and their ilk could be bought over with concessions and gold instead of blood and sacrifice. If it were I, I would be doing just that and sending our men home.'

I was proud. Just listening to such reason, I was proud of my prince. He truly was the son of the great philosopher emperor, with the good of his people at heart. But it was not his decision to make, and the emperor believed the campaign needed to go on.

'I am done with war,' he said quietly.

And he was. While the emperor planned to stay in Carnuntum and proceed with a fresh campaign the next year, Pompeianus surprised us all by persuading the emperor that it would be better for the non-combatants and the extended familia with the court to return to Rome. The winter last year had been hard and, in addition to the still present effects of the plague, the risk to the imperial family and the less martial members of the court was too strong to ignore. The emperor, perhaps mindful of the tenuous nature of imperial succession, and remembering the three days of Verus' vicious demise, commanded Commodus and a number of other courtiers to return to the capital. Thankfully, Quadratus was one of them. I fear that in addition to his lack of talent as a soldier, his attempts to make up for it with sycophancy and constant attention had driven the emperor to push him away. Quadratus was crestfallen and miserable.

As winter's clutches descended on Pannonia, we moved south once more.

VIII

A MAN WHO WOULD ONE DAY BE EMPEROR

Centum Cellae, AD 173

Despite my feeble attempts to avoid the sea, Quadratus would hear nothing of it. We left Carnuntum on the kalends of December and moved at a reasonable pace. This time we were not hampered by slow-moving military units and their endless wagon train. This time we moved at the speed of private citizens, and even the soldiers with us were mounted, part of the imperial horse guard.

We followed almost the same route in reverse, crossing the hilly terrain of Pannonia and heading for north-east Italia. There we crossed the flat plains of Venetia and the narrow northern stretch of the mountains, making for Pisae. I noted oddly that Commodus' mood began to become a little erratic as the journey went on and it was only when I found him one morning looking at the icy, frozen surface of a horse trough while our mounts and vehicles were being made ready that I remembered how the winter's frost and chill were a constant reminder to him of Fulvus. I tried to keep his spirits up and, to some extent, I succeeded, but the connection was always there below the surface, waiting to reappear as long as we remained in winter's grip.

Finally, we took ship at Pisae. It is a near two-hundred-mile journey down the coast from there to Ostia and civilisation, and

I spent days shivering at the thought of that vast swathe of water beyond the ship's all-too-thin hull. In the end, even Quadratus, who rarely thought of more than himself, softened to my fears and did not argue when Commodus persuaded the small party to cut the journey short and dock at Centum Cellae a day early, making the last forty miles to the capital by road.

We settled in at that port city in Januarius and prepared to stay the night while our escort arranged transport for the last leg. Our arrival in Centum Cellae was so unexpected that the authorities did not have time to prepare an appropriate welcome for the prince and his entourage and struggled to put together a banquet in time. Commodus did not really care. We were not in search of pomp or glory, but of comfort and warmth.

As the best quarters in the city were made ready for the imperial party and the members of the *ordo* rushed around making all just so for the banquet, Commodus simply made for one of the city's bathhouses, which was ready to close at the end of the day. Quadratus, robbed of the chance to fawn at his emperor, followed the prince and joined him there, and I was taken along with them. A small group of Praetorians protected the bathhouse to keep the prince safe.

I paused at the entrance, certain that the two men would not want a low-born woman in there with them, despite the mixed nature of such establishments. There was no one else there, the last bathers having left recently, and the place would undoubtedly have been closed to any less important visitor. As it happened, Commodus waved me in. Slaves appeared from somewhere, confused by the sudden change in routine when they were supposed to be closing up for the day, but they managed to provide towels and clogs and all the paraphernalia of bathing.

I waved away the towel and the rest. I like baths. I like to relax in the warm and to be clean and primped, but days at sea had got to me and, despite the luxury available, I had not the remotest urge to sink into yet more water. Instead, I found a manicure kit and prepared to look after my hands, which were suffering somewhat from inattention and the barbaric conditions of Pannonia. While my place as Quadratus' mistress had left me acutely aware of the importance of looking the way he would expect me to, which was almost certainly in that very same way that Mother had once warned me against, the cold lands of the north had been far from ideal for maintaining my appearance to its utmost.

I followed the two men, now wrapped in towels, through the rooms. The floors were not as warm as usual, and I reasoned that this was because we were here after the place officially closed. The failing in the furnaces became apparent as we entered the caldarium and the two men moved to the water's edge, dropped their towels and slid into the bath.

'Shit,' Quadratus barked, then stared in horror at the realisation he had sworn so basely in the presence of the prince.

Commodus waved it aside, clutching his shoulders and wrapping his arms around himself. 'This hot bath would have to warm considerably to just be tepid,' he agreed.

Certainly, there was no steam rising from the water into the cold winter air as was the norm, and the floor was barely above outdoor temperature.

'Marcia, tell someone . . .' Commodus began, but at that moment a slave entered the room, bent double in a careful bow.

'Majesty, we were not expecting a visit at this time.'

Commodus nodded. 'This water is cold. You've not been closed that long. Get the furnace slave to work.'

Quadratus snorted. 'Cold as ice, in fact. Bet it's forming on the surface already. Maybe you should throw the slave into the damned furnace for good measure.'

The attendant rose from his bow, eyes wide, taking this for an imperial command.

I saw Commodus' face then, though. Saw what passed across

it, and shivered. The notion of ice and a frozen surface had cut through Commodus and torn him from Centum Cellae, throwing him forty miles distant and back through the years to his twin, trapped beneath that frozen sheen. All my work across the mountains keeping his spirits up, only to have it all ripped apart by a chance remark from Quadratus, who should have known better. The prince was distracted suddenly, pain flooding his eyes, his gaze on the surface of the water as though he saw Fulvus beneath it.

'I said he should burn the slave,' Quadratus repeated, with a horrible snarl.

'Quite right,' Commodus replied, paying not a jot of attention, eyes locked on the water.

I frowned, but Quadratus leapt upon what sounded like imperial sanction. 'Do it. Send him in.'

The slave backed out, a horrified expression upon his face, and I crossed to where the prince was standing, head cocked to one side.

'Commodus?'

'Mmm?'

'You can't really mean to burn a slave?'

'What?' He was distracted still, not really listening to me, replaying the death of his twin in his head as he had done so many times over the years. I was torn. There was danger here in the path down which his thoughts were taking him, and I knew what could come, but a slave was hurrying down into the bowels of the bathhouse with orders to throw one of his companions into a furnace. As a Christian, I could not let such a thing happen. As a *human*, I could not.

The decision was made for me as Quadratus waved me away. 'Fetch wine while we wait,' he commanded.

I needed no further urging. I left the room and hurried after the slave. I found him by a small door marked as the entrance to the furnace tunnels. He had stopped and was addressing a man in a plain, if good-quality, blue tunic who had an official, competent air about him.

'He asked what?' the man demanded of the slave.

'That I burn Caro in the furnace for letting the water get too cold.'

The man in the blue tunic shook his head in wonder. Behind him, two men were standing impatiently, holding what appeared to be a deflated sheep. One of them cleared his throat, and blue-tunic turned.

'I cannot accept it. Take it back and tell your master that a rug is flat and does not still contain parts of the animal. If I'd wanted a carcass, I'd have asked for one.'

The bath slave made desperate noises, and, with a long-suffering sigh, blue-tunic turned back to him. 'I don't care if it's a prince or the emperor or mighty Neptune himself, I am not about to throw an expensive slave into a furnace just because they have the audacity to turn up when the baths are closed.'

'About this rug—'

He spun again. 'It is not a rug. It is a badly squeezed sheep. The answer is still no.'

'Sir, the furnace . . .'

And back to the slave. 'No. No slaves in the furnace.'

He paused, and a strange smile spread across his face. He turned back to the two men. 'I will take it, after all, though tell your master it is not what I wanted, and I will pay only half.'

They looked as though they might argue, but clearly blue-tunic was determined, and they shrugged, dumped the deflated, filleted sheep on the floor, and left.

Blue-tunic pointed at it. 'Throw that in the furnace.'

'Sir?'

'I know princes and nobles are educated differently to the rest of us, but I doubt even the emperor could tell the difference between a burning slave and a burning sheep when it leaks up through a floor.'

136

With a bow, the slave heaved up the heavy carcass and struggled off through the door with it. The man in the blue tunic sighed and rubbed his head vigorously, turned and noticed me for the first time. He flinched. I was clearly important, from my attire, which meant I was almost certainly connected to the prince and the noble he had just insulted in passing.

'I'm not sure what you heard there, my lady?'

'Enough to label you clever and resourceful.' I smiled. 'I was coming to find someone in an attempt to stop such madness. It is not the prince's order, or would not be if he were thinking straight. He will thank me – and you – later. Quadratus not so much, so let's maintain the fiction this Caro lad was burned, eh? How fast can you warm the bath and floor?'

The man, still cowering a little since I was important, shrugged. 'It will be quick. The bath and floor surfaces cool swiftly when the furnace dies, but the ambient temperature within the hypocaust will still be high and it will not take long to bring it back up. Like a pot of water that's been recently boiled, which does not take long to make bubble again.'

I liked this man straight away. Clever, thoughtful and straight. There was a chance here to repair the bathhouse's reputation and to help break Commodus of the strange spell under which he had so suddenly fallen. Bathhouses had entertainment for their guests, and this was quite a large one. Perhaps it had its own entertainers?

'Do you have wrestlers?'

The man's brow folded. 'We do. They are instructors and masseurs as well, but they put on shows for the clients as required.'

'The prince loves wrestlers. Have them attend. And bring good wine and snacks. Beef. He likes beef. What is your name?'

'Saoterus, my lady.'

'Be quick, Saoterus.'

I returned to the baths to find Commodus sitting on the water's edge with a faraway look in his eye. Quadratus clearly had no idea what was going on with the prince and stood in the water helplessly. I was gratified and impressed to note that, even in such a short time, the floor was already noticeably warmer. The bath would be slower to warm up, of course, due to the volume.

'Where's the wine, girl?' Quadratus snapped.

'They only had a local cheap stock,' I lied glibly. 'The baths' master has gone to fetch wine of appropriate quality.'

My master harrumphed at me irritably, but he would not argue, for he would rather have good wine slowly than poor wine fast, which is something I have found to be a general facet of Roman nature. Moments later, a slave entered with repeated bows and announced, for the prince's entertainment, the 'renowned Sardinian wrestlers Narcissus and Falco'.

Two men with more muscle than any human being had a right to, entered, bowed to their tiny audience, and shuffled along the wall to an area with adequate room for a match.

Quadratus' face was a picture of plum-coloured fury. 'What is the meaning of this? Bringing killer slaves into the prince's presence? I have a mind to . . .'

He tailed off into silence as Commodus, looking present and alert for the first time since he entered the bath, waved him down. 'Quiet, man. I am intrigued.'

And that was it. Commodus was back. I had seen the slippery descent ahead of him and managed to grasp him before he fell. I was sure I was becoming mistress of his melancholia, able to control it and buoy him up when needed, just as my opposite number Cleander was able to constrain his worst temptations.

The wrestlers fought three times, the third time ending with an ignominious fall by Falco into the now-warm pool that had Quadratus scowling just as Commodus roared with laughter. As the bedraggled Sardinian dragged himself from the water sheepishly, the other man bowed low, a hundred muscles rippling.

'Narcissus, was it?' The prince smiled.

'Yes, Majesty,' the wrestler replied in a thick, almost Gallic accent without raising his gaze.

'You are good. Wasted in this place. You need to be in Rome, man.'

I could see a wave of disappointment wash across sodden Falco's face, but as Narcissus straightened, I caught his eyes, and could see something there. He had been showing off for the emperor. He had not been meant to throw Falco in, but had done so to prove his worth. Slaves rarely get the chance to attract the imperial gaze after all. He was shrewd, this Narcissus.

The wrestlers left and Commodus began to swim, enjoying the water that was now beginning to steam in the cooler air once more. The faint aroma of cooked mutton sneaked out through the floor tiles and wall flues, and Saoterus' prediction that a noble could not tell the difference between it and a burning slave proved well founded from the sickeningly smug look on Quadratus' face.

By the time the prince was tiring of the water and I had repaired two winters' damage to my hands and nails, an array of good food was brought in, along with a high-quality Caecuban wine that had probably been expensive and difficult to source at such short notice. A musician entered with a lyre, and a girl came to sing along to it. It was relaxed, peaceful and pleasant, even with Quadratus there. Finally, the supervisor in the blue tunic – a freedman of importance, clearly – entered with a bow.

'This is Saoterus,' I said, indicating him to the prince. 'He is the one who put everything back in order for you.'

Commodus smiled warmly. 'Well met, Saoterus. And not just back in order, but you clearly surpassed yourself. This is excellent fare and your wrestlers good enough that I have a mind to steal them off you. Why, there is nary a bathhouse in Rome that could have achieved such quality with such little notice. You are to be commended.'

Saoterus smiled. 'The owner would be distraught, Majesty, if his wrestlers vanished. What would happen when your illustrious father subsequently visited?'

Quadratus goggled at this insubordinate manner, but Commodus simply laughed. 'My father has less interest in wrestlers even than my cousin here. I like you, Saoterus. You speak plain sense, as well. In fact, I have as much need of you as I have of a good wrestler. Perhaps more. Have you family in Centum Cellae?'

'No, Majesty. Just a room and some personal effects.'

'Gather them up for transport then, man. I have a place for you on the Palatine.'

The blue-tunic-wearing freedman bowed low with a smile. Saoterus, I felt, could be just the very antidote to the odious Cleander who awaited us forty miles away.

We moved on the next day by carriage, leaving early in order to arrive in Rome by nightfall. The roads are good and the going easy, and it is perhaps ironic that I was hale and hearty – if beset by terror – all the way by ship on the rolling winter sea, but by coach on a flat road thereafter I was sick as a dog.

We reached Rome that evening with the erudite Saoterus and the powerful Narcissus in Commodus' personal entourage now. The streets were still stricken with the plague. I thought it less virulent now, though I cannot be certain whether that was truly because of fewer signs in the city or perhaps because I had just become so inured to it that disease and death had become the norm. While the prince was immediately surrounded by those of any position or power seeking news of the north and to ingratiate themselves, and Quadratus drank in praise by association, I made for the Palatine to visit my mother. It turned out however, that Lucilla had sent her to one of her villas in Campania while she accompanied her husband on campaign with the emperor.

And so I returned to the house on the Caelian, still periodically vomiting, attended by the household slaves.

When the illness failed to subside the next day, but faded in the early afternoon, a horrible suspicion settled upon me, and not one that pleased me, either. Sickened with the thoughts that assailed me, and clutching my belly as though it nurtured a demon, I hurried to Quadratus' room, where he lay groaning and hiding from the light, suffering a pounding head from a late night of socialising. One of the standing rules of our association was that *he* came to *me* in my chamber. I was under no circumstances to go to his, for he might be entertaining someone important. But I didn't care, in my labyrinth of loathing. I brushed that aside, just as I did his personal slave who tried to stop me.

'I think I'm pregnant,' I blurted as I walked through the door to find Quadratus half wrapped in a sheet and moaning.

It took my master some time to recover his wits enough to take in this critical news, but finally, sitting on the edge of his bed and rubbing his temples, he fixed me with a fuddled look. 'What?'

'I've been vomiting since Centum Cellae, and it seems to be worst in the morning.'

'Rubbish. I remember my sister being with child. She wasn't sick until it was well advanced. You'd have known by now.'

Possibly. I was hardly versed in such matters. But the coincidence seemed too much. 'I do know for sure. I cannot remember when my last menses occurred,' I replied shakily. The last thing I wanted was to be pregnant. Especially with Quadratus' child. A wave of disgust radiated through me. I didn't want it. I wanted it out of me.

'No. I can't take that chance. I have no intention of siring a child by a worthless pleb; I'll be the laughing stock of Rome. Come.'

He rose and grabbed me by the wrist, dragging me to the kitchens. There, the household slaves dropped into respectful bows in surprise.

'Oysters. Where are the oysters?' the master of the house demanded.

Cook hurriedly dug around in the cold-room and found the slimy seafood delicacy that had been imported from the oyster beds of Neapolis. Under Quadratus' direction, and beneath my worried gaze, cook tipped a dozen raw oysters onto a silver platter.

'Silphium?'

The cook, her brow furrowing in concern, retrieved a small bowl of the chopped herb from a shelf, where it had rested among other similar seasonings. Without care for quantity, Quadratus tipped the entire bowl onto the oysters, shaking the plate so that the seasoning covered as much as possible of the slippery white surfaces. He snatched the platter from her and thrust it under my nose.

'Eat.'

I stared at the plate of slippery crustaceans. Raw oysters were far from my taste, and I found silphium too strong at the best of times. 'No, I . . .' I felt a little sick rise into my mouth.

'Eat the fucking oysters,' he snarled at me in a tone I'd never heard him use. 'They say it kills off a pregnancy. Silphium too. Eat them all.'

I had no choice. Standing in that kitchen, surrounded by watching slaves, I consumed twelve raw oysters. And when I was sick, Quadratus had Cook count the oysters that came up and feed me more to make up the deficiency, finding more silphium and coating the replacements liberally.

When it was over I was shaking, tears streaming down my face. My throat was raw and my mouth gritty from the silphium. All around me the slaves looked on. Pity filled their eyes, and I hated that they had seen me like this. Hated *him*.

When I was finally released, I crept to my room, curled up on my bed and was sicker than I have ever been.

The next morning I bled. I bled as though I were on my period, which for a short while I thought was perhaps true. Perhaps I had been wrong all along, and it had been seasickness after all. The cramps and the blood were familiar enough. But it all changed soon after. Three days I suffered the cramps and the bleeding, and then suddenly, on the third morning, a wave of pain and nausea wracked me from head to toe. I rushed to the latrine.

What happened there is difficult to relate. I had another flow, but this one held something. It was tiny – far from even remotely being a child – yet its nature was unmistakable. I watched it for a moment in sick relief as the pain ebbed. I had lost the life that was growing inside me, a life I could not have nurtured, for it would have been the offspring of my abuser. I stared at the shape below, my body still covered in blood and shaking. Three days of cramps, an hour of pain, and the panic was gone. I would never have to raise Quadratus' child.

It took time to recover from that awful day, both physically and mentally, but throughout the process of healing I found myself granted more freedom. Given what had happened to me, I made discreet enquiries and read much. I learned that Quadratus' sister had aborted her second child, and his knowledge of silphium and oysters was a consequence of that time. It did not take a great deal of research to discover that silphium was a known abortive, used by many physicians, and could be administered painlessly. Raw oysters were more direct and brutal, given to causing bouts of severe digestive agony that would almost certainly carry away any unborn child with them. The fact that at even a hint of pregnancy, Quadratus had used both without concern for my own health said much about him – I suspect that if he had used silphium alone and left out the oysters, much of my pain and discomfort could have been avoided.

Fortunately, as we were back in Rome Quadratus was once more among his elite and with plenty to do, and I was relegated again to being an occasional visit when the lust was upon him. Perhaps it was easy for him to turn away from me after my ordeal. I had likely lost much of my allure to him in the process. For my part, my hatred blossomed into new, fiery depths. Occasionally, I caught his eye straying to one of the prettier house slaves, and I began to wonder how long he would remain interested in keeping me as a mistress after that little episode with the oysters, and what I would do when he finally discarded me. I was a little old now to go back to Mother and help her. Marriage to some tradesman in Lucilla's employ, I supposed.

Despite my earlier ponderings on the necessity of distancing myself from Commodus, I now began to spend more time with the prince again, and our friendship entered a new era of closeness. Indeed, with each passing month, as he grew into a man and a glorious reflection of his great, mourned uncle Verus, I found it harder and harder to ignore the feelings inside me that spiteful Cleander had laughed about so long ago. I was in love with him. And now that I was a woman, and he almost ready to take on the man's toga, it was no longer a laughable, forgivable, childhood infatuation. Furthermore, the way he sometimes looked at me now – his gaze straying down from my face to take in my figure, sometimes seeming to penetrate my physical shell and peer deep into my soul – made it clear that it was reciprocated. Trouble would loom soon if I did not find a way to stop this, but how long could we remain just friends in the knowledge of what simmered beneath the surface?

Winter came with news that the emperor continued to make headway on the Danubius, and more and more tribes were submitting, though each campaign engendered the need for another, and he would remain on the border until he was certain it was secure. Commodus' wry suggestion that war could never truly settle a border, and that trouble would always return, seemed to be more astute and true than ever.

We entered the new year of the Consulship of Gallus and Flaccus on a high point, even though the pestilence still ravaged the poorer districts. Commodus was in grand spirits now, partially because I was there with him, bolstering his mood whenever he felt low, partially because he was grown now, and he was beginning to make a true impact on Rome, and partially because of the influence of the man we had brought back from Centum Cellae: Saoterus. The man had been appointed as Commodus' ab epistulis – his secretary – and had his ear as much as any man at court. I trusted Saoterus, which made him my friend, too. And, to some extent, his presence constricted the influence of Cleander. The slave, who had welcomed his prince back to the palace, hoping perhaps to return to his former position, found that he was playing second to this new favourite. How much that rankled with the man made me smile and left me warm inside. God, but how I hated Cleander.

It was clear how much trust the emperor had in his son for, as the year started, and Aurelius began once more to take steel into the heart of the barbarian world, he started to send letters to Commodus which contained instructions for him to carry out in the capital. The emperor began to administer Rome by proxy, through the prince.

It was a good year. Cleander seethed but lacked the power to do anything about it, Commodus exhibited all the values he would need as an emperor, I kept him happy and Saoterus kept him level. Narcissus the wrestler became more than mere entertainment for Commodus, now residing on the Palatine and acting as a physical trainer to the empire's heir. It was as golden a time as Rome ever had.

The seasons turned once more, and the consuls laid down their authority. This year, one hundred and seventy five since the birth of the saviour, the emperor wrote that he was too busy to devote time to deciding on the consuls and left the matter in the hands of his son. Commodus consulted with several very clever politicians and a number of intuitive freedmen – not even once with Quadratus, which irritated him – and settled upon Calpurnius Piso and a friend of the imperial family, Salvius Julianus.

The year started well enough, but we soon began to see the signs of trouble ahead. One morning a letter arrived from the north, dictated by the emperor through his secretary Eclectus, and the prince opened it hungrily, itching to see what new business he was to undertake. In fact, in the letter there was instruction to begin giving imperial largesse in the forum, though that was but a footnote. The main business was a warning. It seemed that the emperor's good friend Avidius Cassius, an old and trusted colleague who had been Verus' right-hand man in Parthia and who had efficiently put down the revolt in Aegyptus five years ago, had risen against Aurelius, his troops proclaiming him emperor. Commodus found it hard to believe and presumed it a joke. Cassius was as loyal a man as could be found in the empire. Yet there seemed to be no hidden mirth. The letter was genuine and came from the imperial secretary. Further information in that epistle was subtle and understated. Eclectus noted, probably at his own whim and not the dictation of Aurelius, that the emperor was not well. That was all, but the manner of the telling suggested that Eclectus was worried.

'Father is dying, I think,' Commodus said, lowering the letter. His face betrayed no sudden panic or sorrow, and as I looked into his eyes I realised he had donned his mask once more, a mask he had been preparing for this very occasion ever since the death of Verus.

'Surely Eclectus would have said?'

'Not openly. He is certainly more than a "little ill" or Eclectus would not have mentioned it.'

I nodded, trying to imagine the emperor, still sprightly at fifty-four, on his deathbed. It did not sit well in my head. I had never known a world without Marcus Aurelius and could barely imagine such a thing. 'Perhaps he *is* just ill,' I said soothingly. 'He has a weak constitution, after all. You know that. Your uncle always said it. And he is in the cold, dreary north. Perhaps all he needs is to return to warmer climes?'

'Perhaps,' he admitted slowly. 'If word of this has spread elsewhere, I wonder ... Perhaps this is Cassius' reaction to fearing the emperor might fall?'

I frowned. 'But Cassius must know, as all Rome does, that you are the heir?'

The prince turned a strangely bitter, calculating look on me. 'Men who enjoy position fear change. Perhaps Cassius thinks that if the empire passes to me he will not enjoy the same favour he does from my father. Verus knew this problem, I think: that the senators of Rome work for their own advancement, rather than that of the empire. That is why he trusted in freedmen, who could not hope to usurp. Shrewd.'

I tried to picture Cassius rising as a new emperor in the east. I couldn't. I'd only met the man once or twice and I'd been quite young. But I had spent those lonely nights in Carnuntum reading for entertainment, and I had read my histories well. I knew how dangerous a usurper in the east could be. Marcus Antonius and Vespasian had illustrated that point adequately. In fact, the danger of a usurper controlling Aegyptus was precisely the reason no senator could govern the province and it was the remit of a lower prefect.

The months went on, now more than a little tense. Commodus spent time as instructed, in the hall of Trajan, distributing imperial largesse. Some thought it was the emperor and his son alleviating the effects of the plague that continued to claim lives everywhere. Some thought it was a grand way to try and offset the pressure that had been placed on the empire by increased taxes to support the endless wars on the Danubius. Commodus understood the truth, even if no one had said it. There was a usurper threatening the legitimate rule of the Antonines, and the people of Rome had to be reminded where their loyalty lay.

Over those months, more and more reports rolled in. The wars in the north continued, without disaster, but also without clear sight of an end. The situation in the east went from bad to worse. Avidius Cassius, originally with just the backing of the Syrian armies, now had the entire east behind him, including important, perpetually troublesome Aegyptus. The worst news was what came through rumour.

It was said that the emperor had died in the north.

I was shocked when I first heard it. Commodus initially panicked, unable suddenly to maintain that stoic mask he had prepared, but soon he began to calm, reasoning that no matter what had happened, Eclectus or one of the other courtiers or generals in the north would have at least told him, had that truly been the case. When the next news did come from Carnuntum, it confirmed that though the emperor was still not well, he was far from dead. Indeed, he was busy leading a push against the enemy even now. Commodus put away his mask for a time.

Spring rolled on, with a cloying, dung-ridden Roman summer on the way, and I was wondering whether Quadratus intended to move to a country estate, as was the wont of nobles in that season. On one bright, fresh day, Maius the eighteenth, I was on my way to see Commodus, when I rounded a corner to find the most spiteful argument in progress.

Saoterus and Cleander were alone in the corridor and I shrank back before they saw me, listening to them.

'You were like me not long ago,' snarled Cleander. '*Worse* than that. Even as a slave I was close to a prince, while you dug shit from a latrine for a living.'

'It matters not how argumentative you get or where either of us started,' Saoterus replied firmly, 'the fact is that I am a free plebeian of Rome and you are a stinking Phrygian slave who likes to think himself important. Get back to your mopping.'

'When the time comes, Saoterus, you will fall so hard and so far, you won't know what fucking month it is when the boatman comes for you.'

'Your threats mean nothing to me, Cleander. You're no Spartacus, just a palace slave full of ambition and self-importance.'

'And you're no noble,' spat Cleander, just as Commodus emerged unexpectedly around the corner at the far end of the corridor. Two Praetorian guardsmen at his shoulders dropped their hands to the hilts of their weapons at the sight of the two arguing men, just a hair's breadth from openly brawling. I almost wished that would happen, for Saoterus had a good five years on Cleander and was much brighter, and I suspected it would be the latter who came off worst.

'What is the meaning of this?' Commodus demanded of his two favourites, and then glanced up as I rounded the corner.

'Many apologies, Majesty,' Saoterus said smoothly with a bow. 'It will not happen again.'

'See that it doesn't,' the prince barked, his irritated glance enough to make Cleander bow low and flee.

Saoterus straightened. 'Majesty?'

'I have received a summons.'

We both looked at him expectantly.

'There is no mention of Father's condition worsening, but I am summoned to Sirmium. It seems the emperor and his court are on the move. Even a cursory glance at a map suggests that he is on the way from the Danubius to deal with Cassius in the east. Saoterus, have everything made ready and send a missive to Sirmium, informing the emperor and any authorities present that we are on our way in haste.'

149

Saoterus bowed and hurried off, leaving Commodus and I alone in the corridor.

'You're coming too,' he said.

I rubbed my neck in worry. 'I can only go with Quadratus.'

'Then he'll have to come,' snapped Commodus, and I marvelled at how my little prince had grown into a man, and a man who would one day be emperor. Surely the time must be coming for him to take the toga?

'What were those two fighting about?' he asked me as we began to walk.

'Just personal things. But it's not right. I know they are both your favourites, but it's not right listening to a slave speaking to a freedman in that manner.'

I had hoped to elicit some promise of admonishment for Cleander. Never had I seen a plan fail so utterly. The prince nodded his agreement. 'You are quite right. It should not be so. I shall have Cleander freed this very day.'

Shit.

IX

A TRAIL OF CRIMSON

Sirmium, summer AD *175*

Two more years of campaigning in the north had worn down the emperor. The great Marcus Aurelius looked sallow, tired and a little frail. He was, on the other hand, far from the mouldering corpse that rumour would have us believe, and certainly his mind was still sharp and vital. Among his gathered consilium of senior officers stood the competent Pompeianus, and a flick of the eyes confirmed that his sour-faced wife, Lucilla, stood on the edge of proceedings, stabbing the general to death with her eyes.

'Father,' Commodus said with a broad smile as he clacked across the marble floor in his worn travel boots and bowed.

'Lucius,' the emperor greeted his son warmly.

The two men went through the traditional pleasantries of greeting, asking after relations and journeys and the like, while the rest of us stood silent and patient. I scanned the faces around me as I waited, sizing them up. Quadratus was eager, watching intently, hoping for something he could turn to his advantage and waiting for a chance to inveigle his way into the emperor's consilium once more. Saoterus was the picture of stoic calmness, eyes respectfully downcast, the perfect courtier. Behind, Cleander glared at his back.

My attention was torn back to the men who ruled the world

as Commodus straightened and said in a louder, more business-like tone, 'When do we leave for the east?'

The emperor stroked his beard thoughtfully. 'Not until we are ready. The army is divided and spread thin. Much of our force remains committed in the north under Pertinax, fighting back the Iazyges in Dacia, and seven days ago I dispatched Vettius Sabinianus west with a small force to maintain our hold on Illyricum and Italia.'

'Surely Italia is secure?' Commodus asked.

'I would like to think so, but in a time when men can rise against the throne unchecked I would be more comfortable knowing that there is someone I trust with an appropriate force looking after imperial interests at home. But between those men I was forced to send to Dacia, the garrisons settled in northern Pannonia, and the units that went west with Sabinianus, the remaining force will be dwarfed by that upon which Cassius can call. I have commissioned new units from everywhere that can claim even close to sufficient manpower, sent messages to our allies in Armenia and the Bosporan Kingdom seeking support, and drawn what units I can from Africa and Achaea. Within the next two months the bulk of the army will have gathered, and we will be ready to move on Cassius.'

Commodus nodded his understanding, and Quadratus took a step forward hopefully. The emperor, ever a man aware of his surroundings, glanced at the courtier for but a moment.

'Pompeianus will continue to command the gathered force, though I will select other staff officers in due course.'

Pompeianus bowed his head in quiet acceptance, Lucilla's lip twisted at the realisation that this meant she would continue to tour battlefields with the court and, satisfied that the emperor meant him to be among the commanders, Quadratus stepped back once more into the group.

'However,' Marcus Aurelius said, addressing the gathering as a whole now, 'since we are to move against a usurper who has strong support, and since we must be sure to impose our direct rule over the region once more, it would be most appropriate for the locals to see not only their emperor but also their *future* emperor in the best possible light. It is time, my son, that you took the *toga virilis* and lost the bulla of childhood. As Romulus ascended to sit among the gods on the seventh of Iulius, so shall you rise on that day as a man, an emperor-in-waiting, and leader of the knights of Rome.'

I smiled to see the look of pride in my prince's face. He had not been a child, in truth, for some time, except in the legal eyes of Rome, but in a little over a month, not long before his fourteenth birthday, he would officially be a man. He would travel east with his father to put down a rebel as a true officer and leader of men.

We settled in at Sirmium and watched over the ensuing days as new units of soldiers arrived in Pannonia from other climes and bolstered the growing force. Following an overwhelming victory in Dacia, General Pertinax arrived unexpectedly with a force of many thousands, to the great relief of all present. We celebrated Commodus taking the toga, and then, even before his birthday the next month, we began the preparations for journeying east.

Plans changed one warm, balmy morning as I stood in the palace garden, taking in the gentle scent of the flower beds and listening to the bees as they hummed around the lush blooms. Coincidentally, I was also hiding from Quadratus, whose ongoing lack of assigned command was making him irritable enough to take it out on me. He had hit me twice. I had endured it in meek silence, which he probably took to be some Christian weakness, but in truth it was me adding his name to my mental proscription list beneath Cleander and Lucilla. It was remarkably calming in that garden, given the martial activity all around Sirmium that summer. I heard footsteps approaching through the atrium, clicking on the marble, and turned to see

Commodus emerging into the warm sunshine, wearing a smile that warmed the heart.

It seemed now to have been a lifetime ago that my prince had suffered his melancholia, and I was beginning to think that perhaps it had been some childhood malady caused by such deep grief in quick succession, but which maturity and growth had pushed away. Certainly, he had seemed happy and quite positive now for a long time. The last few years had wrought such a change upon the boy I had known, growing him into a man of wit and strength. I smiled in return and noted that he was clutching an opened scroll case that bore the seal of the *cursus publicus*.

'You would not credit it, Marcia,' he grinned.

'Good news, I take it?'

'Perhaps the best. Avidius Cassius is no more. His revolt has collapsed.'

I blinked my surprise. I had privately prayed that I would not be forced to witness a repeat of that awfulness by the river in the north but, with Romans on both sides, I rather doubted the God of Abraham had been instrumental in stopping this.

'One of his own centurions,' Commodus smiled. 'He proclaimed his loyalty to Father and drove his blade through Cassius' heart.'

'You're sure?' It sounded too easy by far.

'*Fairly* sure . . . they sent his head to us with the letter. Father wouldn't look in the box, but I did, and Pompeianus confirmed it was him. The revolt is over without the need for war, Marcia.'

'God be praised,' I said, feeling faintly nauseous about the idea of looking into a box containing a mouldering head.

'Indeed,' he said, giving me a strange, sidelong look, '*all* of them.'

'Then we will return to Rome?' While that would effectively put me back in Quadratus' house and curtail my travels, Rome was a good place to be these days, and we could relax there. Perhaps even the emperor might return with us.

'No,' Commodus replied, still smiling. 'Much of the army will be dispersed, but with the core of it we still go east.'

'But why, if Cassius is dead?'

'Because the people of the eastern provinces need to see us. To see the imperial family, to be reminded of our place in the world. Father is insistent that we both go; Mother too.'

'Surely with Cassius dead, loyalty will be assumed?'

'It is not always that simple,' Commodus said with a shrug. 'Sometimes a rebellious people need to be reminded of their loyalties. Sometimes even on a permanent basis. Look at Jerusalem. Rose against Hadrian and now it has been called Aelia Capitolina after him for half a century, the old Jewish name all but extinct. They will never again forget who rules them, for his name is ingrained in their very streets. Perhaps Antioch, where Cassius' revolt started, could now be Aurelia Capitolina? I shall suggest it to Father.'

I did not know whether to be pleased or afraid. We were to travel east, and I knew that I was to go, else Commodus would not have told me such things himself. Besides, with a foot in the imperial door again, Quadratus was hardly ready to rush off home into obscurity.

East, where the people had rebelled against their lawful emperor, where revolts were commonplace, close to the deadly Parthians, and inevitably crossing more than one large stretch of open water. East, where it was said to be a land of rock and desert and unforgiving sun, where the plague that had almost brought Rome to its knees had been born.

East. Exotic and enticing. Land of Hercules. Land of spice and incense. Land of the Christ child.

Land of change.

There was some discussion as to the route and departure point. The emperor advocated the shortest potential journey at that time of year, to Antioch, the heartland of Cassius' rising. That notion sent shivers down my spine as they marked out the journey on the huge wall map in Sirmium: back to where we had landed on our way here, and then twelve to fourteen days by ship through the Adriatic and around the tip of Achaea to Asia. The very thought of that much water for that long made me shrivel inside. Fortunately, Pompeianus countered with a route he considered more favourable considering the sizeable military contingent we would take. We would travel across Moesia and Thrace to Byzantium, making the briefest of hops across the swift Bosphorus and slogging through dusty Bithynia and Galatia to the former rebel stronghold. The empress and Lucilla were very vocally dismayed at such a long journey over difficult terrain when the same could be achieved by a sea voyage only half as long. I rejoiced, albeit silently.

Despite the long journey ahead, the court that set off from Sirmium on a sun-soaked autumn morning was upbeat and content. The empress, who had spoken to her husband at some length of her feelings on protracted carriage travel, had been reminded delicately that Hadrian, only half a century earlier, had spent some fifteen years extensively touring the provinces with his court, and that *his* wife had accompanied him. It was hard not to smile at her expression in reply, especially given that Hadrian's empress had been rather superfluous, since he had taken his young lover Antinous on much of the journey as well.

I have no idea how large the army was that travelled with us across Thrace and Anatolia, just that it included horsemen and infantry, slowed us interminably, raised a cloud of dust such as I have never seen, and engendered a constant need to gather supplies from each region through which we passed. The small party of illustrious nobles that rode with us included Pompeianus, the heroic general Pertinax, who had saved Dacia from the Iazyges, and a pair of near-identical brothers – the Quintilii. Those two men seemed to me to be every bit as self-serving and smug as Quadratus, though I was quietly told by Commodus that they were respected generals who had shared the consulate a number of years ago and who had been favourites of the emperor Antoninus. Still, I decided at first glance that I would trust neither of them as far as I could spit.

I managed to spend time with Commodus on the journey, except when he was required to ride with his father and the senior generals and plot for the coming days. Oddly, Quadratus was too busy to bother with me except on odd nights when his lust overtook his greed. He had been granted some semi-important logistical role, and was determined to prove his worth to the emperor. Given the size of the army, it occupied much of his time. Saoterus was only peripherally occupied, since everyone with whom the prince might communicate was with us, and Cleander was made somewhat redundant by the presence and competency of the emperor's own *cubicularius*. Thus, the pair made sport of their mutual hatred throughout the journey, constantly bickering, niggling, attempting to one-up each other. They were as circumspect about it as ever, of course, neither wanting the emperor or the prince to witness their bile, but both were happy to argue in front of me.

Consequently, I rode in my carriage in relative silence, watching the varying countryside roll by, often with Commodus riding his white mare alongside. As always, I paid attention to the land and its people as we travelled. As a small girl in that squat building beside the Palatine, helping Mother stitch tunics and cloaks, I had never dreamed of even leaving the great city, let alone touring its provinces.

We followed the Danubius for a short distance, then turned south along a wide valley that brought us to the commercial metropolis of Naissus. From there the going became more troublesome, the road rising to cross numerous passes in the Dardanian mountains. I had thought the Mons Apenninus or the ridged mountains of Illyricum rugged and impressive, but the mountains of Moesia stole my breath. We passed through grand, well-appointed Serdica and began to descend from the heights into a wide, flat land, at the heart of which stood ancient Philippopolis, and from there followed the valley of the Hebros down into the low plains of coastal Thrace to Byzantium, a sight that will remain in my mind and my heart all my life.

As we crossed that wide, green land, something occurred to me, and I leaned close to the carriage window, addressing the prince, who rode alongside with an expression of stoic contentment.

'Have you noticed the people?' I said. 'The land?'

He frowned and looked about himself. Nothing seemed to strike him as noteworthy, so he turned that beetled brow to me.

I smiled. 'I cannot see as many signs of the plague afflicting this region.' While it had only just struck me, thinking back I could remember seeing few signs of the dreadful pestilence since leaving Pannonia. The people were still largely poor and hungry, but there were fewer open indications of the effects of the devastating disease, I was sure. No carts of bodies, no fresh burial pits on the edge of settlements. No village apothecaries with queues of coughing patients waiting outside.

'Is it starting to fade, perhaps?' I questioned. 'Has it moved west and let go its grip on this region? Will it keep drifting west and eventually disappear into the sea?' I liked the idea that Rome might soon be freed from the plague's grasp and allowed to breathe.

Commodus shook his head. 'It's not that easy, Marcia. There are simply fewer people here to suffer. All the men of strength and age and vigour have been drawn into new legions and sent to one war or another, and the plague has long since claimed the weakest of the rest. The burial pits are all full and grassed over. I thought the area was considerably more rural and sparsely populated than I'd expected. I spoke to Pompeianus, and he told me all about it. This was once a thriving area. Now it's a depopulated backwater.'

I shuddered at the idea that a land could look healthy simply because there was no one left alive. 'That's horrible.'

Commodus nodded. 'Things would be better for them, even with the plague, if we'd not been forced to enlist all the menfolk. There has to be an end to these interminable and fruitless border wars, Marcia. We can do nothing about the plague but struggle through it and hope it subsides, no matter what my uncle thought, and poverty is a troublesome hydra with many heads – cut one free and another takes its place. But war can be avoided through treaty and discussion, and that is at least one ill of which Rome could be free. It saddens me that Father, who instilled in me these very values, continues to fight a hopeless war with the dream of a conquest that will last for all time. It is remarkably short-sighted for a man with such vision, do you not think?'

I had no answer to that. And thereafter, as we travelled, what had seemed a peaceful rural region instead resembled a cemetery in my eyes.

Now more than halfway to Antioch, we crossed the blue stretch of water outside Byzantium's walls, in which I was astounded to see myriad jellyfish pulsing, something I had never seen before and which fascinated me enough to overcome my terror of even such a short stretch of water. Then we were in the brown, parched lands of Bithynia. The journey became harder here, the settlements fewer and further between. The farmland seemed harsher and the animals scrawnier. I felt as though we had left the lush world of Rome and passed into the borderlands. Was this the terrain in which Verus had fought the Parthians and found the plague? I could imagine it as the source of misery.

We passed a huge lake on our thirty-third day out of Ancyra that had all but dried up, leaving miles of salty, uninhabitable

159

grey, and began the slow but constant climb through Cappadocia to the Taurus Mountains.

We stopped at a small village called Halala in the high foothills, at the lower end of the great pass known as the Cilician Gates. Though the place was minor and poor in itself, it thrived in other ways due to its position, and boasted a major imperial *mansio* way station for the many officials and couriers that used the pass. The resident visitors had all been moved on to less impressive quarters by the Praetorians who ranged ahead of us, and so the entire mansio was given over to the emperor's court. The bulk of the force that accompanied us camped a little further back down the valley.

The weather was already on the turn and we had noted in the past days of travel a bitter chill in the morning, even in this arid region. It had something to do with our elevation on the edge of the Taurus Mountains, of course, but it most definitely also heralded the cusp of winter, and we could imagine snow awaiting us at the highest points of the range. Still, comfortable and warm in the mansio, we thought little of what awaited us.

As was so often the case in my life, disaster was heralded by Cleander.

I was leaving the comfort of the mansio proper to visit the bathhouse that stood a little apart, down a slope and a small flight of steps, when I heard that hateful voice already raised in anger emerging from another doorway. Cleander appeared, jabbing a finger at Saoterus as though it were a *gladius*, and I rolled my eyes at what resembled a pair of endlessly bickering children.

'You would climb into the prince's *bed* had you the chance,' Cleander sneered.

'You would have me Antinous to his Hadrian?' Saoterus replied loftily. 'A lover and favourite?'

'Me? I would have you skinned and roasted and, who knows, one day I might.'

'You will never have that kind of influence, Cleander. You're just a spoilt, overambitious peasant.'

'And you are a momentary blink of the eye. A bath attendant too big for his boots. Soon you'll be gone, and I will mourn your passing appropriately. With good wine and song.'

I tried to stop listening as they descended into the usual name-calling and concentrated instead on the steps down to the baths, which were slippery. I was startled to see half a dozen Praetorians suddenly emerge from the door below, spreading out, two of them climbing the path towards me as the emperor himself and the empress Faustina appeared from the golden glow of the bathhouse doorway.

Respectfully, I stepped off the path onto the grassy slope some paces away, being careful to maintain my footing as the soldiers climbed. Similarly, Cleander and Saoterus had halted their endless tirade and moved aside in silence. The only noises were the clatter and scrape of the soldiers' boots on the damp stone and the conversation of the man who ruled the world, and his wife.

'I swear,' the empress said gaily, 'that the man's face was so deformed that I honestly wondered if he had been put in the wrong way up.'

The emperor exploded in a shower of mirth at the story that we'd clearly missed much of, rubbing the back of his head and shaking with laughter.

'This, my heart, is why soldiers need their wives on campaign.' He smiled. 'The world can oft appear too bleak without the soft tone and light heart of a woman to heal it.' In an almost unseemly show of affection, Aurelius put his arm around his wife's shoulder and squeezed her to him. 'Come. Warm food and ingratiating, sycophantic company awaits.'

Faustina rolled her eyes. 'And you make it sound so appealing.'

The imperial couple climbed back towards the comforts of the mansio, smiling and easy. Suddenly, with a sharp cry of alarm,

Faustina slipped on the treacherous stone and fell heavily. The emperor made to grab her, but she slipped through his fingers, landing with a hard *crack*. She rose, sheepishly, laughing at her clumsiness even as the six Praetorians turned and hurried to help, their compatriots who guarded the entire perimeter of the mansio complex running to join them. But as she rose, smiling, she yelped and fell again, thudding down onto the cold wet grass beside the steps. I looked at her and winced. The empress' leg was soaked with blood where it had torn on the edge of the stone step, and I could see the white of bone.

The emperor was horrified and called out for help. Moments later, soldiers in white tunics were carefully bearing the empress aloft, carrying her up the steps towards the inn proper, their shields and other equipment discarded on the grass. A trail of crimson climbed the stair behind them. I hurried after the men, my desired soak in a hot bath long forgotten. Faustina was taken to her room and Galen, who had accompanied the court east, fetched to tend to her. Shortly after he arrived and shut himself in the chamber with her and the emperor, Commodus appeared. Cleander and Saoterus immediately flocked to his side, each acting as though the other wasn't there, but Commodus waved them both away irritably, instead crossing to me where I stood nervously, nibbling my manicured nails.

'What happened? I heard she fell?'

I nodded. 'On the bathhouse steps. They were icy. Her leg is a mess.'

We stood there in silence, each moment becoming tenser and more worrying than the last as we waited for someone to leave that room. My fears for the empress gave rise to thoughts of my mother, who I had not now laid eyes upon in four years or more. The one occasion I had managed to secure time and freedom to visit, she had not been there. I had thought of her from time to time, of course, but the empress' predicament somehow flooded me with feelings of guilt over how long it had been since I had spoken to Mother. I resolved to speak to Commodus when the chance arose and beg more time to visit her, sure that we could somehow recapture the closeness of my youth.

It was over an hour before the physician emerged. The gathered faces – everyone who cared for the empress, as well as those who could see an advantage in appearing to be more concerned – leaned forward expectantly. Galen shook his head sadly and I blinked in surprise.

'The empress is not in a good way,' he announced

'You dolt,' Commodus snapped. 'I thought she had died, the way you looked.' I nodded, and I was not the only one, but the physician held up his hands in mollification.

'Please, it is not good. The empress has lost a great deal of blood and the wound is bad – too wide to simply stitch and I cannot attempt to patch the wound with such a flow of blood. She is deathly pale, and her breathing is shallow. I have bound the leg in an attempt to halt the bleeding and clot the wound. If Aesculapius is listening to our prayers and the empress is strong, then she will make it through the night, and if she does and has not lost too much more blood, then I might be able to attempt a surgical graft. For tonight we are in the hands of the gods. I would suggest, your Highness, that you pray for your mother.'

As the crows gathered above Halala, we did. We prayed that night as we had prayed for Annius. As we had prayed for Verus. As we had prayed for Fulvus. Commodus found the mansio's lararium and added to the collection of gods a small statue of Aesculapius that was now a part of his permanent baggage, making libations, lighting expensive incense, praying until exhaustion finally took him. Saoterus did likewise, some respectful distance from the prince, and so did Cleander.

I prayed to God, and, though my relationship with my saviour had been rocky at times, I prayed with all my heart, for

163

the empress had a good soul and her loss would be a disaster for Commodus. Pompeianus took it upon himself, good man that he was, to control the court and keep them informed of all events, allowing the imperial family their privacy. Lucilla put in a brief appearance, a rare display of actual worry and grief as she waited for news of her mother. Quadratus joined us for a while, for once leaving aside all thought of advancement and genuinely praying for his aunt.

I prayed quietly until I was interrupted by a whisper.

'Praying to your lone Jewish god is going to kill the empress.'

'Shut up,' I hissed, casting around my gaze to see if we were being listened to. Quadratus, Pompeianus and Lucilla were all absent. Commodus had retired to his chamber in an attempt to squeeze in an hour or two's sleep, and Saoterus had gone off to check in with the physician. I was alone with Cleander. Had I realised that, I might have left earlier. 'The empress needs all our goodwill,' I said, as patiently as I could manage.

'Not yours,' Cleander snapped. 'Mark my words: in the morning, Aesculapius will turn his back on us because of your Jewish cult and your unwillingness to recognise the true gods. It happened with Prince Fulvus, it happened with Prince Annius, and now your impious rituals will kill the empress, too. How the prince tolerates your kind I shall never understand.'

I turned away from the former slave and ignored his jibes, though with a new, unsettling thought. If the empress did not pull through, *I* knew it would not be because of my beliefs, but Cleander would feel vindicated. What would he do? Christians have rarely been popular in the Roman empire, and more emperors had murdered our kind than had preserved us. Yes, we had freedom and rights under the glorious reign of the Antonines as never before, but how long would that last?

I spent the rest of the night nervous, even when Commodus, unable to sleep, returned to the altar and made a fresh appeal for his dwindling family. 'God has a plan,' my mother would always say, 'but it is not always given to us to understand it or to find meaning or comfort in it.'

She was right about that.

The empress died a little before dawn. We could not quite comprehend it. Mere hours earlier she had been laughing and vital, and now she was grey and still. The emperor emerged from her chamber with the drawn-faced physician, and the two paused in the doorway to deliver the news.

Moans of anguish arose from every quarter, and as I stood, shivering, taking in that scene, I realised that the two people who were not wailing or sobbing were the empress' husband and son. Aurelius had seen enough tragedy in his life and was of a composed and sober enough nature that he was able to box up his raw pain and save it to deal with later. Commodus, in a way that was at once similar and yet so very different, had again drawn that mask of composure down over his face to hide the fact – which I knew full well – that he was screaming inside. It was a habit he must have developed to help deal with his pain whenever I had not been there for him, and the knowledge of that sent fresh waves of guilt through me. How could I let him suffer behind the mask when I was here now to soothe him? I felt that pit of anguish opening up in front of the prince and was reminded of those days I found him closeted away in a dark room, dreaming of death. His descent had to be arrested before he began to wallow, but for a while I had not the chance.

I was ignored for days. Commodus and his father closeted themselves away when they were in private, and the rest of the time they were involved with the inevitable responsibilities of the bereaved. I ached to console my prince but had to let him suffer behind his mask – for a time, anyway. On the eighth day, as was customary, we held the funeral, witnessed only by the court, a grand military presence that had been encamped in the valley below, and the paltry inhabitants of a small provincial stopover. Only when the ceremony had been held and the empress rendered down to ash to lie cooling in her urn did I finally spend any time with Commodus.

I walked into his room at his bidding and closed the door behind me. He looked up, rose from the bed and threw his arms around me. The mask slid from his face and he wept like a heartsore child for hours. That night we talked of death and of loss. Of the ever-diminishing line of the Antonines. I was desperate to push aside such subjects and try to help him find his way back to the light as we had done with the Palatine menagerie, but I also knew that I had to let him vent these emotions to me, first. Grief has to play itself out, as I was already aware. Finally, his body weak from hours wracked with sobbing, his eyes dry and his pillow wet, he slept.

The next day I called again and the Praetorian at the door bade me wait, for the prince already had a visitor. For half an hour I fretted in the corridor until the door opened and Cleander emerged. It was an interesting transition that I saw occur on his face. As he left the room he wore a look of chastened sadness and sympathy, but as he emerged into the corridor it slipped into sour anger, which only deepened as his eyes fell upon me. His lip twitched into a sneer and he stomped away without a word. I was intrigued and entered the prince's room once the guard had confirmed my invitation.

'Highness?'

He was sitting quietly, and his expression was odd, I couldn't place it.

'Is your god an understanding one?' he asked quietly.

I paused, unsure where this was going. 'The *most* understanding. The most forgiving.'

'Cleander claims your impiety killed my mother. Others in the court, I know, would share his opinion, for your god is not popular.'

'God—' I began.

'*Your* god,' he said quietly.

'*My* God,' I conceded, imagining Mother's face at such phrasing, 'would never see an innocent suffer so, and the gods of Rome are said to look after their people, are they not? Only madmen like Nero blame the Christ for tragedies befalling the empire.'

Commodus nodded wearily. 'I had come to a similar conclusion, and I told Cleander precisely what I thought of his theory.'

'He is playing games,' I said, angrily. 'Jostling for position, seeking power and to push down anyone who might get in his way, such as me, or Saoterus.'

'I have known Cleander almost as long as I've known you, Marcia. He helped try to save Fulvus. He saved Annius from a fall. I know you hate him, but you see only what you want to see. There is another side to him. He had often been my friend when I most needed one.'

I nodded, though that cut me deep, partially because I was supposed to be the one he turned to, and partially because I knew even in the bitterest part of my heart that he was right. 'Even a rangy wolf looks like a loyal dog sometimes,' I said meaningfully. He did not look convinced by my analogy. 'Enough of this, now. It is still early morning. Come out. Come with me.'

He threw me a look that suggested he would rather almost anything else at that moment, but I would not relent. We emerged from the room and made our way down the corridor into the light. Two Praetorians fell in behind us protectively as we made our way through the mansio.

'Where are we going?' he asked, his voice still hollow and cracked with grief. I knew my prince. Ahead lay months of despair unless I could help him. And it was not a matter of healing him, but of supplying him with the opportunity and tools to heal himself. I was becoming adept at this, I think.

'We are going to see the world,' I said brightly. He still looked

167

dour and unhappy, but there was just a twinkle of curiosity about him, then. We exited into the chilly, late autumn mountain air, and I beckoned him towards the stables.

'How easy is it to ride?' I asked.

He stared at me. Roman women don't ride. We travel in carriages or litters. But where I had a mind to go only feet or hooves would be possible, and travelling through Pannonia and the east I had seen women on horses – the poor and the semi-barbaric, admittedly, but something bloody-minded in me suggested that if a Thracian peasant woman could manage a horse, then damn well so could I.

'I intend to ride, unless there is an imperial command coming preventing me. Is there?'

Commodus continued to stare at me, but shook his head slowly.

We took the horses from the stable, Commodus selecting his own well-rested mount and the *equisio* giving me the beast he thought the tamest and most steady. After just a few moments of instruction, I laughed at the worry of the stable master.

'I will be fine. Wedged between four horns in this saddle, where could I go? Kick to move, haul back to stop, pull one side to turn. I cannot understand why horsemanship is considered such a skill.'

Commodus actually laughed, then, as much at the equisio's face as at my comment. We set off with twelve Praetorian cavalry keeping us company – a prince's life is too important to expose needlessly – and I soon learned my folly in simple assumption. I had the tamest, calmest horse in the world and damn me if he did not continually go the wrong way, stop when I was busy kicking him in a frenzy, turn left when I pulled the right rein. At least he never ran and never jumped or bucked, but still, he made my first, and last, horse ride difficult. Even with my troubles, more so because of it, in fact, the ride was worth it. My difficulties continually improved Commodus' mood.

We were to ride some ten miles, which the men I had over-heard in the mansio discussing this place had suggested was the work of an hour. In fact, it took me almost three times that, though in addition to my lack of skill the terrain was not easy. Casting my mind back to the conversation I had listened in on at the inn, we followed the road to the south as it rose towards the Cilician Gates, but before we reached that pass we took a small side road to the left. This meandering path led us high up a hill split with several jagged peaks, tapering green trees jutting from the sharp grey scree.

It was principally a logging trail, I think, but it was wide enough and well-trodden enough for us to make our way up without too much difficulty. Nearing the end of our third hour, and with me regretting my curiosity for the saddle, we arrived at the top. The tumbledown remains of an ancient watchtower stood there, and as we reached the crest and reined in, I could understand what the men I'd overheard meant when they said you could see the world. The view allowed for the faint recogni-tion of Halala, whence we had come, some distance north along the snaking road, and valleys stretched out east. To the south we could see the wide, deep vale leading to the Cilician Gates. I had travelled now across mountains in Italia, Illyricum, Moesia and Bithynia, but never had I experienced a view like this.

It was refreshing to say the least, sitting there, wishing my rump was more numb than it was, feeling as though we were atop the world looking down. I could almost feel the pent-up emotion draining from the prince. I had led him to this place. He had done the rest. We returned at leisure and dropped the horses off at the stable. Commodus swore all present to silence about our ride, not at all sure his father would approve of such a frivolous journey – not understanding the need for it – and certain that my reputation would suffer from the tale.

After that day, things slowly picked up again. We had called at Halala for one night and stayed for near half a month. When we left, the prince was almost his old self once more, and his father seemed to have dealt with his grief in his own, private manner. Lucilla urged him to return to Rome, but the emperor's world was ever one of expediency, and even this tragedy could not deter Aurelius from the need to visit the formerly rebellious provinces of the east. The empress' ashes, along with a deputation and a single unit for escort, left us on the other side of the Cilician Gates, making for the port of Hadrianopolis to take ship back to Rome. The appropriate honours would be voted for Faustina and she would go to rest in the mausoleum with the others, though her official funerary observances would wait until the emperor returned. Meanwhile, Aurelius had business in the east.

We forged on quickly now, like an army at war. We passed by Cyrrus, the birthplace and home city of the usurper Cassius, and a lack of interest in visiting the place came as a surprise to no one. We did the same with Antioch, though, the very epicentre of rebellion, which was less anticipated. That city had fallen over itself to do honour to the emperor and his glorious son. The council there had raised monuments and planned games for the emperor's visit, making hasty additions in honour of the lamented empress. They spilled out of the city at the column's approach and were rebuffed by Aurelius, telling them that he had neither the time nor the inclination to spend a night in a city of traitors. Indeed, he dictated a series of punishments for the city, restricting their civic liberty and their status in the world. I knew we had come east to impose imperial will once more, and it seemed to me out of character for the great Marcus Aurelius to so blithely punish and miss an opportunity for glittering largesse. The fact that Commodus shared my opinion suggests to me that the emperor was still beset by grief and out of sorts.

'Leniency might be more productive in the long term, Father,' the prince advised.

'I was lenient with Cassius. I let a man of senatorial rank control Aegyptus despite the law. Look what happened,' was the flat reply.

We moved on across Syria and south throughout the winter, which is the best time to be in that steaming, barren world. Throughout the tour, Cleander remained a canker in the party, though only Saoterus and I saw it, so good was he at playing the good courtier. At least with the other freedman there, Cleander had someone to argue with and rarely started with me. Now that I had realised how bitter the old emperor still was, I watched with fascination as, just as I had urged Commodus to lift himself from his melancholia, the prince repeated the process on his father. By the time Saturnalia was done, the emperor seemed to be something of his old self and closer than ever to his heir. Aurelius vowed to visit Antioch on our return and put right what he had done. The emperor's mellowing led to a more altruistic approach to the rebellious east from then on. Rather than punishment, he embarked upon a campaign of forgiveness, the scale of which would make any Christian priest proud.

Most of the associates of Cassius were pardoned, including whole cities and councils and army officers who had backed him. His head, now little more than a skull covered in brittle parchment carried in a box in the baggage train, was sent to his family at Cyrrus to be reunited with his body for proper interment. Indeed, on the emperor's orders, even the records of the provinces that might contain damning evidence against as yet unidentified people and groups were burned to prevent their ever being used in bringing down punishment upon them.

We kept close to the coast and reached Alexandria in the spring, and I marvelled at this mysterious world of Aegyptus, land of the pharaohs. I had grown up on Mother's tales of cruel Pharaoh and the captivity of Moses and, oddly, I could see an echo of the clear power of that once-great line even now.

Great men such as Trajan and Augustus were carved in their temple walls now, but in the guise of pharaoh, not emperor. No wonder emperors were so watchful of the place as a source of revolt. I was a little disappointed that we had skirted Judea and I never got to visit all those places Mother had told me of in her parables, but I did find that Alexandria had a large community of Jews, and a reasonable number of Christians who seemed to be living openly and in peace. I worshipped with them, to the interest and amusement of Commodus and the mocking derision of Cleander, who seemed perfectly at ease with bird- or lion-headed gods, but could not comprehend my simple faith.

Alexandria had swiftly thrown in its lot with the usurper and now consequently braced themselves to receive much the same treatment as Antioch, but the emperor had mellowed, and Commodus ever whispered words of peace and calm in his ear. Alexandria and Aegyptus were pardoned, though not without exception.

The governor of Aegyptus was allowed to shoulder the entire blame for his province's support of the usurper and accepted the death sentence willingly, proving his Romanitas. Though clearly guilty of treason and unmistakably deserving of death, the nobility of his response impressed Aurelius and his son, and so his death was made correspondingly noble and swift. Kneeling on the warm, flat stones of the forum of Alexandria, he mouthed a swift prayer for his loved ones, and then closed his eyes. The sword of execution was held by Narcissus. Though he was in no way trained with such a blade, his sheer size and strength allowed for an ease of use of the massive weapon and gave a great deal of power to the blow. The edge had been sharpened, which was unusual. An execution blade was often deliberately kept dull to draw out the agony of the process. But between the keen edge and the strength of its wielder, the first blow almost went right through the neck, and the big man withdrew it fast for the second, cutting short the pain for the governor as fast as he could.

Two blows, and the governor's head rolled across the stonework to the raucous cheers of a public who had wholeheartedly supported his treason such a short time ago. Thus did the governor meet his end, swiftly and relatively nobly.

Another death sentence fell upon Cassius' eldest son, who was discovered hiding in the city and preaching hate and revolt against the Antonines. He was less accepting of his fate, struggling and fighting, denouncing the emperor through spit and bile. His death took almost an hour, slowly strangled with each turn of the garrotte in the forum, where he could see the bloodstains that were all that remained of the governor. I managed to find an excuse to leave before the end of that one, but I was later told with glee by some courtier that his eyes filled up with blood before the end.

On a lighter note, a senator involved in the conspiracy and the younger son of Cassius were convicted but the sentence commuted to exile. A few leading lights were punished; most went free. The two legions who had remained loyal in the east were to be given great honours. I spent hours after the executions with my Christian brethren, praying for the souls of the dead, and then I bathed and scrubbed until I was raw, as though I could somehow clean off the impurity of watching that horror. Still, that was one day of nightmare, and some would clearly say *necessary* nightmare. It marred the beginning, but the rest of our time in Alexandria was more uplifting.

During our unexpectedly pleasant stay, the emperor ordered a number of grand new building works, and the Parthians, still at peace with us since Verus' campaign almost a decade ago, sent emissaries with gifts, opening up a whole new era of co-operation with a fresh treaty. All was good.

Inevitably, the summer wore on and we began to move once

173

more. Again, we skirted around the edge of the place that was my spiritual heartland and travelled north. I was never to see Jerusalem or Bethlehem, to stand upon the place where my saviour died.

In the event we travelled along the coast, visiting places that would benefit from the imperial presence, and called finally at Antioch, where the most restrictive punishments were lifted and the festivals finally held, with forgiveness the watchword. Perhaps someone had suggested to the city's ordo that the emperor's heir had had a hand in their pardon, for the greatest games we witnessed there were held in Commodus' name. We travelled on through the coastal provinces, into Asia and finally came to the Greek sea at Miletus at the beginning of autumn. That ancient city celebrated the emperor's arrival and held games and a festival in honour of both he and the heir-apparent. Commodus accepted the honour with the same stoic calm as his father.

Miletus signalled the end of our stay in the east and the beginning of our return to Rome, which I had not seen now for more than a year. Odd how travel and constant demands on the attention dull the ache of homesickness, yet it takes only a single thought for that feeling to come flooding back. Rome awaited, though by a circuitous route. We also began to travel lighter now. The emperor had gradually quartered his troops as we passed through the east, the army diminishing all the time, and we left what remained of the force there on the Asian coast.

In addition to my increasing homesickness, I was tiring of the journey for other reasons. Quadratus was irritable as his constant attempts to inveigle himself into the emperor's personal council failed, and thus when he came to me, less and less often now, he was always in a bad mood. Additionally, Commodus was spending ever more time with his father and involved in affairs of empire, which meant that, although things were still good between us, our meetings had become fewer and fewer as the miles rolled by. I began to acknowledge that perhaps this was a good thing. I loved Commodus, and now that I recognised it, there was no denying it, and no changing it. But for now, at least, I could not be his, and so to save us both pain, I had decided that the time would come when distance became necessary. Maybe events had conspired to make that happen by chance. Whatever the case, things were changing.

While I dreaded what came next – a crossing of three days to Achaea by sea – it turned out to be nowhere near as bad as I had anticipated and was far better than any other sea journey I have undertaken, for that stretch of water is so dotted with myriad small islands that one is rarely out of sight of land for any length of time, and the sea is so shallow that a traveller might think she could even see the bottom if she looked hard enough.

Our arrival in Athens was clearly anticipated. The emperor's plan to spend time in that great land of philosophers had been no secret during our time in Miletus and word had reached Athens in plenty of time for her to prepare. Two grand statues of Marcus Aurelius and Commodus had been erected in the heart of the city and it came as no surprise to see that the prince had been depicted as Hercules in this land of the demigod's birth. I had to smile at the elaborately curled beard on the statue of the prince who, at fifteen, had cultivated all summer something that looked like a dandelion gone to seed. Still, it was the intention to impress that mattered.

As we moved through the city's centre, escorted by the pre-eminent members of the council, more than once I saw a statue of Hercules among the more traditional gods.

'See how they worship him,' Commodus noted, dropping back from the head of the party where the emperor was in deep conversation. The prince's horse clopped across ancient flagstones next to my litter, a great honour for a pleb.

I nodded. 'This is Hercules' own land.'

Commodus gave a strange smile. 'An odd thing. The Greeks are notorious for their sneering at the sport of warriors, yet they so readily worship Hercules, the patron of all gladiators.'

'I suspect their aspect was given first,' I chuckled, and the prince raised one eyebrow wryly. Whatever pithy comment he intended went unheard, for he was summoned back to the emperor that moment. The column came to a halt and with the sudden decrease in noise the ambient sound of the city flooded in. I leaned out of the litter to see what was happening as the general murmur of the great agora nearby closed about me. The column had stopped for the emperor to speak to a man. He looked almost indistinguishable to my mind from the various other elderly, bearded Athenians, but clearly from the way they were at ease, he and the emperor were well acquainted. The pleasant familiarity between them was made all the more noticeable by the seething enmity I couldn't help but feel emanating from other members of our party. Marcus Aurelius might consider this man a friend, but the Quintilii brothers, each mounted among the imperial party, wore expressions of spiteful hate. Some bad blood clearly existed between these people. There was laughter from the speakers and a few moments later the party began to move again, Commodus dropping back to my litter once more.

'Herodes Atticus,' he said by way of explanation.

I gawked at the man now moving ahead with the emperor as though he were part of the imperial family. I had never met Atticus, of course, but I knew of him. *All of Rome* knew of the great man who had been a close personal friend of three emperors, had commissioned some of the greatest buildings in the world, who was former consul, philosopher and statesman, who was as Greek as he was Roman. There was something about the way the prince almost twitched that suggested he had more to say than merely to announce the arrival of a celebrity.

'What is it?'

'Father and I are to be initiated into the Eleusinian Mysteries,' he said with a flood of pride. 'Atticus has arranged for it during the greater mysteries this month.'

He fell expectantly silent. I felt somewhat deflated after the build-up. I had felt that his news would be bigger than his being subjected to yet another weird pagan cult. 'Wonderful,' I said uncertainly, and saw a touch of irritation dance in his eyes.

'This is an extraordinary honour, Marcia.'

'I expect so,' I said, a little unkindly, still sounding more enthusiastic than I felt. 'Like the statue.'

'Far greater than a simple statue. It is rare for a non-Greek to be initiated. Only the greatest Romans are invited. Men like Hadrian. Men like my uncle, who was initiated on his way to Parthia all those years ago.'

'Congratulations,' I replied, unable to produce anything worthier, though I could understand perhaps why he was so eager, since it would be another pace in his beloved uncle's footsteps. The prince gave me a look of irritation and shook his head, digging his heels into his mount and trotting forward once more to join his father. We were escorted to our accommodation and there prepared for a lengthy stay in Athens.

The city was magnificent, of course, but all I wanted now was to go home. Not only had my homesickness taken a new and strong grip on me, along with a fresh desire to visit my mother in the wake of what we'd all felt for the empress, but also our time here was not to my taste, for the prince was always busy with statecraft and religion while I loafed around inside.

Over the coming days, during which I received once more the regular attentions of Quadratus, the emperor and his son kept themselves busy with these weird mysteries of theirs, consorting with endless philosophers in reasoned debates that seemed to me entirely pointless when Commodus excitedly relayed their content, dining with many nobles, including Atticus, and generally making the imperial presence felt in the city.

I spent time reading, as I once had in the border fortress of Pannonia, and managed to acquire a copy of a new work by a local man named Athenagoras, purporting to be a defence of the Christian faith, and was somewhat surprised to find that it had been dedicated to Commodus.

Finally, as winter began to loom, my urge to return home became paramount. I decided that I would even welcome the fifteen-day voyage around the south of Italia and back to Rome. With no sign of the emperor or his son drawing their fascinating debates to a close, and the city revelling in such imperial attention, starved of anything non-Greek I sent a letter back to the palace in Rome, using the cursus publicus and achieving the highest priority with the blessings of the prince. I sought news of Rome and of events there. Had the plague finally faded away? Was Mother bored and listless with so few of the court there to cater for with her work? What was planned for the emperor's return? Surely games at least.

I waited many days in my apartment, hiding from the brutal sexual attentions of Quadratus and the bitter viper's tongue of Cleander, who was at more of a loose end with Commodus so occupied. Finally, one winter morning, I received my reply, delivered by imperial courier.

I snapped the seal bearing the Palatine imagery and slid my mother's news hungrily from the case. The scribe who had penned the missive had perfect handwriting – Mother had never been taught her letters – and I began to read with the first joy I had felt in more than a month.

Then my world soured, and my eyes stung as I read down the neat script.

The palace functionary apologised for the tone of this letter, which was to inform me with regret that my mother had passed away during the spring. A letter had been dispatched to inform me, and the man was heartily apologetic that it had clearly not reached me. With our hurtling around the east, it was no surprise to me that a message meant for a minor companion of the court never found us. The letter did not explain *how* mother had died, though it used the painful words 'lingering illness', which left me in little doubt that the ever-present plague had claimed her.

I was bereft. I had been too young to know what was happening when my father died, and had never truly experienced personal loss. As I sat alone in the room and wept, I finally understood a little of how Commodus had felt each and every time a member of his family had been snatched away like pieces on a game board. How easy it would be to sink into a permanent melancholia.

Blame was easy to come by in my solitude as I let the tear-stained missive fall. Blame at the imperial courier system for not informing me straight away. Blame at an uncaring God, who had let so many good pagans die, but who had now taken one of our own well before her time. Blame at Verus for having brought the damned plague west. Blame at Commodus for not being with me when *I* needed *him* for a change. Almost anything I could blame that helped me avoid the guilt that burned like a cancer deep inside, for I had not visited Mother now for a third of my life.

I wallowed in misery, wishing my prince would come and help me as I had helped him, yet afraid to leave my rooms in case I bumped into Cleander or attracted the further attentions of Quadratus. The last thing I wanted at that moment was abuse of any kind. And the longer I sat in gloomy, angry silence on my own, the less I was concerned with all else, and the more with the failings of a God I had been brought up to believe was good, and loving, but who had torn from me my only family. It occurred to me only on the darkest of nights that perhaps He had forsaken me because I had so often turned from him in favour of the fascinating ways of the pagans.

When Commodus did come, it was many days later and my tears had long since dried. He came to tell me that the time was upon us. We were going back to Rome before Saturnalia.

And I exploded into grieving sobs once more at the thought of what now awaited me there.

X

THE RAGE OF NEPTUNE

Rome, winter, early AD 177

Just as the journey to Athens had been the easiest and calmest voyage I had ever undertaken, so the journey to Rome from there was by far the worst. Had I more pagan leanings, I might have taken it as a bad sign that the ship we took, the *Tigris*, was the same trireme aboard which Verus had returned from Parthia, bringing the plague with him. Around the south of Italia, we were caught in a storm that even the sailors said was one of the most furious they had ever experienced.

The waves hammered at the ship and the gale tore at the sails, and I cowered and shook with fright. My heart lurched as a spar creaked and then gave with a ligneous crack. Those sailors who were not desperately clutching ropes or fastening things down cast up prayers to the gods. One man close to me, who must have been a new crewman, dropped to his knees along with the others but began to intone one of the common prayers to the Lord while clutching his chi-rho symbol of the Christian faith. His open devotions drew the ire of his crewmates, who roared into life despite the wind and waves threatening to sweep them from the deck, blaming him for the damage to the spar and the storm in general, denouncing Christians as unlucky on a ship and having brought forth the rage of Neptune. I watched in horror as they rushed the man and tried to lift him bodily, shouting their displeasure as they manhandled the struggling sailor towards the bucking and dipping rail, their feet sliding around dangerously on the sodden boards. I could see clearly what they planned, as could the ship's trierarch, who stood clutching the steering oars tight, hair plastered across his face, nodding his agreement, unwilling to lift a finger to stop the violence.

God, no. To be thrown into that dreadful endless stretch of water. In an odd way, I instantly identified with the poor man for all our differences, for was he not receiving precisely the same reaction for an innocent gesture as I did from Cleander whenever I showed *my* faith? I staggered to my feet on the slippery deck, the ship lurching as I did so and sending me this way and that as I rushed to the prince, who was in close discussion with Cleander as both men clung to a rope.

'Majesty, you have to stop this,' I yelled breathlessly over the howling winds and crashing water, using his honorific respectfully since we were in public.

Commodus turned to me, frowning, unaware of what was happening, lurching with another sudden movement of the ship. 'What?'

'That poor sailor. They're going to throw him overboard.'

Now the prince was paying attention, his gaze falling on the activity as the struggling man was pushed and heaved to the rail, where the churning, roaring sea awaited.

'Why?'

'Because he's a Christian. That's all.'

'Probably reason enough,' shouted Cleander unpleasantly, and Commodus looked back and forth between us as I was forced to grasp a rail to prevent myself being thrown back away from them. He stood uncertain, torn, pulled this way and that by emotion as much as the tipping of the deck. He had no hatred of Christians, of course, having grown up with one, but he also knew the popular view of them which had pushed Cleander into urging him not to interfere. His gaze fell on Saoterus, who stood nearby, arm coiled in a rope, clutching a mast, and I felt the balance of the scales of justice tip towards me. The secretary gave a slight nod and Commodus turned, pointing at the group of sailors who now had their unfortunate compatriot on the rail, trying to force him to let go, cursing our God as they did so.

'Stop this,' Commodus bellowed. His words were torn away fruitlessly by the gale and he repeated himself twice, bellowing hoarsely above the howling winds. The men fought on for a moment, the prince's voice going unheard, though one or two stopped when the trierarch began to echo the call. The man's life was only truly saved when half a dozen burly Praetorians staggered across and hauled them off him, grabbing the beleaguered sailor and pulling him back aboard, one of their own almost pitching into the water in the process.

The man spent the rest of the journey with the guard, endlessly thanking and praising the prince who had saved him. The ship was battered and torn, tossed from wave to wave, and finally limped, badly damaged, into the harbour at Heracleum. We had also lost one of the two military triremes that escorted us with all hands in the storm. At the port, while I welcomed dry land and turned my back gratefully on the dreadful sea, Commodus had that sailor stricken from the ship's lists and gave him a purse of coins to see him through the month until he could secure a new position.

While we waited for a vessel of appropriate quality to be found to take us onward and an extra escort trireme to be brought from Syracusae, the sailors and many of the court and passengers made their way to the Temple of Neptune to give gifts and make libations in an attempt to appease the sea god before we attempted the next leg of the voyage. I found myself tempted to join them, my legs still shaking from the terror of the sea, then reminded myself what Mother would think if she found out her good Christian daughter had made libations in a pagan temple. That, of course, brought the grief at her passing and the dismay over an uncaring God flooding back in once more, and left me struggling to decide whether it even mattered who I prayed to now. Turning back to Athenagoras' new work, which was perhaps the first philosophical text I had ever cared for, provided some comfort.

Finally, we boarded our replacement ship and sailed on around Sicilia and up the Italian coast to Ostia. I had never hated a journey as much as I did that one, and yet when we bumped against the jetty in Ostia, I found myself oddly reticent, wishing I could stay aboard, given what awaited me in Rome.

Commodus had been largely occupied with his father during our voyage and had continued to spend only a little time in my company. When he did, I took a leaf from his book and bolted on a mask of contentment, letting my heart shatter over and over beneath it. Somehow, the fact that I had always tried to be there when he needed me, yet he had been consorting with philosophers when *I* needed *him*, rankled deeply. He had enquired in Athens when I burst into tears what had made me sad, and I glossed over the whole event, keeping the news of Mother's passing a secret to myself while I gently broiled at his absence during my suffering.

I know it is neither logical nor fair, especially given that I had decided to distance myself from him, but then I never said I was either of those things.

We arrived in Rome to the tumultuous pleasure of the crowd. I was surprised at the change a year and a half had made in the city. While it was clear that the plague was still active in Rome, it was equally evident that it had subsided somewhat. There was still illness, and there were queues outside the many physicians' houses, but not the endless lines of corpse-wagons and piles of bodies there had once been. Silently, unfairly, I cursed Mother for giving in when she did and not lasting another year to ride out the disease.

We returned to the Palatine and the court dispersed in preparation for what was to come. Though the empress Faustina had necessarily undergone a small funeral in Cilicia, Rome expected a grand affair, and so games and processions and banquets and the like would be held to allow the city to properly show its respect for her.

Quadratus gave orders for his household to return to the domus on the Caelian Hill, and as we departed the palace, I took the opportunity to slip away on my own mission. Enquiring of a few of the minor functionaries, I learned what had become of Mother. Two hours later I was outside the city proper, near the fourth mile marker of the Via Latina. A squat, square *columbarium* stood there, plain and unadorned, set slightly back from the road and nestled in shade cast by two much grander tombs. One of the resting places constructed for palace staff. I had acquired a key from the man who directed me here, and quietly, sadly, unlocked the gate and slipped into the gloomy interior. I filled and lit the small oil lamp on the shelf by the door and waited until the glow increased enough to see properly.

I shuddered. Row upon row of small apertures covered each wall, many of them already filled with a cinerary urn and a small stone plaque identifying the occupant. I browsed the more recent additions, grateful that I had not found anyone else I knew, and finally alighted upon Mother's.

Marcia Aurelia Sabinianus.

I wondered oddly whether, when my time came, I would be placed close by. Marcia Aurelia Ceionia Demetriade. No one ever used my full name. I was not important enough.

'Did anyone attend your funeral?' I asked the shade of my mother. I reached out and touched her urn. It was so cold. Months she had been in here while I thought her alive. 'Were there mourners? Did the palace pay for a procession?'

No. Of course they didn't. Mother was a celebrated seam-stress and valued highly by Verus when he lived. But now Lucilla ruled that house, and even had she been in Rome when Mother died, she would likely have drawn the line at paying for the urn and the plaque.

I cried again, then. In that gloomy house of the dead, where Mother, a Christian, sat among so many pagans. At least the columbarium was plain and not painted with gaudy scenes of Roman gods. She would have hated that.

I left the place an hour later, eyes dry once more, vowing that when I had managed to amass adequate funds I would pay for Mother's ashes to be moved to one of the catacombs devoted to our faith. Perhaps Quadratus could be persuaded to pay.

I made my way back to the city and to the domus of Quadratus. The house's master was still on the Palatine and would not want to parade his plebeian mistress there, so I settled into my rooms and I was still there, sitting in silence, lost in my contemplation of Mother and her unexpected and unwelcome passing, when my visitor arrived.

The house was suddenly all abustle in response to the knock at the gate, for Praetorians and lictors waited out in the street. I was unaware, sitting in my room, until the major-domo appeared in a worried shuffle and showed my visitor into the chamber.

Commodus frowned.

'I had thought to find you at the palace, but I was told Quadratus sent you home.'

I looked up, eyes wide, and leapt from the bed to stand respectfully, head bowed. The prince smiled easily and motioned for me to sit. Turning, he bade the staff and his escort leave and shut the door, and with that we were alone. More alone, in fact, than we had been since we left Rome a year and a half ago. And being alone now could be scandalous, though I was only a little concerned. Commodus was fifteen and a man now, unmarried and highly valued. I was almost twenty and a spinster, for all that I was tethered to Quadratus.

'I . . .' I didn't know what to say. I'd not told him about my troubles. In fact, he had been so busy with affairs of state and his father these past months that since that ride to the mountaintop I had spent little time with him at all.

'Something is troubling you, and has been since Athens,' he said, pulling up a chair to sit in front of me.

I did not reply. How could I tell him that Mother had died, that I had needed him when he could not be there for me?

He looked into my eyes for some time and then nodded. 'You are not ready. I can see that. Tell me when you are ready.'

We sat in an odd silence for a while. Not uncomfortable as such, but strained in some way.

'I am to be consul,' he said, finally, breaking the silence. 'Consul and emperor. I am to rule alongside Father the way Verus did. We will rule together.'

'You will do it well,' I said. A formulaic and bland response.

'I fear Father is truly starting to feel his age,' the prince said in a sad voice. 'He is still not well. This illness he suffers may be minor, but it has been with him for so long I fear he thinks of it as a companion. And he has become slower, frailer. He hides it well in public, but he can't hide it from me. I am with him so much – he spends every hour drilling into me the details of state. He is preparing me for when he is not around, and must believe that time is coming soon: there's an urgency to it.'

I shivered. A world without the great Marcus Aurelius. Commodus would be a good successor, of course, but it still felt strange even to think on such a thing.

'And there will be a triumph,' Commodus said, filling that silence again. 'Soon.'

I shook my head. 'The empress' funerary games and rites will go on for some time.'

'And as soon as they end, Father and I share a triumph. Just us, this time, not the whole family.'

I frowned. 'Do you not think that a little unfeeling? So soon after your mother's rites?'

'Propriety sometimes has to take second place to expediency. The triumph is not for me, in truth. Nor even for Father, though it is ostensibly to celebrate the victory over a dangerous usurper. In truth, the triumph is for Rome. The people need it. Gifts and glamour to tear their thoughts away from war and disease and poverty. To remind them that Cassius is nothing and that we rule Rome. Just as we were there in the east, we have to be here in Rome, for the people.'

I said nothing, just nodded my understanding. I was still sad and out of sorts. I could feel the old closeness with my prince hovering on the edge of the room, almost within my grasp, but I knew that it was a fleeting, stupid thing. A promise of something intangible.

He reached out and cupped my chin in his hand, lifting my face from where I gazed at the floor.

'I wish . . .' His voice tailed off. I knew what he had wanted to say. That I was not Quadratus'. That I was a princess or he a pleb. That the divide between us was not so wide and so deep. It had not been as children, but we were adults now, and a social rift widens with age.

I sighed. 'I love you. I always have.'

It felt so strange to say it, and I knew that even uttering those words was dangerous. But perhaps ever since the day Cleander had accused me of that very emotion, I had known it to be true, and I was certain my prince shared the feeling.

'I know,' he said. No reciprocation, of course. He could not.

'But it cannot be. You are the heir to the throne of Rome, and I am Quadratus' mistress. We each have our duty.'

'I would make my cousin give you up,' Commodus said, and

there was something new in his voice – something odd and strangled – 'but it would do no good.'

I nodded. 'We cannot.'

'I still would. I would not be the first emperor to consort so. Hadrian's favourite was the son of a farmer, after all, and he now sits among the hallowed gods.'

Antinous – that great emperor's Adonis. Would I be happy to be mistress to an emperor? Perhaps the distance between us *was* unnecessary. Some women had been very content to be an emperor's mistress. Had not Penthea been Lucius Verus' very willing mistress in Antioch? And it could hardly be any more difficult than being Quadratus' mistress. I would not be his wife, for I could never be that, but like Antinous to Hadrian, or Claudia Acte to Nero, or even Penthea to Verus, I would be the favourite of a married man, for an emperor needs a wife for a legitimate heir. But no, I couldn't cope with sharing him. Better to lose him altogether than share him with another.

I must have let the silence drag out too long, for Commodus was looking increasingly uncomfortable. I readied myself to speak, to send him away as kindly as I could, but he spoke first.

'I am to marry,' he said.

And my world shattered. I was unable to speak. I stared at him.

'Father has betrothed me. Bruttia Crispina. Daughter of a former consul, from a very illustrious line. Pretty girl. Demure, noble, friendly. Perfect in every way. Except that she's not you.'

Damn him, but I had almost managed to convince myself that I could live without him. I had said 'it cannot be' and I had known that. I had been sure, and I had begun to prepare myself for a new, even wider rift to grow between us, but now everything had changed. That I could not have him was bad enough, but to know that someone else *would* made it impossible to accept. To know that he would be tethered to a pretty, probably vacuous, Roman matron whom he did not love, and to know what I had always believed: that he loved me. I tried to keep my face straight, while inside I raged and bellowed, throwing furniture and hammering my fists on the wall at the unfairness of a world that would give my man to another woman. Because I might have been able to deny it while he was single and untouched, but now, tethered to a matron harpy, he suddenly became just that: *my* man.

'Congratulations,' was all I could manage, and as soon as his hand left my chin, my eyes slid to the floor once more.

'It will be soon. There is to be another campaign against the Marcomanni. Father has decreed it. I tried to argue against it, but he is emperor and he is determined. I will go north with him to fight a war, and I will have a wife. And you have Quadratus.'

I nodded silently. He remained in front of me for some time, then rose with a sad sigh.

'I shall look for you at the games,' he said, and left.

I sat in silence in my empty room, shivering. I had lost Mother, and now I was to lose my prince, to a wife and to a war. And Quadratus was hardly a consolation. I waited until Commodus had left the domus, ruminating on my feelings on all that had passed between us in those few short moments. And I discovered that I was not sad. I had been sad over losing Mother, but I was not sad about Commodus. No, I was angry. That God had put me so close to him and made us so perfect together, only to build a wall between us that could not be crossed. Angry that Commodus was to be emperor, the most powerful man in the world, with the ability to write laws at will and kill or pardon with impunity, yet even he could not make it possible for us to be together.

Only moments ago I had been preparing to willingly let him go, until I discovered that I would *have* to do so, whereupon it became critical that I did not.

I ripped open my door and walked out into the corridor. It was empty, just half a dozen painted marble faces staring at me from plinths beneath the windows. The one directly in front of me had a smile. She was mocking me. Who was this stone woman, so happy and silent? So young and pretty and vivacious. Before I even knew what I was doing, I had thrown the bust from its stand to smash into pieces on the marble floor. In my head, she was this Bruttia Crispina, who was to have the man I loved. Damn her.

I suspect that my idiotic reaction and the awfulness of what happened next were as much a final outburst of emotion to Mother's unsung passing as it was to Commodus' betrothal. A slave appeared at the end of the corridor and stopped, openmouthed at what I had done. She was a middle-aged woman I vaguely recognised, and moments later I was in front of her, my eyes wild.

'Where do I get a curse tablet?'

The slave stared in shock.

'Where?' I demanded.

'I . . . I can find you one, Mistress,' she said, still staring past me at the shattered bust that was probably some famed relation of Quadratus'.

'Come, then.'

The slave hurried off, with me right behind her. We went to the storerooms, a part of the domus I had never had reason to approach, and immediately I was taken back to my days as a girl on the Palatine when I had gained an understanding of the world of slaves and servants that the rich will never comprehend. In a matter of heartbeats, the worried slave had found me a lead sheet and a nail. I never even thanked her, so out of sorts was I. I hurried across to the window and placed the lead sheet on the sill, etching into the soft metal with the nail.

I invoked that demon goddess Hekate that I remembered from my youth in the palace. I begged that Bruttia Crispina bear no child to the emperor. I begged that she die a lonely death. I rolled it up and pinned it with the nail, then found a slotted drain in a doorway, just like the one the slave on the Palatine had done all those years ago, and I dropped the dreadful thing into the darkness.

It took only the blink of an eye for me to realise what I had done. Panic overtook me then, driving all my anger out as suddenly as it had flooded in. I had turned my back on God in my fury and had cursed an innocent woman.

I looked down into the dark aperture. I was saved. The lead roll had caught on a lip just half a foot down. I jammed my hand into the hole and huffed, fingers straining to reach it. I felt the touch of cold lead, then my heart froze as it slipped and disappeared into the gloom with a wet plop.

It was gone. The curse was done. I was oddly grateful that Mother was dead, then, that she could not see what had become of her daughter. Could a curse work if Hekate was not real, but just some face of the devil? I prayed to God that it could not.

But somehow, despite all this, somewhere deep inside my cankered heart, a tiny glow still hoped that it would work.

PART THREE

THE GOLDEN AGE

*'Heracles by the might of his arms pulled the weary
rowers along all together'*

– Apollonius Rhodius: Argonautica, trans. Seaton, 1912

XI

ASHES OF THE DEAD

Pannonia, winter AD *179*

Iwas glad to be leaving Rome once more. I had spent the spring and summer following our discussion wallowing. I did manage to have Mother's urn moved to one of the bigger catacombs, where she was interred close to a painted image of the Christ in his majesty, which she would have liked. I could not look that painted face in the eye after what I had done in the domus and scurried back out of there feeling like a pagan heretic. Oh, and I managed to find an excuse for the shattering of the bust that earned me only a few welts and bruises, as well as the gratitude of the slaves who Quadratus had initially blamed.

Commodus had argued against the need for a new war, and might even have succeeded, but then news reached Rome that the Quadi, the troublesome Marcomanni's largest neighbour beyond the river, had revolted against our terms, and further tidings that arrived only worsened matters. The generals in charge of Pannonia at the time were Quintilii – not those sour-faced brothers who had gone east with us, but their sons: young, hungry for glory and, sadly, almost entirely incompetent. It became the common opinion around court that the Quintilii could not possibly hold Pannonia, especially if the Marcomanni began to force the issue too, which they undoubtedly would.

War was inevitable.

I had wondered for a while whether I would join them this

time, but the matter was settled for me in conversation with Quadratus one morning.

'I am, of course, of Antonine blood,' he'd said airily as though we were not all well aware of that. I'd nodded, keeping sullenly quiet. 'While there are those who have a better claim to the throne than I,' he said, a little bitterness creeping into his tone as I pictured Commodus with a sceptre, 'it is unfair how often the emperor passes me over for leading roles.'

I bit back a quote I remembered from Cicero about competence and simply nodded again.

'Pompeianus,' he spat. 'A Syrian nobody who achieves overall command of Rome's forces, repeatedly. Pertinax. Son of a freedman, no less, and heroic general of the Dacian wars. The Quintilii. Noble blood, yes, but from Asia. Herodes Atticus, confidante of the emperor, given lavish gifts and the man's a damn Greek. And here am I, cousin to Commodus, nephew of the emperor, and I struggle to secure command of a fucking legion. Lucilla is right, imperial blood counts for nothing in these days of freedmen.' I took note of that slur on my social status and added it to my list of reasons to dislike Quadratus. 'But no more. I shall demand my right. I shall secure a command this time and not let the emperor send me home.'

He sounded like a petulant child. I sighed. 'How will you persuade the emperor if he has been reticent thus far?'

I was genuinely interested in that. The man was a fool. How could he hope to persuade Aurelius that he wasn't?

'Lucilla backs me. She is well aware of how imperial blood is overlooked. She herself was sold off to a peasant. With her influence and mine, I damn well will secure a command.'

He would. I could imagine it. Not that Lucilla had any better influence over the emperor than Quadratus, but with the two of them badgering Aurelius, I could see him giving in just to shut them up. What a pair they would make. The idiot and the bitch.

Summer came around soon and we left the city. Fortunately,

the army was already gathered in the north, and so we moved at reasonable speed across the Apennine Mountains. We took ship at Ancona and suffered a horrible three-day journey across the Adriatic to Tergeste, during which I constantly shivered in a cold sweat, watching the glassy ocean and waiting for a storm to claim us. We landed easily, though, and moved on once more through Noricum and Pannonia to the Danubius.

I kept very much to myself on the twenty-day journey. I had no desire to be around Commodus, who travelled now with his pretty wife, a fact that taunted me and made my heart burn. And while on my previous journey to that frontier I had been visited regularly by Quadratus, this time, though I travelled with his familia in an expensive carriage, he came to my bed not once during the whole trip. He was becoming tired of me, I think. I had become uninteresting, and he availed himself instead of various young women around the column. And so we arrived in Vindobona. We were swept along into the emperor's new campaign swiftly. If I had thought Carnuntum bleak and martial, then I realised how wrong I had been: Carnuntum was a vibrant, colourful metropolis compared with the grey fortress and small settlement of Vindobona.

Almost immediately, knowing the remaining campaign season to be growing short, the officers gathered the army and forged on northwards across the river, pressing both the rebellious Quadi and the Marcomanni. Quadratus went with them, as did Commodus and his father. In fact, of the senior military men, the only three to remain in Vindobona were the prefect who controlled the place and the two young Quintilii who had managed, by the skin of their teeth, to hold Pannonia over the year but had done little else of merit. Those three, along with a garrison left behind, were given the remit of expanding the place and making it grand enough for an emperor to use as his headquarters, though I didn't notice much happening other than a lot of planning.

The army was gone for more than a month across the great river and I settled into reading quietly in a small, well-heated room for the duration, since every time I left my quarters I invariably bumped into Lucilla or Bruttia Crispina or, on occasion, Cleander. The snake rarely looked at me these days. My withdrawal from the prince's side and replacement with a pretty idiot had made me powerless in Cleander's eyes, and the man obviously no longer saw me as enough of a threat to bother with. That suited me fine, and instead he began to pester Bruttia Crispina, seeing her as the best way to curry imperial favour in Commodus' absence. The two of them would take daily walks along the safe southern bank of the river, soldiers of the Guard following at a discreet but protective distance. What they spoke of I could not know, but I doubted any good would come of it. I hoped the pair of them fell in the great Danubius together.

I was largely alone again.

This time, thank God, I never saw the battle in which the two tribes were battered into submission, but I could imagine readily how awful it had been from the aftermath that I *did* witness. First came the legions and the Praetorian units returning to their garrisons, plus endless cohorts of auxiliaries, dirty, tired and dishevelled. Even to my amateur eye it was clear how much smaller many of these units were than when they had left Vindobona. Then came the slaves. Thousands upon thousands of hairy barbarians, stripped naked to the waist in the cold autumn air, faces still defiant and proud in defeat. The wagon trains came next with supplies and the booty. It would all have been quite grand to look at had not the final stretch of that huge swathe of humanity returning to civilisation been so gruesome.

The wounded were mixed with the dead in the carts. The latter had not been dead when they climbed aboard, of course, but had passed away on the long return journey, and the other occupants had neither the strength nor the inclination to bury them.

I have never seen so many missing limbs or so much visible bone. It was appalling to witness and, given that the only benefit from this war won in the long term would be the slaves and the booty – for these tribes could clearly never be civilised or controlled – it hardly seemed worth it. Despite that, it was said that Aurelius still planned to create a new province across the river before he died, and was pushing to achieve it now, knowing that time was short.

Occasionally I had cause to pass near the hospital district. Imagine, if you can, how dreadful a battle needs to be to require more than just a simple *valetudinarium*, but rather a complex of tents devoted to the differing medical needs of the wounded. The time I passed a surgery tent, holding my breath against the sickly sweet smell of decay, and found the heap of amputated arms, was the last time I went near the place.

As the emperor settled in and the ashes of the dead cooled, Vindobona's reconstruction began in earnest. Grand new buildings arose, blocks of insulae, new roads and more. I joined the court more often now that everyone had returned, but it did not take me long to see how things were progressing. Commodus had returned from battle looking slightly older and stronger; there was a little world-weariness about his expression, but he was hale and powerful, like a conquering emperor of old. Marcus Aurelius, conversely, looked tired, weak and old. Gone was any real glimmer of vitality. He looked like a starving old man: his face drawn, eyes slightly clouded. And whenever Commodus looked at him yet thought himself unobserved, his mask slipped and I could read the immense sadness within him. The *Augusta* Bruttia Crispina simply hung on Commodus' arm like a devoted puppy, completely unaware of the depth of what was happening around her.

My unreasonable, if perhaps understandable, hatred of

Bruttia came to a head one morning. I was standing on a balcony at the building used as the imperial palace, and watching the two emperors, in full regalia, discussing some matter in the square below. There was a whisper of air and suddenly the empress was leaning on the balcony next to me, a demon in white silk.

'Majesty,' I greeted her. It was a term of respect, but the ice and dislike in my voice must have been audible, for she turned to me, one elegantly shaped eyebrow raised. She was almost the antithesis of me. Blonde, pale, quiet, and I had thought shy and retiring until that moment.

'You knew him of old.'

I nodded. 'Yes, Majesty.'

'They say you grew up together, as children. Cleander seems to think you have feelings for him.' She had clearly been doing some prying into my past. She was neither as quiet or as ineffectual as I had thought.

'Cleander says many things, for he hates me, but I know my place, Majesty. We were childhood friends and nothing more.'

'Cleander is a rat, but still, despite your protestation, I discern a grain of truth in this tale. It is also said that you bore a child for Quadratus but tore it out of yourself. Was that because of my husband?'

I stared. Few people knew of that awful incident with the oysters. My pregnancy had hardly been announced, after all. And I had been tortured thus because Quadratus would not have me bear his children, even had I the faintest desire to do so. It had *nothing* to do with Commodus.

'The emperor had nothing to do with it, Majesty. I am but a bed slave to Quadratus. I have no desire to bear him a child, and he would rather see me dead than siring his offspring.'

'A sentiment he and the emperor surely share. Stay away from my husband, Marcia Ceionia. You may have known him all his life, but you are just a pleb, and an ambitious one, I think. He is mine.'

With that she was gone, leaving me in a torrent of emotion. I felt shock at the words, horror at such tales being told of me, fear that I would be somehow ruined by all of this, dismay that a further wedge had been driven between he and I . . . But most of all I felt a new wave of hatred for this woman, and a new determination that Commodus would be mine, and not bound to this angelic-looking harpy. Who was she to take me to task over losing a child? It was nothing to do with her.

I turned back to the tableau below, seething, an emotion that stayed with me the rest of the day.

As the old emperor displayed a notable decline, so the vultures began to gather. Cleander, and even Saoterus, spent much more time with Commodus and the rest of the court. Pompeianus, Quadratus, the Quintilii, anyone with an interest in the potential succession started to become very visible and very close to the heir. Commodus was beset by those who would gain from him, with a wife who was blithely ignorant of his troubles, when all he really wanted was to be shut away with his father.

As autumn moved apace into winter – and Pannonian winters are unkind to say the least – the emperor's fragility continued to worry the entire court, and his time in council with his consilium grew shorter each day. By Saturnalia he was rarely seen in public and, though he put on his most powerful mask for the populace and the legions, everyone could see how weak he was becoming. With the new year, the emperor began to spend whole days in his room and Galen, the famed physician, was now with him almost all the time.

Had I had any real access to Commodus at the time, I would have lost it then, for the young emperor began shutting himself away with his father, receiving advice on what to do in the coming months. Other officers trooped in to see the emperor as required, or whenever their plea to attend him was given the affirmative.

Quadratus, I noted, was not one of those the emperor summoned, and neither were the Quintilii. In fact, the three of them spent a great deal more time now with Lucilla, whose husband *was* one of those the emperor regularly called upon. I could imagine trouble brewing among that disaffected, ambitious group. Had they only recruited the sly Cleander and the cow-faced Bruttia, all the bad eggs of the empire might have been held in one basket.

The day the world changed began with irritation. I had woken and readied myself in my small room in a building that resembled a barrack block. I'd then taken a brief visit to a small bathhouse staffed by grumpy slaves who spoke some awful gruff local language, and then went to see Quadratus to ask politely for a small stipend to keep myself busy buying material for new cloaks and dresses to see me through the horrible northern winter.

I do not know why, but with there being no slaves around to announce me, I walked straight into Quadratus' rooms, expecting him to be up and about at this time. Instead, I found him sprawled naked across his bed next to an equally naked woman. I had known that his interest in me had waned and he was looking elsewhere, but to be confronted with this was difficult. To make matters worse, I swiftly realised that this was no local whore, but the wife of one of the garrison commanders, a woman I had met socially a few times. I ran from the room before they awoke, feeling outraged and confused, despite my hatred of the man.

I wandered aimlessly around the town. Unlike the seedy backstreets of Rome, this Vindobona was safe for a woman of any standing, for Praetorians were in evidence all over the place, precluding the possibility of trouble in the emperor's camp. I had, quite by chance, found my way to the palatial building being used by the emperor and his court and was about to turn and leave when I saw the line of lictors standing patiently outside, and recognised at least two of them as being Commodus' men. I struggled with myself, then. I didn't really think visiting the prince – the *emperor*, I reminded myself yet again – would be a good idea, even if he would see me, but I felt lonely and friendless with the discovery that I was now utterly superfluous, even to Quadratus.

'Oh look, the peasant girl is lost. If you're at a loose end, I can direct you to a whorehouse that needs new girls?'

I sighed. I'd not seen Cleander much recently and, while I still hated him more than any man alive, even Quadratus, it was oddly comforting to be in the presence of his old familiar bile amid all these changes.

'You've visited one? And they would touch you? Poor girls *must* be desperate.'

Cleander simply answered with a sneer. 'Quadratus thrown you out? It was only a matter of time.'

'Go drown in a latrine.'

'Wishful thinking,' he smiled. 'What's it like to be nobody, with no place in the world? What will you be next: a seamstress? A beggar?'

I was too dispirited to rise to it and just shook my head. My attention was then drawn back to the building as the lictors snapped to an attentive stance and Commodus emerged. With him were two Praetorian officers I didn't know. I caught sight for just a moment of Commodus' face and I knew in a flash what had happened. Despite the distance between us, my heart went out to him.

At his instruction, the two officers dispersed. The sight of this commotion had an odd effect. As though the vultures that circled the ailing emperor had been perched on every windowsill, suddenly all those men of importance seemed to be emerging

203

from doors and streets. A soldier sounded a horn with three short blasts and a unit of Praetorians emerged from somewhere and formed up.

I was rooted to the spot. Commodus stood, stony-faced, with his lictors, and finally, as the expectant, tense crowd began to become restive, Pompeianus stepped out of the door behind him, hands raised for silence.

'The emperor is dead,' he announced, eliciting a low moan from all present. They must all, like me, have expected this, yet hearing it was still difficult. 'The legions and cohorts are being assembled on the fields outside Vindobona to be addressed by their new emperor and to give their oath. With the passing of the divine Marcus Aurelius, it is my privilege on behalf of the senate of Rome to acknowledge Caesar Lucius Aurelius Commodus sole emperor of Rome, *Augustus, imperator, pater patriae, pius felix, pontifex maximus*. Hail Aurelius Commodus Augustus!'

I knew Pompeianus to be a well-regarded commander, but I had not realised how skilled a politician and orator he was, too. His very stance and every motion of his hands were carefully tailored, his tone clear and strong, brooking no argument and inviting no interruption, rising towards the end in a crescendo such that the last four words were bellowed like a challenge to God.

I was flooded with emotions. The great emperor, who had ruled Rome all my life, had died. My oldest friend would be sorrowful and lost, and yet would not have time to grieve, for the world would crash in upon him. It was saddening and nerve-wracking. Yet there was something else there. Something glorious and uplifting. The man I always thought of as my prince stood like one of his gods outside that building, strong and tall, hair golden and burgeoning beard gleaming. He looked so powerful, so great, that I could not imagine there being anything he couldn't achieve.

He was becoming the Hercules he had decided to be all those years ago when Fulvus died.

I don't know what made me turn and look. They'd made no noise, but perhaps I just felt the hate wash out across the street like a wave. The emperor's sister, my former mistress Lucilla, was a stony figure of seething resentment, a polite smile bolted on below hate-filled eyes. Quadratus, beside her, switched back and forth with every breath between disappointment and hope. Trouble was definitely brewing in that quarter.

Commodus began his reign with an address to the assembled legions outside Vindobona. I remember it almost word for word, and it stays with me as an example of what an orator he could be.

'I grieve,' he said. 'I grieve for my father, the greatest of emperors, and I know that you share my grief, you who have been our fellow soldiers throughout this bleak and dreadful time of war. And I know that when you take your oath to me, you will be echoing that very oath you took to him, that it will be soldiers making their vow to a fellow soldier, for I am one of you, just as he was. I have spent my childhood with the legions. Grown with you. Learned with you. I owe you all. I owe you for the man I have become, and I hope to enjoy your goodwill throughout my reign.'

He paused for a time for the huge surge of support and cheering that washed across the land from many thousands of voices. Finally, as it died down, he held up his hands.

'For a century we have relied upon adoptions for the succession. Men who were chosen to learn the rule of state from their predecessor. I am the first emperor for a hundred years born to the purple.' Another cheer. 'But I still learned from my father,' he bellowed across the surge. 'My childhood was spent preparing me for this day. I might have been born to be emperor, but it was my father who made me one.'

He paused and gestured at the standards of the legions, gleaming and proud.

'You are soldiers of Rome, and I salute you as the best of men. Would it were that we could conquer even the skies, for I cannot see how you could fail.' Ridiculous praise, of course, but it struck like a lance into the heart of every man listening. 'Whatever the days to come might deliver,' he said, finally, 'I know that you will bring renown and dignity to Rome, such that even my father – *our* father – who has ascended to Heaven, will hear and look down upon us with pride.'

There was a strange silence, and I realised that Commodus had looked down at his feet. Everyone watched, waiting, and suddenly that golden prince, a young Hercules in Roman armour, lifted his gaze to the sky.

'For the senate, and the people of Rome,' he roared, as though addressing his father.

The army exploded into noise.

The greatest emperor Rome had ever known deserved an efficient, respectful and quiet funeral and succession. Whether Christian or pagan, respect for the honoured dead is a prime tenet, I know. Yet what happened with the passing of Marcus Aurelius I can only describe as a feeding frenzy. Those in positions of power and authority sought to solidify their claim to such. Those who felt they had been overlooked or undervalued – such as Quadratus – took the opportunity to seek advancement and change. Those with nothing sought something, anything. And those who knew their place precisely and were confident in it became part of the frenetic activity, Saoterus and Cleander in particular. Neither man seemed to stop moving for days, so busy they did not even have time to argue with one another.

Amid this seething sea of ambition and greed only four figures stood proud as islands amid the crashing waves. Lucilla, who knew well enough that she was unlikely to change her position through her brother, simply watched from the periphery with eyes that bore no filial concern whatsoever. Pompeianus, whose position as Commodus' brother-in-law put him near the top of the heap, was confident enough in his ability and intelligence that he helped the emperor keep an element of control amid surging events. Bruttia Crispina ambled on calmly and overtly happy in the knowledge that she was now the most powerful woman in the world. One might have thought her calm and pleasant, were it not for the acidic looks I occasionally caught her casting at me.

And there was me. I still had ties to Lucilla through her patronage of my mother, though she had clearly not even appended me to her list of things to consider, which was fine by me. Quadratus was nominally my master. Legally, of course, as a grown woman, a spinster, and beholden to no one personally, I could have opted out of being Quadratus' mistress at any time, especially now that Aurelius, who had allowed his spiteful daughter to put me in this position, was gone. But I could not see Quadratus taking such a thing well, and any trouble there would bring me to Lucilla's attention. Besides, what would I do? I had nothing. All my money was given to me by Quadratus. I had no home, no job, no family, no discernible skill apart from a passing talent with needle and thread. That was not strictly true, of course – I was steadily building a whole collection of skills, but there were limited circumstances where they could come into play. I certainly had no intention of being one of those women who used them on street corners. I was wilful and far too well educated for my gender and class, thanks to the palace tutors, so would probably be unlikely to attract attention from men of high class or low as a wife. I was saddled with being Quadratus' mistress until something better came along.

I *was* practical, at least.

What had seemed so simple and glorious then, even amidst the sadness, became complex and fraught now. Though I only saw him from the edge of events, Commodus appeared to me to be drowning in people and supplications, wearing his benign, beatific mask, yet slightly wild-eyed and losing the fight against the flow. Left largely to myself, as I was, and known to be a consort of the imperial family and a childhood friend of the emperor, I was given almost free access to everywhere automatically, though getting close to the emperor was impossible in those days.

Thus it was that I found myself among the lesser attendants at the periphery of the hall when Commodus had finally had enough. I had been sipping good wine sparingly and pinching the bridge of my nose in a vain attempt to ward off a burgeoning headache. I had let myself defocus, both visually and aurally, the seething mass of people just a blur to me and their noise like a gaggle of geese on a lake. I have no idea what had been said, but it had provoked consternation and argument. The geese all began honking at once, as loud as they could. I winced.

Then it stopped.

A single voice that I knew well bellowed, 'Enough!'

As the crowd fell silent, Commodus stepped up on to the dais. 'Silence,' he barked, and the last few stragglers fell quiet.

I concentrated at last, allowing the gathering before me to come into focus. I realised with a start that almost everyone in the room was a military man. They are indistinguishable from the senators and courtiers when they are out of uniform – after all, most of the latter had been military men themselves at some point – but this was a military discussion, obviously, and a largely military gathering. I began to feel a little nervous that I was intruding. Every other meeting had just been filled with people trying to jostle for position. I decided I would slip out quietly, but not before I listened to what came next. Commodus looked irritated. I wouldn't say angry, but definitely not pleased.

'The Marcomanni cannot be conquered,' he snapped. 'Have

you all learned nothing from the dozen years that drained my father of the will to go on?'

Shock rippled across his audience, and I realised people had been asking about plans for the coming season. Most of those present would be hoping or expecting to be in command in some way.

'The Marcomanni,' Commodus shouted, pointing at the huge map on the wall. 'The Quadi. The Iazyges. The Suebi. The Buri. There is an endless list of tribes that go on from the Danubius right to the great encircling sea. And they cannot be conquered or subdued. We have utterly broken the Marcomanni time and again, even while I have been here, and what has it gained us? Some slaves. Some loot. And a huge pile of Roman corpses. And what difference has it made across the river? None at all. A different king. Some empty villages. But the Marcomanni and their allies remain strong. My father's dream was grand, but for all that it was still a dream. A Roman Marcomannia is impossible. And every year we push for it, we lose more men in the legions and depopulate more provinces to create new armies. And every year we drain the treasury drier. And here we are, twelve years later, on the same damned river with different men in a land pockmarked with the graves of thousands of Romans.'

There was a horrible silence. I could almost feel the more martially minded among the crowd lining up their arguments, but no one dared interrupt.

'I am aware,' he went on, slightly calmer now, 'that to simply drop everything is impossible. We will press on for this one season, but we are not campaigning with a view to conquest and the settling of this fabled Marcomannia. We are campaigning to control and strengthen. We will batter the tribes until they are unwilling to cross the river and are happy to sue for peace. We will make them want a permanent border that we have no more desire to cross in anger than they. Even if it takes months, we will do it. And then, when the season is over, we will pay what needs to be paid and agree what needs to be agreed with anyone we need to do it with.'

A brave soul somewhere among the crowd called out in a worried tone, 'If we agree to pay the barbarians good gold from Rome, we will bankrupt the treasury.'

Commodus simply raised an eyebrow. 'And if we commit to another season of mass destruction across the river, we shall do exactly the same. But my way it all ends this year, while war can go on for ever. No. One season and then we are done here. Rome has laboured under twenty years of constant war with Parthia and the Marcomanni. She is poor, sick and dispirited. She needs a respite. We will have peace to heal, and I shall secure it at any price.'

I smiled. I felt pride in the man my prince had become. Years ago, when we had first been here, he had decided that war was not the answer, but it had not been his place to do anything about it. Now he had the power to back up his belief.

A new voice cut through the silence that followed. A quiet yet powerful voice. A voice I hated almost as much as Cleander's.

'You would give up everything our father fought for?' Lucilla said, arms folded. I frowned. She had never to my knowledge shown the slightest interest in the war, or *any* war for that matter. This was a challenge, pure and simple. She had seen a tiny crack between her brother and the generals that he had almost sealed tight once more with his reasoned words, and she was determined to crack it open, the harpy.

Commodus threw her an angry look. He knew what she was doing every bit as much as me.

'Fought for, but did not win,' Commodus replied, and I could hear the pain behind his words. He wanted nothing less than to downplay his father's many achievements, but Lucilla was forcing him to do so, or submit to his generals.

210

There was a murmur of discontent again, now, and Commodus silenced his sister with a glare, though she was content to be quiet now, with the damage already done.

'Rome needs to heal,' he tried again. 'You are leaders of men and victors in the field, but you are also senators and nobles of Rome, with interests in the capital and the provinces. You must have felt your purses thinning these past years? Your business interests slowing and sometimes failing? Your hard-earned land devaluing? Why do you think that is? Mismanagement?'

Now there was a faint chuckle at his gentle jibe. He had them again, was lifting them. 'Twenty years of war. But not just that. Our richest lands have been pillaged and endangered. Precious Aegyptus, with its gold and wheat, for a while in the hands of Cassius' rebels. Dacian gold mine production halted by Iazyges incursions, the cities of Greece sacked, even Italia herself under the barbarian heel, with Aquileia destroyed. And this while we were fighting them. *Our own lands ravaged*. Better, surely, to send a few chests of gold that are too heavy for them to cross the river with?'

Another chuckle.

'Plague. Banditry. The north ruined. The east depopulated. Raiders from Africa in Hispania, farms untended, villages emptied. This is not the golden land that our ancestors enjoyed. This is a land of dust and of death. Of iron and rust. We must rebuild. And to rebuild we must have peace, surely you can see that?'

It was an impassioned appeal, though that last had been a little plaintive to my ears. Still, he had recovered from Lucilla's jab. 'And if it's glory and the grass crown you're seeking and seeing slip past, then take heart. You have one more season to win it and prove your manliness to the women of Rome!'

His grin at this last was the clincher, and the generals roared with laughter, slandering one another in good humour. I could see Lucilla on the far side of the room, seething and

211

plotting, and then Quadratus was suddenly with her. Damn it but they made a dangerous pair. And with Cleander hovering nearby I could foresee only disaster. Oddly, as I looked at them, I noted three crows in quick succession swoop past the window over their heads and I shuddered. I was a Christian, and the old Roman superstitions had been frowned upon by Mother, but it was hard to shake them when they came calling. Three black crows could not be a good sign in anyone's faith.

True to his word, once the old emperor's funeral had been held and all rites observed, the new emperor of Rome, a Hercules in bronze, led campaigns along the Danubius for seven more months, giving his generals plenty of opportunity to win their decorations. He fought not for territory or loot, but to prove the superiority of his forces and the lunacy of taking up arms against them.

And when October came about, and the campaigning season was over, the kings of the great tribes answered when summoned, sending deputations and some even coming in person to Vindobona to meet the man who had so ravaged them for one final year.

The terms were relatively generous. Each and every tribe went home having sworn an oath not to cross into Roman territory or to raid our lands. Some gave men to help fill the dwindling Roman ranks. Some sent their sons as hostages to Rome, where they would be educated and taught why such war was folly. They went home with gold that Rome could scarce afford, but then, as Commodus had so often noted this past year, neither could Rome afford *not* to give it them.

And when it was over and the barbarians had gone back to their own land, some of the generals complained to the emperor about his generous terms. Lucilla, still bitter, still trouble, put in that her father would never have done such a thing. I saw

Commodus properly angry with her, then, his eyes flashing dangerously.

'You think so, dear sister? You think me so much less than he? You think I yield where he would fight? Then think back to those terms our father agreed with the Marcomanni ten years ago, for you will find these just an echo of those. I used Father's terms, Lucilla, more or less. Keep your beak from matters that do not concern you.'

The look she shot him was pure evil and I think that, while I had always known she was dangerous, I had perhaps previously underestimated quite how dangerous.

I was in one of the side rooms of the grand building later that afternoon. I had sought somewhere quiet to pray and knew that to go back to my own rooms would be to risk bumping into Quadratus, who was as sour and mean now as ever, all but ignored by his cousin. I prayed for Mother's soul and for that of the emperor, apologising to God in a strange way for the fact that the man for whom I prayed was also considered a god. Sometimes even *my* religion made my head ache.

The door opened, and I started, feeling guilty for praying such, knowing I was almost certainly the only Christian in the building. I turned to see Commodus in the doorway. He gestured for his men to shut the door behind him.

It was the first time I had been alone with him in almost a year. The first time since he had been emperor, anyway. I sank to my knees, head bowed.

'Majesty.'

'For the love of Jove, Marcia, get up.'

'You are Emperor of Rome,' I reminded him.

'You have seen me having my arse wiped. I think we can dispense with ceremony, don't you?'

I smiled. It was hard sometimes now to remember that this was the boy with whom I had grown up. Commodus was

213

nineteen and well muscled, sporting a full beard. He strolled across the room and leaned back against a table, folding his arms in a manner that reminded me of his sister. 'I understand your mother died while we were in the east, Marcia.'

The simple statement floored me. I had no idea how to respond and therefore stood staring like some dead fish at a market. He gave me a sympathetic smile.

'I can only apologise that I never consoled you for the loss. I remember her only vaguely. A stern woman, for sure, but one with kind eyes and a good heart.'

What an unnervingly accurate picture of her.

'I know we have been ... distant, let's say, for some time. Much of that is my doing, because events have swept me up in their wake and pulled me along. Some, I think, is yours. Are you protecting yourself, Marcia? Or me?'

Or both of us? Still I remained silent. I had the unaccountable urge to cry, and that made me angry, for I am not some wet sponge, but a strong woman.

'How did you grieve?' he asked. An odd question that I'd have had trouble answering even if my voice worked. Did he mean because I was Christian? He seemed to sense my confusion. 'I mean, how did you find time?' he explained. 'I am the master of the world and I have barely two heartbeats to myself before I am once more the centre of someone's attention. I have not yet found time to grieve for Father.'

Guilt flooded through me. In my understanding of how things had changed, I had nearly forgotten how the man before me was prey to black moods beyond his control. I had pulled away and he had gone off to fight a war. Had he suffered out on campaign on his own, as he used to as a boy?

'Are you . . .' I stuttered. 'Did you . . .'

'I made it through, if that is what you're asking. I will not say this has been the brightest year of my life, but somehow Father's passing was different. Fulvus, Annius, Verus, Mother, they were all torn from me unexpectedly through illness or the will of capricious gods. Father I knew was nearing his time. I saw it coming, and so did he. He was prepared. And he prepared me. No, I have not torn at my hair in grief. But I would have liked adequate time to mourn. During the days of his funeral, there was always someone clearing their throat, tugging at my elbow. I was never alone. How did *you* mourn, Marcia?'

I shrugged, 'Alone. I mourned alone. And for a long time. Time and solitude were all I had, after all.'

It sounded like a recrimination, and from the chastened regret in his face, Commodus saw it as one.

'I am sorry, Marcia. Things will change. Once we are home and all this activity and border settlement is complete, things will change.'

'Will they?'

'Yes. We leave this month and will be in Rome and recovered long before Saturnalia. We will have a triumph, for Rome will demand it, and games in memory of Father, but we will settle once more. I know Bruttia is in my life now, and that you cannot be pleased at that, but these are the ways of state and it is not her fault. I beg you to remember that, when you see the woman to whom I am wed. It is not her fault, and it was never her choice.'

Did he already see how much I hated her? God above, but I thought I was subtler than that. Did he have even an inkling that she hated me every bit as much? It came as something of an epiphany that, despite the differences between Bruttia Crispina and myself, we were far more alike than anyone could guess. We both sought only Commodus' heart, and we were both jealous and possessive. God, but that was almost at the root of it. Bruttia and I were reflections of one another. Only one of us could ever be real to Commodus.

'And do not fear,' he went on, 'I will not let Lucilla or

215

Quadratus hurt you in any way. In fact, I would take you from him if you wish it?'

Freedom? From Quadratus? A thrilling prospect if ever I heard one. And I was on the very verge of saying yes, of begging that he do just that, when an image struck me. Lucilla, Quadratus, Cleander. Three black crows. Before I truly knew what I was doing, I found myself saying no, and I think that took him more by surprise than anything. He knew how much I wanted to be away from Quadratus, but really I was in no danger. The man barely registered my existence these days and never came to my chamber. I might as well have been furniture in his house. But there was something about Quadratus and Lucilla – about the way they kept talking together quietly – that made my spine itch. And somehow, being part of his household, I reasoned that I was in a unique position to make sure they did nothing untoward or unexpected.

'However you wish it,' he said eventually, 'but know that I am here, and I will help.'

I thought he would turn and go, then, but instead he reached out and the gesture came so unexpectedly that I failed to react. He gripped me tight before I could fend him off.

'Are you sure? I don't like you being with him any more than you like me with Bruttia. Perhaps there is still a chance for us?' he murmured, caressing my arms, my shoulders, my back, in a way that I had spent years longing for, touching my very soul.

'Oh, God . . .' I was reaching for him now. I had always wanted him, but never so much as in that moment. In that glorious embrace, I saw it all: he could be my love and I could be his empress, and I knew that no one else would ever have that.

Except Bruttia . . .

I must have flinched at the thought, for something changed, the air cooled and Commodus unfolded his arms. When he let go of me, all too quickly, it was like having been given gold and then watching it being taken away again. Duty had reclaimed him once more. For a dangerous moment, his defences had been down. Had we moved on it – had I moved fast enough – he might just have cast his cold witch aside. But no. Despite my fleeting dream, I was still the tagalong friend and Bruttia still his wife. My anger boiled over then, silently and bitterly, locked away deep within, hidden from the young emperor as he straightened and bowed.

'Gather your belongings, Marcia. Within days we leave for Rome.'

I struggled. There is no denying it. In that moment, he had almost been mine, and only Bruttia Crispina had stood between us. God, but she needed to be moved aside.

And in the meantime, Commodus would return to Rome.

Hercules was coming home.

XII

HOPE

Rome, AD 180

The journey south from Pannonia was nothing like those we had undertaken previously, though from what I understand it strongly resembled the journeys of Lucius Verus once upon a time. When we had travelled with Aurelius, he had taken his court and his army purposefully, making for his destination with focus, and dallying along the way only to settle problems or impose the imperial presence where it was most needed. Commodus, however, like his uncle, made pomp and show of his travels.

Perhaps that is a little unfair. Perhaps it would be better to say that the people on our journey made pomp and show for the new emperor. Every settlement we passed through greeted him with garlands and games, sacrifices and honours. And while in some ways that would clearly be seen as an attempt to curry favour for their cities with the new emperor, there was definitely something else to be felt now, too. There was an undercurrent of hope across the land that we had not previously experienced. It was not that the people were relieved at the passing of Aurelius, of course, for he had ever enjoyed a good reputation, but more that it had become known that Commodus intended to end the war and to stabilise the borders. And after two decades of almost constant conflict, and the poverty and anguish that had brought, the people were more

218

than pleased to look forward to an era of peace and, hopefully, prosperity.

The populace celebrated their new emperor and, with him, a new age was felt to have dawned.

It took more than a month to get home, so leisurely was our pace, arriving as winter gripped the city in a white embrace. By that time the armies freed from the war across that great northern river were already back in their long-term garrisons, beginning the task of rebuilding their shattered ranks and settling into border life. All was returning to peace and normality across the empire.

I had never been more grateful to see the glorious city that is the heart of empire. The first time I had returned from the north I had been too concerned with Commodus' recent near dip into melancholia, the machinations of Cleander and my own position in Quadratus' house to truly welcome our return. When I had returned from the east, it was with a distant Commodus and to the ashes of my mother. Now? Now, things were different.

We returned to Rome in glory and I had little over which to worry. We came back in heroic style with a young emperor determined to change the world and bring about a new golden age for Rome. We brought back no corpses and came home to no pyres. Of course, there were still corpses in the streets, but the plague seemed to have abated somewhat and there was nothing like the horror I had seen in previous years. There would be games in honour of the departed emperor, but in truth the funeral and the grieving had been done more than half a year ago in the cold north, and now it was just spectacle for the people. Moreover, Commodus seemed settled into a calm, stable and uplifting mood and, given that he had already offered to rid me of my connection to Quadratus, I knew that nothing bad would befall me now in the man's house, for I could flee at any time. Now, I stayed of my own volition, and for a good reason.

That was one of the only two stains on that golden return: the fear that Lucilla and Quadratus were up to something. The other reared its ugly head mere days after we reached Rome, and it was a familiar, ophidian one.

All that time in Vindobona after the passing of Aurelius, two camps had polarised among the court and the military staff: those who stood against peace with the tribes and advocated only war and conquest, continually wheedling at Commodus to change his mind, and those who supported the new ideal and the man who had decided upon its course. Naturally, the former camp tended to be filled with idealists and men of strength and action, while the latter was largely formed of the sycophantic, but such is always the case when an emperor's choice is involved. It requires men of backbone to stand up against power, and men who bend easily are drawn to support it.

Upon our return, Commodus wasted no time. Those who remained steadfast in opposition to him were given new commands that dispatched them to unimportant peripheral posts, or were simply sent into retirement. The ranks of the emperor's court and his consilium were swiftly filled instead with freedmen of talent, and 'new men' like Commodus' brother-in-law – men who had come from unimpressive backgrounds and had climbed to the top of Rome's heap purely through their own talent. To give Commodus his due, he kept the best of the opposition and removed a number of the less able sycophants from positions of authority and influence. What remained was a council of intelligent and loyal men who largely had no agenda but the tasks laid before them, for they had no web of influence to play. Three men only of those doubters from the north remained in Commodus' circle: Pompeianus, the heroic general Pertinax, and Publius Seius Fuscianus, who had been a childhood friend of Aurelius.

Alongside the reshuffle of the imperial consilium came a reorganisation of staff. During Commodus' time as co-emperor,

Saoterus had served as his secretary, and Cleander his chamberlain. I had, as subtly as possible, suggested that Cleander might not be the perfect material for chamberlain. I reasoned that he had been a slave in the palace these past two decades, and to place him in charge of the freedmen and citizens who he had previously served would be inviting trouble. Commodus agreed, but rather than shuffling him off somewhere unimportant as I had hoped, he simply swapped the roles between his two favourites, appointing Saoterus to the chamberlain's post – a sensible choice, for sure – but making Cleander his personal secretary, which I liked somewhat less. Eclectus, who had been Aurelius' secretary and was now therefore superfluous, was shuffled into the staff of the Palatine, where he seemed content.

Winter rolled past with a grand Saturnalia celebration on a hitherto undreamed-of scale, and gradually the first signs of spring came about. A triumph had been planned to celebrate the 'successful conclusion' of the Marcomannic War. There were, I will admit, a number of dissenters, particularly those who had been dismissed from central positions, who muttered that suing for peace was no reason for a triumph, and I could see a twitch beginning to develop in Commodus' left eyelid whenever rumours of such an opinion circulated. Fortunately for those responsible, they were careful with their words and Commodus was magnanimous enough not to set the imperial agents to uncovering the source of those voices.

Still, the triumph went ahead and no one tried to prevent it. The people of Rome loved a show, after all. *Panem et circenses*, as Juvenal famously wrote – the people need only bread and circuses. Several hundred of the more impressive slaves taken during the past year, who were being held back from sale to keep prices steady, were roped together as part of the celebration.

'Look at them,' Cleander had said derisively, watching the slaves being assembled and tethered. 'Animals. *Less* than animals.'

Commodus had nodded distractedly, his attention elsewhere. As soon as the emperor moved away to discuss the minutiae of organisation, I confronted Cleander, though I knew it was just opening the cage of the rabid beast. Sometimes I cannot help it, though.

'You are so disparaging of your own kind?'

He turned to me with a flash of anger. '*My* kind? Hairy, tree-worshipping, beer-drinking apes. Yes, I came from nothing, but even my *nothing* had culture. The land of Midas, of Cybele, of Achaeus. And if you can compare me with these animals, then what of you, the Greek whore, daughter of a Greek whore slave?'

He smiled viciously and strode off, which at least saved me from struggling with the urge to rip that expression from his face with my neatly manicured nails.

I stood with those of the court who had no place in the triumph on a grey, unimpressive spring morning, waiting for the triumph. The city had turned out almost in its entirety to watch the great spectacle, and the streets were packed and lined with expectant faces all along the circuitous route. Those of us with influence or money found a place among the elite on the balustraded walkways of the old Tiberian palace on the Palatine. Oh, how times had changed for the daughter of a freedwoman who hovered on the periphery as a child. Here, high above the lofty arches of that ancient structure, we had an almost bird's-eye view of the forum and the Via Sacra, along which the procession would pass as it neared its conclusion.

Quadratus was a short distance away, making eyes at some hussy of a senator's wife, and I was surrounded by people with whom I was at best barely acquainted, which suited me fine. Praetorians were very visible everywhere, as well as their counterparts from the urban cohorts, all keeping a watchful eye on the crowd for trouble. Even the vigiles – the watchmen – were in evidence, on the lookout for thieves and other lesser criminals in the crowd. We had little to worry about on our grand perch, of course. Nobles are more subtle criminals.

It took time, the wait seemingly interminable. The procession was known to have gathered in the Campus Martius region almost two hours earlier and would now have been travelling for some time. A triumph necessarily moves at a stately pace so that the crowd can appreciate the victorious general before them, and the recipient can drink in their adoration. We knew where they were in the city at any given time from the noise. Even standing there among an expectant crowd on the Palatine, the din from the distant streets as the emperor passed was astounding. At one point, the route came close to our position from the other direction, where it looped to take in the Forum Boarium and the Forum Holitorium before moving off through the Circus Maximus. In those markets and stadium, there was a great deal of room to fit an adoring crowd, after all.

Then the triumph had moved off, circling the Palatine and making for the colossal Flavian amphitheatre. There, it turned once more and began the climb of the Via Sacra through the forum and towards the Capitol, where it would terminate. Finally, when my legs had begun to tremble with the effort of standing still, the triumph reached us. I watched with a smile as my golden prince was lauded.

First came the ranks of white, toga-clad senators leading the way like an army of swans, preening and proud. They were followed by musicians blasting a repetitive and almost military refrain as they went. I remember wondering how the rear ranks of the senators felt about having so many bronze horns blown right behind them. It must have been deafening. Then came the wagons with the spoils of war from Marcomannia. The representations of the conquered peoples were impressive, as were the trophies made of captured enemy weapons, armour and standards, but only a fool would believe those chests to be full of gold, especially given the meagre Praetorian escort they enjoyed. Besides, those of us who had been in Vindobona knew well that we *paid* money to end the war, rather than reaping it as a reward.

Flautists came next, their more delicate melody largely drowned out by the blaring of the horns, the rumbling of the wagons and the cheering of the crowd, especially at a distance. They were followed by the white sacrificial oxen, then the great black aurochses brought back across the Danubius. A small group came next bearing banners and three golden crowns purported to be those of the Marcomanni, the Quadi and the Iazyges. I doubt any of their kings ever wore such a crown, and they certainly didn't use banners like that, but the Roman crowd were largely unaware of such minor trickery and roared as they passed. Hundreds of downtrodden prisoners came next, eyes lowered as they stumbled, pelted with fruit, vegetables and far, far worse by the jeering crowds.

Finally, the grand heart of the triumph passed. Twenty-four lictors bearing their *fasces* preceded the imperial chariot. I could see Commodus, tall, golden and impressive in his purple and gold toga, and I could almost make out the face of Saoterus, who rode alongside him, holding the victor's wreath above the emperor's head. Behind them would come the military contingent, which interested me not a jot, having spent years watching such a spectacle in the north and the east. Besides, my attention was distracted, then.

Saoterus' presence in the chariot was not universally approved of, you see. A slave standing behind the emperor and holding aloft the wreath, yes, was traditional. A freedman standing alongside the emperor was another thing entirely. It was almost a declaration of the relative importance of freedmen to this new emperor who shunned the senatorial advisors of his father.

I could pick out the occasional barbed remark about the arrangement from the nobles among whom I stood, but one voice in particular I recognised, and it made me turn from the great spectacle and look along the walkway.

'Disgraceful,' sneered Lucilla from where she stood with her children and a few of her closer friends, surrounded by her own guards who kept the hoi polloi away.

'Appalling,' agreed Quadratus, drifting through the crowd to join her. The former empress' guards let the man pass without question, I noted with interest.

'How can my idiot brother allow such a thing? Has he no shame? Does he not realise how this looks to his fellow senators?' she replied, icy and bitter.

I peered around those self-same senators. I can imagine that Commodus did not overly care what they thought. He was his uncle's nephew more than his father's son. And as for 'fellow senators', had any emperor since Tiberius even attempted to maintain that ridiculous fiction of equality?

Whatever else they had to say was lost beneath the arrival of the military in the wake of the imperial chariot. The tromp of thousands of nailed boots made conversation, and eaves-dropping, difficult to say the least, though I watched those two engaged in some sort of private confab for a few moments, my suspicions continuing to get the better of me. It was only some preternatural sense that tore my attention from them, for I felt drawn to look the other way for some reason. I can only see God's hand in that, for the walkway was crowded, and I'd heard nothing, yet I turned on instinct, my gaze piercing the mass like an arrow and thudding home into two more figures standing together in conversation, almost mirroring that from which I'd turned. Cleander and a man in the uniform of one of the most senior officers in the Praetorian Guard. What *that* could be about I had no idea, but, whatever it was, I felt certain it would not be good.

A treacherous snake and a Praetorian officer on one side, a disaffected princess and an ambitious courtier on the other. Suddenly I felt a lot colder than the weather demanded.

I did not enjoy the rest of the day as I'd hoped. There were fights in the arena and races in the circus. A celebrated theatrical troupe performed Plautus to great applause. I was present at them all and, without the disapproval of Mother hanging over me, I could have enjoyed them, but I did not. In fact, I spent most of the day spying out Cleander, Quadratus, Lucilla and that Praetorian officer, who were often in evidence around the celebrations. I did not witness them looking quite so conspiratorial for the rest of the afternoon and evening, even during the lavish meal held in the palace at the close of the day. In fairness, my attention at that banquet was more distracted by the figure of Bruttia Crispina lounging beside Commodus and smiling so sweetly that I hated her all the more. Just looking at her made me question again what might have happened in that brief, open and honest embrace Commodus and I had shared. Still, in my head, I could see the other four in their pairs, whispering and plotting. I was growing ever more convinced that there was real trouble afoot.

I could not confront Commodus about that, though. While I knew what I knew, to accuse Cleander of misdeed without evidence would simply result in the emperor brushing aside my words and the snake himself becoming aware of my suspicions. So, I would have to wait and watch with him, see what transpired. And while Commodus might not particularly feel a familial closeness with his sister and cousin, still I would need some kind of proof before I told the emperor of my suspicions over Quadratus and Lucilla. At least, unlike the Cleander problem, I was in a better position to unpick the mystery of Quadratus.

Over the following months I made it my sole task to keep track of the man who had lost interest in me. I noted everywhere he went over spring and early summer, and everyone to whom he spoke. I had been on good terms with the servants and slaves of Quadratus' domus since the earliest days, given my sympathetic understanding of their position, but now I made it a goal to be close to them all. To have them owe me and feel safe and self-assured in confiding in me. Through them I learned much that I could not see with my own eyes. I learned many of the minutiae of the life of a household that often pass the owners by unseen.

The master of our house began, over the next few months, to disappear on overnight jaunts that were always described as business trips. But I knew Quadratus. Quite apart from the fact that senators did not get their hands dirty with business directly, but rather owned land and estates, Quadratus was far too lazy and selfish to put himself out even for monetary gain.

I got to know his driver, for he preferred to ride in a carriage over distances rather than sit in a saddle. The servant, an Iberian by the name of Alucio, confided in me readily that he often delivered his master to an estate close to Tibur, some twenty miles east of the city. He was never allowed to stay on the estate and was simply instructed with a time to return the next day and collect him.

I had no idea what this place was or why Quadratus would spend so much time there, and it took some digging around to find out. A few hours in the *tabularium* on the Capitol provided a list of estates in the area, and with the help of two of the clerks who I flattered outrageously, I managed to narrow it down to perhaps three or four. Of those, when I checked ownership, the answer became abundantly clear, for one of them was an imperial villa, dating back to Hadrian, and had been left empty for some time. Following up on my suspicion, and with the aid of Saoterus, I was able to confirm that the villa was the current abode of Lucilla and Pompeianus. I could hardly imagine the efficient and loyal Pompeianus consorting with Quadratus, but for him to be spending so much time visiting Lucilla? That made a lot more sense, especially after recent events.

I challenged Quadratus on it a few days later during an unseasonal time of torrential rain. It was late summer now, and his overnight visits had become more frequent.

'Stock up the house with better wine,' he ordered the staff that morning, 'I shall return after noon tomorrow and I will be expecting guests thereafter.'

I was present. I was *always* present now and had gradually changed my habits so that my presence seemed natural, rather than me hiding away in my rooms as had been my wont. As Quadratus made to leave, I cleared my throat.

'Be careful, Marcus. I heard yesterday that several main roads have been flooded this week. Where are you bound?'

He threw me a suspicious look, then announced in bored tones, 'Ostia. A wine thing.'

Idiot. Had he forgotten that only a moment earlier he had commanded his staff to stock up on wine? I tried not to shake my head or roll my eyes at his terrible lying, but to seem supportive and interested instead. 'Might I join you? My favourite seamstress is making me a new *stola*, but the material I want is out of stock. They are apparently having import problems. Perhaps in person I can move things along. I would like to have it ready for Saturnalia.'

His eyes darted about in a shifty manner and I could have laughed. The man was no conspirator. He was far too simple.

'No,' was his straight reply. No explanation or dissembling. He was gone moments later.

As autumn passed and winter closed on us, I settled upon the next stage of my investigation. Though I was mistress to Quadratus, I was nominally still a client of Lucilla's, inherited from Verus. She might have forgotten about it after all these years, but there was a tenuous link there. I spent some time over autumn amassing a small fund from moneys Quadratus threw at me to keep me busy and out of his affairs. When I announced to him that I intended to visit Lucilla, his eyes acquired a flash of panic.

'Why?' he said, tongue darting out to moisten his lips.

'I still owe her. Or rather, I inherited a debt from Mother. I am in a position to pay off our debt and free myself entirely now. The time seems right. After all, one day I might need to marry.'

This last would either disquiet or annoy him normally, but at this particular moment he had other worries than me fleeing his nest. 'I will pay them for you,' he said hurriedly.

'Will you be visiting her?' I asked innocently, and his brow started to bead with sweat.

'No.'

'Then do not put yourself out.' I smiled sweetly. 'You are overcommitted with all your business interests. I shall visit her.'

And that was that. He could not argue further without floundering and looking ever more the fool, so he simply shrugged irritably and stomped off. I had what I wanted: a reason to be away for at least a night and to visit the Tibur villa. I left the next morning. Quadratus let me use his carriage and favourite driver, probably assuming he could be certain of my movements that way, though the driver was my ally now, as were *most* of his staff.

It was a cold day when I arrived at the villa. I noted a mansio in passing on the main road and smiled. Exactly what I needed.

I made my visit to Lucilla short and businesslike. She had no real interest in seeing me and assumed a bored expression when I explained my purpose and offered her a good sum. She accepted, largely to get rid of me, I think, and I left again in the late afternoon. I explained to the driver that it was too late to think about heading back to Rome and we would stay the night at the mansio.

We arrived at the way station not long before dark and I used Quadratus' name and my connections to secure a room. In an attempt to further grow the bond between the driver and I, I gave him plenty of money to get fat and drunk and left him to it. I had my own plans for the night. I spent an hour or so watching the staff and selecting my target, though the man was easy enough to decide upon. I saw him at the desk when a courier arrived, looking tired. The mansio's owner assigned the rider a poor room, as was usually the case for those guests who were part of the imperial network and therefore subsidised. As soon as the owner went about his business, the other man at the desk made marks in a wax ledger on the desk, then a small hushed exchange occurred, a little money changed hands, and the courier was escorted to one of the best-quality rooms.

Pliable and corrupt. Perfect.

I caught the servant's attention some time later in a quiet corner of the room when we were more or less alone.

'You look like a man on paltry wages.'

He flashed me an odd look, then shrugged and grunted.

'Would you like to supplement them?'

Now his ears pricked up. I was dressed well and signed in under a noble name. I was clearly trustworthy. Or at least, as trustworthy as nobles ever get, which is not saying a lot. 'Go on,' he said quietly.

'You keep a track of the names of guests in that book?'

'Yes. Got to keep the records straight.'

'I understand. And I daresay you often exchange a few words with them as they arrive? You probably know where most visitors are bound, eh?'

The man nodded, brow lowering.

'Good.' I produced a small purse of money. A pittance for someone living in a domus on the Caelian or in the palace itself, but a goodly amount for a poor mansio worker. His eyes lit up. 'This is for you. Call it an advance payment for your help. All I ask is that you make a note of the names of anyone who passes through and is visiting the villa across the river. When you have such a name, send a message to me and I will dispatch payment in return. Is that something you think you can do?'

The man nodded eagerly, eyes still on the purse.

I told him that I had powerful friends and did not take well to being crossed or cheated, and then, finally content that the man was corrupt as a month-old body and entirely in my pay, I gave him my address for his missives.

I returned home the next morning with a hungover driver.

Over the next couple of months, I received a number of letters from my hired eyes in the mansio. Most of them were to be entirely expected, and one or two were almost certainly fabrications to earn extra cash, but I was generally able to dismiss those. His veracity was confirmed by the noting of repeated visits by Quadratus.

Names that turned up and were of interest included Quadratus' sister who, as far as I knew, had no connection with the princess, a prefect of the Praetorian Guard by the name of Paternus, and two notables by the name of Salvius Julianus and Didius Julianus. The arrival on the scene of the sour-faced Quintilii brothers I remembered from Athens came as something of a surprise.

As the winter went on, Quadratus began to stay away for longer and longer and finally I decided that something was definitely amiss and was likely to surface rather soon. Biting my lip nervously, I went to the emperor.

I found attaining an audience difficult. Despite our history, I had no official links to the court or the palace any more, and neither the *a libellis*, who dealt with such meetings, nor the Praetorians, who knew me well enough, were of a mind to admit me readily. It was only the happenstance passing of Eclectus on some palace business that secured me my meeting. I was shown into the imperial presence by faceless men and performed all the appropriate greetings and motions before the lackeys left.

Commodus was seated on the grand chair at the heart of the room, a clerk to one side, Cleander to the other, two or three unknown slaves behind, and Praetorians by every door. Truly, the boy Commodus was now gone, grown into a strong emperor, bearded and golden like his beloved uncle. Rome lived in his very bearing. I felt my skin prickle at the sight and forced myself to concentrate, to be proper.

'Marcia,' he said with a smile, 'what a pleasant surprise. I was expecting a tedious delegation from Sardinia.'

I smiled back, uncertain now how to go about this. In the old days I would have spoken to him quietly in a small room. That was seemingly not possible with an emperor.

'I have . . . a private matter to discuss, Majesty.'

Commodus, still smiling, lifted a quizzical eyebrow. 'Alone?'

I nodded, still uncertain. I could see the hatred emanating from Cleander like heatwaves.

'But there are only a few slaves, Cleander here and the guards.'

I nodded. 'Still, Majesty . . .'

He pursed his lips, then made shooing motions with his hands. 'Out, Cleander. And the rest of you. Go. I will send for you shortly.'

The slaves exited in blind obedience. Cleander left slowly,

glaring daggers at me. The Praetorians did not move. I flicked my eyes at them meaningfully, and as the doors shut, leaving us alone with the soldiers, Commodus chuckled. 'I would be lynched by my own prefect if I allowed you an audience without the guard present. Emperors have died in small meetings.'

'Emperors have died at *their* hands,' I reminded him meaningfully.

Again, he laughed. 'They stay, I'm afraid. But be assured that these men are the most loyal to be found in the empire. They are each personally vetted.'

I nodded. This was as private as it was likely to get. And while I was immediately reminded of Cleander speaking to a Praetorian officer in a conspiratorial huddle, though I hated the man I knew him to be loyal to Commodus, which suggested that the Praetorians were, too. Except that one of them had been to Lucilla's villa . . . Ah, but conspiracies give me a headache. I had no choice, anyway.

'I have suspicions that there is some sort of plot afoot.'

He laughed. 'Isn't there always? The mark of an emperor of note is the fact that someone, somewhere, is whetting a knife for him. But it's a little early to worry too much yet. Cassius only rose up against Father when he thought the emperor dead. Anyone who planned to move against me at this point would have done so before I returned from Pannonia. They had ample opportunity to close Rome to me and usurp me then.'

'Not if they were *with* you in Pannonia,' I muttered.

His brow creased. 'What are you saying?'

This was it. Accusations such as the one I was about to make could easily get a person tortured or executed, especially when levelled against the imperial blood. I took a deep breath.

'I think your sister might be conspiring against you.'

233

He laughed, then. 'My sister? Lucilla, you mean, surely? The others are like mice.'

I nodded. 'Lucilla. She has meetings with Quadratus.'

'They are cousins. And since neither of them gets on too well with the rest of us, it is only natural that they should meet from time to time. *Come on*, Marcia.'

'And others,' I blurted. 'The Quintilii? Didius Julianus?'

He frowned. 'The Quintilii? Are you sure?'

'I have it on good authority. And Quadratus is covering his tracks. When he visits her, he tells me he's on business in Ostia or some such.'

He tutted. 'It's tenuous at best, Marcia. Lucilla and I are hardly close, but she is still my sister. We share the same blood.'

I shrugged. 'Caligula's sisters had a hand in *his* death.'

'Come now, Marcia. You've read your Tacitus. Caligula was a madman, and his sisters harpies. Not like our glorious line. You clutch at shadows.'

'Shadows wielding knives.'

He slumped back in his seat. 'You insist this is all true?'

'I cannot say what they plan, but I am absolutely convinced that they plan *something*.'

'And you would take an oath to that on the altar of Apollo?' He caught the look in my eye and chuckled. 'All right, on your Jewish god's altar, then?'

I nodded. 'I would.'

'Very well. I will have the Praetorians and the *frumentarii* look into the matter. They are my hands – one in a gauntlet, the other a calfskin glove. Between them they could uncover a pin in a dung heap.'

I chewed on my lip for a moment. The frumentarii were the emperor's own secret force. Spies and assassins hidden among the military, each fanatically loyal to their master. They frightened me as much as they frightened everyone, but no one could doubt their allegiance. As for the Praetorians . . . I had omitted the name of the prefect from my list when I relayed it to the emperor, acutely aware that I was surrounded by his men. How could I possibly tell Commodus not to trust a Praetorian prefect in front of a dozen of his guards?

I glanced up, as though I might see the shining light of God's countenance beaming through the clouds on the other side of that grand, vaulted ceiling. All I could see were paintings of gods that weren't mine. How much easier it must be to place one's belief in a different deity for everything; how easy to assign blame. I sighed. Mother had always said that God had a plan and, though it might not seem to make sense and would be ineffable, it still mattered. If God did indeed have a plan, then there was a reason for this. I had to trust the divine.

'All right,' I said, as though Commodus needed my consent to assign his guards. He recognised the humour in that and smiled again.

'I had half a notion you would append Cleander's name to the list.'

I frowned. 'Majesty?'

'Oh come now, it's hardly a secret. How much you two dislike one another is clear as day. And when you had me send him out, I was almost waiting for his name.'

I felt chilled by the thought. 'You believe I would lie to have him killed?'

'I'm *sure* you would. And when you go back to Quadratus' house, some small part of you will regret that you hadn't thought of it, I'd wager.'

I bridled. 'My duty is done, Majesty, if that is all?'

A curt dismissal of an emperor by a plebeian. Ridiculous, yet he chuckled. 'I believe so. Unless you think it is time I dipped my net and lifted you from my cousin's pond?'

I glared at him. 'No. Not yet. I might yet be useful there.'

His smile fell away, and he nodded, businesslike.

I left the palace and went home to the house of a conspirator. In the dark of my room that night, I wondered why I hadn't thought of adding Cleander's name to the list. I berated myself for my wickedness well into the night.

XIII

CONSPIRACY

Rome, Maius AD *182*

Months slipped by in a strange sense of tense expectation. I had been sure something important was building to a head with the conspirators at Tibur, but nothing seemed to happen. I visited Commodus as often as I felt I could, which was none too often between affairs of state occupying much of his time and the worry that Quadratus might realise I was on to something.

Much of what I learned over that time came from Eclectus who, though no longer in one of the leading roles at court, was nonetheless privy to almost everything that happened. I had always trusted this man who came to us from Verus' own familia, and he became something of a direct link for me to the corridors of power when Commodus was too busy to see me.

Eclectus had tantalising snippets of information only about the ongoing investigation. The workings of the Praetorian Guard are relatively simple and clear, but their counterparts in the frumentarii, who act as the emperor's eyes and ears, and occasionally his blade, are shrouded in mystery. Certainly, both agencies were at work around the princess' villa. Soldiers infiltrating private mercenary armies, spies hunting one another in the vast estate and the like. All very intriguing and exciting, yet no proof seemed to be coming out of the place. Apart from a few trusted friends and some of her family, no one was admitted to the meetings held by Lucilla, even the slaves.

Commodus, during these months, was busier than ever. The Agonalia festival in Maius was a grand affair at the best of times, and Commodus was determined to make this year's the greatest in living memory. Lavish banquets and great games were planned, leading to jubilation among the people and a constant slew of worried faces from those po-faced men who dealt with the treasury.

The day of the festival dawned clear and bright. I paid closer attention to my grooming than usual on the assumption that I would be attending events with or without Quadratus. I was always rather lucky with my looks, but it was equally important to pay attention to my mode of dress. I chose my finest clothes and the best jewellery, even letting my *ornatrix* put my hair up into an elaborate style, rather than trusting to its natural tumbling tresses. Every bit the imperial lady, if lacking the deportment and the manners true matrons are born to.

Quadratus awoke that morning full of energy and busyness. He shot out orders at the domus staff like an artillerist on the battlefield, for this day was a grand day of races and fights and feasts, and everyone with a place in Rome's hierarchy would be making the most of it. On days like this the public enjoyed the spectacles, and so did the nobility, but for them it was also a time to meet and make deals, be seen to be wealthy and important and build webs of finance and patronage. Quadratus, ever the social climber, was more excitable than I had seen him for some time.

A suspicion began to seep into me. Why the urgency of his actions, though, like a man preparing for a visit from an auditor? I swear he was even twitching a little. I enquired as subtly as I could. 'Am I to attend today?'

'No,' he said in a distracted manner, leaving me determined to do so on my own funds and merit, but then a strange smile

238

slid across his face. 'Actually, yes,' he corrected himself. 'You can hang around with the familia. There will not be room for you with me.'

Hardly a surprise. No matter that I knew I was pretty and common men would envy him for my looks: I was a pleb, and the senators and other nobiles would look down on me.

'I shall be in the imperial box, alongside Lucilla and the rest of the imperial family. You can stand at the back. At least you'll have a good view.'

For a moment I worried that their long planning at the villa had been leading to this day. I worried for Commodus' safety, but logic shouted down my fears. In the *pulvinar* – the imperial box of the amphitheatre – we would be under the watchful eyes of the Praetorians. No one would be able to sneak a weapon in, and if they did they would have scant opportunity to use it before being pinned by guards. Besides, as well as the Praetorians, there would be other trusted men around the emperor. Saoterus, Cleander, Eclectus, Pompeianus. No. Even the nagging memory of a Praetorian prefect's name on the list of visitors the princess had received would not dent my belief. No one could try anything in the amphitheatre and hope to succeed.

Still, my nerves remained taut as we left the domus, and our first meeting did little to diminish them. In front of Quadratus' home on the Caelian Hill stood a group of rough-looking mercenary guards and miserable slaves around a litter. The curtain of the ornate box was pulled back to reveal the sour face of Lucilla, who nodded at Quadratus and then gestured at me with a bony finger.

'You're bringing her?'

'She is a close friend of the emperor,' Quadratus reminded her.

Lucilla looked less than enthusiastic, then shrugged. 'She's your problem, then. Keep her out of the way.'

We set off through Rome, me in a litter somewhat less elegant than Lucilla's, Quadratus on foot, unusually active. It was ironic, I thought, that one of the first structures we passed on the Caelian Hill was the Castra Peregrina, the camp of the secretive frumentarii who had been investigating this woman for months. We met other relations of Lucilla's as we neared our destination, including her sister Fadilla, one of the few young Antonine women with whom I had been on reasonable terms in our youth.

The streets around the great Flavian amphitheatre were a heaving sea of humanity. The emperor had paid for some of the most lavish spectacles in that arena in many decades and it had attracted record crowds. Fantastical beasts had been imported from Africa and Asia and beyond, and the best gladiators to be found across the empire were here, though admittedly there were many fewer to choose from these days since the wars and the plague had thinned their ranks.

The amphitheatre was already open and the seats filling, and the vast majority of the mob outside would not find a place among the stands, relegated to listening to the cheering of the lucky viewers. I reminded myself that many of these people would be here purely to see Commodus as he passed on the way to the games.

'Is the emperor not already in the pulvinar?' I asked, curiously. Commodus habitually watched even the opening parade, such was his love of the games.

Lucilla ignored me entirely as though I'd said nothing. Quadratus too. Fadilla turned to me. 'He's been delayed by some official business or other. He was in a meeting with Sextus Quintilius Condianus when I left the palace, but rest assured he will be here in time for his grand entrance. He was firm on that.'

I nodded as we moved through the crowd. One of the Quintilii, another of the visitors to Lucilla's villa, had delayed

240

the emperor at the palace. My mind snapped back to the histories I'd read in those cold days in Carnuntum. Caesar's murder on the curia steps had only been so straightforward because Cimber had distracted Caesar and directed him to a side room. Before I could mull this over any further, and despite the building conviction in me that something was very wrong, we were ushered through the arch and into the great amphitheatre.

Though the seating and the arena itself are in the open air and occasionally shaded from the bright sun by great canvas awnings, the bulk of the structure consists of darkened tunnels and vertiginous staircases. They are adequately lit on event days with torches and lamps, but there is still an air of oppressive gloom about them. The place seemed to be filled as much with Praetorians as with spectators, which I found slightly heartening. Even if there was something off with a Praetorian prefect, surely rot could not have spread throughout an entire legion of men? Certainly, they looked noble and attentive in their pristine white and shining steel, one man standing in each arch high up, watching every surge of the crowd.

We moved through the tunnels, the private mercenary guard continually surrounding us, moving ahead and clearing our path through the brutal application of knuckles and knees, keeping the public at bay to each side and behind. The Praetorians watched us with a disapproving eye as we made our way to the arena, their dislike of such private forces evident in their expressions, but they made no move to halt the violence. This was the emperor's sister and cousin, after all, and besides, even the lowliest noble of Rome had his mercenaries for security.

Somewhere in the bowels of the place as we climbed towards our seats, a young man called to us. Quadratus acknowledged him with an offhand wave, while Lucilla ignored him entirely. I had no idea who he was, but the lad's colouring and facial

241

features reminded me closely of Pompeianus, suggesting he was some relative.

We emerged into the stands at the pulvinar and were admitted to that hallowed space by more Praetorians. Already the stands were almost full, the hum and murmur of thousands of people filling the great arena. Lucilla, Quadratus and Fadilla took their places in comfortable, expensive seats with an unimpeded view of the entire place. I was relegated to the periphery with some mercenary that smelled of *garum*, and Quadratus' personal slave, present in case he needed anything.

I waited, the sense of anticipation building in me all the time. Other notables and bearers of the Antonine blood arrived and were admitted, and finally the opening parade began. The Gate of Life at the eastern edge of the arena opened to great fanfare. The musicians emerged first, blasting their horns and rapping their drums. A troupe of eastern acrobats appeared through the gate behind them onto the as yet bloodless sand, leaping and tumbling, and I could see the shapes of carts behind them, decorated lavishly, trundling through the shadow towards the light. It was a grand spectacle, and one that I usually enjoyed, right down to the arrival of the gladiators at the end, but my attention was drawn away from it as the pulvinar's door opened. I turned to see Bruttia Crispina, her ash-blonde hair elegantly curled and piled up, clad in an ensemble that cost enough to outfit a small navy. She entered with her slave, her guards gathering outside with the others, awaiting our time to depart. The only soldiers in the box other than Lucilla's own bodyguard, who smelled of dead fish, were half a dozen rigid Praetorians.

Bruttia flashed a pleasant smile around and greeted me warmly, the only hint of anything other than joviality a flintiness in her eyes as they locked with mine. It was a great honour for someone as low-born as I, and I managed to return the smile and the greeting with polite formality, stepping carefully well out of the way as the empress moved across to her seat, greeting Quadratus and Lucilla with equal ease and civility. Lord, but she was pleasant and quiet and pretty, at least on the surface. Lord, how I hated her. The very sight of her reminded me that I had locked my heart away in a box because I could not have the man I loved, while this pretty little viper had him all to herself. I fought down my need and my anger, though. This was not the time. It might be worth noting that this was likely the only thing upon which Lucilla and I ever agreed. The princess was equally warm and polite in her greeting to the empress, but I saw her eyes and the fiery bolts of hatred they unleashed.

I suddenly felt very claustrophobic, sharing this box with two women and one man whom I hated in varying degrees. I would happily miss the rest of the parade and the announcements, the pre-game entertainment and the rest, while they waited for the emperor's grand arrival. I would do almost anything at that point not to be in that place with those people.

'I feel a little queasy, I'm afraid,' I said suddenly, gulping in air. It was true, in fact. I was standing too close to that mercenary who reeked of fish sauce.

'I can understand that,' Lucilla said nastily, making sure not to look as though she was referring to the empress, though a quick flick of her eyes confirmed that for me. 'Go and throw up somewhere.'

'Yes,' Quadratus snapped irritably. 'I don't want to spend the day with the aroma of your stomach contents around me. Go on.'

I needed no further urging, and knocked on the door. The Praetorians let me past and I heaved a sigh of relief as I returned to the tunnels. Two of Quadratus' bodyguards fell in behind me and I almost waved them away, but the amphitheatre can be as dangerous as any backstreet of Rome. Despite the Praetorians in evidence around us, thugs and robbers would be at work wherever they could, and a woman would not be safe in these tunnels without a strong escort.

There would be time, I reasoned, to stretch my legs and explore a little before I needed to be back in the pulvinar. As long as I was there when Commodus arrived. I could see, as I descended a stairwell, the line of white-clad guardsmen clearing the route for their emperor's arrival, and decided that, just like any other member of his adoring public, I would watch his arrival in glory. As long as I stayed on this side, ahead of his route, then I could be back in my place in the box before him.

With a little time to kill, I bought a couple of trinkets from a stall in one of the archways, treated myself to a sweet pastry and then a small cup of good wine. I almost began to enjoy myself, not focusing on those women and that ape in a toga that occupied the pulvinar above.

I was definitely feeling more relaxed. My earlier fears seemed so far-fetched now. All those I mistrusted were in the pulvinar under the watchful eye of the Praetorians. White-clad soldiers seemed to line every passageway and stand in every arch. It was simply ridiculous to think that someone might do something today.

I was enjoying the sight of the gladiators finishing their parade, seen through one of the arches that opened onto the seating, when a fanfare announced the emperor's arrival. I smiled. Just in time. Turning my eyes from the last of the parade, I peered down the dimly lit tunnel, past the ranks of Praetorians, to see movement at the entrance to the amphitheatre. The corridors in the place had swiftly filled with desperate spectators hoping to catch a glimpse of the young emperor. I could see Praetorians holding them back and occasionally applying necessary force to prevent them breaking out into the open. The Guard were good. They knew exactly what they were doing. The noise rose, crescendoing both inside the arena and out, the former as the opening parade finished and the gladiators disappeared to prepare for the afternoon's matches, the latter from the crowds adoring their emperor.

Noise and a press of humanity, all surrounding the calm, professional soldiers in white.

I saw Commodus at last, striding down the clear passage, waving to the mass of spectators on either side. At his shoulder was a Praetorian officer, with Saoterus, Cleander, Eclectus and a dozen other notables following on, yet more of the ever-present Praetorians bringing up the rear.

I eased back, ready to retreat up the stairs ahead of the emperor, preparing to settle in for the day's events, and then I saw it. Just an odd face in the crowd that somehow grabbed my attention. I peered into the dim light to be sure.

Slightly ahead of Commodus, the Praetorian lines at the side were struggling to hold back the excited mass in the side passages, and where the cordon of white-clad men bulged, I could see a familiar face. It was the boy we had seen as we entered the place, the one who reminded me so of Pompeianus. A sickening feeling welled in the pit of my stomach, and I realised now how well founded my fears had been. Those bastards in the pulvinar didn't *have* to lie in wait. They had someone to do it for them. Though there were Praetorians everywhere, the emperor was exposed, in the open. It would only take one swift blow. Yes, the boy would die in a heartbeat, but by then it would be too late. Commodus would be lying on the stone flags, bleeding his last, like Caesar before him.

I yelled a warning. I can't remember what I shouted, but it was urgent and loud. Unfortunately, fifty thousand people all around me were also shouting urgently and loudly.

Commodus strode forward, oblivious, sharing a joke with the Praetorian officer.

The young man suddenly burst through the cordon of white-clad soldiers, ducking beneath grasping hands. He was running now, straight for Commodus, and as he ran his hand tore a blade from his voluminous tunic. I stared in horror. He had the jump on everyone. No one would be able to react before he struck.

To my surprise, the young man pulled himself up in front of the shocked emperor, gladius raised to strike, and bellowed in a voice that cut through the sound of a thousand indrawn breaths, 'See what the senate sends for tyrants!'

His blade wavered for just a moment and then began its descent. Commodus threw himself backwards, but the blade nicked his raised forearm. Thus, he escaped the deadly initial blow: the lad had been foolish enough to delay his attack to deliver a message. The idiot. Soldiers were running to defend the emperor. A Praetorian spear came from somewhere, gleaming in the lamplight, and struck the would-be assassin in the shoulder of his sword arm, sending him spinning in agony and dropping to the floor as his weapon clattered off across stone.

The young man shrieked and coughed up a gout of blood, struggling to rise. My fears over the loyalty of the Praetorian officer dissolved in an instant as the man took charge, sending his soldiers this way and that, sealing the area and driving all spectators back. Limbs were broken and heads bashed in an attempt to clear the corridor, but no one cared. The emperor's safety was paramount.

Commodus was shaken but unwounded, apart from the scored red line across his arm.

The lad on the floor was in more pain, though. He writhed, bleeding, trying to get to his sword. Two Praetorians reached down and grasped him, pinning his arms and lifting him upright painfully, making him screech anew.

I could see shock and anger both in Commodus' face as he stepped forward. There was a brief exchange between Commodus, his would-be killer, the Praetorian officer and a few of his men, though with the sudden surge of shocked noise from the crowd and the bellowing of soldiers trying to clear the passageways, I could not make out the words. I stared as the emperor took the boy's sword and examined it with a professional eye, then I jumped as Commodus suddenly slammed the blade into the lad's chest, twisting it this way and that, then releasing the hilt to step back, leaving the weapon in place.

The boy collapsed the moment the two Praetorians let go of him, blood pouring out onto the flags, filling the gaps between the stones first, then thickening into a sea of crimson around the dying attacker. I stared. I'd not been expecting such a thing, though I probably should have, given both what he had tried to do and Commodus' martial nature. This was the same Commodus who had ridden back from Marcomannia with a king's head swinging from his saddle, after all.

It took only moments for the Praetorians to clear the way, remove the body and put everything right. I could see a brief argument going on between the emperor and his officer, and I could imagine it: the Praetorian insistent that the emperor be escorted back to the safety of the palace, Commodus refusing, determined instead on continuing with the day for his public.

He resumed his climb towards the imperial box, ashen-faced Saoterus, Cleander and Eclectus with him, white-robed soldiers moving ahead and following on, watching every dark corner. Two of the Praetorians reached me where I stood ahead and made to move me out of the way, but Commodus waved them aside.

'Marcia?'

'I wanted . . . I wanted to see you arrive, Majesty.' I felt frozen to the core, gooseflesh prickling. I appeared to be in shock far more than he, though I suspected that calm and businesslike face to be one of the masks he wore when he needed to hide his true emotions.

'Come on. The games will start soon.'

My eyes widened. 'No. You can't. Not the pulvinar. This wasn't just the boy . . .'

He smiled easily. 'I know. Lucilla. Quadratus. The Quintilii.

247

Everyone you warned me about. Perennis just confirmed it all from his agents. The Praetorians know them all.'

'If they were that well informed, how did this happen?'

The emperor shrugged. 'Sometimes we are in the hands of the gods, Marcia. All we can do is work with what they provide. The fact remains that I am alive and well, and my assassin is dead. Now come, we have games to watch.'

We entered the pulvinar, where we settled in for one of the weirdest days of my life. The ring of conspirators who had meant to murder the emperor in the tunnels below sat alongside us and watched the games in a polite, tense silence. We knew they were guilty, and so did they. They must have had at least a suspicion that we knew, and I believe that is why Commodus had us sit calmly through the day's proceedings. It was a small, subtle flash of revenge to make them sweat through the whole event.

When the closing ceremony finished at the end of the day and the imperial box opened for us all to depart, only then was Commodus' displeasure made manifest. Quadratus and Lucilla were seized by the Praetorians and detained, as were three others, though Pompeianus and Fadilla were not among them, which relieved me. I liked both, and neither had been potential conspirators on my list, even though Pompeianus naturally lived in his wife's villa.

I observed the conspirators being bundled away with mixed feelings. I had never liked Lucilla or Quadratus, and they deserved everything they would get for attempting to kill the emperor, and yet that part of me that had been weaned on a diet of understanding and forgiveness rebelled a little.

'What will happen to them?' I said, quietly.

'Death,' interrupted that Praetorian prefect with a stony face as his men led the prisoners away.

'*Exile*, I think,' corrected Commodus carefully. 'Remember that these are my family.'

The prefect – Perennis, his name was – gave his emperor a black look. 'A sister's blade is as deadly as any other. Exile is not enough, Majesty.'

I was torn. In one way, it truly was. In another, it really was not.

'Time will tell us what they deserve. Perennis, I need you to unpick this conspiracy down to the very threads now the deed is done and find out everything there is to find. Anyone involved is to be taken in, and we shall decide appropriate punishments in due course.'

And so ended an attempt on the life of Commodus. I fell somewhat by the wayside after the games, uncertain what to do with myself. The emperor, clearly, had plenty to occupy him and, under the scrutiny and influence of Saoterus, Cleander, Eclectus and this prefect, he was immediately whisked off for the rest of the day.

I really did not know even where to go. I was finally a free woman, of course, with Quadratus now permanently out of the scene, yet I was totally alone. The only home I had known, for a decade now, was not even mine, but the house of that very conspirator. I tried to wrap my mind around the concept of not being his mistress, not to be summoned at will and dismissed abruptly. Not to be beaten when something annoyed him. I was free. I had no home, no money, no job. But I was free, and I knew that Commodus would not see me starving and destitute. I wondered whether the domus on the Caelian would pass down to Quadratus' equally unpleasant adopted son. If so, I would make sure to leave before he came anywhere near it. More likely, given what had happened, the house would be impounded by the palace and become imperial property. Once more that old quandary returned. Could I find myself close to Commodus? My heart begged yes, but my mind reminded me that there was a wife there to stand between us. I might have to find a way to scratch that particular itch before long.

For the time being, I went back to the house on the Caelian Hill, and the staff treated it as only natural that I should return. I stayed there for a month, receiving occasional updates from Eclectus concerning progress on the Palatine, though the brutal reaction of the administration to the attempted assassination was well known even by the lowliest street urchin.

Lucilla, her daughter and Quadratus' sister were sent into disgraced exile on the island of Capri and the archaic villas of Tiberius. They were the lucky ones. The Quintilii brothers were arrested by Praetorians and dispatched, though rather more humanely than anyone expected, their property impounded by the palace. Salvius Julianus met a violent end at the tip of a Praetorian blade, though his cousin Didius was pardoned for any wrongdoing given that, apart from that one noted visit to the villa of the princess, he had apparently refused to be involved in the conspiracy any further and had argued against it. Half a dozen notables who I did not know by name were said to have met the edge of a blade for involvement, though there was a murmured belief among the nobility that the proscription lists that killed so many important people were largely compiled and approved by the Praetorian prefects and the palace freedmen.

I could quite believe that.

Norbanus, Paralius, Vitruvius Secundus, Vitrasia Faustina, Velius Rufus, Egnatius Capito. The list went on. Even the consuls Aemilius and Atilius went into exile. At least half of them were outspoken opponents of the emperor's reliance upon freedmen, which is somewhat telling.

The only punishment that I witnessed personally came the day after the games. The crowd that gathered to watch the end of Quadratus, the emperor's treasonous cousin, was almost as large and excited as the crowds at the games the day before.

I may have hated the man, but even I, with every reason to wish him a humiliating death, felt my gorge rise as I watched from between the columns of the Temple of Concord. Half a

dozen Praetorians appeared at the top of the infamous Gemonian Stairs, where their fellows had kept the entire place free
of citizens. The mass of observers had gathered in the forum
below or, like me, on the steps of temples where the view was
better.

Quadratus was ruined. He had spent the night and the morning in the cellars below the Palatine with some very unfriendly
professionals, who had prised out of him every last detail of the
conspiracy. He was tortured and abused, a mere mockery of
a human, now. His flesh was cut, burned, sloughed away. He
had been left one eye with which to watch, terrified, his fate.
His ears were gone, his fingers trimmed down. His body was
naked, his flesh purple and blue, beaten and torn. In truth, he
had been hurt beyond all reason and was probably now praying
to his gods for death, a collection of expertly tied ropes the only
thing that held him up in a parody of a whole man.

The Praetorian centurion Adrastus, the man who commanded
the Palatine's executioners, stepped forward and bellowed out
the traditional accusations, convictions and sentences for a
citizen who committed treason against his emperor, though I
heard only staccato bursts over the general buzz of the blood-
hungry crowd.

I forced myself not to turn away as the executioner produced
his sword. This was a man who had not only tried to assassinate
his emperor, but a man who had enslaved, whored and abused
me throughout our association. A man with no moral fibre,
whom I owed nothing but disdain. I had watched that governor
in Alexandria go under the sword like a true Roman, and his
quiet nobility had earned him a razor-sharp blade. Quadratus
was no such man. Not even a shadow of Romanitas fell upon
him, and I knew that the sword would have been kept suitably
blunt for him. That belief was borne out as the executioner
swung and the first blow only cut deep into the side of the victim's neck, breaking bones and snapping tendons. Quadratus

screamed then. He might have thought he had reached the pinnacle of his pain. He had been wrong. It took six blows in all to remove the head, and Quadratus must have felt every one, each delivered with agonising slowness.

The head was cast down the stairs, where it bounced numerous times with dull clonks, before vanishing into the crowd below. Moments later, it was raised in triumph by some grisly spectator, a souvenir of the day. The rest of the body was then hurled out down the steps, where it bounced and slithered to a halt perhaps a third of the way down.

Their task complete, the Praetorians withdrew and their cordon collapsed, the crowd surging with a roar up the steps to pull and dismember Quadratus' remains, each hoping to take some souvenir of the day. I turned and left them to it. I was becoming inured to such vile things, but at least Quadratus had deserved his fate.

I did see Commodus occasionally after that, while the other sentences were being announced and carried out, and I noted with relief that he seemed to have remained blessedly free of the black moods that had beset his youth. Perhaps it was because this was no loss of a loved one, but more a cleansing fire clearing out the chaff that had accumulated around him. He and Lucilla had never been particularly cordial, and he held Quadratus in much the same low regard as I.

Finally, I received a message from my friend in the palace that the Caelian house was to be cleared. Rooms had been made available for me on the Palatine. I was to have my own apartment in the palace for the first time since I had been a girl. And with that I found myself confronting something I had buried for a long time and had not been able to face since that day in the arena. I was free. I had been kept from the man that I loved partially by my tie to Quadratus, but now that tie was severed. There was still the somewhat troublesome obstacle of

Bruttia Crispina, of course. I wanted Commodus, I realised, as much as ever I had, but it had now become clear to me that I could not share him, even if I could never be an empress. Still, if there were a way to remove Bruttia from the picture, it would be easier to find it on the Palatine. And when I sometimes felt the needle of guilt in even thinking about how to deal with that pretty little empress, I simply reminded myself of her words back in Vindobona:

'Stay away from my husband, Marcia Ceionia. You may have known him all his life, but you are just a pleb, and an ambitious one, I think. He is mine.'

The prospect of being close to my golden prince again made me inordinately happy, and I reached the imperial palace one bright, sunny morning with a cart and a handful of slaves following on bringing all my worldly goods. In truth, and against every Christian value that had been drummed into me as a child, I had spent days going through Quadratus' house like a swarm of locusts, swiping anything I liked or thought might be worth holding on to and claiming it as my own. I could perhaps argue Christian charity in urging the slaves and servants to do the same.

I arrived at the palace doors and was shown inside by some functionary I did not know. I was told that Eclectus attended the emperor and would be with me shortly, and left in a comfortable room in which I had not sat for over ten years. I leaned back, enjoying being in the palace once more. I could wait; Commodus was a busy man.

The door to the chamber suddenly burst open as though a runaway cart had struck the far side, and the emperor emerged, his face puce with rage. I shrank back in my seat at the sight of such fury, and then remembered at the last moment to stand and bow appropriately. Commodus did not even notice me.

'Fetch me Paternus!' he bellowed, and Eclectus, appearing at his shoulder, white-faced, nodded and ran off. The emperor came to a halt, shaking. Another figure entered the room through that same door and I was surprised to see that it was Perennis, the Praetorian prefect. It was only the sight of his uniform that jogged my memory. *Paternus*. He was the other prefect, the one who had been to visit Lucilla. I contemplated drawing attention to myself, but decided against it.

'His name *was* on the list, Majesty,' Perennis said quietly.

'Then it should not have been,' snarled Commodus, rounding on the prefect. 'And even if it was, no executions should be carried out without *my* sanction.'

My skin prickled. Executions?

Perennis, clearly a brave man, spread his arms wide. 'In defence of my colleague, Majesty, throughout this investigation you have made it clear that we had the authority to do just that.'

Commodus glared at him, but said nothing, his silence confirming the truth of Perennis' words.

'Tell me that *you* would have butchered him out of hand without consulting me first?'

Perennis shook his head. 'I would not, Majesty. But Paternus is not me.'

'He will not be *himself* for long, either,' snapped the emperor.

A moment later the outer door opened once more and another man in a Praetorian prefect's uniform entered, Eclectus at his heel. He must have been close by, then. 'Majesty?'

'Why, Paternus? And without consulting me first?'

The prefect stood straight and stony. 'You refer to Saoterus, Majesty?'

My blood ran cold and I fell back into the seat. Saoterus? Executed?

'His name appeared on the list of those who visited the empress more than once. We had agreed that multiple visits suggested a potential major conspirator.'

'He was my chamberlain.'

'And a consort of your sister, Majesty. Before he died, he confessed all.'

Commodus' glare could have cut through steel. At that moment, Cleander stepped into the room from the other door and I caught, entirely by chance, a knowing exchange in a single glance between he and Paternus. With cold certainty, I felt I knew what had happened. Saoterus was the emperor's favourite. A more loyal man I could not imagine in the palace. He had never visited the villa to my knowledge, though whether he had or not, it would be remarkably easy for certain folk – say, for instance, the imperial secretary – to add a name to a list. Cleander was at the heart of this, ink still wet from the execution order for his opponent. He had wanted Saoterus out of the way since the day they met. I knew him for a devious snake, but his ruthlessness was clearly greater than even I had appreciated. I found myself seeing him now as a far greater danger than ever before.

Eclectus, who was only peripherally involved in the rest of the exchange, finally noticed me. With a bow to the emperor, he crossed the chamber, bade me rise, and led me from the room to show me the apartment that would be my new home.

Paternus died that same day for his part in it all, his traitor's ravaged body dumped in the Tiber to float away with the refuse, and with him went any possible proof that Cleander had been behind the death. Over the coming days, I watched with sickened dismay as a number of other names were attached to funeral urns, now far outside the original web of conspirators, each one carefully selected by Cleander, I was sure, and then approved by the emperor before they met the edge of the executioner's blade.

I went to see Commodus a few days after I had settled in as the latest handful of dead 'conspirators' was announced. I was admitted to his presence by the guard only with Eclectus' support, though I was once more a palace resident. Even then, I was not alone. Two Praetorians and a palace slave entered with me. I found Commodus sitting by a window, looking out at a grey sky where birds wheeled carelessly. He turned at my arrival and my heart sank.

There, once more, were the dark circles and the sallow complexion. That age-old problem had not faded with youth but merely become dormant as disaster and heartache faded. Saoterus' death had brought it all back.

There was one person in the whole empire who knew what to do about it: me. Commodus turned to me with a bleak, dark face and pointed at the door.

'Out.'

I had been dismissed.

XIV

THE FATE OF THE EMPIRE

Rome, AD 185

Everything changed after the day Lucilla tried to kill her brother. When Pompeianus' son, a willing conspirator in the plot even without his father's knowledge, had thrust a blade at the emperor, he'd announced that the senate had sent it. In truth, I think we all knew the attack had precious little to do with the senate. Lucilla had instigated the plot in an attempt to place her own children on the throne, as she felt was only right, being offspring of the emperor Verus, and she had dragged in disaffected friends and family. Yet the fact remained that several of those who were linked to the plot, even if only peripherally, were senators, which, when added to the assassin's words, cast a permanent doubt over the loyalty of all their ilk.

The emperor severed his ties with the senate thereafter, removing himself from the traditional relationship he shared with that august body. Even Pompeianus, who had ever been recognised as the most loyal of subjects, was cast out in light of his connections to both senate and conspirators. Those other advisors of his father he had kept on were thrust away, Pertinax to provincial commands, Seius Fuscianus into roles of urban authority.

For a few days after the death of his favourite, Commodus donned his impenetrable mask of well-being over that turbulent sea of sorrow. Saoterus could not be properly mourned, for as a denounced traitor there had been little left of the body to mourn, even before it had been cast into the river. Instead, Commodus threw himself into a brief, fierce and critical reorganisation, his mood clearly constantly wavering between ire and depression. Cleander was once more made chamberlain and placed in control of the palace, grinning with glee, with Eclectus returning to the role of secretary, also lodged on the Palatine. Both men would serve the palace and the empire, but neither would serve the emperor as such, for Commodus withdrew from Rome, hiding away with that sow of a wife in a grand villa on the Via Appia that had belonged to the Quintilii until their recent demise. Whether he continued to wallow in despair there or had since recovered I had no idea, but he clearly had no intention of returning to public life. Naturally I feared the worst, but, stung by his rejection following the disaster, I no longer tried to visit him. I seemed to flip about like an eel these days between my urgent need to be part of his life and my refusal to do so, when he so bluntly refused me, yet let Bruttia Crispina into his bed.

I was something of a mess.

In Commodus' place in the city, Perennis, now one of the few men the emperor seemed to trust, was given free rein as sole prefect of the Guard. I wanted to visit Commodus, to make sure that his slide into melancholia was neither critical nor permanent, but it took me a long time to fight down my own objections to doing so. In the end, like everyone else, I was refused permission to visit the villa anyway. A blessing in a way, since I really did not want to have to pass the time of day with his wife.

That year was bad for everyone, even though the plague seemed finally to be abating. The people of Rome began to worry instead about their absent emperor. All public business with Commodus went through a trusted few. Perennis, a man with a solid legal background as well as military talent, became much more than just the commander of the Praetorians. He began to answer petitions on behalf of the emperor, and make legal judgements in his name, even with his seal. He held banquets for the emperor. He bridged that ever-widening gap with the senate. In many ways, while Commodus wallowed in privacy, Perennis ran the business of empire for him. Eclectus remained important as secretary, though now working mostly with the prefect. Cleander, who had begun initially to take on the emperor's tasks for him, soon found himself with little more authority than any house's major-domo. After all, he had no training or experience in law, politics, or military matters and it was only natural that most of the work should fall to Perennis. Cleander's hate for the prefect soon overtook his hatred for me.

The year rolled on and I became more and more lonely in that palace of a thousand people.

As winter sent us its last icy throes before the advent of spring, I met with the Praetorian prefect quite by chance. I stepped out into the cold, my breath frosting as I crossed the balcony that looked down upon the valley of the circus. Tigidius Perennis was leaning on the balustrade with a cup of wine. He started as I appeared and then, recognising me, relaxed and sank back to the rail. I was simply seeking company, for much of my time now was spent in solitude, and even the company of a man I didn't know very well, like this vital character, was welcome.

'Lady,' he acknowledged me with more respect than most would. I warmed to him for that if nothing else.

'Prefect.'

He looked tired, and I realised that while I had left my rooms in search of human interaction, he had almost certainly come here for quite the opposite reason.

'How is the emperor?' I asked, quietly.

'I have no idea,' he replied wearily. 'He remains on his estate away from Rome, and I see him no more than anyone else. I am beginning to tire of his duties, though. Months ago, it seemed so sensible. I think I even enjoyed wielding the authority. But now? It is just work, and *endless* work at that. The senate have not taken to me at all. An equestrian, beneath their social circles and yet wielding power over them? They are polite and deferential in words, but their eyes carry the constant desire to see me fall.' He sighed. 'Cleander too. That rat sees me as opposition. I apologise for my candour, but the emperor once confided in me how little love was lost between you two. I can quite see why. I worry that the empire is faltering, Lady Marcia. Once, back in the early days, Tiberius retired to his island and left a Praetorian prefect to run Rome. No good came of that.'

I nodded. Tiberius' madness and the vicious cruelty of the prefect Sejanus were the stuff of legend. 'But you do not seek the throne as he did, and Commodus is not mad.'

'*I* know that,' he sighed, 'and so do you, but what does it look like to the senate and the people? I hear my name whispered in the same breath as the word *usurper*. My future is uncertain, Lady, at best. Certain at worst.'

'The emperor trusts you. And he will return.'

He looked unconvinced as he returned to his silent contemplation of the valley below us, and I decided there and then that I had had enough of this. For the better part of a year Commodus had been gone from public life and I, in my weak and flappable inability to decide what I wanted out of life, had let him do so. I, the only person who could really regulate his mood when it fell. Perennis was suffering in his place though now, Eclectus was powerless, and Cleander dangerous. And I was just lonely.

I left the palace that day with just two slaves and two guards as company, courtesy of Eclectus. We travelled the five or six miles along the queen of roads to the grand villa, following the secretary's instructions, and arrived at the gate in the late afternoon.

Despite the seriousness and urgency of my task, I had to marvel as we halted before the villa gates. I could understand now how the emperor could lower himself to living in a former senator's villa. The place was quite magnificent. The great arched portico entrance was flanked with colonnades and statues, sheathed in expensive marble and towering high, yet dwarfed by a great nymphaeum that gushed with crystal-clear torrents, jets arcing high into the air, statues of gods and weird creatures that would have no place on Noah's ship amid the flow. If this was just the entrance . . .

One of the slaves hurried over and rapped on the metal gate as the other helped me down from the carriage we had used. A surly doorman appeared through a smaller side door and barked at us, demanding to know what we wanted. I was grateful when one of the two Praetorians accompanying me stepped forward and took it upon himself to interfere.

'The lady Marcia brings greetings to his Majesty from the Palatine, and I bear a message for him from my prefect.' Of course, Perennis sent his men here daily with missives for one reason or another.

'The emperor is not accepting visitors,' the doorman rumbled, then held his hand out for the letter. His eyes bulged in shock as the soldier took a step forward and grasped him beneath the chin, bunching his tunic and yanking him forth from the door.

'Take us to someone of authority.'

All sense of self-importance dissipated in the slave as he recoiled from the soldier's directness. The Praetorian let go, and the man scurried inside and held the door open. That wonderful soldier smiled at me and gestured for me to proceed. I did so, with one soldier and one slave, the other two remaining with the carriage. I felt, possibly for the first time ever, like a noblewoman. Bless that guardsman.

I marvelled once more inside the place. Behind that grand façade and the huge nymphaeum lay a beautifully landscaped garden, perhaps a hundred paces wide and three hundred long, bounded by an aqueduct and a decorative wall. Neatly tended flower beds, ponds, cunningly placed trees and hedges stretched ahead as far as the villa, which was itself palatial. Also evident were members of the Praetorian Guard at strategic points around the entrance and the entire garden's periphery.

I passed through the garden in awe. The Quintilii had clearly been very rich men. We reached the main complex swiftly and the slave hurried in through a large set of doors that stood open despite the cold weather. I heard a brief murmur inside and then another functionary, this one wearing an expensive silk tunic, emerged.

'Please come in, Domina. If you would wait in the ante-chamber, I shall petition his Majesty for an audience on your behalf.'

I nodded and thanked the man, moving through the corridor and to the room he indicated. I had expected to fight and argue for such an audience. I had expected to be refused while the emperor wallowed in the dark, possibly tearing out his beautiful golden hair. What was I to expect now? I waited there for perhaps a quarter of an hour under the watchful eye of two more Praetorians. The focal point of the chamber was a grand statue of Hercules in painted marble. Was this who I had come to see? I wondered. Was my Herculean prince in residence, or was it the sorrowful young man who lived in the dark? He had been here for some time, after all, away from public eyes.

Finally, the man in the silk tunic returned and bade me follow him. I did so, through the labyrinthine villa and out into a small, well-tended courtyard garden. Across that space stood a high, curved wall. Moving around the outer edge, I could hear the sounds of blades clashing and the grunts of men exerting themselves. I shivered. A small amphitheatre, clearly, for private performances. Just being here took me straight back to that day when Commodus had almost died in the tunnels of just such a place. We reached a flight of steps and climbed into the light on a small arc of marble seats covered with plush red cushions.

I felt a surge of joint dismay and dislike to discover that the *cavea*'s only occupant was Bruttia Crispina. Why had the slave shown me to the empress? My gaze then slid to the arena itself and my eyes widened at the sight of Commodus engaged in combat with a gladiator in the armour of a murmillo.

I stopped and stared. He was the same Commodus I had always known, yet different. He had let his beard grow out; it was longer and curlier than his father's had been. Gone were the sallow complexion and black circles beneath the eyes I remembered from our last meeting, and which I'd expected to find. Instead, he looked bronzed and healthy, alert and alive – for now. His opponent's blade came for him and only failed to draw blood because the emperor pivoted lithely and danced out of the way. He was holding a spear and made to jab with it, then noticed me in the stands.

Commodus stopped, waving his opponent away. The murmillo bowed and retreated through a doorway, leaving us alone, or at least with only the empress. Commodus flashed me a smile and cast his spear. I marvelled at how straight and true it flew with such a negligent toss, striking one of the three targets set up at the far edge of the arena, almost centrally.

'Marcia,' he said, still smiling, and jogged over to the door at this side of the arena, opening it and climbing up to the stands. The weather was still chilly, and I was shivering, even little Bruttia was wrapped in a cloak. Not Commodus. Stripped to the waist, he wore only gauntlets and a loincloth, his skin slick with sweat, though starting to come up in gooseflesh now he had stopped exercising.

'Majesty,' I said politely as Bruttia smiled pleasantly at me with everything but her eyes. Here I was once again: a challenge to her primacy. She saw me as a threat, and that was without knowing how we had embraced . . . how close I had come to perhaps supplanting her.

'I was not expecting visitors.' He smiled.

'Clearly,' I noted with an arched eyebrow.

He laughed. 'I have been training for months. I'm getting rather good, if I say so myself.'

I shook my head. 'It is not . . . an emperor shouldn't . . .' I didn't quite know how to say it, but he laughed easily again.

'I know. You disapprove. So does Bruttia. Most of them do, in fact, but it's only exercise. No one minds if I run or swim, but somehow fighting is beneath me. I like it, though.'

He always did. I remembered him sparring as a child with Cleander in the palace. More, still: he had been reborn in the cauldron of the empire's strife. 'I am, it seems, made for war,' he had once told me in the cold and barren north.

'I am pleased,' I said, haltingly, 'and surprised, to find you so well.'

His look grew serious for a moment. 'I wasn't for some time after . . . you know. I was not myself. But Bruttia brought a lanista here and hired a stable of gladiators for the villa. I came to watch them more and more, and then eventually walked down among them. It is very liberating, fighting. I cannot express adequately how it has pulled me out of deep sadness.'

Good. I didn't particularly like him fighting, but he had found a way to lift himself back up where I could not. I tried not to admit that his wife had clearly had a large part in it. A

264

bell of warning chimed somewhere deep within as I remembered those days of his youth when he would be seized by excitement and explore dangerous pastimes with his brothers. Damn it, but I also had to admit that it had been Cleander who had tamed him then, honing those games into something less perilous.

'Do come inside,' he said, smiling again. 'Get yourself warm. You too, Bruttia. It's too cold out here for you.'

'I like the cold,' she replied lightly, eyes narrowing slightly as they passed over me. 'I think I shall take a walk. I will be along presently.'

Shrugging, Commodus gestured for me to descend the stairs. In a nearby room, he eschewed modesty entirely and put on his tunic in the room where I waited. I almost averted my eyes from his lithe and powerful form. Almost, but not quite. I suspect he caught me looking, for he smiled wickedly for just a moment before seriousness fell across him once more.

'Is too much fresh air bad for a woman's fertility?' he asked in a weirdly offhand way. His arms reached out in an oddly imploring fashion and for a moment I thought he might embrace me as he had once before. But no, that was not going to happen. This wasn't about me. This was about Bruttia, the witch that kept him from me.

I frowned. 'I have no idea, but I cannot imagine so. Why?' But even as I said it, I knew the answer, and my heart lurched, my blood turned to ice.

No. Do not make a child with that woman . . .

'Bruttia seems not to be fertile,' he replied. 'I wondered if it was to do with her obsession with being out in the cold air or something. It's not like we haven't tried.' He smoothed the clean tunic down over his perfect, perspiring form and grinned. 'Sometimes I try five times a night.'

Heartless bastard. Had he no idea how those words cut me? In my head, I drove daggers into the breast of Bruttia Crispina.

Then the reality of what he was saying hit me and I shivered in a manner that had nothing to do with the cold, remembering that lead tablet I had inscribed with a curse and pushed into the darkness. I had sweated over my guilt in that act ever since, and yet in my more bitter moments I found myself admitting that I would do it again in a heartbeat to keep her from being the mother of his child. I changed the subject rather bluntly.

'You should return to Rome,' I said.

'Why?'

He turned again, from where he'd been fastening his belt, with a look of genuine unconcern. My frown deepened. 'Because you are the emperor. Because the people think you have abandoned them. Perennis is running the empire on your behalf, and Eclectus is his secretary. That cannot go on.'

Commodus smiled. 'I see no reason why not. Perennis has the skill for it. I rule, but he governs. It is an excellent arrangement.'

'But it isn't,' I insisted. 'Perennis and the senate cannot get along. He is an equestrian. They do not respect him.'

'I am at best barely concerned with keeping the senate happy,' Commodus replied, his smile sliding away. 'Perennis likely treats them better than I would.'

'Nevertheless, you see a man governing for you, but the people will start to see you as Tiberius and Perennis as Sejanus. You must come back. Be your people's emperor again.'

'Come back to Rome for the summer? The season the rich and the noble leave the city for the countryside? Come, now, Marcia.'

I had to concede that. No one of note spent the summer in the city, after all. 'Then when summer ends. Come back for autumn.'

He laughed. 'I will consider it, though I am truly enjoying my time here. Will you stay with us? There is plenty of room.'

266

I almost snapped up the offer, before my imagination cursed me with thoughts of what it would be like sharing the place with Bruttia Crispina. Sharing *Commodus* with her. No, I had decided long ago that I could not do that. He would be all mine or not at all. A small, wicked, part of me noted how many would-be empresses had been cast aside by their husbands for not bearing an heir. Perhaps my curse had worked, and soon he would discard her. That brought a faintly wicked smile to my face, but I still could not stay there.

'No, Majesty. I will return to the palace. And I shall then eagerly await your return.'

I left the villa and the imperial couple in a flurry of mixed emotions. I had been expecting to find Commodus moping in the dark. Instead, I found him the true Hercules I knew lay inside. And in his mind he had not abandoned Rome, just left a skilled deputy running it. He would come back in the autumn, I was sure. So many things to be happy about. But the realisation that where it should have been me helping lift him from his misery it had been Bruttia soured the whole thing for me.

I returned to Rome for the summer. Now, in my boundless free time, I began to observe. Feeling rather better acquainted with Perennis, and somewhat pleased that his taking up of imperial authority had defanged Cleander, I took an interest. And given that I now knew Commodus was well, everything seemed a little brighter.

The people were still concerned about their emperor, but Perennis repeatedly announced largesse on behalf of Commodus, and this imperial generosity kept them relatively content. The senate continued to hold the prefect in low esteem, but few were willing to do more than mutter, given the immense power Perennis now wielded.

I noted over the summer months a number of arrests and

267

executions of influential nobles on various serious charges, and when I asked Eclectus about them, he confirmed only that appropriate evidence had been produced in each case. His expression, though, suggested something more, and a little investigation made it clear to me that the men who had died were uniformly those who had opposed Perennis at every turn. It was cruel, clearly. It was also expedient. Does the one make the other acceptable? For my own soul, I hope so.

It was September when the emperor returned to Rome. A messenger came ahead a few days earlier to warn the palace, and so the streets were lined with people cheering. Commodus appeared in style, preceded by his lictors, dressed in his most majestic garb and riding in a rich chariot, the empress in a litter behind him and Praetorians all around.

If Cleander had hoped that the emperor's return might mean an end to Perennis' supremacy and a return of his own authority, he was sadly mistaken. Commodus still had little intention of taking on the day-to-day administration of empire and continued to rely on the prefect for that. Instead, he took to being the *face* of empire, if not the voice. He began to hold the traditional evening dinner parties once more and to pay for, and attend, races in the circus and games in the amphitheatre, yet it continued to be Perennis who administered everything.

That October, during the festival of Jupiter Capitolinus and the associated games, the first figurative artillery shot was launched against the beleaguered prefect Perennis. We were gathered at the great theatre of Pompey in the Campus Martius to watch Hosidius Geta's latest masterpiece, *Arrius Varus*, the tale of a Praetorian prefect in the civil war a century ago, which had been playing to great appreciative crowds in Sicilia. The bulk of the attendees sat in the vast arc of tiered seats, though the emperor and his party were seated on plush couches in the orchestra. The empress was there, of course, as well as Eclectus, Cleander, Perennis, myself and several other people lucky enough to have been invited to sit with Commodus. Praetorians were everywhere, lining the orchestra, the highest tier, by every entrance and exit. After what had once almost happened in the great amphitheatre, the prefect was taking no chances of a repeat performance.

As I watched Cleander and Perennis glaring daggers at one another the way he and Saoterus used to do, two men scurried onto the stage and began to set a scene with furnishings and props. An emperor's luxurious apartment unfolded before our eyes to a gentle hum of conversation that filled the auditorium. The weather was chilly, though the sky remained clear and sprinkled with stars. Someone in the crowd exploded in a coughing fit and Commodus paused in his conversation with Perennis to turn and peer up into the seats. A man with a purple face was standing now, choking and waving his arms as friends tried to help him.

'Pray contain yourself, Aelius Rufus,' called the emperor with a quizzically tilted eyebrow. 'If the stage props have such an effect on you, I fear for your health when the real action begins.'

The crowd roared in appreciation as the man took his seat once more. Moments later, while the emperor and his prefect were still engaged in conversation, the chorus emerged from the wings and arranged themselves ready, four musicians moving to the side, preparing to issue a fanfare. They had barely started when a lone figure suddenly burst from one of the doors at the rear of the stage and ran forward, coming to a halt at the stage front.

I watched, rapt. I was not certain whether this was supposed to be part of the act. It seemed oddly out of place, but Hosidius Geta's work did have a reputation as being unpredictable and unusual. Certainly, the many Praetorians on duty had not reacted. The bearded, ragged-haired man on the stage was naked barring a loincloth, with a gnarled staff in his hand and a satchel over his shoulder.

The man threw out both arms wide in oratorical style and a murmur of excitement filled the crowd, Commodus exchanging a quiet joke with Cleander that sent the chamberlain off in fits of exaggerated laughter. With a sweep of an arm, the weird, half-naked man spoke.

'You come to see Praetorian fight Praetorian before the gates of Rome. You come to celebrate the great festival of Jupiter.' His sweeping arm became a pointing finger now, jabbing towards the emperor. 'But, great Commodus, son of Aurelius, this is no time to celebrate such festivals with the serpents of your court.'

Commodus' expression shifted between a smile and a frown, and Perennis' face suggested that something was wrong. A whistle shrieked above the seats and Praetorians were moving now, converging on the stage. Those soldiers with us in the orchestra were moving too, ready to defend their master.

'Majesty,' the man went on, watching the Praetorians closing on him from all sides, 'the blade of the snake Perennis sits at your throat! The danger is not in your provinces, Emperor of Rome. Not in Britannia, or Dacia or Hispania. It is by your side, and death will stalk and take you if you do not heed the warnings.'

Praetorians were on the stage now and running for the man. I sat, as rapt as any play might make me. Oddly, there did not seem to be much danger. This may be unplanned, but the man was unarmed apart from a stick, and seemed to be shouting words of warning and support for the emperor, rather than threats.

As the Praetorians reached the bearded man, he made one last impassioned speech, pulling away from men trying to grasp him, pointing still at Commodus. 'Majesty, your prefect fills his own coffers and raises an army to unseat you. Already his sons command the swelling armies of Pannonia, and his favourite equestrians take control of the legions in Britannia.'

White-clad soldiers now had him and forced him down to the stage, ripping the staff away. The man must have been stronger than he looked, for he tore himself free for a moment and lurched to his knees.

'Act or die, Commodus. Act or die.'

That was the last he said, as he disappeared beneath a pile of Praetorians, who dragged him from the stage, leaving a bloody trail. I turned to the others beside me. Commodus was staring in shock, then spun to look at his Praetorian prefect, who had gone puce with rage. As the emperor reached out to steady Perennis, nothing but disbelief in his eyes, I caught sight of Cleander behind him, and I knew in that moment that the chamberlain was behind this. I had no idea how, but somehow the snake had engineered this accusation, which I found impossible to credit.

One glance around the theatre told me I was in the minority. The people of Rome had been watching the prefect ruling them and occasionally doing away with difficult senators while their emperor languished in exquisite exile. Now they saw him as a new Sejanus. It mattered not whether the accusation was true or false, for the damage had been done. Doubt would flood outwards through the city and the empire like the ripples from a stone cast into a pond.

I fumed and deliberated that night. Back in the safety of my quiet apartment, I decided I wanted to save Perennis from what seemed to be lurking in his future. He was innocent, but his reputation had been tarnished, possibly irreparably. Cleander was so clearly behind it, but only he and I knew that, and I had not a jot of evidence. I was more than tempted to go to Commodus and tell him what I thought, but finally reasoned the move would be foolish. Cleander was a master of manipulation, and the emperor knew how much we disliked one another. Commodus would be unlikely to give credence to my theory, and voicing it would give Cleander new ammunition to use in his war against any who might oppose him.

I spoke to Eclectus and aired my concerns. Even he was doubtful, and he had always been one of those few to whom I felt close.

Winter came, and as the days rolled by I watched Perennis' reputation turn to ashes in the fire of public condemnation. It transpired that the prefect's two sons were indeed in command of Pannonia now, and they were certainly militarily strong, though there seemed to be no evidence of wrongdoing, just mile upon mile of suspicion and accusation.

The prefect's authority more or less collapsed. Even his own Praetorians began to turn on him.

Then came the final hammer blow. During the spring a small force of soldiers arrived at the palace, disarmed, of course, and travel-worn. They were led by a provincial officer and claimed to be from some cohort stationed in far-off Britannia. What they did have, and I have no idea how they acquired them, was a large number of coins stamped with the likeness of Perennis, portraying him as an emperor.

Perennis was dumbfounded, and vehement in his denial. He had never seen them before and most certainly had not commissioned them. I believed him. I think that even then, with the evidence mounting against him, Commodus believed him too. But the pressure to deal with the powerful prefect had risen to a critical point. The senators universally called for his prosecution and now the ordinary populace gathered daily outside the palace walls, demanding that the prefect be brought to justice.

I met Perennis for the final time on that same balcony, over-looking the Circus Maximus, he again with a cup of wine, I with a sad expression. I had only known Perennis for four years, since that first attempt on the emperor's life in the amphitheatre, and yet in that short time I had come to see him as an honourable and noble man, with more grace in his soul than almost any of those who called for his head, and certainly far better than the man I was sure had somehow engineered the soldiers and the coins. Few men could manage to arrange for the minting of coins, and even fewer had the skill and the guts to cover their tracks and bare-face their way out of it.

'This was all Cleander,' I said with a sigh, leaning on the rail.

'Of that I am certain,' he replied. 'I have done what I can to protect my family. With luck, they will escape the worst of what is about to happen. A man should never see his sons die.'

I tried to say something, but choked. I had no words.

'When my head rolls down those steps and the crowd tears me apart, be watchful, Marcia. Cleander is on the cusp of true power. He will find a way to slip into my position, mark my words. He can never hope to rise higher than my post, but I guarantee that his sights will fall there.'

I felt a chill at that thought. Cleander in command of the Praetorians? Could such a thing be imaginable? A man who had once been a slave, sweeping the floors of the Palatine, aiming for such a lofty position?

'And if he manages it, then only the emperor will have the authority to oppose him. Eclectus will be his next victim. Eclectus or you.'

Again, I shivered. Cleander had threatened to see me fall since we were children, but then it was a threat I had also flung at him. Was that to be the way of it, then? The two of us locked in a secret duel until only one remained?

Perennis died the next day, just as he'd predicted, his head separated from his body and the remains cast down the Gemonian Stairs into the hungry crowd. Commodus wept when he sealed the order, but seal it he did, and with it the fate of the empire.

XV

GOD'S PLAN

Rome, AD 185

War.

This time not against Parthians or Germanic savages. This time against a wily serpent in whose lair we all slept. And this time not with a gathering of legions under an emperor, but me, and me alone. A secret war, but one that I had known was both impending and unavoidable. Cleander had systematically removed his opposition in his rise to power. In the twenty years I had now known him, he had climbed from a lowly palace slave, cleaning latrines and up to his elbows in shit, to the lofty heights of the emperor's chamberlain and senior palace functionary. Now, men, women and children who served on the Palatine and across Rome lived or died at his whim. Such power for someone of such humble origins. The great Marcus Aurelius, I suspect, would have been appalled to see it.

Commodus was not. Like Verus before him, he saw the value in freedmen who had no power base to strengthen, and shunned the senate, who tended to disagree and argue with his decisions. Commodus, of course, could not see the stair that Cleander had ascended and planned yet to climb – an impressive gradient built upon the backs of those of whom he casually disposed.

I knew he was behind the death of his first great opponent,

Saoterus, even though I had no proof of it. I knew that he had been instrumental in the fall of Perennis. I wonder to this day how many of those who perished in the aftermath of Lucilla's plot were simply innocents that Cleander saw as obstacles in his path. And now that I was paying attention, I noted that perhaps a dozen, even a score, of the palace staff that Eclectus and I had considered trustworthy had gone. Undoubtedly the work of Cleander, clearing out those who might stand against him. Now, all eyes and ears on the Palatine belonged to the chamberlain. It was a dangerous place to be.

But chamberlain clearly was not the apex for which Cleander strove. He saw himself more powerful still than that. The death of the Praetorian prefect Perennis, along with that of his colleague Paternus a few years earlier, left the most powerful non-senatorial positions in the empire open. As emperor, it was Commodus' right to appoint the Praetorian prefects. As a man reliant upon his freedmen, though, Commodus simply accepted the names Cleander provided and placed them in power. Thus did a former slave appoint his own creatures to command the emperor's guard.

As the months rolled past following Perennis' death, I watched with horror as strand after strand in the web of power fell into Cleander's hands, and all with the emperor's blessing. By the winter of that year, senatorial appointments were only likely with Cleander's favour. He controlled the careers of half of Rome, and the important, the rich and the influential all came to owe the chamberlain. He also became rich, unsurprisingly.

Eclectus and I, as the only two people in the palace who saw what Cleander was doing and claimed a resolve to stop it, began to conspire. Our first move was to try and halt the serpent's influence with the emperor. We both secured audiences with Commodus. I have no idea what transpired between the emperor and his secretary, but when he returned to his rooms,

Eclectus wore a face like thunder. He had been removed from his position and left the palace forthwith to retire to a small estate outside Rome. I had no chance to speak to him beyond one brief exchange as he left.

'Watch your back, Marcia,' my friend had said. 'Cleander pulls the strings now to make the emperor dance.'

'Impossible,' I replied, remembering the golden prince I had always known, ever a man of his own mind.

'Yet the government and the military both now answer to the chamberlain and his honeyed words sooth the emperor. Be careful.'

And then he was gone. Cleander had removed another obstacle, and I could only be grateful that Eclectus had simply retired, rather than meeting the edge of a blade.

My audience with Commodus was no better. Worse, in fact, in so many ways. I managed to secure the most private audience possible in these troubled times, which meant that only half a dozen other pairs of ears were present. I chose a time when I knew Cleander would be absent from the palace. Instead, I met Commodus under the gaze of Atilius Aebutianus, Cleander's pet Praetorian prefect, Iphiclus, the new secretary, also appointed by Cleander, and four Praetorian soldiers.

I had to be careful. Cleander knew I both hated and opposed him, and undoubtedly his attention would soon turn to me after he had removed anyone more immediately troublesome, but at that time he was busying himself with others. To directly accuse him would be to draw his gaze and climb the ladder of his targets.

'Marcia,' Commodus greeted me in a warm, friendly manner.

'Majesty.' Those old emotions came flooding back in. I missed this glorious golden man, this new Hercules. I missed his company and his easy laugh. I missed his humour and his excitement. He looked well. In fact, he looked as untroubled as I had ever seen him, and with that realisation a number of things fell into place.

Commodus had allowed Cleander the latitude he had because Cleander removed from his master all the cares of empire, just as Perennis had done before him. Commodus was a good man, and clever for sure, but he cared more for the excitement of command than its administration and detail. By gathering power, Cleander was making life carefree for the emperor.

'It has been too long,' Commodus said, a smile creasing that handsome face between his moustache and a beard that was now bushy and golden, well-tended and luxuriant.

I nodded. It had. We were not close as once we were. Partially he was kept from me by the chamberlain, and partially Bruttia Crispina, who remained a barrier between us. Yet I still longed to spend time in his company.

'The business of empire keeps you busy, Majesty,' I said. A prompt. A probe.

'The empire is in safe hands with Cleander at the steering oars. I have my own focus. The succession. Marcia, the empress is with child.'

The bottom fell out of my world. Everything I had come to say drifted away like smoke in a breeze. A child? I suppose I ought to have been relieved that the lead curse I had cast those years ago clearly had not worked, but in my shrivelling heart, at that moment I truly wished it had. I had never liked Bruttia Crispina, and she had shown that she too could be barbed in her disdain for me, but now she rose to become an enemy of import, on a par perhaps with Cleander himself. He merely wanted power. Bruttia wanted my prince.

'Congratulations,' was all I could manage in a strangled voice.

'You are not . . . pleased?'

How to tell him? Surely, he knew?

'That you have an heir? The whole empire will rejoice, Majesty.'

But his eyes cut through such dissembling. He knew I loved him. And beneath all this imperial pomp and façade, he loved me still. His gaze told me everything I needed to know. He had been obsessively focused on the succession to the exclusion of all else. He was the first emperor born to the purple in a century and was determined that he would not be the last.

'You wanted to see me about something important?' he asked, changing the subject, much to my relief.

I was horribly aware of the ears and eyes all around me. 'I happened to meet Pompeianus,' I said. It was untrue. I'd not seen Pompeianus for years, but I knew that he had retired to an estate in the country, out of sight of his enemies, and that therefore no one would be able to deny it conclusively. And I needed a respected name that carried weight. Pompeianus may have been Lucilla's husband, but it had been clear that he was not involved in the conspiracy, and in fact had detested his wife as much as she detested him, and no stigma had attached to him. He had simply seen the direction the capital was taking and had removed himself from danger.

'A good man,' the emperor nodded.

Yes. And one of the few Cleander had not yet removed.

'I wondered why a man of his talent and loyalty is not in the senate, backing your decisions, Majesty. When I mentioned such a thing to him, he trotted out a list of names he felt would be much more advantageous in the senate than he. Yet, to my confusion, none of those names are among that august body.' All lies. All my imaginings, but enough to make him think. 'Nonius Macrinus, Saturninus, Julianus, Pertinax?' I went on. Men who had been loyal and whom Commodus respected. Men who had been bright enough to retire or seek appointment somewhere outside Cleander's current reach. Men Cleander would hate to see in the senate.

Commodus nodded, his brow folded. 'Interesting. Yes, such

279

men should be helping guide the ship of state. I shall speak to Cleander.'

Damn it. So carefully constructed a plan demolished so simply. But I had no argument against it that would not work its way straight back to the chamberlain via one of those listening, so I simply had to accept that as I had accepted the news of Bruttia Crispina, with iron discipline and a mask of content.

The rest of my meeting was cut short by a rap at the door. Commodus, frowning, gave the guard a nod and the portal was opened. Cleander strode into the room with a sharp bow. He was supposed to be in Ostia. Surely the man couldn't have heard I was to see the emperor and rushed back? But that was not the case, for as the snake's gaze took in my presence it registered passing surprise before he painted me out of his mental picture.

'Majesty, there are grave tidings from Gaul.'

I stepped aside. This sounded important, and there were still things that might have to take precedence over the war between Cleander and myself.

'What is it?'

'The reports we've had of the rise in banditry across Gaul turn out to be well founded. It would appear that these so-called "bandits" are, in fact, a strong group of military deserters, led by a former officer. More, in fact, of a criminal army than mere bandits. They are not simply preying on merchants on the road, but interfering with the administration of the province, endangering our control. I seek imperial permission to send the general Pescennius Niger with a force of men to clear up the mess?'

Commodus nodded, and I swiftly ran through names in my head. Among those we had discussed, Eclectus and I, Niger was one we had attached to Cleander. A man either in the chamberlain's pay or in his debt. I could see danger in this, though I was not sure how.

The emperor nodded. His gaze flashed to me. Names I had mentioned as absent from the senate were clearly circling in his mind. Great military men like Pompeianus. 'Granted,' he replied to Cleander. 'And have Pertinax assigned also. He has been in Britannia for some months now and his experience will be invaluable in putting down these deserters.'

I could see the disappointment in Cleander's eyes that the emperor had interfered in his affairs when all he'd expected was to be given blank permission to do as he pleased. Whatever his plans for Niger, they would probably be scuppered by the introduction of Pertinax into the scene. Cleander's gaze fell upon me, and it was clear that he suspected my influence somehow. I smiled sweetly at him, which made his face sour further.

I left them to it. There was little I could do now with the chamberlain present.

Bitterly, I departed the room and exited into the corridor outside. My mood, already black, became positively Stygian as I turned to see the pretty, diminutive figure of Bruttia Crispina pass by. She flashed me a look of unbearable smugness, laced with cold dislike.

In that particular moment I would have dropped a thousand lead curses into the darkness and prayed to Hekate in defiance of my faith. The hate bloomed as it had when I had first been told about her and had smashed that bust of Quadratus' cousin.

Unbidden, brief flashes of memory popped into my head, images of my time with Quadratus. The pit of hell opened in my heart at the realisation that she was growing poor Commodus' child inside that tiny belly, while all my withered womb had carried was the offspring of my abuser . . . until it had been forced from me. A frisson ran through my womb and for one tiny moment I think I felt God's plan being enacted about me. How else might I explain a memory so disconnected and yet so influential filling my mind at that very moment.

I had been planning to return to my rooms for *prandium*, the noon meal, which was undoubtedly where Bruttia was also bound. Moments later I was instead hurrying through the palace into its bowels. The kitchens of the Palatine were a complex rarely visited by anyone other than slaves. The residents of the palace proper would have little idea where the kitchens were, let alone what went on in them. Not I. As the daughter of a freedwoman, I had had the run of such places in my youth, and from my time among Quadratus' household, I knew their ways well. I knew the kitchens and the storerooms – had hidden in them so many times during games of hide and find.

I reached them already out of breath. I had a plan, born of that awful knowledge that she carried the child that should have been mine, while I had been forced to abort the one that should not. It was a wicked plan, but had not the very notion come to me in an epiphany? With every step I had run, my heart switched back and forth between horrified disbelief at what I planned and a strangely calm acceptance that somehow God had planted the idea in me as part of his grand plan. Commodus may be a pagan, but perhaps God's ineffable strategy did not involve the offspring of the imperial couple. Certainly mine did not.

Timing mattered. I found the specific kitchen where the meals for the emperor and empress were being prepared without difficulty. Their lunches were, naturally, prepared separately from any others, and the emperor's food taster was employed there to check each ingredient before they were added. I arrived at the most fortuitous moment. Lunch was largely prepared, and the taster had already done his work on each individual foodstuff, confirming that the meals were safe. Commodus might well have the taster in attendance once more at his side during the meal, but it mattered not. It was not his food that I sought to alter, and it would do him no harm anyway. Now the two platters sat waiting on a table while the slaves and the taster moved to another room to check the wine that was to be served. Beside the platters were four small bowls of herbs and spices waiting to be applied. They had probably already been tested, but it mattered not, in truth. I was not going to try anything that would show up on the palate of a food taster.

I had initially thought of oysters. But over and above the fact that such a thing would be rather difficult to administer unnoticed, I still felt uncomfortable causing more pain than necessary in the process – perhaps an echo of my Christian upbringing. And, in truth, despite her attitude and the chasm that lay between Bruttia and I, I did not want to *kill* her, but she must not be allowed to carry my children.

You may remember that following my own horrific and painful abortion, I had done my research. Raw oysters were a good bet, but they only removed the babe by poisoning the mother. I needed to be much subtler than that.

Silphium, though . . .

Silphium was used in medicinal compounds by midwives who needed to abort a pregnancy, partially because it was one of the most effective methods, partially because it did the least damage to the mother, and partially because it could be ingested without trouble, since it was a common seasoning in the kitchen, often used interchangeably with coriander.

All I had to do was stop the offspring, not poison the mother.

The shelves of seasonings, spices and herbs were mere feet away, since they were the final thing applied to a dish. It was the work of mere moments to swap the small bowl of coriander on the table by the plates with a similar one of silphium, handily labelled such on the shelf. I was gone before the slaves and the taster returned. It had all taken less than twenty heartbeats.

I waited for the Guard to come and arrest me, though realistically, even if anyone discovered what had happened, how they could have learned who was responsible, I know not. But guilt and fear when hand in hand make a powerful couple, and so I cowered in my room.

Nothing came of it. In fact, when I tentatively struck up a conversation with one of the cooks the following day, it transpired that the empress had complimented the kitchens on one of the best meals she had tasted in some time.

I struggled then with the morality of what I had done. It took a while this time for me to squarely lay the blame with the divine plan, but lay it there I did. And consequently, over the next eight days, I made the most of my relationship with the servants and my understanding of the workings of the kitchens. Despite the danger and difficulties of doing so, I managed to add silphium to two more meals.

Bruttia Crispina miscarried in her sixth month. I felt wretched. I spent hours on my knees in the privacy of my own room seeking God's forgiveness. But while I felt terrible at what I had done, and in form I repented, in my heart I knew that I would not have undone it if I could.

'God has a plan for the world,' I told myself, wondering how long I would continue to believe it.

'Does God plan for his people to poison one another? Is the mindful murder of the unborn part of his plan?' the shade of my mother asked.

'What must be, must be,' I replied. 'Perhaps it is not God's will that the empress bear Commodus a child.'

No. For that was *my* job and mine alone . . .

A miscarriage was unfortunate but would have no comeback for anyone else.

Commodus grieved, and Cleander had no idea how to handle this particular development. Consequently, there I was once again when my golden prince plummeted into misery and needed me. Bruttia Crispina was mercifully absent in the month or two that followed, undertaking a protracted visit to the sanctuary of Venus on Cyprus, island of the fertility goddess' birth, in an effort to seek her blessing on a restored womb.

During her absence I visited Commodus often and, though Cleander tried to find ways to prevent it, he failed, for the emperor sought my company now. My tarnished soul glowed with satisfaction. I was close to Commodus, had temporarily ousted Cleander, had ended the empress' pregnancy and perhaps even put doubt in her husband's mind.

I am not proud of what I became that year on the Palatine, but I have heard it said that creatures adapt to their habitat as required for survival, and that is precisely what I did. To supplant Bruttia Crispina I devalued her worth, and to play the game against Cleander I became as devious as he, and as unrepentantly unprincipled.

I began to build a clientele of my own, as though I were some senatorial patriarch. Where a nobleman would hold a grand morning *salutatio* and hear the petitions of his clients, I did so whenever was convenient and in secret. Just as Cleander openly sold positions to those who sought them, so I sought favour with the emperor for those who needed it. I started to find allies. Despite Cleander's efforts to remove all opposition, there were men in Rome, even rich and important ones, who despised the chamberlain. And when I gained their confidence, they could often point me in the direction of other such men.

I found Laetus, a centurion in the Praetorian Guard who hated Cleander and feared him taking the reins of the Guard. And Laetus introduced me to one of the Praetorian prefects, Rufus, who had been installed in that position by Cleander but had since grown to dislike and fear his benefactor. Arrius Antoninus and Antistius Burrus, two men of senatorial rank who saw Cleander as the nadir of everything they believed in, to such an extent that they were willing to submit to the will of a pleb like me if it meant the possible fall of the chamberlain.

More, still. I was introduced to Papirius Dionysius, who was one of the more important wheels in the machine of state, as well as Rufinus, the prefect of the Misenum Fleet, and Nicomedes, the *Praefectus Vehiculorum*, who controlled the courier service across the empire. I discovered the fierce general Septimius Severus. Men of strength and importance, each of whom loathed Cleander.

Some were desperate to act, others more patient. I knew Cleander well enough to not try anything too precipitous, and plans began to be made by men I trusted. In a way, it was I who had brought them together, who became the linchpin.

Only once did all my web of conspirators meet in the same place, for to do so was to invite disaster, but it had become necessary to pool our thoughts and settle upon a path. It was that one time that polarised the gathering. We chose our time and location carefully. Thanks to my contacts among the Praetorians, we made sure that Cleander and his pet officers were well out of the way, dealing with some issue in Ostia. We could not meet on the Palatine, or anywhere central, clearly. I know not how the others slipped away from their roles and made their way, but for me, I claimed to be visiting my Christian brethren for a baptismal ceremony. It is amazing how one disappears from people's notice the moment the faith crops up. Before I left, I saw Laetus speaking quietly to two of his men and the pair left the palace in my wake, providing much-needed protection. I silently thanked him for that. Just in case, I did actually visit one of our gatherings in the city, made brief prayers with them, and then slipped out among the crowd and moved off up the slopes of the Aventine, trying not to look suspicious. The two Praetorians had vanished during my prayers, though I suspected they were still out there, somewhere, watching me on Laetus' orders.

Few experiences in my life set me as on edge as moving through the dangerous and plague-ridden streets of Rome at night. Every alley seemed filled with disease and peril, and every figure who passed me felt like a robber or rapist just waiting for someone like me. I suspect that I would have swiftly given up my surreptitious journey and fled back to the safety of my rooms, but I had the inescapable feeling that I was still being protected as I walked. Not the all-pervading and ethereal protection of the Lord, either, but the very real presence of those Praetorian allies watching my back. Nevertheless, I was immensely relieved when I reached my destination.

The warehouse, one of many identical buildings atop that hill, belonged to a client of Antistius Burrus, and several others were already there, suspicious, eyeing one another warily, when I entered. Some of their nerves dissipated with my arrival, but it was the appearance of Prefect Rufus who took most of the tension from the air. Somewhat unfairly, I believe, since it was I who had threaded this web together.

I could see how things would go even as the various remaining members drifted in and took a seat. They might not have noticed, but I had talked to all these men individually, and I knew which ones favoured immediate and brutal action, and which preferred a slow, cautious approach. The two groups had coalesced to face one another without any intentional plan.

As Senator Antistius closed and locked the door, hired men of his in a cordon around the building to make sure we were neither disturbed nor overheard, I looked at Rufus, who shrugged and gestured back at me.

I rose.

'I see no reason to tread lightly around matters. We all know why we are here, and we may as well now speak openly of it. If our enemy's spies are at work, then we are already doomed.'

There was an uneasy nod of acknowledgement around me.

Some of these men were happy with me speaking to them, but I could see the misogynist tendencies rising. I was the source of this meeting, and the only person in the room they had all spoken to, yet I was both a pleb and a woman, and there was little chance of my controlling a room of powerful men.

'Cleander has to be removed from power,' I said, flatly, hoping the basic raw truth might cut through and bring things to order. Instead, half the room perhaps nodded, while the other half looked uncomfortable and unhappy with me. I sighed. Sometimes things were better done through an intermediary. We all knew why we were here, so I nodded at Laetus, who smiled apologetically, and rose.

'Friends, we cannot afford to tarry here longer than necessary. Any of us could be missed and cause concern. The reason we are here is to discern a way to bring about that which we all desire.'

'Carefully,' came a response in a deep, powerful tone. The whole room looked across at Septimius Severus, who sat with folded arms, the young naval prefect Rufinus on one side and the gaunt figure of Papirius Dionysius on the other. The triad looked odd together, but they represented what I saw as perhaps the subtlest men in the room.

'No one ever butchered an animal carefully,' Senator Arrius snorted.

'You have clearly never seen a butcher at work,' Severus replied. 'There are many ways to go about this, but we have to consider the results of everything we do. A knife in the dark has several disadvantages. Firstly, if it fails, it opens up all those involved to scrutiny, and I suspect none of us wants that. Secondly, it requires putting all our faith into the hand that wields the blade, and if the empress' conspiracy against her brother taught us anything, it should be that such a choice is foolish. Thirdly, if it succeeds, then it is simply a murder, and not *justice*.

As such, there would have to be an investigation and culprits found and dealt with.'

Prefect Rufus shook his head. 'It is considerably more black and white than you suggest, Severus. You'd be surprised what the Guard has witnessed. How then would you go about this?'

'Carefully,' repeated Severus. 'Take note of Perennis' fall. He died by the emperor's own will, despite the fact that the emperor believed him innocent and counted him a friend. His power and respect were gradually whittled away beneath him by a cunning opponent, leaving him perilously balanced and awaiting a simple push to fall. This is how Cleander needs to be dealt with.'

'Severus,' one of the senators put in, 'every day Cleander gains more power and targets more enemies. If we do not act soon, it will be us under the sword and all will come to naught.'

'Act too precipitously and you invite defeat,' Severus replied. 'I suspect I am the only one here who has fought a war. Believe me when I say everything needs to be carefully co-ordinated. Rushing off to find a knifeman is idiotic.'

But it was clear from the senator's manner that he disagreed. Prefect Rufus was the one to voice the last.

'I have no stomach for conspiracy and clandestine meetings. I favour a simple fight. Looking down my blade at my enemy.' The two senators at his side nodded.

My gaze raked the gathering. I could see it polarising as I watched, like cream separating. As if to draw a vote, Severus rose, arms still folded. 'I have a number of ideas. The fleet play a part in it. Dionysius here has a role, I think. It will take a good time to put things in place, but I can expound upon my plan as it forms, and include all of you who wish to play your part. Those who do not want to be involved need to stay well clear, for the more voices in a conspiracy, the more chance of someone being overheard. Do I presume that you gentlemen wish to have no part?'

His gaze fell upon Rufus and the two senators, who rose and stood together in a group. Rufus, as Praetorian prefect, looked pointedly at his centurion Laetus, but the latter simply shook his head sadly, and came to stand by my side. Rufus rumbled his disapproval. 'You may feel free to play what games you wish, Severus, but there shall be no acknowledgement of your value when we plant a blade in Cleander's neck.'

'Good,' the bearded African responded. 'Be certain, when you fail, to keep any name from your lips, no matter how many fingernails they pull out.'

I saw the naval commander, Rufinus, wince next to him, yet he stood staunchly by Severus' side. Nicomedes, the master of the couriers, dithered uncertainly for a time, and then paced over to Severus. Two groups. And, by the looks of it, two plots. I sighed, but before I or Laetus could try and reconcile matters, Prefect Rufus threw out a finger at the men on the far side of the room. 'The same goes for you. While you plot and plan like low criminals, remember to keep our names out of your workings.'

And with that the three men left, and I was alone with the others. Beside me, Laetus cleared his throat. 'Do you think it can be done?'

Severus nodded. 'But I think the fewer people involved, the better. You are daily among the Guard, which contains not only Cleander's men but also Rufus'. Bend all your own time to staying safe and out of matters. And the lady here? She is far too central to power to be personally involved. Cleander already hates her. Domina, you must, like Laetus, look to your own safety.'

And that was that. The conspirators I had brought together had gone two separate ways, and neither of them included me. I returned to the palace filled with a nervy mix of fear and hope.

As the year wore on, Commodus, having much recuperated from the sadness of losing a potential heir, recovered his spirit and, irritatingly, began to spend more time with his freshly returned and newly purposeful wife again. I would normally have truly hated that, but such were my machinations now against Cleander that I was grateful for the time to devote to my own care.

The seasons turned again and in the spring there was much rejoicing as Bruttia Crispina announced in close circles that she was pregnant again. God forgive me, I actually almost repeated my dreadful deed, but I was already deep enough in a moral mire, and I trusted to God now to see me through. After all, if it had been God's great plan that her first pregnancy fail, then surely the same would hold true now.

It was in the late summer of the year of the consuls Aurelius and Glabrio that the empress miscarried again. I had not realised how soul-sick I had been over what I had done the first time until I discovered that, in fact, it *had* been God's plan. He had simply used me as a tool of His divine will. This time there had been complications, and Bruttia Crispina almost joined her unborn child in crossing the final river. The physician gingerly admitted to the emperor that if Bruttia were ever to fall pregnant again, he would be astonished, for he believed this latest disaster had left her barren. I spent the winter consoling Commodus and attempting to keep him from the darkness into which he repeatedly threatened to slip. I was failing. I noticed cracks appearing in his soul. His melancholia took a new and worrying turn, slipping occasionally into a dark rage, sometimes directed at himself, sometimes directed at whatever or whoever was in front of him.

And when I failed, Cleander was there, like the serpent he was. Where I tried to bring my golden emperor back to the light with gentle encouragement and nurturing, the despicable chamberlain discovered another way to haul Commodus from the dark: playing to his excesses, urging him to feats of almost manic folly. I tried to argue, but my voice was lost sometimes in the glee.

Saturnalia passed and proved not to be the bright festival it usually was. Winter turned into spring once more, and then, without warning and entirely unexpectedly, the plotting senators and the prefect made their move. Unfortunately for them, they had made the mistake of letting their plans be known among the more disaffected of the senate.

I was in the aula regia along with numerous other hopefuls, waiting for a chance to speak to the emperor, when the plot erupted into disaster. Commodus had just entered and taken his seat, murmuring to the *ad admissionibus*, who would have the list of those wishing to be heard, when the doors thumped open unexpectedly and most improperly.

Commodus looked up in surprise and the entire waiting crowd turned even as the hand of every Praetorian in the room went to his sword hilt. In the doorway stood the toga-clad and ashen-faced figure of Publius Seius Fuscianus, the urban prefect, whose soldiers policed the city of Rome. The Praetorians tensed, for there has ever been a rivalry between these two branches of the military, but Fuscianus was a commander, appointed by the throne, and so he entered unmolested, two of his men in his wake.

'Dismiss these people,' he barked at the nearest Praetorian, whose face reflected what he thought of being ordered around by the urban cohorts. Ignoring both Praetorians and civilians further, Fuscianus closed on the throne. Soldiers moved protectively close to Commodus, but he motioned for them to disperse a little as the urban prefect approached and dropped respectfully to a knee.

'I bear critical tidings, Majesty.'

Commodus frowned, but motioned for the prefect to stand. 'Go on?'

'I regret to inform you of a plot against the throne.'

My heart lurched at the words. Had we been discovered? Our meeting in that warehouse? Was my web of plotters unravelled? I almost ran. In fact, I actually began to slip through the shocked attendees, making subtly for the door, sure that my life would be forfeit any moment.

'Two senators, Majesty.'

I paused. Two senators? And had I been under suspicion, surely soldiers would have me by the arms even now? I forced myself to stay calm, relax, watch, act as shocked and horrified as everyone else.

Commodus chewed his lip. 'Two senators?'

'Yes, Majesty. Two of those who I suspect might be tied to the web her Majesty Lucilla wove years ago. Arrius Antoninus and Antistius Burrus. Their conspiracy was reported through trustworthy sources, Majesty. I have spoken to the Praetorian prefect and his men are already on the way to arrest them.'

Commodus shook his head. 'But I barely even know them. What could they have against me?'

'Praetorian knives will clarify that in good time, Majesty,' the prefect said with vicious certainty. Once more my heart thundered. Torture. Under torture those two men might reveal any number of co-conspirators, even down to a well-dressed Christian who had slipped into a warehouse on the Aventine. Even as the prefect explained what had happened to the emperor, in my head I was racing through my alibis, working out how to deny any involvement.

Something was clearly wrong with the discovery anyway, for I above all knew that the two senators held nothing but loyalty to the emperor, and that it was Cleander they sought to destroy. But how could I explain this without causing my own downfall.

No. Deniability. That was all that mattered now.

I waited until the emperor confirmed that the morning session was cancelled. So busy was he that I do not think he ever even noticed I was present among the rest. The Praetorians ushered us out, and as the crowd was escorted from the palace, I found myself drawn aside.

Laetus, the centurion of the Guard who had also been present at our clandestine meeting, pulled me close. 'All is in hand. Do not worry, and do not show weakness or guilt.'

And with that he was gone.

Not exhibiting guilt was difficult. Over the proceeding days, the backlash from the uncovered plot caused vast commotion, and I did all I could to appear totally loyal and almost as totally invisible.

Laetus had been correct, though. He had known in advance. Those named by the senators in that first night of torture were other patrician conspirators of whom I was unaware, and each and every one had managed to open his veins and bleed out before the Praetorians came for them. Worse still, or perhaps *better* for me, the men in charge of extracting information proved to be overzealous, and the two senators died quickly in the Palatine cellars before any truly dangerous names could escape their lips.

The Praetorian prefect Rufus was reprimanded harshly for his utter failures in carrying out his investigations. He bowed out in disgrace, resigning his commission and disappearing into private life. He had failed in his job, but only I and the other conspirators would ever know just how much he had done to save us all and himself.

It was disheartening, but hardly unexpected, what happened next. Despite carefully worded warnings from the more sensible in the court, Commodus sanctioned Cleander moving into the role of Praetorian prefect. The second most powerful man in Rome after the emperor doubled his influence and strength. The other prefect, Aebutianus, was removed as unsuitable, despite having done nothing wrong, and Cleander appointed two mindless lackeys as co-prefects beneath him.

We approached the winter of the year with Cleander seemingly all-powerful. He now controlled the palace, the imperial bodyguard, had impressive influence over the army, and had put his own creatures in most positions of power in the administration. He was untouchable.

I still had my friends, and they remained confident as their plans moved towards fruition, but I could no longer see how a few minor officials, an admiral and a former general could possibly stand a chance against Cleander and his ever-growing web.

I could do little to help them and had to trust in their plans. Instead, I moved on to my next plot. Any hope of a natural imperial succession having ended, now I had to remove Bruttia Crispina from the picture entirely.

XVI

ADOPTING DISGUISES

Rome, AD 187

I came close to ruining the emperor that year, or at least the unhealthy combination of Cleander and I did. Beset by political issues such as the army of deserters in Gaul that continued to cause trouble, plagued by the loss of now two potential heirs and the prospect of a barren wife, Commodus sank repeatedly into bleak misery, buoyed up with my careful ministrations on the occasions I could get to him, but more often carried to heights of pleasure by the chamberlain – *Cleander's* antidote. At his bidding, Commodus would hold great drunken parties in the baths and invite only those people he considered 'fun'. He would lock himself away in the circus with the green team and race chariots, drunk as a Gaulish poet. He was becoming visibly out of control, while clearly *in* the control of his own chamberlain. Once, all those years ago on the high wall with little Annius, it had been only the guiding hand of Cleander that kept him from falling. As I had been the woman to keep the prince from the depths of gloom, so Cleander had been the man to keep his potential excess in check. It seemed that was no longer possible. Now, Cleander simply urged him on. *My* Commodus was the golden prince who held so much promise. The one Cleander was slowly promoting was the sweat-soaked gladiator emperor I had met at the Quintilii villa, and I was not sure that I liked this new Commodus.

While I worried about him, I felt a little like a gladiator myself, beset from all sides and parrying blow after blow. For Commodus was not Cleander's sole concern. My return to the imperial presence had seen me rise up the chamberlain's list of targets to the top. I was not so easy to ruin as others, though, and so our silent war was waged across the Palatine.

Twice in one month I found Praetorians in my room, rummaging through my things. Once upon a time I had trusted the Praetorians. They had kept us safe in the mountains of Asia and fought valiantly for Rome on the Danubius. Now, they were little more than the armoured agents of Cleander. I had a small but trusted cadre of palace slaves that I relied upon for information and aid, and gradually over the months they disappeared, either arrested on some ridiculous charge and taken to the cellars to scream out their tortured confessions or simply gone with no explanation. I was being systematically disarmed.

On one occasion I managed to speak to Commodus, briefly, although not out of earshot of the Praetorians, so I was forced to be oblique and careful.

'My privacy has been cast to the wind,' I muttered. There was no harm in that. Of all people, the Praetorians knew it, for they were the very prying eyes and ears responsible, and it would be natural for me to complain. 'The Guard feel free to ransack my room and question my slaves.'

'*Your* slaves?' Commodus raised an eyebrow. Clearly, all slaves in the palace were his or the imperial family's. I actually owned none of them. But he smiled and let that go. 'Since that day with my sister and the arena, the Guard are more watchful than ever. If anything, it does them credit. They are just being thorough.'

'They think to find an assassin's blade beneath *my* pillow? I am being targeted, and you know precisely who by.'

He rolled his eyes. 'I'm not having that old argument again, Marcia.'

'With respect,' I said, though I suspect there was little indication of that in my tone, 'I think you are ignoring what is going on around you. You let people run the empire for you.' Praetorians were paying attention to me now. I was breaking my own promise to be careful. 'But while your favourite drives you to extravagant gestures and wild ideas, those gestures are taking root in people's minds differently. What to you is recreation to them looks like excess. The population of Rome only sees the heights to which Cleander drives you.' Damn it, I'd said it now. 'They talk of orgies and profligacy. Even of incest. Rumours abound because, while you should be dealing with your people, you are instead driving chariots and holding parties, leaving the business of empire to Cleander.'

He pulled away from me then, angry. 'You think me blind to unhealthy influences, Marcia, yet here you are trying to persuade me to distrust my own guard. Curb your tongue when you speak to me.'

With that he stalked away angrily and I, all too aware of the Praetorians watching me, also went my own way.

While all this was happening I at least knew that other good men were moving towards the inexorable goal of tipping Cleander from his lofty perch, so I settled into palace life, waiting for the inevitable, or rather, for what I *presumed* to be inevitable. Despite everything, Commodus remained with Bruttia Crispina. She was no longer a smiling little thing, but a sad, moping, bitter creature with little hope of a future. I had torn that away from her. Perhaps out of some childish loyalty, Commodus remained steadfastly married to his barren empress, though he never slept with her.

I was devious enough to work like Cleander, but not quite as corrupt in the soul. I had taken from Bruttia Crispina the chance to bear the emperor's children, but had stopped short of seeking harm to Bruttia herself. And even now, while Commodus clung to her despite everything, I would not seek her fall.

The inevitable. Soon, the importance of the succession would force him to cast her aside without my interference.

Winter rolled into spring with the news that the revolt of the deserters in Gaul had finally been put down. Between the generals Niger and Pertinax, the rebellious force had been utterly smashed and control reasserted over the roads and towns of the province. The ringleader and a small number of his men escaped, and the authorities continued to investigate in Gaul, attempting to track him down, but the danger was clearly over, and even the emperor heaved a sigh of relief.

Urged on to unnecessary extravagance as always by Cleander, Commodus decided to celebrate the return to peace in as grand a manner as possible. Beginning on that least auspicious of days, the Ides of Martius, the festival of the mother of the gods, Cybele, lasted a whole week and was one of the more anticipated celebrations of the pagan year. I had seen the festival numerous times and was prepared to witness licence, abandon and even debauchery. Commodus, however, planned grand games and parades and plays.

The Ides came around and we prepared for the opening procession. With no rigid mother to stop me these days, I threw myself into the fun of the festival. At least for a few days neither Cleander nor Bruttia would be troubling me, for everyone would be busy.

I deliberated for some time on what to wear, for it is the custom during the festival to dress in whatever manner one desires, regardless of station or gender, adopting disguises. Even soldiers, senators and priests would be there in their costumes and masks. This was the only time of the year in which I could legitimately and without fear adopt any mode of dress I wished and it was clearly important, at least in my head, that I make a statement. I thought long and hard about it. I wanted to appeal to Commodus for obvious reasons, but I had had my time as a concubine, a plaything for a rich animal, and I would not demean myself so again. I considered a goddess, but even in these days of relative freedom from Mother's disapproval, my fear of the Lord and his commandments on idols and worship made me flinch from doing so. I needed something sensual and alluring, but temporal. It needed to be enticing and yet strong. It needed to draw the emperor's eye and the empress' ire. I settled upon my disguise of an evening while reading Juvenal's satires. The very notion leapt from the vellum. It was everything I required and more.

I waited on the morning of the festival outside the temple of the Magna Mater on the Palatine, the sacred sanctuary of Cybele. I was dressed as a gladiatrix and could see all male eyes lingering on me. In little more than a leather wrap for my breast and a leather loincloth, I held a wooden sword and a small wooden shield, my hair held back by a simple leather thong and my face covered with an expressionless yet very feminine steel mask.

Juvenal was my guide and my muse that day. *'What modesty can you expect in a woman who wears a helmet, abjures her own sex, and delights in feats of strength? Yet she would not choose to be a man, knowing the superior joys of womanhood.'*

Lysandra the gladiatrix awaited her emperor.

I smiled as the last two figures emerged from the palace, making their way to the temple under the escort of half a dozen men who had foregone the chance to dress as they liked and wore the traditional white toga of the Praetorians. The group of soldiers surrounded a small man dressed as the goat-god Pan, and a tall one wearing the lion skin and carrying the club of Hercules. Despite the gold mask covering his face between beard and hair, no one in Rome would be in any doubt of the true identity of the god walking among them. I might have baulked at impersonating a pagan deity, but I found delight, oddly, in seeing him dressed as one.

The emperor and Cleander joined the group, and Commodus

300

gave me an appraising look. I clearly came down favourably and silently I thanked Juvenal for his inspiration. What would Bruttia make of me when she saw me? Other notables and guests joined us, then finally there was a fanfare from the temple and the *Galli* – the eunuch priests – emerged at a stately pace. Leading them was the reed-bearer with his simple piece of flora on a perfect cushion of white. Behind him came more and more of his ilk, each carrying the paraphernalia of the goddess and her associates. Finally, the statue of the great mother herself, seated in a rich chair, appeared on the shoulders of six priests, sweating under the weight.

The procession moved off, heading along an age-old route that took it through the streets to the adulation of the people. The emperor and his escort, along with myself and various other notables, fell in behind the priests. All was jubilant and good-humoured. Men and women shared jokes, unaware with whom they were laughing. At the end of the day, when the rites were done with and the taverns seduced the populace, there would be more than jokes shared between hidden identities. I smiled at the thought. Everywhere we went, two figures in the procession attracted attention above all others: the golden Hercules at its heart, and the lithe, swarthy, alluring gladiatrix nearby.

We picked up more and more followers in the crowd as we travelled, for figures would fall into the procession and join as we moved, such that it would be a long, snaking line by the time we arrived in the forum. Initially I worried about the emperor's safety, given the proximity of so many hidden faces, but Commodus was no fool. He was separated from the public by Praetorians, who were fierce and undisguised.

We moved through the city and I laughed and joked. It felt good, even for just a day, to be free of machinations and dark thoughts, and I revelled in the opportunity to enjoy myself for a change. Even Cleander seemed untroubled and in high spirits.

The only stern faces were the Praetorians, and they had a job to do. That was simply professionalism.

Finally, as the sun neared its zenith, we reached the forum, passing the great amphitheatre and the Temple of Venus and Rome, watching with mirth as the priests struggled to manoeuvre the seated goddess through Titus' arch, then on again, down the Via Sacra.

It was as we passed the Temple of the Divine Caesar that it happened.

So suddenly we had no chance to stop it, one of the Praetorians around the emperor ripped his sword from its hidden place beneath the folds of his toga and turned on the emperor. Two more followed suit, then another. I realised in the blink of an eye that there were far many more Praetorians around us now than there had been at the temple when we departed.

Commodus was doomed.

Two more Praetorians ripped their swords free and went for the emperor. It seemed his entire escort were assassins in the guise of his guard. For a horrifying moment I panicked that Laetus had foresworn his association with our conspirators and launched an attack of his own, but I swiftly pushed down that idea. Laetus was no fool.

'Men of the Eighth Augusta! Protect the emperor,' bellowed a voice, and suddenly soldiers were launching themselves at one another, their identities baffling as true Praetorians and assassins fought, all dressed identically.

The assassins had the edge, and though there were many more true Praetorians around the procession, the crowd and the priests kept them from coming to the emperor's aid. I caught sight for a moment of Laetus, struggling to reach the action, which confirmed for me that this had nothing to do with him. Now figures were fleeing the fighting, senators and plebs alike, colourful tunics and rich togas hurtling away into the forum in panic, Cleander was unarmed and useless. He did what he could, to his credit, placing himself between the attackers and the emperor and waving his pipes menacingly, though he flinched away when a sword came near him. But the assassins had not reckoned with the Hercules they faced. Commodus was no shrinking flower. I had seen him train with gladiators, hunt animals, throw spears. This was a man who had been blooded at ten years old in Marcomannia. And suddenly I was glad he was Cleander's extravagant gladiator emperor.

The emperor swung that great Herculean club and the effect was devastating, for it was no facsimile of papyrus and reeds, but a real ash staff bound in rings of iron. The huge weapon took two attackers from their feet, shattering the arm of one. I marvelled, but my own attention was distracted a moment later as another would-be assassin was trying to push past me and get to the emperor. Clearly, as a woman, I was no threat. I had not trained like a gladiator or ridden to war in Marcomannia. But I was strong, I was determined, and I had a three-foot ash-wood gladius.

I slammed the tip of the weapon into the man's ribs as he passed and was rewarded with a violent explosion of breath as the man fell. I am sure I at least cracked a few ribs. I had no chance to follow up on my blow, though, for he was dispatched easily a moment later by a Praetorian with a real sword.

By the time I recovered from the shock of the whole incident, and my unexpected part in it, the danger was over. Nine Praetorians lay dead on the paving around us. There were screams and moans from the gathered crowd and from the priests, but Commodus was unharmed, his club smeared with blood.

'You,' the emperor called, pointing at one of the white-togate, sword-wielding men who had leapt to his defence. The soldier bowed his head respectfully, sword lowered.

'You,' Commodus repeated. 'You identified them as men of the Eighth. That's a Gallic legion. Maternus' men. How did you know?'

The man, his head still bowed, cleared his throat. 'Because I was one of them, Majesty. Aulus Rutilius Secundus, Eighth Augusta, formerly.'

Commodus stared. This was one of those men who had ravaged Gaul until the two generals put down the revolt.

'Explain,' Commodus said in a dangerous voice.

'Majesty, some of us lads, we left the legions for good reasons. Bastard centurions who beat us and stole our pay, kept us on the worst duties, and all 'cause they didn't like our faces. We had to leave, and we had to survive, but it was never our intention to cause harm to the emperor. That was Maternus and four of his cronies, Majesty.'

Commodus stared, his face unreadable.

'Execution is the only answer for a deserter,' Cleander said quietly, and to his credit the soldier remained calm and accepting. I stepped forward.

'He and his friends *saved* you, Majesty.'

The emperor nodded thoughtfully. 'A condemned deserter who saves the emperor from harm. I would wager there is no precedent for dealing with such a thing.' He straightened and turned to Cleander. 'Identify the intruders among the living and the dead. Every man who fought alongside Rutilius Secundus here is to be pardoned his desertion and to be offered the choice of returning to his legion or receiving honourable discharge with pension.'

I was paying only passing attention. My quick mind was making calculations. Maternus and four of his cronies, the deserter had said. But I remembered six men attacking the emperor. I ran the scene back through my head once more but was sure it was six.

'Which one of these is Maternus?' Cleander snapped at the

deserter, gesturing at the bodies that were now being laid side by side.

'None of them, sir. You'll find him in the temple we just passed, I'll wager.'

True Praetorians were dispatched to search the Temple of the Divine Caesar, but that only made my math that bit more shocking. Only four deserters then, but six attackers. And there was only one explanation. The other two would have to be actual Praetorians from Rome, who had attacked the emperor.

For a sickening moment, I blamed Cleander. Praetorians had tried to assassinate emperors before, some even succeeding, but why? Who had led this? Certainly, no guard in Rome would be working for the leader of the Gallic deserters, which pinned culpability in my mind to Cleander. But what could he hope to gain? Even if Commodus had been struck down, the senate and the people would not accept the accession of Cleander. He could not be emperor. Never. So, what was going on? Even if Laetus *had* been involved in the attack, which he clearly was not, he'd have been trying for Cleander, not the emperor.

Whatever the case, what meagre trust I had left in the Praetorians withered.

I watched, sick to the stomach, as the rebel leader Maternus, who had fled among those many running figures to the temple the moment the fight started, realising it was doomed to failure, was dragged before the emperor. Commodus had been merciful to the men who had saved him, but there was no clemency in him for Maternus. The former officer was held down as he spat bile and hatred, and one of the Guard lifted his gladius. The standard weapon of the Roman army is a multi-purpose blade but is most dangerous when stabbing. The edge can be keen, but still, as the man swept it down into Maternus' neck, it did little more than cripple him and leave his head lolling in agony. The man tried to scream, but his pipe had been severed and only a strange whistle emerged. It took the soldier two more blows to take off the head. I watched the entire grisly scene, my mind casting me images of the governor of Aegyptus accepting such a blade stoically, and of Quadratus, hacked at and screaming for what seemed an eternity. I am no wallflower, and blood does not overly concern me, but this was appalling.

The rest of the day was exceedingly strange. While I could see an edge to Commodus' expression that spoke of uncertainty and even anger, he was safe, the would-be assassins were all dead, and loyalty and aid had come from unexpected sources. Commodus was determined to go on. Indeed, he launched into the rest of the procession and festivities with renewed vigour, adding to the planned prayers and speeches new thanks to the gods for his deliverance. The public echoed that very sentiment, too. Their emperor was saved, and on an auspicious day: that same day upon which the assassins of Caesar had *not* failed in their task.

It was only when the day was done and we returned to the palace that I had a chance to air my concerns to the emperor. Bruttia Crispina was in her room preparing for the grand banquet that was planned, and Cleander was seeing to the security arrangements in the company of his two sycophantic prefects. I went looking for Commodus and found him in an unexpected location. Clearly, he had been more shaken by today's events than he had shown, for he was in a place I had not seen since we were children. Oddly, it was when I was passing that open door, and smiling about our childhood games of hide and find, that I realised this was where he had been on the day of Fulvus' accident.

The Palatine is a complicated palace, with many different regions and built on numerous levels. There are cellars upon cellars in some places and those that are infamous for their Praetorian interrogators are only one such area. The one that Commodus had found his way to is a dank area beneath the heart of the palace.

I found him sitting at the bottom of a stairway lit only by a small oil lamp. He turned, startled, at the sound of my approach, then relaxed as he saw who it was.

'I came seeking solitude.'

'Solitude is not always good for you,' I replied quietly.

He acknowledged this with a sigh. 'When will people stop trying to kill me?'

I laughed mirthlessly. 'When someone succeeds. You are the most powerful man in the world. There will always be those who covet what you have.'

'Emperors seem made to be killed,' he added, rather darkly. Before I could interject, he pointed back up the stairs. 'Up there? The Flavian palace built by Domitian, stabbed in the groin at his writing desk not more than two hundred paces from here. The room down there? Part of what was Nero's house before it was ravaged and built over. It might have been in that very room that Nero, knowing his reign was over and the wolves were coming for him, spent his last night in the city before waking to find all his guards and servants fled. See that corridor?'

I peered myopically into the gloom. A wide, arched passage led off into the subterranean world.

'Somewhere at the other end of that, just outside Tiberius' palace, was where Caligula was butchered. This is not a palace. This is a mausoleum.'

I shivered. Down here in the darkness it actually *felt* like one. 'Come with me. Back to the light.'

He was not deep in a black mood, just hovering on the maudlin, and he nodded and followed me back up the stairs. As we climbed, while we were alone, I confided in him.

'The bodies in the forum did not add up.'

Commodus frowned. 'How so?'

'Your saviour said the enemy numbered Maternus and four

307

others. There were six attackers slain, even before Maternus was found.'

The emperor dismissed it with a wave of his hand. 'The man was probably just estimating numbers.'

'Perhaps,' I admitted. 'But it was impossible to tell who was a real Praetorian and who was not with the white togas and the blades. What if two men of your own guard were part of the attack?'

'There was no way they could have been in touch with the plotters.'

'No,' I admitted, 'but if they happened to be there when the attack occurred and felt that they might be able to achieve a despicable goal of their own by supporting the assassins? Opportunists? I know you trust Cleander—'

'Not this again, Marcia. Yes, I trust Cleander. He has protected my back since I was a boy. And I know you two do not like one another, but that does not mean that either of you is my enemy. He speaks of you just as you speak of him, you know? Cleander will not move against me. There are few things in life about which I am certain, but that is one. Just as I am sure you will never turn on me.'

I nodded. It was unthinkable. And perhaps, while I hated Cleander, I was doing him a disservice to suggest that he might be plotting against the emperor. 'But Cleander is not the only man with authority over Praetorians,' I insisted, a dog with a bone, not willing to let it go. 'There are two prefects. Numerous tribunes. The commander of the cavalry. What if one of them has reason to hate you? Remember those emperors you spoke of in the ruins down there? Caligula: murdered by a Praetorian. Nero: betrayed and abandoned by his Praetorian prefect. Domitian, whose prefect had been part of the plot to drive in that knife.'

As we reached the top of the stairs, I could see that my words had had an impact. It was all speculation and might be built on nothing but flights of fancy, but there was truth in the danger of placing too much faith in the imperial bodyguard. Like all men, they could be bought.

'I must see out the rest of the festival, Marcia. I have planned great things. But like all right-thinking citizens, I intend to abandon the stink of the city in summer. When the week is over, we shall quit Rome early and move to one of the country estates. It will be more pleasant and, if there is anything in your fears, we shall be safer there.'

I nodded uncertainly. Was that *we*, he and I, or he and his wife? 'Will I come?'

'Yes,' he replied, and I tried not to sigh with relief. 'Bruttia too,' he added, casting a pall over my brief joy. 'Cleander can stay in Rome and keep things in order for me.'

I nodded again. While leaving Cleander in control of Rome was far from ideal and putting up with the presence of the empress was a loathsome thought, it was still a good idea. How things had changed. A few years earlier I had visited that same villa to drag Commodus back to Rome, fearing he was becoming a new Tiberius. Now here I was urging him to retreat there.

At least I would be free of Cleander.

XVII

WICKED BLADES

Via Appia, 6 miles from Rome, AD 187

The villa that had formerly belonged to the sour-faced Quintilii brothers was a self-contained world. Surrounded by a huge, walled estate and fed by its own aqueduct, it provided everything a person could need for months of retreat. Sporting two bathhouses, an amphitheatre, a small auditorium and even a private race circuit, it really did cater for the luxurious life.

Indeed, being just a few short miles from both Rome and Albanum, there was always a ready source for anything we desired. If we wanted an amphora of Setinian wine, we could have it in little more than an hour, and, Commodus being Commodus, ever a man given to life's luxuries, we had those indulgences.

He had them, in particular. His pet lanista, who had been brought here two years ago by the empress in an attempt to draw her husband out of his gloom, had been far from idle during his time here. He had increased the stable of gladiators, trained them and improved the facilities. When we arrived at the villa, it transpired that those brutal fighters were now guarding the estate as well as practising for bouts in the small private arena.

Commodus launched into the world of gladiators again with gusto. It was no place for the emperor, standing on the sand of the arena and swinging steel at a slave. His place, like mine, was to sit in the stands and watch. But Commodus was of a different mind.

'Must you?' I asked as he stepped out of the doorway clad in linen padding and streamers, carrying a gleaming bronze helmet and a wicked-looking blade. He was oiled and showing much lean, muscled flesh. If the stuffy senators of Rome had seen him like this they would have collapsed in shock.

'It is a sport, Marcia.' He rolled his eyes.

'There are other sports that are less demeaning. Less dangerous.'

'But this serves a secondary purpose,' Commodus said, and his face took on a more serious cast. 'I was attacked, Marcia. In the streets, by soldiers, and my guard could do nothing, for they could not even tell who the enemy was. Only the fact that I was armed and knew how to wield my club saved me from death. That will not happen again. I shall become a killer, Marcia.'

I shuddered. I didn't like that word.

'But a *soldier* can teach you to use a sword. Other emperors have had a strong pedigree in war.'

Commodus fixed me with a look. 'I have told you before of my thoughts on war. It is indiscriminate and wasteful. I have no desire to learn how to stand in a wall of shields and be part of the legion, hacking at barbarians in rotation. I need to learn from *true* warriors. Men who can kill with a stick, a stone, a finger. I need gladiators. I shall train for the summer and beyond. I shall be the best, the Hercules I *should* be.'

There was a certain logic there, I had to admit. He had avoided the assassin's blade twice now, largely through luck and the intervention of others. If he could defend himself against any opponent? Well, then he would not join the ranks of Caligula, Nero and Domitian amid the ghosts under the Palatine.

'And they have been guarding the estate well,' he added. 'If they can guard something the size of the villa, then they can guard something the size of me. I shall add to the Praetorians from the ranks of these men.'

And he did, despite argument to the contrary. The Praetorian centurions were less than thrilled to have gladiator units mixed among their ranks, but they had little say in the matter. I cannot say how it was organised, but certainly I saw well-padded, half-naked killers standing stoically by doors that year as often as I saw a gleaming, stuffy Praetorian.

He trained. Not just on the sand, but wrestling on the palaestra with them, stretching and boxing, running and swimming. Narcissus, the wrestler we had brought back from Centum Cellae all those years ago, became a favourite, teaching the emperor and pushing him, strengthening and encouraging. Commodus was all but one of them at times. Bruttia Crispina disapproved in her quiet, mousy way. With her slide from popularity, her veneer of friendship with me had corroded somewhat. Some time, a month or so after we settled in, I was sitting on a marble bench overlooking a pond when, to my joy, Bruttia appeared. I tried not to glare at her.

'Marcia?'

I looked up, startled. She rarely spoke to me, and certainly never in a familiar manner, using my given name.

'Majesty?'

'I know there is no love lost between us. We are opponents and ever have been, and I will continue to fight for my place.'

I acknowledged this with a nod, lacking any emotion.

'But he has to stop this, and while I would tear out your gut with hooks, I know that you share that opinion, and you have known my husband longer than most. How do I stop this madness with the arena?'

I frowned. Neutral ground? I had never thought to find it.

'I'm not sure you can. If there is a way to divert his attentions it is only by raising the stakes. Find him something even more distracting than his current diversion. When we were children and I needed to change his direction, I took him to see Maximus, the Palatine lion. He loved that lion. He is clever, but he is permanently slave to his emotions. He obsesses over the arena? Find him something better.'

She nodded, deep in thought. 'A lion.'

I honestly thought she might go and get a lion then, but in actual fact she left the villa for a number of days, and when she came back it was as much a surprise as anything she could have brought.

In her wake, she fetched a menagerie of fierce beasts. A famed *bestiarius* from Syria had come to Rome for Commodus' great festival of Cybele. I vaguely remembered seeing the fellow in beast shows, leading his teams of men in the amphitheatre as they hunted animals, and now here he was, entering the villa. Behind him came his troupe of half a dozen expert *bestiarii* and more than a dozen vehicles carrying animals. I stared, wide-eyed, as enclosed timber wagons rolled past, shaking and lurching as their occupants roared and huffed and bellowed.

Commodus emerged from the bathhouse and stared in amazement as Julius Alexander, with the empress at his side, took a bow. It took me a moment to realise why Bruttia was so comfortable in the man's company, while it had taken her years to use my name. He was of a royal line himself, with blood as old and as noble as hers, albeit Emesene rather than Roman.

'What is this?' Commodus breathed, watching the wagons with breathless anticipation.

'Hunting,' Bruttia Crispina said with more determination than was her norm. 'A good, noble pastime. Julius Alexander here brings wild beasts to release in the estate. You can hunt in the privacy of your own villa.'

It was a masterstroke, I have to admit. I knew from the sudden gleam in Commodus' eyes that he was instantly hooked. Over the following days the bestiarii were lodged in the villa,

313

the animals released into the extended estate, and new safety measures instituted at the villa proper. After all, no one wanted to emerge from their bedchamber, yawning, to find a lion waiting outside. I had to grudgingly nod my approval to the empress, but the look she returned confirmed for me that our neutral ground had slid away once more to leave that same bitter chasm.

The new diversion did not quite have the results the empress expected, though. Commodus began to hunt with the bestiarii across the estate, sometimes on foot and sometimes either on horseback or by chariot, and he threw himself into the sport. However, rather than this exotic hunting supplanting his apparent desire to fight in the arena, it simply added to it. Now his time was divided between the two. More, even, for he began to race chariots around the private track, as well. I saw him less and less. Had he spent any time with his empress these days, she would have noticed that lessen too.

The height of his beast-hunting came one summer night as the evening began to draw in and the sky glowed with that glorious indigo twilight. As I emerged from the villa onto a wide path, taking the air, I peered carefully into the dim light in every direction. The guards were everywhere and in all the time we had been there not one of the beasts loose in the park had actually come up to the villa, especially with well-armed and skilled gladiators all around, but it was still wise to check as you left the structures.

In the gloom, I could see a column of men and animals returning to the villa. I stood and watched, fascinated. Three of the bestiarii came first, then Commodus, with a wry smile. Behind him, four huge slaves carried a stout wooden staff with the body of a lion dangling from it. Then came Julius Alexander, and then various other hunters and slaves. There had been only one lion among those beasts released into the estate, and it had evaded the hunters for months. Out of respect and nostalgia,

Commodus had named him Maximus and had more than once vowed that he would bring down the beast himself.

I smiled as they approached. He had finally achieved his goal.

'Your hunt went well, Majesty.' I grinned. This was better than watching him risk his life on the sands any day, though hunting a lion clearly carried its own special perils.

Commodus shot me a look that for just a blink of an eye I thought was one of anger, but then he laughed. 'Well indeed. After months, I had my javelin ready. There was Maximus, upwind, unaware. I brought my horse to a position where I had a good throw, waiting for the wind to pick up and rustle the trees, covering the sound. I managed to get into position, and you know how I am a master of the thrown spear. Maximus was mine.'

'I am impressed, Majesty.'

'I am not,' snorted Commodus. 'I pulled back my arm, ready to throw, and suddenly the lion was hurled across the clearing, howling, a javelin through his neck. I stared in shock, and then Julius was there, whooping like a lunatic. The bastard had taken it with his first throw. Beat me to it by a heartbeat, and no more. The lion is Alexander's, not mine.'

Julius Alexander threw out a horribly apologetic look, and Commodus burst out laughing. 'If I were the sort of man to kill for something so small, you'd never have made it back to the villa, Julius. Come, we must have wine and talk about javelin weights. Then, tonight, we shall dine on the most exotic of meats.'

And we did. That night we ate lion. It was the first time I did so, and the last. I will admit that I found it to my taste, as much for the fascination as the meat itself. The roasted flesh was rich and pungent and added to a wild array of aromas in the dining room. Julius Alexander, not the least, had a very individual scent, strong enough to override the spiced meat of the meal and the burning incense. There is something about Emesenes that makes them smell like a heady combination of sweat and warm spices. I spotted signs that night of what was to come, though I did not recognise them at the time. Had I realised, I'm even now not sure what I would have done.

The days rolled on, then. More hunting, more racing, more fighting. More of Bruttia Crispina watching in dismay as her somewhat estranged husband raced and fought with men and beasts rather than the rhetoric and literature she clearly thought more appropriate.

One night, quite by chance, I entered the empress' section of the villa – she and her husband were no longer living as man and wife – simply on the way through to visit Commodus. I climbed the stairs quietly. I had removed my sandals for the blessed cool of cold marble on my feet in the warm, sultry, breezeless summer night. I was, therefore, almost entirely silent. I had neared the top of the staircase when I heard a door open. I'm not sure precisely why, but I slowed. As I reached the upper steps, with a view along the lamplit corridor, I could see a figure leaving at the far end. I noticed the door from which the figure had emerged click shut, and my blood chilled.

It was the empress' chamber, and the unidentifiable figure I'd seen disappear at the far end was most certainly not Commodus. In fact, there is a way conspirators move that identifies them more than any evidence, and the figure had moved like that. I stood at the top of the stairs for a long time, dithering, wondering what to do next. Then I took a step, then another. Moments later, I was outside the empress' door. But before I even considered whether or not to knock, my nose wrinkled.

There was just a whiff of a heady scent in the corridor. Spicy, sweaty.

I felt cold, even in the heat of the summer evening. I knew that scent. And now that evening of the lion meal came back to me. The looks shared between Julius Alexander and Bruttia. I knew then that their affair had been going on for months, right under our noses, possibly since the day the Emesene hunter had arrived. In fairness, while Bruttia was apparently barren, she was still a warm-blooded woman, and the emperor had not lain with her in so long. I can hardly blame her for her actions – what woman wants to live her life solitarily, without the touch of another? But an empress cannot be as forward as any other woman, and how dare she cling to my Commodus while bedding another?

Bruttia Crispina and Julius Alexander.

There was no time to lose. A vapour stays in the air for mere heartbeats, even in an enclosed space. I hurried away.

The emperor's door was guarded by two gladiators rather than Praetorians, and I am still not sure how I feel about that. I nodded to them. While I did not know them, they had to know me.

'I need to see the emperor.'

'Na, no see,' grunted one of them in barely recognisable Latin, with a thick Numidian accent. I rounded upon him angrily.

'This is critical imperial business, and I am a close friend of the emperor. Fetch him!'

Perhaps there was something in my expression or my voice. I was part of the emperor's court, but I was still in truth little more than a pleb, yet something made one of the gladiators bow his head and open the door, disappearing inside.

Commodus emerged from his rooms a moment later with the gladiator. I had no idea what he planned, but he seemed to be dressed as Hercules again, down to the lion pelt and the huge club. I like to think that he was preparing for some strange pagan ceremony of which I was unaware, or perhaps readying himself for some kind of ritual bout in the arena. Whatever the case, he was clearly surprised to see me.

'Marcia?'

I bowed. 'Majesty. I have . . . You need to come with me.'

317

It is perhaps testament to what existed between us that he came without question. A moment later we were moving through the corridors of the villa with two gladiators at our back. Before we reached our destination, I tried to decide what to say. If I made it too clear, I could, in theory, be accused of leading his logic, especially if that scent had faded.

In the event, I need not have worried. Even as we neared the empress' door, Commodus' nose wrinkled, and I knew that he smelled it.

'No.'

His eyes were suddenly afire. I started to worry about the wisdom of what I'd done. My eyes dropped to that monstrous Herculean club he carried, nervously. We reached Bruttia's door and, without knocking, Commodus reached out and grasped the handle, flinging it open. The empress was lounging on a couch. I felt a chill run through me from the aroma that washed over me. There was the warm glow of charcoal and burning oil, there was the empress' rose-petal perfume, but there was more than that. The spicy-sweat aroma of an Emesene body and the unmistakable smell of sex.

I flinched as Commodus stepped into the doorway. Oddly, as though attracted by disaster, a pair of Praetorians were suddenly in attendance. I never heard them arrive. By the time Commodus stepped into his horrified wife's room, two trained killers and two elite soldiers were with him, all with weapons drawn.

'You faithless *harpy*,' Commodus snarled.

Bruttia Crispina recoiled as though struck.

'Whore. Adulteress. You kill my heirs repeatedly, yet retain your honour and place. And how do you repay me? Betrayal. With him? *Him?*'

Bruttia clearly knew there was little point in attempting to dissemble. The odour alone condemned her. 'You . . . you never come to me, my love.'

Commodus' lip curled. 'Why would I? Why would I come to a barren wife who cannot do what needs to be done?'

Bruttia quivered and, just for a moment, I actually felt sorry for her.

'I am still a woman.'

'No.' Commodus spun and extended a digit at her. 'You are an *empress*. That carries almost the same weight as being emperor. You must be the very embodiment of Romanitas, and if there is a single duty you have that is paramount, it is to produce an heir, a duty that you clearly cannot perform.'

Bruttia wailed. 'I tried. I tried and I almost died.'

Commodus, still shuddering with heaving breaths of anger, gestured at the guards that accompanied us. 'Take the empress to Rome this night. Gather her personal effects and then give her an escort of a century of Praetorians and put her on the first ship to Capri. She will not leave the island thenceforth.'

Bruttia's eyes widened. Exile? 'No, husband. No . . .'

Commodus' lip twitched. 'Do not test me, woman. You know the law. The punishment of both of you is my decision. I am inclined to leniency given our long and contented time together, and that is why you will go to blessed Capri and not meet some fate that would make you wish you'd died with one of those unborn heirs.'

'But exile . . .'

Commodus had already turned his back on her and left the room. I glanced after him and then back to Bruttia. She fixed me with a look and I knew at that moment that she blamed me for the revelation of her adultery. Conflicting emotions flooded through me, and I threw her a sympathetic look and left. Yes, I am aware of the hypocrisy. Throughout that maelstrom of complex emotions that followed my actions and her fall, the feeling that rose paramount above the others was one of victory. I never saw her again and my final memory of her is that dreadful expression as she was condemned to exile.

Then we were marching off in the direction of the guest quarters where Julius Alexander was staying. I felt a tingle of anticipation. Commodus was angry and, while he had been lenient on Bruttia, I could not see the same clemency being levelled at his Syrian guest. I scurried along in his wake and we arrived at the guest quarters to the surprise of the two Praetorians on guard. They snapped to attention.

'Majesty.'

'Which room is Prince Julius Alexander's?' Commodus said, his voice carrying a leaden toll of doom.

The soldiers exchanged a look. 'He and his protégé have gone night hunting, Majesty. They went to the stables just now.'

'Night hunting indeed,' snarled Commodus. 'I have no idea how he knew, but he is running. Have the Nymphaeum gate sealed and alert the boundary guards. Julius Alexander is not to leave the estate.'

The Praetorians saluted and both dashed off about that duty, leaving just us and our four-man escort. Commodus turned to the two gladiators among them. 'Go to the *ludus*. Rouse your fellows. Scour the estate and bring me Julius Alexander alive or dead. A bag of gold to the man who achieves it.'

With no need for further urging, the gladiators hurried off to stir their companions. I could see the twitch in Commodus' lip. He felt furious and impotent. He was a man of action, and in a perfect world it would be him hunting down the cuckolding Emesene. Gently taking his arm, I steered him through the villa to the *triclinium*, where the wine from our evening symposium still stood on the table, unfinished. The two Praetorians remained with us, yet with just four of us it felt like solitude. I poured a cup of Caecuban and passed it to him, reaching for the jug of water, but he put his hand over the cup top and shook his head. It was a measure of his state of mind, since he liked his wine for sure, but always cut it with an appropriate quantity of water.

We strolled from the room onto the balcony, where the evening air had picked up into a gentle, warm breeze and the atmosphere was less cloyed with braziers. Standing on that balustrade, with Commodus occasionally supping from his unwatered wine, felt oddly perfect. As though we were the couple we had always been meant to be. It was all too easy to imagine, mentally discarding the empress who would, even now, be hurrying for the Via Appia under escort. I almost slid my arm into his, but stopped short. The evening air was quiet with the night-time susurration of insects and the fresh smell of night-blooming flowers. It was only partially marred by the muffled distant shouts of the men guarding the estate, who were scouring the periphery, looking for Julius Alexander. Despite the sprawling estate and the huge boundary, it was well protected and there were many guards. I doubted he would escape.

'Will you divorce her?' I asked quietly.

'I don't know,' he said in reply. 'I ought to. But I still feel somehow responsible for her. She has suffered so much, and she never really wanted me, as you can imagine. She is from a very powerful and popular family. Merely *exiling* her will make me enemies.'

'But you will *have* to divorce her. Or take her back,' I responded, urging him. Completely free of her, he could be mine . . .

'I cannot take her back. Under ancient statutes, I would be in violation of the law myself if I remained with an adulterous wife. I just . . . I can't think about it now, Marcia.'

I smiled sympathetically while inside I screamed DIVORCE at him. The moment was broken by sudden shouting. Commodus drained his cup and slapped it down on the balustrade as figures emerged from the woods that were part of the eastern grounds of the estate. I felt tense, suddenly.

The lead figure was most definitely Julius Alexander, and on the horse close behind had to be the man he'd taken with him.

Just heartbeats after them, three gladiators emerged on horseback, each armed with gleaming iron and urging their beasts on. They were going to overtake the second refugee any moment.

It was like sitting in the stands of the amphitheatre, watching this chase and combat play out. Alexander, suddenly aware that his friend was in danger, wheeled his horse and raced at the gladiators. As he rode, he lifted a javelin to shoulder height and steadied it. I watched, tense, as the two groups of riders neared.

The javelin launched and the expert hunter's aim was true. One of the pursuing gladiators fell to the missile, though at such a distance all I could see was it strike him and throw him from his mount. More shouts of consternation and anger, and the two remaining gladiators went for Alexander, ignoring his friend – the second man was not worth a bag of coins, after all.

Julius Alexander was a master of his craft, though. He had come all the way from Syria at the bidding of the imperial consilium to entertain the crowds with his skills. And while the gladiators were good men, the best of their ilk had gone to fight in wars years ago and only now was a new generation of fighters blooming.

The horses met with a crash and again there was just a distant blur from our viewpoint at the villa, but the initial impact left the two gladiators dead or dying, one lolling sideways in his saddle, the other fallen somewhere. Satisfied that he had dealt with the pursuit and saved his friend, Alexander turned and started for the woodland again, where they would stand more chance of losing themselves and making it to the edge of the estate.

As they neared the treeline once more, a veritable sea of figures burst forth from the shadowy canopy. Gladiators, roaring, some on horseback and others on foot. Someone must have had a bow and a passing ability with it, for before they even closed, the younger hunter's horse suddenly reared and screamed, throwing its rider with a cry of alarm.

Alexander wheeled his own steed ready to ride away again, but as he turned to flee he realised that his friend had fallen. He hauled on the reins and, as his mount stopped, slipped from the saddle, running across to the other hunter.

I watched, my breath held. I had never once believed that Julius Alexander would escape the grounds, but if he had stood a chance, then he cast it aside by stopping to help his friend. I watched the two men, Alexander crouched over the younger man, who must have been wounded in his fall, for he was not rising.

The gladiators began to howl. A variety of wicked blades were brandished and I could see them gleaming in the evening light. Death was closing in on the two fugitive hunters, and it would be brutal, each of those men wanting to be the one to deliver the killing blow and win the prize. I could picture it, a dozen blows at once, slashing and stabbing, trying each to be the first.

Julius Alexander must have come to a similar conclusion. I could not quite see what happened, but the hunter crouched lower over his friend and a moment later they both fell flat. The gladiators reached the two fallen hunters and paused. Clearly their prey were already either dead or mortally wounded. Still not prepared to be robbed of their gold, the gladiators lunged at the hunters and began to stab and hack. They only stopped when one whooped and rose, his hand shooting up into the air, a large object swinging from it. Even at this distance I knew what that was. I felt sick.

'It is done,' Commodus said, and his voice was as empty of satisfaction as I had ever heard.

'What now?' I whispered.

'The villa has lost its shine for me,' he replied sadly. 'It is time to return to Rome. Even with the stink of the streets, it will smell sweet after this place.'

He turned and disappeared indoors, leaving me alone on

the walkway, with howling gladiators carrying a severed head towards me.

After all my work to ruin Bruttia, to keep her from bearing an heir, in the end it had been she who had condemned herself. It was difficult, though, to feel regret or remorse. I had never been closer to Commodus. In Rome, as summer turned to autumn, we could finally be together.

XVIII

THE LIFE OF GODS AND GODDESSES

Rome, AD 188

In the event, Rome was a short-lived return for us, albeit a welcome one. We settled into the palace and, without even consulting me, Commodus had my effects moved into his apartment. I was his. He was mine. That for which I had been yearning, and often working, for more than twenty years had finally come to pass. And now it no longer felt strange, thinking back on those jibes of Cleander so long ago.

Commodus and I were not lovers immediately. I think that perhaps what had transpired with Bruttia had shaken him and made him too careful to leap into bed with me. But he had moved me close, and our time would come soon enough. I was more than willing to allow him the room he needed. After all, we had all the time we wished for, now. I was happy. I was so blissful in our togetherness, in fact, that I became all but oblivious to important things happening around me.

I barely registered as we passed through the city to the Palatine the signs of the plague that were clearly on the rise once more. We had assumed with the visible decline in its effects that the terrible pestilence that had now been with us for more than two decades was fading away. But what it was doing was ebbing and flowing like a dreadful sea, and we were just beginning to see the tide rising once more. The plague carts were at work again and new burial pits were being dug. The populace wandered, deaf to their own misery, their ears and noses stuffed with petals coated with fragrant oils and perfumes to keep the poison at bay.

A more personal omission in my attention was Cleander. I barely noticed the man as he met us and bowed deep to the emperor. While he had always been my nemesis, I had achieved that which I had sought, so I temporarily allowed myself to forget about him. Foolish. Had I been paying more attention, I might have noted that he was the master of Rome, now. The whole palace bowed to him before they even looked to the emperor. Rome was staffed, paid and punished at the whim of Cleander. And had I noticed, I would have seen the look he must have given me as we returned. His old enemy now in the most dangerous position possible, for him.

And I should have noticed Rome. Rome was not at its best. Even had the plague not troubled the city, it languished under the pestilence that was Cleander. Not one face wore a smile in that city. There was starvation among the poor – those who were not dying of the plague anyway. Those of the senatorial class wore expressions of glassy-eyed hatred, for their world was being ruled by a man who was, in their eyes, a slave, and the emperor had allowed this to happen. I would have felt panic had I really noticed how the aged aristocracy of Rome glared at their emperor. We had been gone from Rome for half a year, and Cleander had consolidated his power.

Commodus, of course, left the man to his work and threw himself into sponsoring games in the arena and races in the circus in a Cleander-inspired and partially successful attempt to keep the populace content. I was cocooned in my comfortable world in the palace, and in the late autumn I was in my chamber reading some of the more wicked poems of Catullus when there was a rap on the door. I responded 'Enter,' and my visitor did so. Commodus, in just his tunic and boots with a warm smile. My Hercules finally came to me as I had hoped he would all those years ago in Vindobona when he first enfolded me in an embrace.

I had known the touch of only one man in my life, and he had been forced upon me, a pig of a man. I realised suddenly as Commodus closed the door behind him that I had absolutely no idea how to approach a meeting of lovers.

He came to the bed languidly, and I struggled to decide what I should do. Had this been Quadratus, all animal instinct and wine-soaked desperation, I would have risen up with arched brows and prepared myself to lead him through the night. That would not do with the man I loved. The man I had yearned for all these years. The master of the world.

He slid from his tunic and boots, and to me he was truly Hercules, his body toned and muscular from his years of train-ing and exercise, his flesh taut and smooth, his hair and beard twinkling golden in the lamplight. I held my breath.

I should have removed my own tunic, I suppose, but in the strangest way for a woman who had become a whore and an Amazon to survive her unwanted master, I was suddenly extremely self-conscious and nervous.

His smile eased my spirit a little, but I was still almost shiver-ing with tense anticipation as he slid across the bed and slipped my tunic up over my head. I folded my arms across my breasts.

'I am not Quadratus.'

That was it. A simple phrase, and yet it sank in, flooding me with relief. It meant that he understood. He knew what I was feeling, and he knew how to deal with it. Just as I had so many times urged him back from the dark with slow, careful words, so he knew how to coax me from my odd shyness. He pushed me gently back to my pillow and we lay side by side, his fingers tracing delicate designs on my shoulders, my neck, my thigh.

Everything I had learned in those years under Quadratus melted away. With Commodus I did not need to struggle. With Commodus I could be a woman. I lay, enjoying his touch, anticipated for so many years. He was surprisingly gentle and delicate. We were there for a day, or it felt as much to me, he enjoying my presence and me enjoying his touch, neither of us willing to push the other into anything. In fact, I think we would have simply laid beside one another like that the whole night, had I not finally plucked up the courage to raise my head from the bed and kiss him.

That kiss changed my world. As though he had been waiting for it, he was unleashed.

We made love. Not the animal sex that I remembered with Quadratus, but a sensual, caring, exciting and daring meeting of lovers. I had never known such ecstasy. And he was insatiable, in the most perfect way.

The birds were already tweeting their greeting to the day when we finally lay, exhausted and still. Even then he returned to tracing delicate designs on my skin with his fingertips, and that was the last thing I felt before an exhausted, contented sleep claimed me.

The autumn rolled into winter, passed through Saturnalia, and emerged into a new year in something of a dreamy blur for me. If I could have frozen time in a moment, it would have been sometime that season I would choose. But even the happiest beasts deep in hibernation eventually have to emerge into the cold light of day and seek sustenance.

I began to become aware of what was going on around me.

Dulius Silanus and Servilius Silanus became consuls, both bowing their heads in acknowledgement to Cleander, both seething at their patrician blood being forced to obeisance before a former slave. An undercurrent of disaffection that rippled across the city. It was not aimed at the emperor, for Commodus was still Rome's golden prince, and a man of unsurpassed breeding; it was aimed at Cleander, and inevitably there was a growing dismay that the emperor was doing nothing to curtail the situation.

I wondered occasionally at how Septimius Severus and his fellow conspirators were faring. I had been forbidden from becoming involved and it had taken an effort of conscious will to stay away. On the one hand, neither Severus, Rufinus nor Dionysius had been mentioned in any untoward way, and all had steered clear of proscriptions, so they were still clearly free to work. On the other hand, they had seemed so convinced that they would be able to bring down the upstart chamberlain, and yet thus far things had only become worse.

Even had I not been urged to leave them to their work, in the tight imperial circles I now moved, in a city where every wall held Cleander's eyes and ears, I was hardly in a position to start enquiring anyway.

I watched with dismay what was happening in the streets, though. Food was becoming scarce. Whether that was the fault of the plague preventing farms from being harvested, or some other crisis, I did not know, but when added to the disaffection under Cleander's hard rule and the constant ravaging of the disease in the streets, it helped to turn the mood of Rome sour. Despite our happy closeness, I began to regret returning to the city.

Cleander started working against me once more. He had removed every other opponent in the regime and now, once he got rid of me, only the emperor could gainsay him. He was very circumspect, very careful. He *had* to be. Now that I was the emperor's mistress and sharing his apartment I was almost untouchable. *Almost.* Yet twice I found among my things love letters from men purporting to be waiting for me to do away with the emperor so that we could be together. I had never heard of one of the men. The other was Eclectus, who had disappeared entirely from the scene some time ago. Subtle and dangerous. I kept a close watch, even as I burned each piece of spurious evidence that appeared in my chamber. And, of course, I did not go everywhere with Commodus. When I was on my own, I swiftly became aware that I was never *truly* alone. Men trailed me and watched my every move. I am certain there was a ledger in Cleander's office that told where I was and what I was doing every moment of every day. He felt sure I would trip myself up. And I could do nothing to aid that happening. I lived an exemplary life that season, willing Severus and his companions to work their hidden magic.

I did make inroads with *one* old acquaintance, though.

In the winter, Galen came to court once more. He had remained in Rome during our absence, healing the wealthy and influential, putting into place once more those responses of his to the ravaging disease and, I understand, working on a treatise on the temperaments. I found him one morning waiting to seek an audience with the emperor. Oddly, it was about the only time I could claim even the remotest level of privacy outside the bedchamber. The vestibule in which the physician sat quietly was almost empty. None of the ubiquitous pursuers had followed me in here. It would have been too obvious, and was almost certainly deemed unnecessary on the Palatine, for the Praetorians had eyes and ears everywhere here anyway. But the only other two people in the room were tunic-clad figures who from their very look and stance I knew to be Commodus' gladiatorial guardsmen. The Praetorians who habitually waited here had entered the room beyond to petition the emperor for Galen's audience. I had only moments before they returned, but for that brief spell, I could trust everyone in the room.

'Galen?'

His head turned slowly, wearily, and his brow knit for a moment, then recognition dawned on him.

'Young lady. Yes, I remember you. Verus' seamstress girl. The emperor's consort, no less, I understand.'

I smiled. 'Marcia, and yes. You've come about the trouble in the city?'

Galen nodded sadly. 'I once left Rome, with no wish to become part of its charnel landscape like so many other thousand mouldering souls. The emperor's father called me back to care for his family. I have done so where that was possible, but it seems so redundant now. The emperor rides chariots and fights with gladiators. He is clearly determined to maim or kill himself. And each day in this city is a die roll for my survival. I seek to return to the calm of Pergamon.'

Would that *we* could flee Rome so easily. To be free of both the plague and the chamberlain . . .

I frowned. Perhaps we could. There were plenty of places we could go that weren't that Quintilian villa, after all. Would it be dangerous leaving Cleander in sole control again? Last time we had done so he had consolidated his power considerably. Could he be allowed to do so again? But then what difference were we making here anyway? Commodus was spending time at his favourite hobbies and leaving Cleander in control. I could do nothing with the man's eyes on me constantly anyway.

'What would your advice be to the emperor?' I said quietly.

'Stop fighting and racing before he kills himself.'

I chuckled hollowly. 'I mean with regards to the plague.'

'Staying in the city is foolish. Even here on the Palatine it is never far from the door. I have seen palace slaves struck by it.'

'So you would advise the emperor to depart the city.'

'Yes. And I shall.'

'Perhaps you could remain court physician if we left? Must it be Pergamon you leave for?'

He looked wistfully into a distance only he could see. 'To be back in that sultry homeland, its red roofs nestled between the heights, lofty and graceful homes of the gods. It is my heart's desire.' He sighed. 'But there is also my duty to my work and to an old friend to do what I can for his son.'

331

We were interrupted then by the door to the imperial aula regia, and the Praetorians called Galen in. I left, aware that my time of privacy had passed, but that night when Commodus came to me, I learned more. We lay, tangled in sheets, resting and touching, content.

'Galen wants me to leave Rome,' he said in little more than a whisper, his breath on the nape of my neck.

'Oh?' I shivered. His fingers twined themselves in my dark hair, and I sighed contentedly.

'He says that Rome festers and no good comes of staying here. He wishes to leave. If I go, he will accompany the court. But if I stay, he begs leave to return to his home.'

I rolled over and snuggled into the crook of his arm, my Hercules. It was still new for me. I still relished every touch.

'What will you do?'

He stroked my hair again, and gave me an odd smile. 'What do you think I should do? You've always had the answers, since we were young. When I was in despair, you found me Maximus the lion. When Mother died, you made me climb a mountain to look down on the world like a god. What do I do now?'

'You leave,' I replied, quietly but without a hint of hesitation and doubt.

'Rome will not take it well. They need their emperor visible. I remember telling you that years ago when we went east and then came back and held triumphs, all to remind the people who it is that rules Rome.'

Cleander rules Rome. It almost passed between my lips and I clamped them shut to stop it. He caressed my side as I pondered, and I felt a thrill of desire pass through me again. It made me think along new lines.

'I would say your prime concern would be the succession.'

His face darkened, for that brought back unwanted memories of Bruttia Crispina and her betrayal, but he sighed. 'With you? Don't think I haven't considered it. But if the senate are so set against a freedman with power – yes, I am aware that Cleander is not universally popular – imagine how they would feel about an emperor who is half born of the purple and half to the daughter of a freedwoman. The succession would be argued. There are ways, of course. If we were to marry, then it would be legitimate. But for that you would need raising from your current status. And I cannot simply make you a patrician. It doesn't work like that. Yet perhaps someone would be willing to adopt you?'

I frowned in confusion. 'Adopt?'

'It is not unknown. Quadratus wanted no wife but needed an heir, so he adopted one. Back in the days of the Republic, even as a grown man, the wily patrician Publius Claudius Pulcher wanted to lower his class to secure a tribunate and had himself adopted by a much lesser equestrian family, becoming Clodius Pulcher. These things can be done. But they must be done right. Carefully.'

I continued to frown. The very idea of renouncing my link to Mother and allowing another woman to call me daughter? Strange. And no new family would likely be as welcoming of my unpopular beliefs, either. Still, along that road . . .

Empress?

I stretched. I was daydreaming now, and straying from the point. 'We should leave Rome. The plague. It claimed your uncle. Don't let it claim you.'

That was the correct tack to take. Verus remained his idol. To be reminded of how swiftly the glorious co-emperor had succumbed to the pestilence brought it all a little more into focus for my love.

'Where, though? I shall not go back to the villa on the Via Appia. It is lost to me now. And the great Tibur villa was where Lucilla plotted her murder. The Tiberian island is now home to Bruttia. There are many other imperial villas, though.' He wrapped me in his arms. 'Would you live by the sea?'

I shivered, despite everything. Would I? Ever since that first night of the flood in Rome, great swathes of water and crashing waves have plucked at my courage and filled me with dread. Yet when I had endured the sea time and again, I had always been on a ship, at its mercy. Perhaps if I were on land? But then had I not been on dry land when the Tiber tried to take Mother . . .

'I don't know,' was my honest answer.

'There is a grand villa at Laurentinum, just up from that owned by the great Pliny once upon a time. It is perfect. Well-appointed and grand, with a guardable perimeter, close to the market and emporia at Ostia, and only a day's travel from Rome. It has excellent gardens.'

I smiled. It would make him happy, and it would get us away from Rome, the plague, Cleander.

'Laurentinum it is.'

It is a rare occasion when the imperial court can move at short notice and this was certainly not one of those times. Indeed, some parts of the administration were only now beginning to normalise after our return from the Via Appia. We left the city before spring began to show her luscious wares, though, and moved to Laurentinum.

I need not have worried too much about the sea. Though the villa was officially a seaside residence of the imperial family, in fact the bulk of the complex lay some distance from the shore, with one wing lancing out towards the water, ending in some sort of promontory and viewing area-cum-dining room. I nodded and smiled politely while I was shown it, fighting down the faint signs of unease at such huge quantities of water. And thereafter, I stayed as much as possible in the garden wing. Despite the constant aroma of brine and the cawing of gulls, it was a refreshing place to be. Best of all, it was purely a villa in which to relax, which meant it had no amphitheatres or race tracks, and the boundary was much shorter than the previous villa's. The consequences suited me fine.

No entertainment venues meant that he and I made our own entertainment. And the shorter boundary meant fewer men on patrol. Consequently, the villa was almost entirely guarded by my love's chosen gladiators, his only nod to the authority of, and necessity for, the Praetorian Guard being a small detachment housed in a separate complex on the grounds. Cleander was rendered all but blind, deaf and impotent at the villa.

Galen attended us as court physician, warning Commodus to curtail his love of the rarer seafoods and giving me a check-over, proclaiming that I was in the best of health and, with a nod to Commodus that suggested it had been his idea, that there was no reason I could not bear children.

We revelled in our love that spring and summer. It was the most carefree and happy I have ever been, and the same was true for Commodus, I'm sure. We walked and dined, laughed, talked, made love, listened to songs I'd never heard, even took a few days out to the theatre at Ostia and down to Antium for a change. It was simply the best time of my life.

Such things always come at a cost, in my experience. While we were living the life of gods and goddesses, Rome was suffering. Galen occasionally returned to the city and, though he rarely detailed what he witnessed, I could see in his eyes how bad it must have been. Rome was reaching the height of this latest wave of death. On one occasion when we did get him to speak of it, he told us bleakly that two thousand people a day were dying in the city. He then told the emperor that we were in the best possible place and to stay here until the sickness ebbed again. Then he got drunk.

Only occasionally during that time did I think of Cleander, and when I did, I found myself praying that he might be one of the plague's latest victims. Then I would curse myself for my uncharitable thoughts, apologise to God and feel contrite, though somewhere deep in my cankered soul I would go on wishing it.

The year rolled on and it was wonderful, even with the nagging knowledge that Rome suffered. But all good things come to an end, and Saturnalia had passed in our private retreat when finally, as we waited out the last frosts of winter and looked forward to the budding Laurentine spring, the world came crashing through our door.

We could hide away no longer. Cleander had finally broken Rome.

XIX

A DANGEROUS MOB

Laurentinum, AD 190

Like many of the more expensive villas along the Laurentine coast, each owned by one of the greatest names in the empire, the one in which we spent that sojourn was connected to the main road by a long drive. The approach was lined with well-tended poplars reaching into the late Februarius sky in ordered rows, like an army on parade. Statues of gods were interspersed with the trees along the route, though pride of place, close to the villa itself, had been given to a grand likeness of Hercules that Commodus had acquired at ridiculous expense from some source in Ostia. Opposite it stood another new marble, and this one was female. It did not resemble any god of whom I was aware, but the presence of a quiver at her hip and her chiton hanging open to show one breast led me to suspect she was an Amazon. Commodus clearly saw the Hercules as himself and I had the nagging feeling that the half-exposed warrior woman was therefore supposed to be me. I did not ask. I wasn't sure I would like the answer, whatever it turned out to be. She was shapely enough, though nowhere as pretty as the real me, if I might say.

The drive led to the villa's gate: a beautiful oak door in a whitewashed wall flanked by two small rooms, each of which held several gladiators at any time. More were garrisoned around the periphery and in the house. The small Praetorian unit was housed off to one side, close to the beach, which was patrolled at all times. Inside that main gate lay an intricate garden formed of circular paths of white stone chippings between neat lawns and low hedges, carefully dotted with flower beds and bushes, across which stood the somewhat monumental arched entrance to the villa proper.

Commodus and I were in the atrium that morning, wrapped tight in preparation for our morning walk around the estate. It was still early in the year and the sea carried a salty chill inland. We had paused at the impluvium pool, which tinkled lightly as the water tumbled down from the bronze satyr fountain. Commodus had been happier this past year or two than I had ever seen him. I had almost forgotten what it used to be like when I found him wallowing in the mire of his misery, contemplating death and pain on a personal, philosophical level. These last few mornings, though, and I could not explain why, there was a sadness about the edge of my love's eyes, and I began to worry that we were bound for one of those same troughs of melancholia. Perhaps it was something to do with the season or the weather. Perhaps it was because it was this time of year that Fulvus, his twin, had lived his last few gasps of life. Whatever the reason, I was determined that he would not sink into a black mood. When I had woken in the middle of the night to find him gone from the bed and standing at the window looking out across the night, I was doubly determined.

'We should go to Puteoli for a few days,' I said, watching the satyr dance within the fountain's flow.

'Puteoli?'

'Verus used to like Puteoli. Mother talked of it. He took his whole court there once for a few days. There are sulphur springs and baths that ease away aches and pains. It is said to be very good for you. Given the cold, why not? We can manage, what, four or five days' journey?'

'*Two* by ship,' reminded Commodus, but nodded. 'I know,

no ships. But Puteoli is more than healing baths. There lies also one of the gates to Hades. And close by is Cumae, where the Sibyl resides with her prophecies.'

I smiled to see the sadness at the edge of his expression slowly being subsumed by excitement at a new prospect. He might not be worried about sulphur baths, but a pagan prophecy? To be honest, despite what Mother would have thought, I was fascinated at the very idea. I would love to visit Cumae myself. And apologise profusely to the Lord afterwards, of course, but not at the expense of the visit.

'We shall go, if you wish to bathe in the vapours of Hades.' Commodus grinned. 'Or are Christians immune to such things? I mean, you do not acknowledge the gods, so what happens when they toast your backside? Do you just not believe it and it stops?'

'Mock me all you like,' I said, lifting my chin defiantly. 'Yet it's to me you come.'

He peered at me intensely for a moment, then pinched my chin between thumb and forefinger, pulling my haughty face back down and planting a forceful kiss that went wrong because we were both grinning too much.

People laud the great Vespasian and the magnificent Trajan and Hadrian. Yet Vespasian destroyed the Jews' whole world. Trajan was no friend of the Christian. Hadrian obliterated Holy Jerusalem and renamed it for himself. In *Commodus* was a man of true tolerance. My people could go far under his rule.

It was a perfect, tranquil moment, framed by the tinkling of the water. Like all perfect, tranquil moments, it passed too soon.

Voices outside were being raised in alarm. I looked to Commodus, whose brow lowered. He nodded and we both hurried out, past the shrine of the household gods and the doorman's cubbyhole, through the arch and into the cold morning air, pulling our cloaks around us.

The gardens were in turmoil. The gladiator guards were

swarming to the wall, armed and shouting to one another. Off to the side, out of sight, we could hear the metallic thunder as the Praetorian detachment emerged from their quarters and hurried around towards the villa's front. Still holding my hand, Commodus began to stride out across the circular garden towards the gate, where men were gathering. The walls were but eight feet high. Tall enough for privacy, yet paltry for defence. Along the inside were raised steps that allowed a guard to see over the top, and men on these steps were gesticulating outside.

I felt very tense suddenly. Beneath the buzz of action and voices around the villa there was a rumbling undercurrent. It was not dissimilar to that deep grumble that the vast armoured column made when we travelled north with the emperor's army. That very notion set me even more on edge. The noise was coming from somewhere along the drive, I was sure.

As we moved towards the gate, a man turned from bellowing orders at the gladiators and started waving at us. 'Majesty, you must return to the villa.'

'Why?' Commodus asked. 'What is happening?'

'A mob. A huge mob, Majesty.'

A mob? Here? The very idea seemed far-fetched. Yet that low rumble, like distant thunder, seemed to confirm it. The gates were opened and three gladiators hurried in, men whose duty it had been to keep watch on the surrounding area. Past the three men, we could see down the long drive to the main road, perhaps half a mile distant. There was a cloud of dust and many, many people. A mob it was. And mobs are a very specific thing. They are always seeking something, and no one ever heard of a happy mob. I was ready to do just as the gladiator officer had said and hurry back to safety when Commodus let go of my hand and shrugged off his cloak.

'Sword.'

'Majesty, inside you—'

'Give me a sword.'

Without further argument, the officer passed over his weapon. It was not a glorious, decorative officer's weapon or an emperor's blade. It was the tool of a killer, hard iron pitted with the marks of a hundred fights. Commodus hefted it expertly.

'Cowards run from trouble. Cowards like Nero. Cowards cannot rule an empire.' He turned to me. 'You go inside, Marcia. I will come for you when this is over.'

I shook my head. No way in Hell was I going inside and leaving him to face an angry mob.

'Ten men,' bellowed Commodus. 'The best ten, with me.'

The Praetorians were now falling in in two rows of eight, looking more than a little irritated that their emperor was relying upon his gladiators when his official elite guard was also present. Still, their centurion stood, blank-faced, awaiting orders that would never come.

To the shock of all present, except possibly me, Commodus brandished the sword and strode out of the gate onto the drive, the ten gladiators around him. I made to hurry after him, but the guards stopped me from leaving the villa. Foiled, I ducked to the side and climbed the steps so that I could see over the wall.

The mob was a mass of a few hundred souls, by my estimation. Mostly plebs in poor dress, though there were a few among them who were certainly equestrians. They were running, but not in anger. A *turma* of Praetorian cavalry was racing down the drive after them, spears levelled, blades brandished high. My heart leapt into my throat. These men were out for battle. They were not going to stop.

The civilians made it more than halfway to the villa before the cavalry ploughed into their rear ranks. I watched in horror as white-clad imperial guardsmen with their unique hexagonal, scorpion-motif shields began to butcher what appeared to be innocent Roman citizens. The first few were run through with spears, jerking and lurching to the side, falling in agony to be

341

pulped beneath the hooves of their killers' mounts. Then the swords began their work, cleaving and slicing.

I stared. How could this be happening?

The front of the crowd was closing on us now, howling for mercy as though it had been us who had commanded such violence. Commodus turned to look back at me and I could see the fury in his expression. He wheeled once more and began to bellow. One thing about my love that I may not have mentioned is his voice. He had a powerful baritone that was capable of carrying over most noise. In another life he would have made a great actor.

'Halt!' he bellowed.

The mob ground to a halt, stumbling into one another. Behind them the Praetorians, as yet unaware amid the dust cloud raised by so many feet and hooves, were still busy killing indiscriminately.

'Praetorians,' he called out at the top of his voice, 'form ranks!'

Oddly, where a single order had gone unnoticed, a more military command in an authoritative tone seemed to have the desired effect. The massacre slowed and stopped as the horsemen pulled back and returned to form a column, four men wide.

Commodus pointed at them with his raised blade. 'The next Praetorian who raises a hand against a Roman citizen without my express permission will be thrown into the Tiber in a bag full of vipers. Do I make myself clear?'

There was a rumble of acceptance among the soldiers.

'Now, what is the meaning of this?'

A dozen voices started to clamour at once. Commodus raised his hands to stop them, his scowl still angry. And then, as the noise subsided once more, a single horseman emerged from the ranks of the Praetorians like some figure from nightmare, trotting forward. He was in the uniform of a senior Praetorian and it was only as he broke clear of the worst of the dust cloud that I recognised the chamberlain.

'What is this, Cleander?' Commodus demanded angrily.

The chamberlain and commander of Praetorians reined in and sat straight in the saddle, looking down at the emperor. I noted with anger that he did not even bow his head in respect.

'Rome seethes with riots. I had word that a mob was bound for the villa, so we came to protect the imperial person.'

'Horse shit,' bellowed someone in the crowd, earning a fiery look from the rider. Commodus' head snapped back and forth between them. 'They are curiously unarmed for a dangerous mob, Cleander.'

'An enraged man can kill with his hands. Think what hundreds can do.'

'He lies, Majesty,' called that same voice from the crowd.

'I will have your fucking tongue, maggot, before you are nailed up,' Cleander spat.

The crowd parted and the speaker emerged. It took a moment for me to recognise Eclectus. He had lost weight and looked older. He wore the simple garb of a country man now, but it was most definitely him, despite the long hair and the matted beard. From secretary to the great Marcus Aurelius to angry revolutionary pleb. How far he had fallen. How far had he been *pushed*, I reminded myself.

Clearly, neither Commodus nor Cleander recognised the man.

'Is your appetite for torture not sated yet?' Eclectus spat back at him. I could see the indecision in Commodus. There seemed little grounding to the belief that this crowd meant harm, and yet he had always relied so heavily upon Cleander. Even I had to admit that the snake had never once shown a sign that he was anything other than loyal to the emperor.

'Let him speak,' I yelled from the wall-top into the silence that followed. Such a command issued at a critical time by a woman was shock enough to draw every pair of eyes in my direction. Most gazes were surprised or disapproving. I saw relief in Eclectus', interest in Commodus' . . . and blind fury in Cleander's.

'Marcia?' Commodus prompted, still craning over his shoulder to look at me.

'It is Eclectus, Majesty.'

His head snapped back to the dusty civilian. I could not see his face but could quite imagine what it looked like.

'You should have been put down when we had the chance,' snarled Cleander, but Commodus' hand, still brandishing that blade, shot out at him.

'Quiet, Cleander. Speak, Eclectus.'

'This man has turned Rome to revolt, Majesty. To the very brink of a civil war, in fact. Even now, the streets run with blood, for good men will no longer take his oppression and raise blades to defy him, even as he has his Praetorians gut the populace in the forum.'

He threw out a hand, pointing at Cleander. 'As the Praetorian commander, he has become overlord of Rome, master of spies and butcher of citizens. He casually murders those who oppose him and takes their lands. As chamberlain he is worse. Rome starves, Majesty. In times of such dreadful famine, the best of emperors past have increased the grain dole, doubled shipments, even diverted the navy to ease the crisis. What does this man do? Hoard what little is left in private granaries and put to the sword any man who tries to feed his family from what should be public grain.'

Unease crossed Cleander's face now.

'Is this true, Cleander?' the emperor asked, turning to the mounted man.

'After a fashion. On the advice of the grain commissioner, I began to stockpile the grain against the time of greatest crisis.'

I felt a strange lurch inside. *The grain commissioner.* Years

344

ago, when I began to build my web of allies on the Palatine, I had been introduced to Papirius Dionysius, who filled that role. Was it still he? Connections began to fall into place. Rufinus, the prefect of the fleet. A man who could impede or aid the flow of grain at will without the knowledge of the administration, probably in conjunction with Nicomedes, who could ease or restrict the flow of information at will with his couriers.

'You do not feel that starvation in the streets is the time of greatest crisis?'

I realised as Cleander opened his mouth again that not only was he not bowing his head, but he was also repeatedly failing to address the emperor with any kind of title or honorific.

'Things can always get worse. I was preparing for disaster.' His voice was becoming edgy.

'You were *causing* disaster,' Commodus snapped. 'What do the consuls have to say on all of this?'

Cleander's eyes narrowed. I could see him thinking his way around the problem, but he was too late.

Eclectus cleared his throat. 'Majesty, Consul Vitellius has fled the city, fearing Praetorian blades in the night, for he has already lost a son and most of his property to Cleander. Severus is one of those lionhearts in the city who wields a blade in defiance.'

Severus. Another of my conspirators. A city pushed to the point of revolt by oppression, starvation and disease. It had not taken much to finally burst the dam. Just the failure to feed the starving. A consul, a grain commissioner and an admiral. How neat. And how very hard to prove. Cleander must be sweating.

Commodus turned back to the chamberlain, who thrust out an angry finger at Eclectus. 'This man is twisting the truth. I followed the advice of the grain commissioner. He assured me more supplies were on the way. The Misenum fleet has been dispatched to speed the flow. The consuls should be helping to keep the peace in Rome so that I can do my job . . .'

It almost sounded plaintive. Almost like a child attempting to excuse some clear failure of their own.

'Yet you have driven one consul from the city and turned the other against you as a champion of the starving?'

Cleander shook his head. 'No.'

Still no sign of deference to the emperor. I could see Commodus' free hand constantly clenching and unclenching. He was becoming truly angry.

'And these people are such a danger that you thought to bring a turma of cavalry and slay hundreds of Roman citizens in my driveway?'

Cleander again, still shaking his head. 'No, but—'

'But you could not allow news of your mismanagement and cruelty to reach my ears?'

'No.'

'That would be no, *Majesty*.'

Cleander suddenly realised what he was doing and dropped his head. 'I sought only to serve.'

'I can see that now. I have been blind. Perennis once warned me. He said that you paid me lip service but only ever served yourself.'

Cleander was in the grip of panic now. 'No. Perennis was a traitor.'

'Was he? The evidence was always so uncertain to my eye. And Marcia has been telling me all my life that you only ever sought your own glory.'

'The whore is a liar.'

That was a mistake. I watched Commodus' hand fall very still as he spoke again.

'I should have listened to her years ago. Who knows, perhaps I would still have Saoterus. Eclectus would still be in the palace. Rome would not be under siege by its own populace and citizens would not be butchered on my drive by the imperial guard.'

'Listen, I—'

'You are hereby removed from the Praetorian prefecture and the office of cubicularius. I imagine there are legal hoops through which to jump with the senate, but they will not deny me when I brand you an enemy of Rome.'

Cleander's face blanched. *Enemy of Rome.* A traitor in the eyes of the empire. No chance of clemency. Even a swift death would be too much to hope for. '*No*, Majesty!'

Commodus took a few steps, the mob pulling back in fear and respect. Only Eclectus remained in place, head bowed. The emperor stopped before him. 'You are chamberlain and friend of the emperor. Deal with this animal.'

He handed his sword to Eclectus, who stared at it in shock, and then bowed. Commodus turned and strode back towards the gate, his gladiators pulling in behind him. Outside, the scene played out to its inevitable end. Eclectus brandished the blade and repeated, 'Enemy of Rome.'

Cleander, desperation flooding him, turned to the cavalry he had brought. 'Defend me!'

But the horsemen did nothing. Stripped of his command and labelled an enemy of Rome, Cleander had no authority over them. Instead, they fanned out, barricading the route back to the main road. The former prefect, aware now that all were against him, wheeled his horse. The Praetorians were blocking his path of escape. The emperor and his gladiators had reached the gate and were standing in the open space, preventing entry. The mob were starting to chant.

'Enemy of Rome.

'Enemy of Rome.

'Enemy of Rome.'

Had I been capable of even one iota of sympathy for the man, it would have come then. He was trapped, and he was doomed. The sides of the drive were lined with trees and statues and there was no space through which to safely guide a horse. In desperation, he turned his mount towards a seated statue of

Vulcan. Digging in his heels, he raced towards it and tried to jump.

Cleander was no horseman. He'd learned enough to ride convincingly, but he had no mastery of the beast. There was not enough space to make such an insane attempt, and the statue was too high, and the horse knew both. It refused, stamping to a halt and sending Cleander lurching in the saddle. The mob surged towards him, still chanting.

At the last moment, Cleander tried to draw the sword at his side, but suddenly arms were grabbing him, heedless of the nervous horse, people swarming all around mount and rider. Cleander was pulled from the saddle and disappeared amid the mass of bodies. I lost sight of him then, though my searching eyes scoured the crowd.

There was a scream. Then another. Then a long, blood-curdling howl, such as might be made by a soul in unimaginable torment. I know from what later remained that he was literally cut and torn to pieces while still alive by that crowd of furious citizens. What I saw next at the time was his head suddenly lifted above the mass to a whooping accompaniment. The sword Commodus had given Eclectus appeared from somewhere and the tip was jammed into the gore of the neck so that it could be held aloft, trailing matter and dripping dark blood.

Cleander was no more.

'Take him to Rome,' Commodus bellowed, and the crowd fell silent, that head bobbing around several feet above the others. 'Take him to the forum and make sure all of Rome knows his crime and his fate. Eclectus? Take the cavalry to the Palatine, attire yourself appropriately, and call a public address in the forum in my name. Take to the rostrum and tell the people of Rome that I am on the way home. And when I arrive, I will open the grain stores, reinstate the disenfranchised and con-struct a new grain fleet to double the imports from Africa and Aegyptus. Tell the people their emperor hears their cries.'

With that he returned to the villa with his men, the gates were closed and the mob, along with the cavalry and their grisly prize, turned and began the journey back to Rome. I stood at the wall for a moment while Commodus began issuing commands to his staff and guards. As the dust settled, all that remained were the bodies of two dozen or so civilians, and the unsightly lumps of meat that were all that was left of the man who had been my nemesis since childhood.

I should never have doubted Severus, Dionysius or Rufinus. Their plan had been long in the making, but it had achieved what no direct action could. They had brought down the unassailable tyrant.

I was free. Commodus was mine and all my opponents had gone: first Quadratus, then Lucilla, then Bruttia, now Cleander. Rome was ours. The *world* was ours. And I was going back to it on the arm of my Hercules.

PART FOUR

A ROMAN ICARUS

'As the thinning blood ebbed from Hercules' body:
so may the baleful venom devour your body'

– *Ovid: Ibis*, trans. Kline, 2003

XX

NO MERCY

Rome, AD 190

Anger and misery may be the blackest of twins, but they are not the same. In fact, anger can be every bit as much the antidote to misery as can joy. Thus it was that Commodus' anticipated slide into that old, familiar melancholy was arrested by his ire at Cleander and what he had done to Rome in the emperor's name.

We returned to the Palatine to the surging acclaim of the people. Even wallowing in starvation, eaten at by plague and impoverished by Cleander's constant taxation, the people had heard Eclectus in the forum. The emperor was coming home and he would make things right.

That began with killing, of course.

Cleander had been in power now for so many years that his tentacles had worked their way into every aspect of government and administration. With the aid of Eclectus, the emperor set about identifying any person who owed their career or position to Cleander alone. Each one was brought to the Basilica Iulia and there their accounts were examined, their deeds in office reported, evidence produced and witnesses located for and against. Any man found to have gained at the expense of Rome, been part of Cleander's corrupt web, been a detriment to society, or found to have abused their power or position, was condemned. And there was no mercy. No clemency. Those men who had been Cleander's creatures were killed. Few were given the treatment of traitors and tortured and abused, thankfully – most were simply executed, their families allowed to go on. A few knew what was coming and threw themselves upon the points of their blades like failed generals of old, preferring that to the ignominy of trial.

The two prefects of the Praetorian Guard who had been little more than Cleander's sword and dagger were removed. Regillus and Gratus met their end publicly with unexpected stoicism and professionalism. Pompeianus, that wily old dog who had been Aurelius' top general and had survived a coup led by his wife, stood trial, denounced by several of his fellows, yet no evidence could be produced against him. He returned home in peace, his honour intact, as he always did.

One sad morning was that upon which I watched the grain commissioner, Papirius Dionysius, bow his head in acceptance of the verdict at his trial. I was nervous for a time. Dionysius was one of those three conspirators I had found who, together, had engineered Cleander's downfall. Few in Rome knew how he had been part of a convoluted plan to starve his own city purely in order to bring about the end of the corrupt chamberlain. But he could not proclaim his innocence without condemning all who were part of the plan, and on the surface he appeared to have worked in collusion with Cleander to withhold the grain. Fortunately there was no torture, and Dionysius went to the grave with his lips sealed as I, Septimius Severus and Prefect Rufinus, among many others, watched the blade fall.

It was a bloody time. I saw men I had known for years go to the sword, men I was surprised to find had been in Cleander's purse. Yet no man went without there being evidence against him. This was not a massacre, but a purge.

The people cheered and thrilled to see their corrupt masters being punished.

The senate watched, silent, pensive. Many of those sent to Elysium were of that class, and while the people saw this as a rightful cleansing of corruption, to a certain sector of society it looked as though a wildfire were tearing through their world. The senators began to wonder who would go next. Commodus was, as ever, seemingly oblivious of the danger from that quarter. He had always shared his uncle Verus' unshakable belief in the power of skill over blood and continued to rely upon freedmen in spite of that august body that had once ruled Rome alone, without an emperor.

The senators, initially hopeful at the fall of Cleander, began to seethe as Eclectus slid neatly into his place as chamberlain. Indeed, matters were hardly helped when Commodus, so long removed from the corridors of power, put onto Eclectus' shoulders the burden of selecting new Praetorian prefects. In the event, he selected only one, returning the Guard to the sole command of the competent African Laetus, that very same man who I had once enlisted in my network of conspirators when he had been but a centurion in the Guard. Once again, the senate watched a powerful freedman choose a friend from the equestrian class to command. I knew Eclectus well enough to know that his motivations were good, and undoubtedly Laetus would prove to be the right choice, but to the senate this looked like an echo of Cleander's rise.

In the cold light of day I might be forced to acknowledge a certain level of overreaction in Commodus that spring. Certainly there will have been men who died in those months who had been driven to such acts by fear or coercion. Still, a cleansing fire was necessary to clear out the chaff of Cleander's regime, and that is what Rome got. In some ways it reminded me of that horrendous list of proscriptions after Lucilla's plot, though this time the list was not *by* Cleander's influence, but *of* it.

Servilius and Dulius Silanus, Antius Lupus, Petronius Sura

Mamertinus, Antoninus, Allius Fuscus, Caelius Felix, Lucceius Torquatus, Larcius Eurupianus, Valerius Bassianus, Pactumeius Magnus, Sulpicius Crassus, Julius Proculus, Claudius Lucanus. The catalogue read like a guest list for a consular dinner . . .

Against the background of this death and the growing worry of the senate, Commodus did many good things. True to his word, a new grain fleet was ordered, and construction began in the great shipyards of Carthage. The entire Misenum fleet was put at the city's disposal by its new prefect, ferrying vast quantities of grain, which the emperor paid for out of the imperial coffers. The storehouses guarded by Cleander's Praetorians in Rome were thrown open, their contents distributed among the poor and starving.

Still, it was not enough. Once the grain flowed and Cleander's men were gone, the world of the ordinary Roman returned to one of disease and poverty. The senate continued to bristle.

The subject of finance came to a head one balmy afternoon. Commodus and I were sitting in the octagonal fountain garden of the palace when a deputation of senators sought an extraordinary audience. The ad admissionibus bowed and retreated, and a party of half a dozen toga-clad luminaries entered, along with two men I knew to be involved in finance from their repeated presence at such meetings. The senators stopped a respectful distance from us and bowed as the Praetorians and gladiators standing guard watched them carefully.

'Gentlemen.'

'Majesty. It has come to the attention of the senate that the recent increase in taxation, which was a far from popular measure but was ratified on the understanding that it was connected to the need for new grain import, is being gathered for an imperial expedition instead?'

356

Commodus' left eyebrow rose a little.

'I was not aware that I was required to detail every nuance for the senate. But since you ask, yes. I have gathered together funds for a journey to Africa to see the commissioning of the new grain fleet enacted and to personally oversee the organisation of the new flow that will help ease matters in Rome. So in a way, the tax will most certainly be connected with new grain import.'

The senators shared a number of looks, and then another man spoke up.

'It is the belief of the senate that direct imperial oversight is not necessary in such matters, Majesty. It is suggested that such a use of tax is a waste.'

I saw Commodus' hand begin to twitch. He did not like to be spoken to like that, and less so to be dictated to by the senate.

'Is it?'

A third man tried another tack. 'Even the plebs, Majesty, might take offence at their emperor using newly gathered funds to visit far provinces when the city struggles in the grip of hunger and plague. They will wonder why no one pays to alleviate their troubles.'

Commodus spoke again, and now his voice had a hard edge to it that suggested peril for a number of dignitaries in the garden. 'I had no idea the senate cared so for the plebs. I honestly thought that the vast majority of senators saw the people as little more than livestock. Very well. I shall call off the trip.'

That first speaker bowed his head obsequiously. 'Might the tax be rescinded and repaid, Majesty?'

'Gods, no,' snorted Commodus. 'The senate can afford to bleed a little gold. Since you are so concerned with the plight of the commoner, the funds shall go on public games. We shall take the people's mind off their misery with your money, senator. How philanthropic you must be feeling.'

The men, their expressions of gratitude painted over sour faces, bowed, made appropriate noises, and retreated.

Once we were alone again, I smiled. 'Bravo, my love. Your uncle would applaud you. Your father too, I think.'

Commodus nodded. 'It is a small thing, though. I alleviate the people's burdens, punish their detractors, feed and entertain them, but I still cannot make Rome smile. The people are simply too broken. The plague has ravaged the city for so many years now that it seems like an old friend. The plebs have become used to starvation and oppression. Gone are those happy faces that greeted us ten years ago when we came back from Vindobona with my father's ashes, commanding a new golden era for all.'

'You do all you can. No emperor could do more.'

'But I must,' he said. 'Can you not see? Whatever I do it is not enough. The senators disapprove of me, and they resent what I do, but they obey sullenly. I do not worry about the senate. And the army is loyal, for sure. In the last ten years they have known peace for the first time in nearly half a century. They are loyal to the core. But the people have always been mine. I have always been their golden son. Yet now they have become quiet and miserable. Such cheering I hear is rote and strained. These are not the people I remember from when we came to Rome. Something must be done. When I acceded to the purple, Rome hailed that new golden age. I must bring it about. If I am to do anything for my empire, I must do that.'

I nodded. 'With the corruption gone, you have a chance. But it is about you, my love. All about you. When you were the new golden emperor of Rome, the people thrilled. But for years now they have seen only the pitted iron monster of Cleander. They must see you in your imperial glory once more.'

He nodded his agreement.

The rebirth of the empire began slowly, but it began then, in the aftermath of that meeting.

Despite the worries of the bean-counters in the administration, Commodus funded more games. He drained the treasuries to a new low, keeping them alive with a trickle of fresh taxes or the sale of unwanted imperial estates. But before long, rarely a day passed when there was not a race on at the circus, or a day of events in the amphitheatre, or some play in one of the great theatres.

The grandest of the shows in the amphitheatre was one of the strangest for me, as a Christian. It is a long-standing tradition, of course, to recreate ancient tales and legends in the arena, from the battles of Achilles' Myrmidons in the form of the eponymous gladiators, to the great recreation of the Battle of Actium replayed in the *naumachia*. But one day a reworking of the war between the gods and the giants was held in the Flavian amphitheatre, and I think that event in some ways spurred on what was to come.

The doors of the Gate of Life swung open and the entire crowd of the colossal amphitheatre hushed, tense, waiting to see what spectacle the emperor had planned for them that day. Then, into that expectant silence, stumped twelve men, dragging their way through the sand. Each one was enormous. The lanistas must have scoured the empire to find a dozen such giants. Each man carried a huge, iron-bound club and was dressed only in a loincloth and leg wrappings that had been fashioned to look as though serpents writhed around their shins as they moved. I was not sure how it had been engineered, but somehow those leg wraps hobbled the giants to some extent and they moved slowly and with difficulty to an appointed space at the centre of the arena.

The crowd cheered as the twelve giants moved into position. They truly were imposing men and I pitied whoever they were set against. My knowledge of pagan myth is not strong, and I had only a passing understanding of this tale of the dawn of gods and men.

The twelve deities of Olympus entered next, each dressed as their character, some armoured, others in only a robe, some naked. They were men and women, small and lithe, deliberately chosen to look diminutive against the giants. I smiled oddly, reminded of myself garbed as a gladiatrix for that festival three years earlier.

Jupiter came first, a purple robe draped around him as befitted the king of the gods. He brandished a long bronze javelin with a zigzag, lightning-bolt-shaped head. Juno wore a white robe and a gleaming bronze helm, a narrow-bladed spear in hand. Neptune was naked but for a gold crown, and carried a trident. Apollo, likewise stripped and oiled, carried a bow in one hand and but two arrows in the other. Ceres, the goddess of the harvest among other things, wore a white robe and carried a sickle. Minerva, armed for war, had a spear, while similarly attired Mars bore a short sword and shield. Diana, like her brother Apollo, carried a bow and twin arrows. Half-naked Vulcan with his leather skirt bore a dreadful-looking hammer, and Mercury a staff, fashioned like the caduceus, of bronze. Finally came Venus, naked but for a myrtle crown. She carried nothing.

I could see how the matching had been made. The difference in physical terms of the giants to their opponents had been cancelled out by partially hobbling them. They had heavy clubs with long reaches, but the gods bore a variety of weapons. In individual pairings some would clearly be doomed, but if the gods were to work together to bring down the giants, they could do so.

The crowd rumbled in anticipation, their woes of plague and hunger forgotten in the glamour of the vicious action about to unfold. *Bread and circuses, eh, Juvenal?*

The emperor rose and, as always, I thrilled to be seated next to him, where only a few years ago Bruttia would have been. The announcer down on the sands explained the tale of the gods and the giants and that this would be a rare contest, to the annihilation of one team or the other. I was hardly listening. I was having ideas. The crowd had been restive in their seats, as they had been all across the city since Cleander's deprivations. The giants had entered and a hush had fallen. But it had been when the gods appeared that the crowd truly fell into reverent awe. It was only now as I watched the preparation for an epic battle that I realised that to the bulk of the Roman populace their many gods were as much a cause for piety and awe as God was for me. Possibly more so, given my tendency to stray. I think the average Roman is far more pious, and certainly more credulous, than I.

Commodus needed to capture that. If his very presence could instil that same awe and reverence in the crowd, then wherever he went he would bring about that very golden empire of which he dreamed.

I thought on the matter at length as the fight began. The giants, aware that they were facing missiles, immediately broke from their centre and burst outwards like a dropped pomegranate's seeds, each making for an opponent. They moved in lurches, painfully, hampered by whatever lay beneath those wrappings.

Apollo and Diana both nocked arrows and released, then nocked and released once more, using early their only two missiles. To their credit, they were both clearly excellent archers and both struck with each shot, yet their arrows were enough only to wound and not to kill.

The first true combat occurred when Jupiter hurled his thunderbolt javelin, striking his giant in the torso, where the weapon penetrated deep. The hobbled victim howled and yet came on, struggling and yelping, aware that to pause here was to die, trying to swing his club even with a five-foot weapon hanging from his belly and dragging on the ground. The father of the gods nimbly ducked the pained clumsy swing of the club and grabbed his thunderbolt, tearing a huge hole in his opponent's belly as he dragged it back out.

Even as he dispatched his giant with a cry of glory, my attention was caught by Apollo, whose giant had reached him, despite the twin arrows jutting from his torso. The archer god tried to duck left or right, but other fights were going on there and no safe haven was to be found. He retreated towards the arena wall, panicking, aware he was becoming trapped. Finally, as he bumped into the stone periphery, the giant lifted back his great iron-bound club with a grunt of pain from his wounds and swung.

Apollo ducked, but the giant had anticipated the move and adjusted downwards as he swung. I winced as the great weapon smashed straight into the god's face, rupturing his head like an overripe melon and mashing it against the stone. Headless Apollo's twitching corpse collapsed to the sand, but he was avenged a moment later as his sister Diana appeared from somewhere with an arrow in her hand, which she slammed into the giant's neck, ripping open his artery.

The crowd roared with each horror.

I was impressed to see poor unarmed Venus, who I had thought doomed, riding the back of a giant, her arms around his neck, rapidly squeezing the life from her mount's throat.

It was over in perhaps a quarter of an hour, and five gods remained standing, all dozen giants gone.

It had won over the crowds with its innovation and glamour, but my mind was still whirring. Commodus the god. Had not he *said* that he would be a god? Even all those years ago as children, while Fulvus suffered his last, Commodus had said he would be Hercules. He had *been* the glorious demigod, in fact, that day he had fought off Maternus' killers in Praetorian white.

It was almost meant to be . . .

God's great plan. Did all gods have a plan, I wondered idly, or was it all my god?

Bread and circuses was a formula that Commodus began to turn to daily. No matter what the senate thought of his lavish presentations, he was keeping the people content. He was shepherding them into that golden age they had anticipated. Chariots thundered around the circus and gladiators and bestiarii fought in the arena. Plays new and old were performed. The people began to forget the plague that still stalked the streets of Rome, at least for a time. And with the new grain fleet now at work and the extra dole being delivered from Africa, hunger had abated.

I spoke to Commodus one night, finally content my reasoning from that day in the arena was sound.

'The people seem happier.'

Commodus, lying beside me, and toying idly with locks of my glossy black hair, nodded. I felt the movement on the pillow. 'Juvenal was astute. Would that I could remove the underlying cause of their ill and banish the plague. But neither my father nor the best physician in the world could manage such a feat. Yet we are at peace, starvation is forgotten, and only that Parthian sickness remains to ruin lives.'

'You are loved.'

He sighed and leaned over, kissing my neck, which sent a delicious shiver through me. 'Not by the senate,' he said as he leaned back again. 'But then do I care for the love of the senate? I most certainly don't *love* them. Not the way I love you,' he added, and kissed my forehead now, then my nose, then my lips, lingering for a long moment. He leaned back with a huff. 'But the men in charge of the treasury are beginning to worry about the funds I lavish on the people. To keep the plebs happy costs money, and we run low. I must soon choose what to do about it. The clear solution is to tax those men of property who we all know can afford it. But then my relationship with the senate will erode even more. And while I do not care overmuch for them, it would be foolish indeed not to consider the danger they might represent should they take against me.'

So he did consider the danger, then.

'You are of divine blood, are you not?' I asked, with a silent apology to God for even the notion. I knew there was no more divinity in Commodus than there was in me, but sometimes I had to play to the pagan in people.

'So they say.'

'The people need to *see* that,' I replied. 'Caesar built his temple to Venus Genetrix in the forum, reminding the whole world that he carried that goddess' blood. You told me about Hadrian and Jerusalem? Well, I read more upon that. Did Hadrian not build a temple of Jupiter upon the ruins of the Jews' holy site and place in it a statue of his deified self? These were the men who were walking gods. You are no Venus, nor Jove . . .' I prompted.

'I am Hercules,' said Commodus softly. It was said so quietly, so matter-of-fact, that I wondered then if perhaps he was beginning to believe in his own divinity. Still, despite everything, I did nothing to disabuse him of the notion. Rome hung in the balance now. He had almost healed the wounds caused during Cleander's reign of terror, but if this was to truly be the golden age of Rome, he could not stop and rely upon having done enough. He must always build. Always strive. Always improve.

'You are their Hercules. *Be* their Hercules.'

He nodded, then leaned over me. 'Then I must issue my first divine command,' he grinned, and rolled on top of me as I laughed breathlessly.

That summer there was a shaking of the ground in Rome, such as is recorded happening from time to time. The people panic, believing that Vulcan is angry, a few buildings develop cracks, there are a few injuries. It happens occasionally. But this particular tremor was much worse for one of the neighbouring towns. A deputation from Lanuvium reached Rome in the month of Augustus. I wonder what they thought to arrive at the front of the palace and be greeted by statues of Jove and Hercules, the latter bearing more than a passing resemblance to the emperor, for busts and statues of Commodus in the guise of his patron deity were beginning to appear in all corners now.

The men were shown into the aula regia. I was becoming known as the emperor's consort, an empress in all but name these days, and no longer did anyone blink to find me seated in the presence of Commodus during official engagements.

'My friends, welcome,' Commodus called warmly, rising from his seat and greeting the newcomers. 'How fares my city?'

I frowned for a moment at his choice of phrase, then realised that it was at Lanuvium that he had been born, in a villa that had belonged to Antoninus Pius upon a time.

The representatives from that town were unhappy, their faces downcast. 'Majesty, Lanuvium is in dire trouble. The city suffered a fire last year that was devastating. Much of the city's funding went to the extensive repairs that were carried out over the proceeding months. Indeed, the wealthy landowners and the ordo have all donated of their own purses to the effort. Then, a few days ago, the shaking of the ground came and caused fresh disaster. Much of our town is in rubble again, only having been reconstructed after the fire for mere months. Majesty, we simply do not have the funds to rebuild after this new disaster and we must throw ourselves upon the emperor's mercy and beg for his aid.'

Commodus nodded slowly. 'It would seem I am to be Titus to your Pompeii. Be of good cheer, dear friends, for Lanuvium is a city close to my heart. Though the treasury is low, I shall find ways and means to do what must be done. Return to Lanuvium and begin planning your rebuild. Nay, not just a rebuild, but a *refounding*. Lanuvium shall be greater, grander and better than ever. I vow it.'

The ambassadors left a short while later with endless words of praise for the emperor, bowing to kiss the statue of his Herculean self outside the door.

'Where will you find the money?' I asked.

He sighed. 'I fear it is time to make myself even less popular with the senate.'

But while he continued over the following months to widen that divide, he became ever more the people's emperor. Even during my rare encounters with the ordinary folk of Rome, I became aware that he was spoken of in the same breath as Hercules, in the same reverential tones as the gods. Statues of the curly-haired and bearded Hercules emperor appeared at strategic sites around the city and beyond. I heard it said that statues of Hercules in Athens had been reworked to bear the emperor's face. I felt quietly smug, for my initiative, born of observing a hungry crowd at the arena watching their gods, seemed to be working. Commodus was becoming a god to his people.

I suspect that my place in Hell has been earned by that as much as anything I have done in my life. All followers of Christ know that one of the inviolable rules of the faith is not to worship at false idols. How much worse is it, then, to *create* one?

Perhaps my very presence as a known Christian by the side of the emperor did some good, though, for my people had ever suffered ills at the hands of Rome. Worse under some emperors than others, admittedly, but never had we had a glory time. Yet now, people were beginning to think before they chided. Christians were beginning to identify themselves openly in the streets. Vicious governors and soldiers were being lenient with the faith, where before they would torture and condemn.

A chance at the redemption of my corroding soul came that autumn. Commodus was at his bath, which was sometimes a lengthy visit, and I was simply relaxing in one of the Palatine libraries, looking into the history and legends of Hercules, when one of the palace slaves found me and approached, bowing deeply. Odd how I had arrived first on this hill almost twenty years ago as a penniless peasant at whom even slaves looked askance, and now here I was bedecked in finery in a library, being bowed to by palace functionaries.

'Highness?'

That took me by surprise. It was not the first time I'd been referred to in such a manner this past year or so, but it always stunned me to be treated as though I were some kind of princess.

'Yes?'

The slave remained bowed.

'Someone seeks an audience with you, Domina.'

I frowned. This was new. 'With me?'

'Yes, Domina. He is some sort of priest, I think.'

Still beneath a furrowed brow, I pursed my lips. I was just the emperor's mistress. I did not hold audiences. I had no place to do so, and certainly the emperor's aula regia was out of the question.

'Show him to the library,' I said quietly. Was that appropriate? Would he be impressed? I was aware that in some odd way I would represent imperial authority and whatever I did would reflect on Commodus. While the slave was gone, I ducked outside and found a couple of Praetorians on guard.

'You. I need you in the library for an imperial audience.'

The soldiers looked at one another, each seeking guidance

from his friend. I had no official authority whatsoever over the Praetorians, but I was known to have the emperor's ear and was seated with him in public as though I were an empress. Refusing me could be a fatal career move. Both men bowed their heads and followed. Thus, when my guest arrived, I was seated in one of the city's most erudite places of learning, perfectly arranged and pretty, with two mean-looking Praetorians in attendance.

I boggled as my guest was shown in and the slave announced him.

'The high priest of the Christians.' He paused as he wrapped his tongue around an unfamiliar word. 'Bishop of Rome and pontifex of the Church, Aelius Victor.'

The servant left, and the man who was the head of my faith stood in the doorway, a long white robe covering a grey tunic, hair short and curly and beard neat and trimmed. Victor was clearly of African origin, his skin tone that of cinnamon, his flesh like well-worked leather. His eyes were a warm brown and he was tall.

'Highness.' He greeted me with a slight incline of the head.

I was baffled by how this worked. He was the high priest of a church that no one respected, while I was the de-facto empress, yet low-born and one of Victor's flock. I could see from his uneasiness that he was as unsure as to the realities of this as I.

I chuckled. 'We edge around this as though we wish to dance but neither knows how to begin.'

Victor gave a relieved grin. He was young for a man in his position, and I know that his predecessor in the office had died only the last month. He was still finding his feet in a world that was all new to him.

'Please, sit.'

He did so, sinking into a seat opposite me. 'It is said with surprising openness that you are of the faith, Highness. I do not know if you attend our meetings? I have not seen you at mine.'

I felt sheepish, looked it too. Mother would have disapproved to know that I had not attended meetings of the faith. But then she had lived a relatively unimportant life and had been free to do so.

'Sadly, in my position the opportunity is not often forthcoming,' I admitted. I probably could. It did not occur to me often. I lived my relationship with God largely in private.

He nodded. 'I understand. The world interferes with our faith all too often, and a lady in your position must have many demands upon her time.'

A few. A touch of guilt struck me, though, as he went on. 'I am here to petition you, Lady Marcia, and to beg you to intercede with the emperor.' I felt nerves touch me then. This sounded important. 'The governor of Sardinia,' he said, 'is a notorious hater of Christians. While the reign of the blessed Commodus has been a boon to our people and across the empire, much of the pressure has lifted as men have chosen paths of tolerance, the governor of Sardinia is steadfast in his hatred. On that cursed island, many sons and daughters of the Church are endangered and harmed. When a Christian is identified, they are charged with impiety and condemned to the mines, where they are worked to death on behalf of the Roman state. Is this, I ask you, a way for man to treat his brother? Would the emperor approve?'

In fairness, I doubted the emperor would care much one way or another, but the situation did sound appalling. I would like to say that I agreed to help through the altruistic nature of my Christian soul. It would be a lie. Like most of the less devout, my piety becomes greater when I perceive danger, and I knew that I had been a corrupt soul these past few years, my virtue on the decline. I perceived a way to perhaps redress the balance somewhat and make my heart a little more pure.

'I will speak with the emperor,' I said to the head of my faith. 'I will seek his support for your plight. Such things should not be allowed.'

He left with a grateful bow and I felt if anything more fraud-ulent than ever with the idea that I might buy redemption with the help of my love.

I did not want it to be official. To register such things in the annals of Rome might not be the best of ideas. I waited until we were alone that night, lounging in our bed, sated and content. If ever there were a time to ask something of a man, that was it.

'I have a favour to ask.'

He leaned close, his piercing blue eyes fixing me with their gaze. 'Ask.'

'Who is the governor of Sardinia?'

He frowned at me in confusion. 'A man called Sempronius. Huge eyebrows and no chin. Sense of humour of a drowned cat. Hates Christians. You'd love him.'

Sounded likely. 'Is Sempronius important?'

He snorted. 'Is *any* senator important?' He fell serious again for a moment. 'Not especially. He has connections. Old family. A few cousins and a brother in various positions. After Sardinia he'll probably just retire. I expect he will have skimmed enough gold off the top of Sardinia's coffers to make his retirement more than a little comfortable in that corrupt way all senators do. Why?'

'Are you willing to pit yourself against him for me?'

His frown deepened. 'What can he have done to you when you don't even know his name?'

'He persecutes Christians.'

Commodus sighed. 'There is no law against that, Marcia. Indeed, from time to time it is positively encouraged.'

'Not by you.'

'No,' he admitted. 'I have never seen the danger in Chris-tians. Perhaps that is your doing. Some say they anger the true gods. In my opinion the gods would be petty if they cared too much about the wayward wanderings of a small part of Roman society.'

'Would you be willing to intervene in his affairs?'

Now he shot me with a meaningful look. 'Officially, it is the policy of Rome to punish those who deny our gods – in particular the divinity of the emperors. It smacks of defiance and disrespect. In that manner, Sempronius is only supporting Roman policy. Interfering in such a thing would not be without its consequences. Would saving a few criminals in Sardinia make a grand difference to you? What of Gaul, then, whose governors use identified Christians to pad out the ranks of the gladiators since the plague thinned their numbers?'

I shuddered. That happened too? I bit down on my lip. I could not save everyone, but I could at least save some. 'Those on Sardinia I know are worked to death in the mines for nothing more than having faith in the same god as me. Would you send *me* to the mines?'

'Of course not.'

'And the only difference between me and those men and women is that you *know* me.'

'I might suggest there is a little more to it than that,' chuckled Commodus, but subsided as he saw the set of my chin and my determined expression. 'Very well. For you. For you, I shall have Sempronius recalled and given a nice little stipend to send him to happy obscurity. I shall make sure to appoint someone tolerant in his place and have all extant Christians in the mines freed. Does this make you happy?'

I smiled. 'Did you know that when we were in Athens I bought a new book called *An Embassy for the Christians* by a man called Athenagoras, and he had dedicated it to you?'

He laughed aloud. 'The man clearly had foresight. Then perhaps I had better do something about Gaul too, before he scratches out my name and replaces it.'

He was joking, but there was that about Commodus which meant he rarely said he would do something without at least attempting to carry it through. 'Will you?'

He rolled his eyes at me. 'That is an easy proclamation, to end their punishment as gladiators. It won't end your people's troubles, though, Marcia. Cruel men will always find a new way to abuse the weak. But for now it will close one door for them.' He laughed. 'D'you know, I rather *like* Christians? I wish all of Rome was as easy to please as your people. To make a Christian deliriously happy all you have to do is not set fire to him.'

I smiled and kissed him then, my glorious golden prince, champion of the just.

Hercules completing a new labour.

XXI

THE ROME OF COMMODUS

Italia, Maius AD 191

That spring we quit Rome for the summer. The city was settled. The people were as content as could be expected, given that the city was still ravaged daily by the ongoing plague and carts continued to ferry the dead out across the Quirinal in a macabre convoy. Still, chariots hurtled at a sickening pace around the circus and men fought in the arena for the gruesome entertainment of the mob. The senators still grumbled about the repeated increases in their taxes, yet they continued to pay and somehow still managed to get by with their amassed personal fortunes. The borders remained quiet and the armies of Rome continued to nestle in their garrisons, acting mostly as a peacekeeping force and living more as an army of builders and engineers than soldiers.

Happy that Rome was not going to become a seething hotbed of resentment in our absence and that Eclectus was trustworthy enough to leave at the reins of state, we abandoned the city when the temperature began to rise in late spring and moved south.

We had decided to take the journey we'd talked about during our last time away at Laurentinum, down to Puteoli where the gate to Hades and the sulphur baths waited. Imperial estates lay everywhere, having been confiscated when their original owners fell foul of the emperor of the day, and the Neapolis

Bay was no different. The main luxurious estate of the imperial family there had been buried during the disaster of Titus' reign a century earlier, when the mountain exploded and the city of Pompeii vanished beneath the earth. But there were still a couple of lesser estates, including a seaside villa at Surrentum, for which we were bound.

The journey along the Via Appia took seven days, for we were travelling at leisure and with no pressing timescale. The road passed through the landscape of Latium and I drank it all in as we went, for I did not have to worry about the sea this time. We were accompanied only by a couple of units of guards rather than a vast field army, which made travel easier, and we were heading in a direction that was new to me.

For two days the Via Appia marched through a gradually changing world, with the high craters and peaks of the Alban Hills on our left and on our right flat agricultural lands stretching out to the Tyrrhenian Sea some ten miles distant, the coast running parallel to us. At Tarracina we met the water and followed it onwards from there.

Though my attention was regularly swept up in the landscape or the fascinating and noteworthy places we passed – Caligula's Alban villa, the favoured estate of Antoninus Pius, and so on – I found myself pondering odd questions, one of which concerned the route that we travelled. The Via Appia is indisputably Rome's most famous road. She is often called the 'queen of roads' in fact, and it occurred to me that I had no idea what the name meant. This was compounded when, as the road moved from good solid land into the Pontine Marshes causeway, we passed through the small town of Forum Appii, where we spent the night.

'What does the name mean?' I asked over our evening meal. 'What?'

'Via Appia. Forum Appii. What are they named for?'

Commodus smiled. 'And here was I thinking that you knew

everything, always with your nose in a book. The road was the first real purpose-built military road in the empire. It was built half a millennium ago by a man called Appius Claudius. That's where the name comes from.'

I nodded, turning over this new knowledge in my mind. The great and the good of Rome often had buildings named for them. The Basilica Iulia. The Flavian amphitheatre. Even the Servian Wall. It was a way of remembering the great after their death, but it was also a way of honouring those luminaries while they lived, for not all such names were given posthumously.

An idea began to filter in at Forum Appii, and it strengthened and grew as we travelled. When we reached the Bay of Neapolis, we passed through the ancient port city of Puteoli and rounded the headland to Neapolis itself. Then, little more than a few miles from that sprawling metropolis, we passed through the latest of the innumerable small settlements on the route and my eyes widened at the place's name as we crossed the boundary into the village.

Marcianum.

I had the entire column stop and pointed it out excitedly to Commodus, who smiled and soothed my sudden activity as though I were an overreacting child. A town with my name! It was such a thrill to find. I had the tiniest hope that perhaps Commodus had had the place founded a few years ago in my honour, though that was clearly fantasy and the place was a lot older than that. But the name sank in and joined Forum Appii in my growing idea.

Rome was beginning to identify Commodus with Hercules, you see. The statues and friezes and paintings that had appeared in public places across the empire were received with appreciation. The people did not resent his association with Hercules, in fact they loved it. Romans always like to think they are special, more important than all other people, and having their emperor seen as a divine hero fitted well in their philosophy. Had not

375

Caesar been descended from Venus, or so he claimed? My faith allowed me something of an outsider's view on the matter, and I could see well how it worked.

Commodus was Rome's new Hercules, and all it had taken was a few statues to embed the notion in the minds of the people. But it did not have to end there. Commodus had become Hercules in the eyes of the people, but Rome remained Rome and as such languished under the twin torture of plague and taxation.

What is in a name, though? Names are mutable, changeable things. Commodus himself had been born Lucius Aurelius Commodus. On his accession he had dropped the Lucius and taken his father's name Marcus, identifying him as the successor. A simple name change but an important one. The land through which we were passing was once the land of the Aurunci before it became Rome. What did *they* call the place? What about when Neapolis was Greek, before the days even of the Republic? Names change.

Better still, names were given to identify with important people. Just as Forum Appii was named for this Appius Claudius fellow in the distant past, there was a long tradition of such things. Forum Iulii in Gaul, named for Caesar. Pompelo in Hispania, named for his enemy Pompey. And Jerusalem that, as Commodus himself had told me, had become Aelia Capitolina under Hadrian, named for his own family. If other great men could have places named for them, why not Commodus? Why stop at the new image of the Herculean emperor?

It was an exciting idea, and the more I thought about it as we travelled, the more I realised it could be done without seeming ridiculous. Had not whole months been renamed for Julius Caesar and his heir Augustus? I knew of legions that bore the names of emperors they served well: the Thirtieth Ulpia Victrix of Trajan; the Fourth Flavia Felix of Vespasian. I began to see possibilities.

376

Commodus wanted a new golden age for Rome, and his people had been anticipating it ever since he ended the Marcomannic War and brought peace to the empire. It had not come about, though, through the constant deprivations of the plague and the mismanagement of men like Cleander. Well, there was little we could do about the plague, but the corruption had been cut out of Rome, and now was the time for Commodus to rebuild, to glorify, to create. Now that golden age could begin, at last

I smiled all the way down the remaining coast towards the villa. I kept my thoughts to myself, letting the idea bubble away like a soup of invention. Commodus kept throwing me intrigued glances. He knew I was up to something, and was interested, but I wasn't quite ready. Perhaps what I needed was the catalyst to bring my half-conceived idea into the light of day. I smiled at his intrigue as we passed through the great urban sprawl of Neapolis, of which my overriding memory is the smell of old fish. We travelled past the high peak of Vesuvius, which had exploded and buried those poor towns nearby, causing the death of that same admiral Pliny whose estate at Laurentinum had bordered ours. Somewhere under those lush fields lay one of the old imperial estates, lost at the same time as the whole city.

Then it happened. I found my catalyst. My trigger.

We passed through a small shanty village that bore a rather grand sign proclaiming its ancient name. The true town, equipped with all the paraphernalia of a grand Roman *urbs*, had been yet another victim of that terrifying mountain, but its name lived on in the village built atop its ruins.

I stared.

Herculaneum.

In fact, I was so astounded to see the name that I gasped, drawing Commodus' attention.

'What is it?'

'It's a sign,' I breathed, reverentially.

'It is. It's a sign for Herculaneum,' he said prosaically.

I rolled my eyes. 'You're a follower of omens and portents. What else could this be, this city of Hercules?'

He frowned. The connection had clearly not struck him before. 'It was supposedly founded by the demigod himself. Here was where he defeated Cacus and built a city. I always wanted to come as a boy, as a sort of pilgrimage, but Father would never devote the time to visiting the site of a city that is no more. Too many living places to take care of, he said.'

I nodded, still distracted, still marvelling.

'But this is your city. This is the land of Hercules. And it is God telling me that I am thinking along the correct line. It is time, my love.'

He frowned, but his interest was clearly piqued.

'Time for what?'

'Time for your golden age in Rome. You say you still want to see it happen? Now is the time, and portents have been assailing me all the way here. Appius. Marcianum. Herculaneum. It's all in the names.'

'You speak in riddles, Marcia.'

'No. No, it's very clear. You told me the story of Hadrian and the Jews. That dreadful revolt and the unsettled nature of Judea. Hadrian wanted a new age. He wanted to wash away the rebellious past and create a proper Roman province there. He did it with names and symbols. He swept away their ancient temple and built a Roman one, and in it he put himself as a god. And because even the name Jerusalem carried the taint of rebellion, even that name had to go. It became Aelia Capitolina – the capital of Hadrian. He rewrote the very identity of Jerusalem to make it a new place.'

He was still frowning, but I could see a sparkle in his eyes now. He had caught some of the fever of excitement from me. He nodded, encouraging me.

'It's not unknown,' I went on, almost breathless, 'in fact, there is a long tradition of great men stamping their name on the empire. The Fourth Flavia Felix. The Via Appia. The Basilica Iulia. Even the Dacian king's old capital became Ulpia Traiana after Trajan's own name. And these names have stayed. They have changed the very identity of that to which they are applied. I mean, think of the months that were Quintilis and Sextilis? How long is it since those names were used? Now the summer months are Iulius and Augustus.'

He was nodding now, but I had the bit between my teeth.

'A golden age needs a line to differentiate it. There needs to be a clear point at which you can say, "This is when things change. This is when dirty old Rome, weighed down by war and disease, seething under the corruption of bad men, ends. This is when the new Rome begins. The Rome of Commodus. The *golden* Rome."'

His eyes were bright as he caught up with me on the run and took the baton. He leaned forward, gesturing wildly. 'A new foundation. As Romulus founded Rome and Venus founded the first imperial dynasty, so a new divine hero. A new foundation. A Rome of Commodus, yes, but also a Rome of Hercules. Hadrian may have rebuilt Jerusalem as Aelia Capitolina, but of equal importance was the statue of himself in the temple of Jupiter. A statement. That Hadrian was the king of gods in that place that now bore his name. So I cannot just be Commodus. I must also be Hercules.'

I nodded. 'Your statues are already in place.'

'No, Marcia. Don't you see? That is just me in the clothes of a god. Me dressed as the man. And the people know that. But that is not enough. I must *become* Hercules.'

I could almost feel the energy vibrating from him and I nearly fell into the vision alongside him, so seductive was it. But he was *too* energetic. Manic, almost. This was not just excitement. This was a momentary flash of that same Commodus who had oiled his flesh and strapped on bronze plates to fight in the arena. This was Cleander's Commodus. I felt just a tinge of warning at that realisation.

'I'm not sure you need go so far,' I said quietly.

'Nonsense. I am strong like Hercules. I am a twin like Hercules. I am of divine blood just as he. I can fight. I can run. I can overcome any labour that great hero managed. Fetch me Geryon and I shall loose a deadly arrow true to his skull.'

'Listen . . .'

But he was beyond mere listening now. I had stoked something and let it loose, and Commodus was running with the idea. 'All things. Not just a month. Why one month? Why not all of them?'

'You cannot call every month Commodus. No one would know what time of year it was.'

He shot me an exasperated look. 'Don't be facetious, Marcia. You know what I mean. And I shall attach the name to the legions. The Herculians or the Commodiana? Or both?'

'Which legion? It is peacetime, so none have really had the chance to distinguish themselves.'

'All of them, then. Why not? An honour to every soldier of Rome, not just one unit.'

I shook my head. 'That's too much.'

'No. That's the thing. It isn't. Watch.'

He leaned out of the window of the carriage and waved over a Praetorian cavalryman who'd been riding alongside. 'With whom did you serve before you were transferred to the Praetorians, soldier?'

The man frowned. 'The Seventh, Majesty.'

Commodus nodded. 'The iron that holds Moesia together. Veterans of Caesar's wars and of Trajan's. A good legion. You must be proud.'

'Prouder to be Praetorian, Majesty, but yes. The Seventh were my home for many years. My family.'

'And what is their full title, soldier?'

'The Seventh Claudia Pia Fidelis, Majesty.'

'And why is that?'

'Because we supported that emperor and put down the usurper Scribonianus, Majesty. Proud to be the Claudian legion, loyal and faithful.'

Commodus nodded. 'Of course you are, and rightly so. Once upon a time, they were just the Seventh, fighting in Gaul under Caesar. But under Augustus, when they were already known as *Paterna* – the old ones – they acquired the name Macedonica for their time in garrison there. But for more than a century they have been the Claudia Pia Fidelis, and proudly so.'

He waved the rider away, and the cavalryman moved back into position. Commodus gestured at me. 'You see? They are proud of their name. But I would wager that before then they were proud of being the Macedonica. And before that they were proud of being the Paterna. Every name carries a tale, Marcia, and a new name just adds to the pedigree.'

I was less convinced. 'Slowly. Carefully. Draw a line, but do not aggravate people with it.'

'You worry too much, Marcia.'

And that was it. For the remaining twenty miles that brought us into Surrentum at the close of day on a balmy spring night, Commodus enthused about the possibilities for his new golden Rome. I had to repeatedly haul myself back and be objective, for it was almost hypnotic and was most definitely enticing, listening to the litany of possibility. Commodus' vision of the new world was grand. Grander than reality generally allows, of course, but then I have heard it said that only dreamers change the world. I was exhausted from listening to the plans by the time we arrived at the villa, and I slept well that night.

I awoke the next morning to find myself alone. I had woken beside Commodus now for long enough that it felt odd and worrying to do otherwise. I rose, performed my morning ablutions and dressed, allowing my hair to simply hang wild. I scoured the apartments, but there was no sign of him.

I enquired of the guard, but all I could glean was that the emperor had gone out for the day and would return in the evening. A little investigation revealed that wherever he had gone he had taken Praetorians and gladiators both. There was little I could do about it, and so I spent the day exploring the estate and perusing the market and shops of Surrentum with an appropriate escort. It was a pleasant way to spend the day, and the Sorrentine peninsula is a ridiculously beautiful spur of land. I even appreciated the sea, partially because it was some distance below me over the cliffs and therefore safely far away. Still, I did not linger at the sea views. By mid-afternoon I was starting to become a little twitchy. I did not like Commodus being away from me, and I liked not knowing where he was even less.

He returned just before the evening meal, looking tired and pale. I hurried over to him and asked if he was all right. Was he unwell? He shrugged it all off and waved me away, telling me everything was fine, though his expression suggested otherwise. There was a haunted aspect to those glorious blue eyes that had not been there the day before. In fact, I had not seen that particular look since he had been forced to order the execution of Perennis, despite believing the man to be innocent.

I pressed him for information as he bathed and changed.

'I crossed to Capri,' he said quietly.

'Bruttia.'

'Yes. It was part of my reason for coming here. It had to end, Marcia.'

'Is she . . . ?' But the answer to that was evident in his eyes.

'I made sure it was quick and as painless as possible. Bruttia had changed, Marcia.'

I could understand that. Exile on an island for more than a

year, away from everything you knew and loved, could hardly fail to affect someone.

'Was she contrite?'

'She said things, Marcia. Terrible things. I . . .'

He walked away then, his sentence unfinished. I tried to speak to him about it for the rest of the evening, but once he had stopped, he refused to be drawn further. He had closed off that part of his life and sealed it away now. I felt a tiny thrill of worry over what Bruttia might have said, but no matter how I worried at it, the fact was that she knew nothing of anything underhand I had ever done. She could hardly incriminate me. What, then, had she said that was so terrible for Commodus to hear?

That evening he began to talk more on his plans for his new Rome, though he felt different. Less enthusiastic. More subdued.

We would cut short our summer at Surrentum and return to Rome to institute his grand new plan. He continued to feel odd and distant. I hoped that returning to the city would change that, but hopes are like clouds – the slightest breeze and they tear apart and drift away.

XXII

BLACK CLOUDS

Rome, Maius AD *191*

Whatever had passed between Commodus and Bruttia Crispina as she waited for the blade to descend on that island of exile had changed everything. On the surface, the emperor was the same man with whom I had fallen in love, but there was something new beneath the surface. It was as though he wore a new mask, but this one was impenetrable and I could no longer tell why he wore it. It certainly wasn't the old familiar melancholia that I knew how to deal with.

We continued to share a bed, and even a life, but I could feel him pulling away from me, infinitesimally slowly, but doing so all the same. And I did not like the direction he was taking, either. Where he had spent a year or more holding great races in the circus and cheering on the victors, lavishing gifts and praise on them, now he would take part himself, against all the advice of his friends and family. Chariot racing is the most dangerous sport in the world. More charioteers die per event than gladiators, for the fights are often to first blood, while a man whose chariot fails him is invariably dead when he is carted from the sand. I stopped going to the races altogether. I could not watch him endanger himself so.

The new quiet distance that had settled upon us meant that when I tried to persuade him of the folly of his endeavours it only spurred him on to greater heights. It was appalling. I could almost feel the spectre of Cleander hovering over both of us, laughing. Damn the man, but even in death his shade still cast a pall.

And while the emperor thus far stopped short of actually taking part in the gladiator fights in the arena, he did begin to join the bestiarii and the *venators* there, hunting beasts before the crowd. Again, I would not go and watch, though I knew from all our time together that he was a master huntsman, and I did not really fear for him in those events. But in addition to widening the growing rift between us, his participation also increased the gulf between him and the senatorial class, who disapproved utterly of his activities.

It was as though he had no fear of death. It was as though he challenged death to take him. Perhaps I was wrong, and there *was* an element of that old familiar melancholia there, after all. That same little boy who tore out his hair and dreamed of how it would feel to die. Still, I could not get through to him, could not persuade him to change his course.

And perhaps the most agonising thing about it all was not knowing why this change was occurring. It had something to do with that visit to Bruttia on Capri, but he would not discuss what happened there. He continued with a glazed smile as though nothing was wrong. We walked together, ate together, made love, but it felt different now – a life by rote. Perhaps this was how his wife had felt all those long years of their arranged marriage. I did not like it. I was losing the Commodus I loved and gaining in his place that Commodus that had been born of Cleander's influence, given to dangerous extravagance.

Summer came with its oppressive heat and dust, and the rich, already unhappy with the emperor's actions, disappeared to their country estates, leaving only a populace of the poor and diseased. The undercurrent of misery in the plague-ridden streets was glossed over with the excitement of the games and of the golden Hercules who took a personal role in much of it. Indeed, he began to wear a Greek-style chlamys of white and gold in public, instead of the staid Roman toga, and had his lictors carry before him the lion skin and club of Hercules, further identifying himself with that great hero. The people drank it in. We walked side by side in public as though I were an empress, yet that invisible wall between us remained, seemingly built by Bruttia Crispina even as she died.

Still at night he came to me and we lived our lie for a little longer, though even as he lay next to me I fretted over how I could repair a wound when I could not identify the cause. I did everything the physicians said in an attempt to sire him an heir, hoping that a pregnancy would close that rift somehow, but nothing happened. The prosaic woman in me had decided that those oysters and silphium Quadratus had forced into me years ago had ripped from me the ability to bear a child. The Christian in me told me that I had become so wicked that God would not let me procreate.

So we drifted on.

We were lying wrapped in our sheets one sultry Roman summer night. Commodus, tired by a day's exertions, lay on his back, snoring gently. I lay on my side, facing away from him, wide awake and yet again trying to reason through a way to close the open wound in our relationship.

The first sign that anything was wrong was, for me, a preternatural feeling. Suddenly, gooseflesh prickled my skin and the hair rose on the nape of my neck. Something was out of place. I rose and crossed to the window, which looked out from our lofty perch over the valley of the circus. I shivered as I reached the window, unwilling for a moment to twitch aside the drapes, reminded of that day as a young girl I had made these very same moves to see a vast wall of water crashing along the street towards me.

Not this time. Still cold and skin-prickled, I half expected to see water everywhere, but there was nothing. The streets beside the great circus were dry and poorly lit, beggars, whores and drunks the only occupants at this time, half of those busy dying on their feet.

But I was aware of something else. There was a distant murmur. The sound of a huge din muffled by distance and direction. Something was happening, but it was happening at the far side of the city centre, beyond the Palatine, perhaps in the forum. My pulse began to quicken. The forum was where trouble often began. It was the main public gathering space where grievances were so often aired. I wondered whether someone had finally taken against Commodus' new sports or his lion skin and club, enough to gather supporters and demonstrate.

Surely not. The senators who disapproved were largely absent, and rousing a rabble in the forum would be too much like real work for their sort anyway. No, it had to be something else.

Leaving Commodus to sleep, I padded across to the door and opened it. The corridor was empty and I paced along it and through the building, taking several turns and passing through doorways. I did not want to leave the complex and encounter the Praetorians on guard when I was still in just a silken tunic that left little to the imagination, but I did want more of an inkling as to what was happening. Most of the imperial apartments are angled to face the circus valley rather than the more level, public areas of the Palatine, but the complex is huge, and lightly traipsing up a flight of stairs and crossing several rooms I rarely visited, I moved to one of the few viewpoints facing north.

The windows here were neither shuttered nor covered with drapes, allowing the night air to waft in and out with what paltry breeze there was. I shivered as I approached, despite the heat. At first there still appeared to be nothing wrong. I could not

387

see the forum from here, nestled in its valley, and my view was largely of the palace rooftops, but I could see the distant twinkling lights of the Quirinal, Viminal and Esquiline hills beyond, and the deep, dark purple night sky, heavy, like a blanket.

The one thing that was wrong with the view slowly insisted itself upon me. That blank sky. It was high summer and there had been little more than light, high, wispy clouds for many days now, and rarely even them. Where, then, were the stars?

It was now that I realised the sky was moving. That dark blanket was not the sky itself, but a vast cloud of smoke pouring across it. Even as my eyes widened, the huge pall of black billowed and blotted out those tiny myriad lights on Rome's northern hills.

I squinted. The source must be somewhere in the forum dip. This was too big to be a deliberate fire set by a man, though. This was clearly a conflagration of some magnitude. I hurried back through the rooms of the palace now, desperate. On my journey through those night-time rooms trying to find a high window, I had seen not another soul, not even a slave. Now, though, as I returned, the place was coming to life. Servants and slaves hurried about in a panicked manner, calling to one another. Pairs of Praetorians scurried this way and that.

I reached my room to find the door open and the interior lit with lamps. Two Praetorians stood outside and as I entered I found Commodus pulling on a clean tunic and hurrying to find his boots. Slaves rushed in carrying my clothes and a toga for him, as well as his now customary Greek attire.

'This is no time for such things,' Commodus snapped at the slaves, belting his purple tunic and slipping his feet into his calfskin boots. He noticed me as he looked up. It is perhaps a sign of how things had changed that he never even bothered to question why I had not been in the room with him when he awoke. 'You've heard?'

'I have seen, from a high window. The forum, I think.'

Commodus shook his head. 'The guards tell me it seems to have started in the Subura, but had spread to the Temple of Peace before the vigiles could even get their fire carts from the sheds. Rome is ablaze, Marcia.'

And then he was off. I hurriedly threw on my saffron stola and lilac palla, pinning them in place as I scurried along behind the emperor and his men. A slave running at my heel carried my sandals, but I let him continue to do so as I did not have time to pause and slip them on.

'Have all the vigiles been called out across the city?' Commodus asked as Eclectus appeared from nowhere and fell in alongside us, a pile of wax tablets in his grip.

'They have, Majesty. And I have dispatched riders to Ostia, Veii and Bovillae to seek extra manpower.'

Commodus nodded. 'How bad is it? Bad enough to call on other towns, clearly.'

'This is a disaster in the making, Majesty. Already the flames have reached the *horrea piperataria*, the storehouses of the eastern spice merchants. The only saving grace at the moment is that what breeze there is blows to the south and the fire comes this way, towards more spacious open areas. If the breeze changes and the flames spread through the Subura, we could be looking at a citywide blaze.'

I shivered at the thought. Such a disaster would be as bad as that flood in my youth. Worse, even.

'Deploy the Praetorians and the urban cohorts,' Commodus said, waving at the chamberlain. 'Set them to keeping order where necessary, but also to the creation of firebreaks. We can do little with the forum and Palatine, and must just hope and prepare, but we can tear down the poor housing in the Subura and hopefully prevent the blaze extending that way.' He paused as Eclectus struggled to open a map, and the two peered at it. 'Send word for the men of the fleet at the Navalia to join with the vigiles and set up extra water sources here, here and here.'

His finger stabbed at the map and just for a moment I saw in Commodus a flash of his uncle that first night, the eve of the flood, when Verus and his co-emperor had taken in hand the protection and safety of the city themselves. Commodus was glorious again, then, his love for the city overwhelming anything else.

Even me.

For as we dashed from that place, officers and administrators flocking to Commodus' side, not once did he look at me. Once he would have sought advice from me. Not that night. Not any more. Somehow Bruttia had ended that.

We hurried from the palace and emerged into a city in chaos. As Commodus paused to issue a stream of orders to the men around him, who then ran off in all directions, I took the opportunity at last to slip on my sandals. Then we were off again, heading for the northern slope of the Palatine. The huge, roiling black clouds now filled the entire sky like some dreadful portent, blotting out moon and stars alike. The heat from the conflagration was intense enough that it could be felt even here, more than two hundred and fifty paces from the flames, and the noise of the panicked population was audible even over the deep, throaty roar of the fire.

The scale of the nightmare was staggering.

From our high vantage point, the path of the inferno was clearly visible. A small portion of the Subura was already little more than the charred bones of buildings amid a glowing golden mass. The first act of the vigiles had been to pull down the adjacent houses to impede the spread, but now, following Commodus' initial orders, Praetorians and men of the urban cohorts were moving into position too. The fire was already leaping the gap of the demolished buildings, embers carried on the breeze catching at the next tinder-dry house, clawing at it until it burst into flame. The soldiers were using long poles with hooks and ropes with grapples to haul at walls and tear them down, filling the streets with rubble and creating wide spaces to stop the fire.

The Subura could be saved, but if the long history of fires in Rome has taught anything, it is that a conflagration in the city will run amok as it pleases and defy all attempts of men to halt it. In the event, those firebreaks did work, and the northern side of the city was saved by the loss of a few housing blocks.

The other directions were a different matter entirely.

From the starting point of the blaze, the fire had leapt to the Temple of Peace, that grand marble space at the forum's edge built by the Flavian emperors to celebrate the suppression of Judean revolts and the end of the civil war. The temple was now all but gone. The glorious white marble was black and charred, the roof caved in, the interior gutted and all the glorious paint burned off. I realised with a start that this temple was also used as a vault by some of the richest men in Rome – a sort of personal treasury in the same manner as the Temple of Saturn served for state finances. The blaze here would have made paupers of some very important men.

Leaving the temple little more than a marble carcass, the blaze had leapt into the warehouses at the eastern end of the forum, including those spice stores that had been mentioned before. Oddly, when you took a deep breath, which we tried not to do too often, being downwind of the fire, as well as smoke and soot there was an odd heady scent of super-heated incense. It was quite strange.

The vigiles were at work trying to prevent the blaze extending to the great temple of Venus and Rome, and they truly had their work cut out. Every time they managed to force back a tendril of fire that threatened the temple, another place would suddenly explode in a great orange fireball, engulfing screaming firefighters and scoring the walls of neighbouring structures. I could see Commodus deliberating whether it would be acceptable to pull down part of that most significant temple in order to save the rest, but to do so would be the worst kind of impiety and would be seen by Rome as some kind of sign. I was reminded unpleasantly of that rumour that had spread in our youth that Verus' sacking of the Temple of Apollo had been the cause of the great plague that had been with us ever since. While I did not like to lend credence to superstitious pagan talk, even I worried about what next great ill might befall us if we pulled down the temple to Rome itself.

At the far end of the disaster the blaze was more easily contained, as the wind did not currently threaten the forum proper, though men were in position to stop it as best they could should the breeze change.

The real danger lay at the centre of our view, directly ahead. The blaze was crossing the Via Sacra in the form of sparks and burning debris and already shops and warehouses on this side of that important road were bursting into golden flame. I watched, heart in throat, as more vigiles arrived, panting and sweating, having driven their vehicle from some distant quarter of the city. Even as I watched, they began to pump the wooden handles on the cart, forcing water from the mobile reservoir into a pipe that they could aim at the critical spots. Others were creating human chains, passing buckets in a constant line from any of the numerous water sources.

It was having little effect. Some three thousand men were already at work in a relatively small area, armed with everything they needed to fight a fire, and yet they were losing this war. For every building they managed to douse and extinguish, another two caught and exploded into fireballs.

The blaze was coming our way.

The Praetorian prefect appeared from somewhere and gestured to Commodus.

'You must leave, Majesty.'

'What?' The emperor turned to his officer.

'The peril is too great. I have men ready to convey you to safety in the Praetorian fortress. From there a convoy can take you from the city to one of the imperial estates while this is dealt with.'

'I am going nowhere, Prefect.'

The Praetorian looked troubled, but pulled himself up straight. 'Respectfully, Majesty, I must insist on conveying you to safety. The emperor cannot risk his life in such a manner. The fire is moving towards the palace rapidly and clearly nothing will stop it.'

Commodus fixed him with a look. 'A hundred years ago Rome burned almost to the ground. The emperor – that universally despised degenerate, Nero – acted like a hero for days, seeing to the safety of the people, organising relief, commanding his men in an attempt to halt the blaze. Are you seriously suggesting that I quit the city like a coward and let my people burn when even *Nero* stayed to help?'

The prefect lurched back from the vehemence of the emperor's angry tone, but he acceded readily. The emperor would stay.

I stood there, rooted to that spot, coughing in the hot, smoky air, for the next two hours as Commodus continued to oversee the war against the blaze. A constant flow of men, both military and civilian, attended him, and a small army of scribes and runners hurtled this way and that with questions and commands.

I watched.

The fire had caught swiftly in two more temples in the forum, and men struggled to prevent it spreading any further that way, where the heart of the ancient city lay, including its most powerful and critical temples and basilicas.

Worse still, the flames that had leapt the Via Sacra and set ablaze rows of shops and stores at the bottom of the Palatine slope had now spread to one of the most important buildings in the city. The eternal flame that burned in the heart of the Temple of Vesta was now utterly lost amid a much greater blaze that ripped and roared around that building. The adjacent grand House of the Vestals had gone up like dry tinder and the flames that danced on its roofs were now threatening the lower reaches of the palace of Tiberius and Caligula at the western end of the Palatine.

I watched in shock and dismay as the virgins of Vesta escaped their blazing sacred house, already missing one of their number, and threaded their way through clouds of billowing smoke, a thousand dancing motes of orange and desperate, filthy fire-fighters, and made their way up towards the Palatine. Ahead of them they bore the Palladium, the sacred wooden statue of Athena that had come to Rome after the fall of Troy and which was kept hidden under permanent guard, never seen by the eyes of the world. Not so, now. The misshapen ancient lumpy goddess was black, and I feared for a moment that one of the city's most sacred relics had been burned, though apparently that was how it always looked. It was ancient, after all, and had been carried from a burning city all those centuries ago.

The Vestals were escorted into the palace by Praetorians and the battle against the deadly blaze before us continued. I realised just how perilous things were as the night wore on, and began to wonder whether the Praetorian prefect had been right. The breeze remained a slight, yet steady southerly, and the flames continued to advance on the Palatine.

The teams of men dealing with the fire began to concentrate on the lowest slopes of the Palatine, dousing the roof of the Vestals' house, hurling endless buckets of water into the shops on the Via Nova, buildings whose very bones were built into the foundations of the palaces above. Despite the many men working there, they were still losing. Some enterprising soul at the Tiberian palace had set up another three bucket chains fed by the fountains and ponds in the palace gardens, which were soaking the northern edge of the palace constantly, preventing the flames that licked all around it from taking hold. There were no such easy sources of water where we were or on that part of the palace closer to the amphitheatre, though, and the fire was making inroads there despite the best efforts of all concerned.

Finally, as the pre-dawn light began to show beyond the Caelian Hill, barely visible beneath the cloud of choking black, we had to move. The fire was advancing across the Palatine. Due to a happy combination of wind direction and those three bucket chains, it neatly avoided the Tiberian palace and the atrium of Caligula, but the recently reconstructed Temple of Jupiter Palatinus and the various civil structures on these slopes were at great risk.

At the emperor's command, the remaining men set out to save the temple, abandoning the Via Nova and what remained of the Vestals' house to the conflagration. A thousand men worked tirelessly, fetching water and throwing it endlessly at the endangered northern side of the temple complex. Even then, the portico caught and was already badly damaged before the vigiles, supplemented by every Praetorian who could be spared and a number of civically motivated citizens, managed to get it under control and save the temple itself.

The sad fact was that in saving the Tiberian palace and the Temple of Jove, there were not enough men and resources to protect what lay between them. Even with reinforcements arriving now from Veii and Ostia, hurrying to help fight the blaze, the fire roared between those two soaked bulwarks, leaping from building to building like some athletic Minoan dancer, leaving charring infernos in its wake as it advanced on the main palace. We who had been observing, including the emperor himself, were steadily forced back by the blaze and before long we were in our palace once more, watching as hellfires gnawed at the edge of it.

Given the direction of the prevailing breeze and the general advance of the blaze, we acquiesced to the Praetorian prefect's next request and abandoned much of the palace, leaving it to the firefighters. We exited the palace and moved up past the Temple of Apollo and those houses that had once accommodated the very first emperor and empress, to the heights of the Temple of the Magna Mater on the highest corner of the Palatine hill, where we had gathered years ago for our masquerade festival on the day of Maternus' attack, Commodus dressed as Hercules and me a gladiatrix. Now I was dressed as an empress and he, though attired as a prince, was the god he had once impersonated.

From the heights of that ancient place we watched our palace consumed by flames. Here alone of all the southern edge of the Palatine was a ready escape route in the form of the staircase that led down to the Forum Boarium. Down, strangely, past the old bathhouse and the squat two-storey residence and workshop of an imperial seamstress where I had grown up. My eyes strayed down those steps uncomfortably. I had not once trodden those stairs since I was a girl, first arriving in the palace, and I had no wish to descend them now. Somehow it felt as though to do so would be final. An end to my time in the imperial household. Had we now half the water I had run away from on that day, we could have stopped the blaze in its tracks. Despite my own faith, I felt a frisson ripple across my flesh at the thought of the fire reaching this place and consuming the Temple of Apollo, in a horrible echo of that wartime disaster that was said to have brought us the plague.

Some enterprising soul had given the order to clear parts of the palace complex of their most prized contents, carrying them to the Capitol or down past the circus to the Aventine where they would be safer. I watched as a huge line of men carried priceless, irreplaceable documents from the library of Augustus even as the flames from the neighbouring palace began to lick at it. I learned later, to my dismay, that they failed to evacuate the entire building and at least a quarter of the knowledge it held was lost when it burned.

The sun was rising now on a new day, still oppressed by that huge cloud of boiling smoke which announced to the world that Rome burned. We stayed there like refugees, watching our world char for the better part of a day.

In the event, it was nature herself who saved Rome. Mother would have said it was God, though I doubt he had much to do with it on this occasion. Most of those present put it down to the million prayers that had been cast up to Jupiter over the night. Commodus believed that mighty Jove himself had deigned to save Rome because of the effort the emperor had bent to saving that lofty temple from the fire. Piety begat divine intervention in the minds of Rome. I usually find in my own faith that all piety begets is guilt.

Whatever the cause, be it divine or natural, Rome experienced a rainstorm of the sort it does get in summer, though only on very rare occasions. One might even label the timing miraculous since, without that sudden unexpected rain, likely the whole city would have burned to ash.

In the end we lost several temples and warehouses, a huge swathe of shops and stores, some ancillary palace structures and maybe a quarter of the palace complex itself, mainly comprising the public spaces from the aula regia to the libraries above the circus. The damage was appalling, but it did not take a lot of imagination to realise how much worse it could have been. And in the end the majority of the damage was to public buildings or the imperial complex, with surprisingly little impact on the ordinary folk of Rome. Had the wind blown north or east that night, a third of the city would have gone in hours, and much of it would have been commercial or residential.

That evening, as the sun slid slowly into the west and the fine sprinkling of rain continued, we stood where we had spent much of the night, amid the charred bones of the Palatine, inspecting the blackened world around us. Commodus and I, Eclectus and the Praetorian prefect, Laetus, as well as various men of the Roman administration and other officers of the Guard, vigiles and urban cohorts. We pondered on what had happened and, with some relief, on what *could* have happened had not luck or divine providence been with us.

'It is time,' Commodus said, suddenly.

We all turned to him in surprise. He was suddenly oddly divine in the way he stood there, simply dressed, a man who had stayed amid the burning of Rome and helped plan its defence. Hercules incarnate. *My* Hercules, if only he would come back to me.

'Time, Majesty?' Eclectus prompted quietly, and for the first time that night and day, Commodus turned and looked directly into my eyes.

'Time to change. The gods have swept away old, foul, corrupt, pestilential Rome. Now is the time for the golden age. Now is the time to expunge old Rome and to build anew. To build Colonia Commodiana.'

I shivered. I nodded with the others, of course, for he was right. It *was* time. And the plan had been as much my idea as his, if not more so. But there was something that troubled me about it, and it was not until I was lying awake once more, unable to sleep, quite apart from the ever-present stench of smoke, that I realised what it was.

Once, long ago, another emperor had watched the city burn and had leapt to the aid of its people. That emperor had, just the same, planned to build anew on the carbonised bones of Rome. And he might not have planned a golden age for his people so much as a golden house for himself, but history carries warnings, and Commodus was becoming a living echo of Nero at that moment.

Sleep evaded me entirely with that thought.

XXIII

DEMOLISHING MY DEFENCES

Rome, spring AD 192

We continued as Rome's glassy-eyed emperor and empress throughout the autumn and winter that followed that dreadful fire. It took until the cold winds and frost came just to clear away the debris and shore up the buildings that could be at least partially saved. True work on the rebuilding would start with the spring thaw. In the meantime, the imperial brickworks at Pollinarium worked long days throughout the inclement weather, turning out stack after stack of materials for the rebuilding the following year.

True to his word, Commodus set about the refounding of the city in his image even before the structures could be repaired. In the forum, the great *Fasti* calendar was replaced with Commodus' new months. I wondered what the great Caesar and his heir would think about the loss of Iulius and Augustus in the summer months. Indeed, how would the pagan gods feel about the loss of their own months? Confusion reigned in the markets and preparation for festivals as people tried to remember the sequence of the new month names: *Lucius, Aelius, Aurelius, Commodus, Augustus, Herculeus, Romanus, Exsuperatorius, Amazonius, Invictus, Felix, Pius*. Of course, though I cannot say for certain, I can only imagine that most of the public went about privately using the traditional month names. The populace took that change in good enough humour, though it baffled people all that winter, and a number of folk missed celebrating the first day of Saturnalia through date confusion.

The order also went out to append the honorific 'Commodiana' to each legion's name. This, at least, was a simple change and a welcome one. Every military unit liked to be honoured by their emperor, of course, and even if that honour was shared across the entire army, it was still an honour.

All this happened on the Ides of Aelius, which had once been Februarius. The day was labelled the *Dies Commodianus*, for clear reasons. The day of the refounding of Rome as *Colonia Lucia Aurelia Nova Commodiana*. The day of the dawning of the *Saeculum Aureum Commodianum* – the golden age of Commodus.

The people revelled in the changes. Their emperor was stamping his mark on the world and each transformation helped herald a new world that was dawning. For the people, there seemed to be divine validation for the emperor's new world, too. The fire that could have utterly destroyed the city in fact burned away some of the more notable symbols of the old Rome and previous regimes, the Flavian temple and the palace of Domitian. It burned with a strangely sweet and spicy smell from the eastern warehouses, and almost miraculously barely touched the world of the common man before it was extinguished seemingly by divine intervention. Far from seeing the fire as a bad sign, it seemed to be the gods clearing the way for Commodus' new age. Perhaps most miraculous of all, the plague abated that winter. As if the fire had burned through the strain of disease in the city, cases of the pestilence dried up seemingly overnight. It truly was remarkable. By late autumn there were no longer carts in the street. By early winter the burial pits that had been used for over a decade, constantly extended and replaced, were sealed over and planted with grass. Physicians returned to their ordinary practices in confusion, given that the plague had been the main focus of their work for decades.

Even I, as a Christian, found it hard to deny the evidence of some sort of divine strategy at work. Perhaps God's plan had a place for Commodus even if he was not one of us. After all, he *had* been the first emperor in all of Roman history to save Christians from persecution.

If only that strange wall between us would crumble and fall. There was still a distance that I could not overcome, and when I tried to discuss it, Commodus would have none of it, refusing to acknowledge the subject or, occasionally, storming off in a mood.

The senate disapproved of all this, of course, because disapproval is the standard expression of a senator. Lord, but they had something in common with Christian priests. And yet for all their disapproval, they too fell readily into line with the new regime. Despite dissenting voices in that great body, namely Sosius Falco, Cassius Dio, Marius Maximus and their ilk, the bulk of the senators, in the most revoltingly obsequious manner, voted to rename the senate the 'Commodian Fortunate Senate'. Their sycophancy knows no bounds. Even Commodus snorted at the news.

As well as the changes in name that the empire adopted, the new age was heralded by a veritable explosion in Herculean imagery. Statues and busts appeared everywhere. New coins were issued with Commodus in his lion pelt, the Roman Hercules. Some appeared with my image on, which took me somewhat by surprise, though to my distaste I was depicted variously as Minerva or an Amazon or some other pagan symbol. I wondered what the Bishop of Rome thought of his wayward sheep when he handled coins of her as a goddess.

One statue that caused something of a fuss appeared outside the senate house that winter. Hercules, clearly Commodus in the guise, with an iron bow, pulling back the string, an arrow nocked and aimed. The target? The doorway of the senate house. It was clearly a statement and could be saying any one of several things, though none of them were good for the Commodian Fortunate Senate. Several leading lights had already petitioned the palace to have the statue moved, voices led by that same Falco who had argued against the renaming of the senate, but thus far their entreaties had not made it through the palace doors.

The breaking point for me came not even with my Minervian coinage, but when I emerged from my room one morning, with Commodus already long gone about his day's business, to find two new busts in the corridor outside, staring at me. An ornate marble head of Commodus with that ubiquitous lion skin over head and shoulders, paws knotted across his naked chest, great club held casually over one shoulder and a hand raised, containing the apples of the Hesperides. His expression was one of benign superiority and, while there is always a little variation in marble representation from artist to artist, clearly the men responsible for the carving and painting of this particular work had done so from a live model. It was him in perfect painted marble, right down to his eye colour and the golden shimmer of his hair. I was used to seeing such statues now, of course. They appeared wherever a statement needed to be made or where the easily influenced public would be most prevalent. To find one outside my room watching me was new and unsettling.

Possibly worse, beside him, I saw myself. Equally, that painted marble likeness of me had been fashioned by men who had seen me, *known* me even. It was me in perfect reflection. The sculptor had left my hair down in the manner I used when I could not be bothered to fashion it up in high Roman style. Somehow that seemed to suit the fact that I was clearly an Amazon again. I will admit that I was far from the most attentive and pious of Christians, but with every new vision of myself in pagan glory it began to worry and annoy me more.

I knew why it was happening, of course. The memory of his deceased wife had to be swept away entirely. Her busts had

402

gone with her exile, but it is harder to remove a memory than a physical reminder. Thus I was being used as counterpoint to his Hercules to add legitimacy to the new regime. A god needed a suitable consort. That was why we still walked as though we were man and wife despite the chasm between us. Something would have to give soon. Things could not go on like this, with the gulf in our relationship unexplained and not discussed. Either he would have to discard me, which I felt sure the senators would have liked, or heal that rift and take me to wife so that I could truly be part of his new world. This strange half-life was killing me inside.

Dressed and ready for the world, I emerged from my apartments and found the pair of Praetorians on duty by the door.

'Where is the emperor?'

One of the soldiers turned a strange, almost apologetic look on me. 'He left early for the colossus, Domina.'

I nodded. He had been there several times over the past few days. I gathered my servants and a few of the Guard, collected my litter and bearers and began the journey to the colossus. We passed through the bones of the burned public palace where once, as a child, I had watched the emperor's twin almost drown in a pool, and across the Palatine towards the forum valley.

At the eastern end of the forum, when Nero's Golden House was torn down, the Flavian emperors had constructed their great amphitheatre, watched over by the Temple of Venus and Rome. But while the greater part of Nero's lavish palace was destroyed or reused as foundations, one part remained in glory. That narcissistic young despot had had a colossal statue of himself fashioned in bronze. Over a hundred feet tall, it had stood upon a time in the atrium of his great house. After his death, and not wanting to waste such a grand monument, the thing was moved to a position between the temple and the amphitheatre, the identifying features of Nero struck from it and refashioned as the image of the god Sol Invictus. Thus it had stood for so long beside that grand amphitheatre that the plebs had even started to call the place the Colosseum.

The colossus had been Nero for not quite five years. It had been Sol for over a century. Soon it would change again. I saw the great bronze god even before we emerged into the open space nearby. The paved area between the conical fountain, the temple, the arena and the colossus was devoid of citizens, for the Praetorians had created a security cordon around their emperor and his companions. They let me past, of course, and I alighted from my litter below the steps of the temple.

Commodus was in conversation with men who were likely engineers and architects, he in his now common Greek chiton garb, his lictors standing nearby with their bundles of rods and their Herculean accoutrements on a cushion. Of the small gathering of officials, clerks and other functionaries, one figure broke away and hurried over to me.

I smiled at Eclectus, one of my oldest friends.

'I imagine you are as appalled as I?' he said quietly as he closed on me and painted a smile on his face.

I frowned. 'Over what?'

'You know he plans to change the colossus. After a century he wants to make it Hercules. Or at least, himself as Hercules. Do you realise he's in animated discussion as to how they can attach a beard to make it look more like him? It's going too far, Marcia. I don't know whether it's sacrilege to tear away the image of a god if you're replacing it with another god, but I cannot see any good coming of it. It's appalling.'

'I think you overestimate my concern,' I sighed. 'You know what I am. What should *I* care which pagan idol stands guard here? They are all equally meaningless to me.'

'A strange attitude for a woman who oscillates between being an Amazon and the goddess of war and wisdom.'

I could not tell whether he was mocking me, or being serious, so I ignored the comment. Eclectus sighed and turned,

404

gesturing to the great arcade of the amphitheatre. 'It did not take too long for people to start calling it the Colosseum. How long d'you think before it becomes the Commodium? Whether through public assimilation or by imperial design, I can see it happening. How long before we all have to discard togas and wear a Greek chiton, Marcia?'

I looked about me in consternation. This sounded like a dangerous conversation to be having in the open, even these days without men like Cleander around to clamp down on dissent. But the problem was that Eclectus was right. This was all a little bit much. The world had that pre-thunder feeling. You know when a storm is nigh and the pressure builds in the air. You can feel it in your ears, applying force, making things tense. Your hair begins to crackle. There is lightning in the very air. In some odd, indefinable way, this felt like that: as though a giant storm were building. I was not sure I wanted to be in the open when it broke.

An officer called to Eclectus and he made his apologies and hurried off to discuss some nuance of administration, leaving me to my own devices. By coincidence, at that moment Commodus' engineers and architects came to a decision and wandered off with a slate containing a set of technical drawings. Commodus stood on his own, hands on hips, gazing up at that impressive, clean-shaven bronze countenance that lorded it over the square.

I took my opportunity and hurried over.

'This is too precipitous,' I said. Perhaps not the gentlest way to begin, but I think the words of Eclectus had sunk in and lodged.

Commodus turned and I took a step back. There was something in his eyes that worried me. Something manic and wild, like the intoxicated, crazed look the worshippers of the wine god get during Bacchanalia.

'What?' A sharp retort.

'This. It's all acceptable, of course, but you're pushing it too far, too quickly.'

'No.'

I sighed. 'Dies Commodianus was a political masterstroke, I admit. A complete new beginning, and people are adjusting, some more readily than others. But your plans continue to gain momentum like a runaway cart on a hill. Perhaps you could just apply the brake a little and slow the process. Let people become used to what has already happened before they are presented with the next change. I know I said there needed to be a line drawn to mark the beginning of it all, but not *everything* has to begin at the same time.'

Commodus was glaring at me, a strange, faraway mania dancing in his eyes like motes of dust in the light. It was extremely unsettling. I had seen that look when I first proposed these ideas on the way to Surrentum. I had seen similar when he raced chariots around the circus, when he fought in his private arena. This was the Commodus of Cleander again. It distressed me to realise that though the bastard had now been gone for years, I would never be rid of his influence. Just as I had managed to develop a way to calm his melancholia, Cleander had awoken something manic in him and instead of calming it and reining it in as he had in the early days, he had later begun to guide and exacerbate it. And though he was gone, his work lived on. I had no idea how to deal with it all.

'This is a new foundation,' he said in a flat tone, though his lip twitched. 'This is no longer Rome. Rome had become corrupt and chaotic. Driven by fat senators who want only war and conquest. Driven by men who want only what they do not yet have. Driven by greed, beset by war and poverty and disease. But I am changing it, Marcia. Dreadful Rome is gone. Colonia Commodiana is here. And in this new world there is no costly, endless war. Disease has fled and peace reigns. Grain comes in abundance with the new fleet I built. I have men prospecting

– looking for new deposits of silver and gold. We need not rely on putting the barbarian to the sword to fill our coffers when new wealth lies under the earth. All will be glorious in this golden age.'

That wild, agitated look in his eyes was increasing with every word.

'There shall be games and races every day. Food for all. Peace and glory. A new golden age. And it will be in my name. *All* in my name. The greatest emperors brought loot and expansion to the empire. I shall bring peace and contentment. Who could ask for more?'

And the problem was that, despite the strange wildness of his manner, he was speaking what sounded like absolute sense. Who *would* wish for war when they could have peace? No wonder the people were so ready to accept his changes. But the senate would still baulk at such a notion.

'It is all a good idea,' I said, soothingly, touching his elbow with a brush of my fingers. 'It really is. But if you want it all to settle in smoothly, you must introduce it slowly. Like a trickle from a leaky pipe that slowly floods a room, rather than a tidal wave that smashes down walls.'

His eyes narrowed and I felt a tinge of nerves then. 'This was *your* idea, Marcia. *All* your idea. When I struggled to keep Rome content, I did it all on my own, with bread and circuses, while you pottered along happily in your own world, no help at all.'

I started in shock. He sounded angry. And yes, he had kept the people happy with entertainment. But he had not *needed* my help at the time, nor asked for it.

'Then,' he continued, jabbing a finger at me, 'you come to me with this idea. This notion, totally unlooked for. And it was seductive. It was a good idea. It built on my own expansion of the Hercules emperor. I took your advice yet again, as I ever did, and made it happen. And now that I do precisely what you yourself advocated, you want me to slow? To stop, even?'

I recoiled from the anger in his tone.

'I did not mean to provoke you. I have only your welfare in mind, my love. I am trying to protect you from—'

He snarled and my voice died in my throat. I became aware that guards and engineers were all watching us. He seemed not to care.

'Is it not enough, Marcia, daughter of a freedwoman, that you control the very direction I take at every turn, but now you must control the pace at which I take it?'

I shuddered. What was this?

'I sought only to help. You came to me for advice all our lives, ever since we were children.'

'They were right about you, Marcia.'

'What?' My blood ran cold now. What was he talking about?

'Cleander. Just as you spent every moment you could pouring your poison into my ear, telling me that Cleander was wicked and sought only his own power, yes, he did the same. He warned me over and over again that you sought power and influence. That you would control me if you could. Not just guide, but control. I dismissed it. I loved you. I always did, but love is dangerous. Love is blind to fault. Love hid from me the controlling nature in my Marcia. I saw only the woman who aided me, never the puppet mistress tugging on my strings.'

No. This was not true. This was not happening. I realised with dread that this was the culmination of that gulf that had been widening ever since his visit to Capri. This was what lay at the root of all that distance between us. I had so longed to bring that matter to a head, out in the open, and discuss it. And now that we were, I changed my mind. I didn't want to hear this. Despite the discomfort, I suddenly wanted the strained silence back.

'What you said about Cleander might be true,' he went on, growling. 'He might only ever have had his own destiny in mind, but never once did he set himself against me. Never did he steer me or push me. He helped. He supported. Maybe he was not the best person for Rome, but, by the gods, he was better for me than you.'

I lurched back. I felt as though he had jammed a blade through my heart. This was not true. I was always better for him than Cleander. And I never sought to control or to master him. Just to guide and encourage, surely? But somehow, even deep in my heart, a realisation was dawning that perhaps that was not quite true. I had once been encouraging and guiding, but I had learned things in my time with Quadratus. I had learned how to stop being a victim, or at least how to stop seeing myself as the victim. Had I done that with Commodus without even realising it, so used to it was I?

The emperor was not done. His ire was in control now.

'And I may never have realised the truth of Cleander's words, but that I went to Capri. I went to sever my final ties with a wife I never loved so that I could be with a woman I did. And she laid bleak truths before me. And I knew them for truths. You know why?'

I shook my head, not trusting myself to speak.

'Because Bruttia Crispina was the most innocent soul I ever met in my life. She never set out to harm anyone. She knew you hated her and yet for all our marriage she only ever tried to befriend you. Still you shunned her. Estranged her. Made her feel as though she did not belong in the palace, while you did.'

I shook my head. That wasn't true. That was not Bruttia. He didn't know how very much like me Bruttia could be. How she had warned me off. How she could smile like a dove beneath eyes that carried daggers. But I couldn't tell him that. How could I? I could hardly defame the dead, and even if I could bring myself to do so, would he believe me? I doubted that.

'She had no cause to lie to me on Capri,' he went on. 'We were there for her death and she knew it. She was resigned. She

409

even thought that you were somehow behind her miscarriages, though she cannot say how. But she warned me, just as Cleander had in his time. She said that she had been inconvenient and that you wanted me all for yourself and had finally found a way to get rid of her.'

I felt an utterly unmanageable wave of guilt flow through me then. Curse tablets. Silphium. Revealing her affair with Julius Alexander. I *had* been despicable to the empress. I had been everything she accused me of and more.

'She told me flat,' he said. 'She told me that within the year you would be all but regent of Rome and I your mewling child.

'I . . .' How did I respond to this? Bruttia had crucified me with her final words. After a life of tame silence, she had turned on me with her last breath and destroyed me in the emperor's eyes.

'Bruttia was convinced that you had done away with anyone who stood in your way,' Commodus snarled. 'I didn't believe it at first, but the more I thought about it on the boat back to Surrentum, the more I realised it was true. You have been at the turning point of everything. You are a catalyst that is always there when things change for me, and rarely for the better.'

Now, the Praetorians were unsure what to do. Some had begun to move closer, wondering if their services might be required. Others had backed away, widening the cordon, believing they should not be overhearing all this. I wished they were not. This was not a conversation I would ever wish for, and least of all in public.

'Isn't it odd,' he said now, his tone accusatory as he took a step towards me, towering over me, 'how all those years ago, I favoured visiting the evening race, but you wanted to see Hosidius Geta's *Arrius Varus* at the theatre? And so we went to the theatre, where Perennis was denounced.'

That had not been me. Well, it *had*, but purely because I

wanted to see the play and not more death on the racetrack. There had been no ulterior motive. 'You *like* innovative theatre,' I said defensively. 'Geta's reputation—'

'That when we were in the villa on the Via Appia,' he interrupted, 'it was you who came to my room to warn me about my wife and Julius Alexander?'

Yes, it had been, but I had not engineered that. That was simply God's will.

'That was an unhappy accident. I—'

'Cleander tried to explain his actions at Laurentinum,' he went on, 'but you urged me to ignore him and listen to Eclectus. That same Eclectus who now echoes your concerns over my new plan. How strange that you two should share opinions, eh? The only two of my circle of friends and advisors who have outlasted the many dead.'

'I cannot—'

But he was in no mood to listen to my defence. He rode roughshod over me again. 'You. All you. You got rid of Cleander. You got rid of Bruttia. I wouldn't be at all surprised to find that you were somehow behind my sister's fall, for I know you hated her too. And Quadratus. And, curiously, just after the lad tried to stick a sword in me, who do I find lurking on the stairs of the amphitheatre mere paces away? You.'

God, no. That had been pure chance. I had gone to watch him in glory, not to oversee some kind of plot!

'You are *always* there Marcia. And when you're not doing away with those who are inconvenient, you're pushing me. Getting me to ban Christian gladiators in Gaul. To free convicted criminals in the mines of Sardinia. Using me for your impious Christian agenda.'

'I—'

'They were right about you. They were both right. Did you poison my unborn sons somehow, Marcia? Did you?'

I shivered. I couldn't answer that. Whatever he accused me

of, I could not face that, for I was well aware of the depth of my guilt.

'How did you do that?' he snarled. 'Was it some weird Christian rite that killed my heirs? I should have your Minerva portrait reworked and your Amazon busts rechiselled to resemble Hekate.'

My shivers came again now at that name, the goddess I had once begged that Bruttia die alone and childless. He was not *quite* right, but, Lord, he came so close to the facts.

'None of this is true,' I managed in a hollow voice.

Some of it was true.

Much of it was true. But some things are difficult to admit, even to oneself.

'Get out of my sight,' he snapped. 'This is my new age and I am in a forgiving mood. Be thankful for that, lest you join Bruttia's ashes on Capri.'

I stared.

This was what had been festering beneath his veneer since those days in Surrentum. No wonder it had eaten away at him. Had he spoken of them to me earlier, I might have been prepared. I could have dealt with such accusations one at a time, but not like this. Not like a barrage. Not like that dreadful wave, sweeping along the street, demolishing my defences with ease. And it would certainly take some thinking about, for though some of his comments were wild and erroneous or simply the result of chance, there was a dangerous element of truth in some of them, and I could hardly let that knowledge out into the world. Those truths were to be shared only between me and God when I am judged.

I left shaken, close to panic. I looked back only once to find that Commodus was already in discussion with another engineer, gesturing this way and that as they planned his new world. I was shivering, cold with dread, as I climbed into my litter and gave the tremulous command to return to the Palatine.

I had lost Commodus. I only just finally had him to myself, and then I had lost him again.

I clenched my hands so that the nails bit deep into my palms and forced myself to stop trembling. What was this? A few hard words from him and I had become a pathetic girl? This was not Marcia. This was not me. I would gain control of myself. And then I would begin to work it all out. I had built plans that had brought down the serpent Cleander. I could certainly deal with this, now that I knew what I was facing. All was not as lost as it seemed.

There was time.

I would get my Commodus back.

XXIV

A WAVE OF POPULARITY

Rome, autumn AD 192

There was simply nothing for it. I had to prove I was anything other than what I truly was in order to stand a chance of winning back the trust of the man I loved. A tough proposition, and one that would require me to become a much better person than I had been in recent years. I prayed. I beseeched God to forgive me my many, many sins. I became a regular visitor to the services of the Bishop of Rome or any other priest I could find when I felt the need to unburden myself.

I became attentive to the emperor's needs, which was again a difficult proposition. Now that the trouble between us had been aired, there was little need for the strained fiction we had lived. We were noticeably, publicly drifting apart now. I was not always invited to things, but where I *could* be with him, I was, and I played the perfect empress. I made sure to support his decisions, whatever they were. That alone made me shiver, for he seemed to be assailed by ever more adventurous and outlandish ideas. Yet still I blindly agreed and supported, making sure not to pry my opinion into matters. I would not be the woman who directed and drove Commodus. I *could* not be. Not only would it mean accepting the loss of our relationship for good, it might well mean much, much worse for me, remembering his veiled threat at the colossus.

*

414

Over the summer I watched as Hercules began to dominate Rome. He was going too far, and I knew it. I could see the senators bridling over it all, even if the bulk of the faceless populace continued to cheer for their divine, golden lord. Senators are to be ignored at an emperor's peril. They and the Praetorian Guard are people with the power and influence to make or break rulers, no matter how divine their blood.

Newly issued coins now rarely showed anything other than the club-wielding, lion-wearing demigod emperor. Statues were everywhere. The ongoing disgruntlement over the archer Hercules threatening the door of the senate house caused dissent and an ever greater number of the members of that ancient body began to add their voices to the call to remove the offending artwork. Commodus' answer was simply to exacerbate the problem. One of the most potent symbols of Rome is that of its founders. At some of the most critical places in the city, a bronze or marble wolf suckled two babes above the grand slogan *Senatus Populusque Romanus* – 'For the Senate and the People of Rome'. These began to be moved out of the light and be replaced by that ever-present Hercules.

It was too much.

There were rumbles in the senate constantly. Any other time, I would have warned Commodus, urged him to release the tension in the cable, make peace with the senate, slow his changes, but I could not do so now. I had to watch as he took umbrage at the senate's dissent and instead of stitching closed the wound, opened it ever wider. A new slogan began to appear in Rome, one that had no other purpose than to offend those same senators.

Coins. Statues. Inscriptions. Especially in the forum, near the senate house.

Populus Senatuseque Romanus.

What a challenge. 'For the People and the Senate of Rome'. Openly, blatantly, the emperor had put the people above their

415

ancient senate. A guaranteed move to create love and devotion among the people, and the soldiery and the equites were content enough, but to the senate it was the ultimate insult. And that affront was compounded by new taxes levelled solely at the rich, refilling the imperial coffers at their expense. The people watched their grand entertainments, satisfied in the knowledge that they were being paid for by those sour old oligarchs.

The divided opinion of the different classes was clearest around the colossus by the amphitheatre. There, flowers and offerings were left daily by the public on the grand pedestal, for now that grand bronze figure bore the beard and accoutrements of Hercules and Commodus, the great club and a lion at its feet. The emperor's many titles were listed on the base, along with the new addition: 'Champion of Secutors', as though that were some kind of imperial title. And slogans were scratched on the stone. *Herculi Commodiano*. He was, if anything, more beloved than ever of the people of the new city of Colonia Commodiana.

But those who still thought of it as Rome – the old blood and the old money who sat impotent in the curia, dreaming of the days they had made a difference – refused to look up at that colossus as they passed.

Not that they passed it often. The majority of those who came near the great statue were heading to or from the amphitheatre, and the senators rarely attended games now. For some of the more impressive events over the summer, the closest tier of seating to the action in the amphitheatre stood largely empty, for it was reserved for the Roman elite and, of that class, only the emperor and his consilium now attended. Then, towards the end of summer, the senatorial seating rule was abolished altogether and the equites moved forward, filling the best seats in the venue. Another dagger in the back of the senate's supremacy, not that they hadn't invited that one.

Once, ten years ago, a young man had tried to put a blade in Commodus in these very stands. He had claimed to be acting on behalf of the senate, though the plot was in truth limited to the emperor's sister and her cronies. Now, the situation had changed. Now, I half expected to see a similar blade appear, truly on behalf of that order.

Indeed, Senator Clarus had begun making speeches in the curia openly disparaging the emperor's treatment of their order and his lavish gifts to the lower class. His words carried weight among the powerful, and the seething resentment of their entire class was almost tangible. Falco, another outspoken aristocrat, began to harangue the populace, telling them that they were devoting too much praise to Hercules and that the other gods would become angry. I worried about the effects these men were having, though I had my own troubles at that time.

The emperor ignored the danger of the senate, for the common people loved him. Commodus rode high on a wave of popularity, and he bathed in it.

All I could do was encourage it, when every fibre in my body screamed at me to suppress this grandiosity before it triggered something dreadful. He never asked my advice, and I could not give it anyway. He stopped coming to my bed, sleeping in a different apartment in the palace. We even sat apart in public. Slowly, I came to accept that I needed to do more than simply be supportive and accepting. But what? Without being accused of trying to control him again, how could I hope to win him over?

I had started attending the races and the games again. I had to. If I ever wanted Commodus back, I had to always be there for him, and never pushing, and while I worked out how best to win him, I had to continue being the woman he wanted. So I watched him race chariots around the circus as though he were a low-born sportsman, enjoying the extreme danger. In fairness, he was very good at it. Had he been born in another life, he would have made a champion driver. But still, such low and perilous entertainment was not the place for an emperor, and even I agreed with the senate on that. I watched him hunt beasts – all manner of great animals imported from across the empire – in the arena with the venators. Huge grey things with a horn on their heads that gored a dozen men before they fell, yet Commodus was there, among them. Lions. Panthers. Bears. Wolves. He faced them all with his low-born and enslaved companions. Even the equites now were beginning to feel uncomfortable with such displays, for all the general populace cheered him on. I watched it all. And when Commodus sat in the pulvinar with me, he was never truly *with* me. Our seats had been separated, and Praetorians filled the gap between us.

The message was clear. I tried endlessly to close that gulf between us, to play the perfect wife, but it was having little effect. I began to fear that the shades of Cleander and Bruttia had ruined us for good and, try as I might, I could not see the way to improve matters.

Summer rolled into autumn, and autumn gave way to winter, all with continued grandness and dangerous exploits that thrilled the public and offended the senate. All that time I sat with the emperor and yet I sat alone. Even when he deigned to look at me, there was a horrible mix of disappointment and mistrust in his eyes. Nothing I could do changed that look.

The disaffection of the senate continued to grow. Those stuffy old men made certain to use the old months, refused to acknowledge that their city was anything other than Rome, refused to accept Hercules as a god, or anything other than a Greek hero. They came a hair's breadth from openly insulting the emperor and I could see Commodus seething about it – or, at least at the time, I thought that was what it was. Worse still, there was a rash of vandalism, with Herculean statues defaced, their inscriptions scratched out. Even the new inscription on the base of the colossus was chiselled away one night.

Soon, things would come to a head with the senate, and I

thanked God that at least it would be tolerant Commodus that would deal with it, and not the vile Cleander or strict Perennis, though it was hard to ignore the fact that this Commodus was the one that Cleander had created, not I.

November came – now the month of Invictus – and brought with it the Plebeian Games. Unlike the majority of the festivals of Rome, which had been instigated by the nobles with the aim of pleasing Rome's various social strata in order of precedence, the *Ludi Plebeii* had been created by the plebeian *aediles* in the distant past purely for the lower classes, perhaps in answer to the grand designs of their betters. The festival had, over the years, grown into an annual event that even the higher classes enjoyed, for it was a grand celebration. Over fourteen days of that month there were athletic contests, races and fights, spectacles and plays.

Commodus, of course, paid particular attention to the Plebeian Games. Their very nature suited him, for he was a man of the people and eschewed that same aristocratic order that the games had been created to snub. The senators' money was yet again drained into the imperial coffers and thrown at events to please the plebs.

I was at the Circus Flaminius for the opening event of the games. The venue was considerably smaller than the great Circus Maximus, and was used for foot and horse races rather than chariots. Over the centuries, it had been encroached upon by the city's blocks such that now, when events were held and temporary wooden seating stands created, they backed directly onto other buildings. I sat on my wooden seat with a thick purple cushion, while on the other side of a couple of expressionless guards sat Commodus, bathing in the vocal adulation of the crowd.

For this first special day of the festival, he had gone a step further than usual. Though he still wore his Greek white and gold chiton, now he had a lion's pelt around his shoulders as

419

some sort of cloak and a huge club rested beside his chair. Hercules himself had come to the games.

There was a procession of priests and lower-class notables, musicians and dancers, and then, after a short but impressive speech from the emperor, the games began.

I watched thirty horse races in the space of two hours. Never had I seen so many horses. The prizes alone must have bled the vaults of the Temple of Saturn dry. Golden wreaths and chests of coin, parcels of land and property across Italia. Men became rich that day. One racer, I heard, went from being a freedman with a talent for racing to being a knight of Rome in the space of an hour, for he had won sufficient land and coin to qualify him for that honour.

And as if the lavishness of that opening event was not enough, Commodus then gave a signal as the last prize was dished out, and his men appeared in strategic positions all around the circus and proceeded to throw purses of coins into the crowd at random. I wept inside for the fact that I knew he was going too far and I was utterly helpless, unable to stop it.

There was a break, then, for a noon meal and for the people to recover and then settle on any further events they wished to attend, for there were two or three venues in use at all times over the fourteen days, such was the volume of gold thrown at the games.

Much to my relief, Commodus rode in only one chariot race that festival, though it was the first and the most important. I heard afterwards that folk came from as far afield as Africa and Hispania to watch the emperor race that day. He drove for the Greens, and managed to achieve a respectable third place.

Respectable. As if an emperor racing at the circus could ever be such a thing.

I sat and watched the race. I cheered enthusiastically while dying inside a little. I waited until Commodus had bathed, changed, had a couple of abrasions and cuts dealt with and then joined me in the pulvinar. I congratulated him on his good place in the race. He acknowledged me with just a faint nod, but with that nod came something unexpected.

A smile.

It had been more than half a year since he had smiled at me. I had been convinced that my role as good, supportive little Marcia was not enough and I would have to do more. I had begun to think his shell of distrust unbreakable. But with that upturn of the mouth came hope. Perhaps the gap between us could be bridged after all.

That night I thanked God and made promises that no good Christian should ever have had to make in the first place. To be faithful and loyal. Not to seek the death of my countrymen, whether they be friends or enemies. Not to poison or curse or betray. All things I had done in my time, but I would be a new woman. I would be a good woman. And, in being so, perhaps once again I would be *his* woman.

I half hoped he would come to me that night, though in truth I did not expect such a change so swiftly. I promised myself that, since it seemed I did not need to find a new path to healing, I would not only continue my campaign of support, but would even build upon it. I took a chance. It was perhaps ill-advised, and I'm sure my reputation suffered, but I was becoming desperate to repair the breach. Perhaps I was even becoming as manic as he, in my own slightly more staid way. I certainly worried that I was going too far, just as my love was now wont to do.

The first day of games in the amphitheatre that he attended, which was the third day of the festival, he emerged from the imperial apartments once more dressed as Hercules, that great club over his shoulder. There was a purpose to his mode of dress today, for I knew at least something of what he had planned. Commodus stepped out into the cold garden, followed by Eclectus with his now common frown of disapproval, and a dozen Praetorians and gladiator guards. And he saw me.

His smile told me I had done something good.

I had deliberated for some time in the small hours over what to do, and when I had settled on a course and sent out my slaves to find everything I needed, I then deliberated on whether it was a good idea. I had made vows to be a good woman, and not to manipulate or control, yet in essence what I was doing, currying favour this way, was dangerously close to doing just that.

I shivered in the chilly late autumn air, for I was clad in the garb of the ancient warrior woman I had been in that statue, Greek-style dress, hair held back with a circlet, bow over my shoulder and quiver at my side. I drew the line at exposing a breast, but still my appearance was clear. My identity obvious.

'An Amazon?' He smiled appreciatively. 'Will your god not punish you?'

It sounded harsh, but it was said with the inflection of a friendly jibe, and I smiled back.

'For your great day, I'm sure I shall be forgiven.'

We left for the Flavian amphitheatre together. We rode in the same carriage for the first time in half a year, a clear sign that what I was doing was working and that the wound was slowly closing and healing. We arrived at the arena, though not in a grand display for the public as I had expected. We arrived in all but secret, making our way into the dark halls of that great structure unseen by the people of Colonia Commodiana. We parted ways there, in those shadowy corridors, and I was escorted to my seat. Somehow, the knowledge that the emperor and his mistress were close once more had gone ahead of us. Our seats were together, though his remained empty.

I watched with the rest of the people as the day's games began.

The opening parade was grander than usual, which in itself was no surprise to any of us, given Commodus' love of ostentatious display. We watched, the crowd hungry and cheering, as the gladiators, the musicians, dancers, jugglers, everyone they expected, entered through the Gate of Life and circled to the adulation of the crowd, then returned to the darkness of the working area beneath the stands. Then came the Vestals and the priests, reverent and stately, making their way to their seats. At other times, the senate would be with them, but the paltry handful of toga-clad hopefuls that attended were hardly deserving of such a grand appellation. Only two of the more important luminaries of that ancient body attended, and Clarus and Falco would only have deigned to do so because they had been selected as next year's consuls and they would want the people to see them. The public didn't really care about the senate or the consuls, though. They cheered the priests and priestesses, and then the senior officers and prefects as they made their way into the stands.

A hush fell. This was when the emperor traditionally put in his appearance, entering the pulvinar and bowing to the roar of the spectators, possibly throwing a few gifts into the crowd. The silence dragged out. The emperor did not come.

Suddenly there was a creak, and a door below the lowest row of the seating opened, leading out onto a wooden walkway that ran around the entire circuit of the arena, marked out at points around the circumference with stacks of javelins and pots of glowing fire. A grand fanfare played high in the stands, and the crowd, confused, looked back and forth between the imperial box where they anticipated the arrival of Commodus and the small door where action seemed more imminent.

Hercules entered the amphitheatre through that small door.

Commodus was clad in the demigod's garb, though he had discarded his club, which was being carried uncomfortably by one of the lictors who emerged after him. Instead, he bore a bow and a quiver. This was still Hercules, though. This was the Hercules who had shot the Nemean lion, the Hercules who had

423

slain the Lernaean Hydra with flaming arrows ... the reason for the burning bowls of pitch I had noted all around the edge of the arena suddenly became clear.

Commodus threw out his arms in triumph and the crowd roared. He jogged around the entire circuit of the place, arms raised, bow in hand, drinking in the praise of the crowd. It was an impressive entrance, I had to admit. The senators would hate it, but the people could imagine nothing better.

The emperor completed his circuit and stood, powerful and impressive, above the sand of the arena proper on his timber walkway, as the crowd continued to roar, so loud and approving that they even drowned out the fanfare that accompanied the arrival of the sacrifice.

A white bull was led across the sand to the altar that had been reverentially placed at the centre, and where the few priests who were not seated in the stands stood waiting for their part in proceedings. The bull was sacrificed in the traditional manner and the invocations and offerings made to Jupiter. Half the crowd followed the ceremony, the rest still watching their golden emperor, half expecting some strange activity to occur. Commodus, though, waited respectfully for the rituals to end, for the altar and the carcass to be removed, for the priests to leave in silent procession and even for the slaves to rake the beast's blood into the sand.

Finally, the show was ready to begin. Traditionally, the beast hunts are the first event, and the crowd rumbled in anticipation as more slaves emerged onto the sand with wooden hoardings that they proceeded to use to divide the arena into four parts. It took perhaps a quarter of an hour to make everything ready, then the slaves vanished again, leaving the oval quartered and an expectant crowd. Finally, the animals were released. A bear into one section, a lion in another, a leopard in the third and a wolf into the last. The crowd fell into a hush, which was filled with the varied sounds of the vicious beasts prowling in their enclosures. The emperor gave an almost imperceptible nod, which was picked up by some unseen functionary. Leaning his bow against the rail, he moved from foot to foot, limbering up, preparing for his show.

The pits in the ground opened up in all four enclosures and suddenly herds of animals were running up onto the sand in panic: goats, deer and sheep. As soon as half a dozen animals were released into each arc, the doors shut down again and the predators began to move, racing for the ready meat that ran, panicked and startled, among them.

Then Commodus also started to run.

If ever there was a more impressive show of speed, strength and skill, I have yet to hear of it. The emperor moved like a racer at the games, slowing as he reached the first of those stooks of javelins. He selected one and lifted it. Standing at the edge of the rail, a hundred paces from where the wolf was busy cornering a sheep, he settled into position, pulling back his arm, javelin angled just right, a Greek-style throwing strap in evidence.

He adjusted, shifted a foot, breathed quietly . . .

And threw the missile.

It sailed out silently across the gap and, to the astonishment and delight of the crowd, struck the wolf in the back even as the frenzied beast lunged for the sheep. The weapon pinned it to the sand and it lay there, thrashing and howling, dark blood gushing out onto the arena floor. The sheep scurried away from the transfixed predator and milled in confusion and panic with its herd at the far end.

Commodus turned and essayed a quick bow to the people, which elicited a fresh roar from them all, and then he was running again. Clearly, he was gaining in confidence as he moved, for he entered the quarter with the leopard and grasped a javelin from the next stack, pivoting, turning, and hurling the thing without taking time to prepare and sight. Admittedly, the beast was closer to him than the wolf had been, but the javelin flew true, smashing into the thing's hindquarters and sending it skittering across the sand to lie crippled and in agony.

The crowd erupted like a tidal wave of humanity. Men hurtled from their seats to their feet, cheering and waving their arms at this display of prowess. But the emperor wasn't done yet. He approached the lion enclosure. This time he was too late to save the other animals, and a goat was already being devoured. The lion lay still, tearing at the carcass. The emperor stood in frustration for a short while. Killing a stationary animal was not the display he had in mind, but time wore on and the animal was happy to lie still and consume its kill. The crowd started to become restive. They had been treated, and they wanted more. With a clear sigh of regret over the ease of the kill, Commodus hefted the next javelin. In order to make it somewhat more skilful, he spun a full circle before he let go. The weapon hit the lion square on, and he was moving again even as the crowd roared once more.

He reached the bear. It had slain two animals already, but was more intent on the killing than the eating, enraged and angry. It hurtled around the sand, howling, chasing the other prey. Commodus selected a javelin and aimed.

He threw. The beast moved at the last moment, and it is to Commodus' credit that the weapon hit the bear at all. It tore a piece of flesh from the ursine monster in its passage and the bear suddenly registered the new threat. It spun and dropped to all fours, thundering towards its aggressor. The crowd fell into an awed silence. The animal was a large example and as it closed on that temporary wooden walkway that ran around the edge, it occurred to everyone that the beast might just be able to reach the emperor.

Commodus had perhaps realised the same, for he grasped a second javelin and threw it hurriedly.

This one struck the bear in its shoulder, throwing it off to one side, though the wound was far from fatal and a moment later it had brushed off the weapon and was rearing up, closing on the walkway. Even I felt the danger, then. The walkway was fifteen feet above the sand. The bear was perhaps twelve feet tall, but its reaching paws would easily be able to touch the timber.

Commodus danced to the side as a paw swung and tore through wooden planks and joists as though they were made of papyrus. I swallowed nervously. The emperor grabbed a javelin just before another powerful paw swept through the wood at the base of the stack and sent them scattering all over the place. Half the stack fell down onto the sand, the others forming a dangerous hazard underfoot on the walkway.

This was Commodus' opportunity to escape. He could run past the dividing timber wall to another quarter. He did not. He hefted his javelin as though it were a stabbing spear. I felt my pulse quicken, my blood chill. This was true danger. A bear will not hold back where a gladiator might. Commodus danced past the bear once more. The paw struck the pot with the glowing pitch in it now, and the liquid slopped out onto the wood, immediately setting fire to the walkway.

The bear thrashed and tore at the timbers, gradually shredding its way through.

Commodus found his optimal place and prepared. The beast closed, a paw raised to smash through the wood at the emperor's feet.

The glorious Hercules of the arena jabbed out with the javelin, punching it into the animal's eye. The bear howled and dropped back, half-blinded and in rage-filled agony. Commodus was not about to allow it time to recover. Steadying himself and changing his grip, he threw the weapon, which slammed into the bear's neck so hard it emerged from the far side amid a torrent of blood.

The bear fell.

It spent a long time dying on the arena floor, and Commodus, perhaps honouring the power of the beast, retrieved another two javelins and struck it well twice more, finishing it off and putting it out of its pain.

The crowd went wild.

I thought that anything he might do after that would be an anticlimax, but I was wrong. Slaves appeared with buckets of water, extinguishing the fire on the walkway, and others with extra timbers that they proceeded to use to shore up the damaged sections. The herds were shifted from the arena and the dividing walls swiftly taken down. The corpses were removed and the sand raked over. All this took less than a quarter of an hour, during which a girl entered the arena with a cup of wine, handing it reverentially to the emperor, who quaffed it thirstily, then handed it back with a grin. The crowd erupted again, wishing him long life, and chanting the new slogan that filled Rome.

Herculi Commodiano.

It would be difficult to deny that he was their golden emperor that day, but what came next only added to his legend. More beasts were released once everything was ready. This time it became a free-for-all, and every animal in that arena was a killer in its own right. Dozens of them, each more fierce than the last. Needless to say, fights erupted between the animals instantly, and the crowd bayed hungrily. Then the emperor began his next display. Sweeping up the bow with which he had first arrived, he stretched and prepared and then, taking a deep breath, started to run. As he passed the first container of pitch, he produced an arrow from his quiver, dipped it in the flames and nocked it without slowing his pace. The missiles must have been treated with flammable material for the arrow ignited easily. He released the string and the arrow thrummed through the air, his aim true, striking a tiger in the neck. He never slowed. On he went, pulling out another arrow and igniting it as he passed the next bowl, nocking it, drawing back and loosing even as he pelted along the timbers. It struck some strange, vicious-looking thing in the rump and made it roar in pain and shock and turn from its fight. On he ran. I watched him with the same awe as the rest of the crowd. He repeated the process over and over, never once slowing his pace, circling the arena more than twice, repeatedly loosing flaming arrows until his quiver was empty. In all that time, with perhaps twenty arrows, I saw him miss only four times. Three of his shots killed on impact. I had not even known he could handle a bow, and I marvelled. It must have been one of the skills he had learned from his cadre of gladiator instructors.

The bestiarii arrived then, emerging through the Gate of Life and making for the numerous wild predators on the sand. Perhaps some of the roar of adulation from the crowd was for these professional hunters, but I suspect the large part of it was for the incredible prowess displayed by the Herculean emperor before them.

An hour later, the emperor was back in his white and gold chiton, bathed and brushed, clean and relaxed as he entered the pulvinar. We watched the rest of the day's events together and for the first time that year I was able to laud him and his achievements and support him without a hint of underlying regret or falsehood. I was proud of my golden prince.

The games went on, day after day, and each time Commodus involved himself in some way. Sometimes he hunted beasts with the others on the sand. Sometimes he armed himself as a gladiator and took to the sand with other professional killers.

With the rest of the crowd, I watched, heart in throat, as the emperor deftly leapt from side to side, barefoot in the bloodied sand, shield on one arm, gleaming blade in the other. I held my breath as a trident tore three jagged rents in the coloured surface of his shield, mangled the bronze strip on the edge and then clanged off that smooth, eerie helmet.

But Commodus the *Champion of Secutors* had trained with

429

the best the empire had to offer in that private arena on the Via Appia, and in other venues thereafter. A quick pivot on one greaved leg and his blade came up, neatly hacking the trident in half and leaving the retiarius poorly armed. The shocked man tried to back away, but Commodus' questing foot found the man's net and stamped down, pinning it to the sand. Off balance, the net man fell and the emperor's blade was at his neck in a heartbeat, hovering over the kill-point. Then it was withdrawn and Commodus tore the helm off and cast it down to the ground, grinning and complimenting his opponent before reaching down to give him a hand up to the roared delight of the crowd.

He was never truly in danger with the men he fought, though. The gladiators would have been instructed not to inflict harm upon the imperial person, but to test his ability. There were a few inevitable grazes and small cuts, of course, but nothing crippling or life-threatening. Equally, Commodus delivered a few wounds, but stopped short of killing his opponents. These were contests of skill, after all, not executions. Listen to me so calmly describing damage to the imperial person. How inured to such dangerous excess I was becoming.

I watched for days and could not help but be impressed. And when he was observing and not taking part, we were seated together in the pulvinar.

Things were almost back to normal. He had even lost that hint of suspicion, for the most part, when he looked at me, though there was something undefinable still about his eyes. I could not say what it was, but it still made me a little uneasy, though it was not just there for me, it was there even as he drank in the adulation of his public.

I deliberately ignored it. Whatever it was, it was not specifically aimed at me, and so I concentrated on other matters. The wound was almost closed now, and I had to bind it and keep it safe.

Then, one night, Commodus came to my bed.

'I apologise,' he said quietly, 'I have not had time to bathe. I will smell of sweat.'

You smell of death and bloodshed, was what danced through my mind, though I simply smiled and forced that down as I drank in the sight of the gladiator lord of Rome.

'You have astounded everyone. No one can doubt your power, now.'

He nodded. His smile was easy, though I still could not help but note that odd something shadowed in the back of his eyes.

'Let me show you something about power,' he said, oddly, then rolled on top of me, and kissed me. My breath caught in my throat as I took in the great demigod above me.

My Hercules had returned.

XXV

BLACK WITH SORROW, CRIMSON WITH RAGE

Rome, 31 December AD *192*

Life's joys are fleeting.

The wound that had existed in our relationship for a year or more had scabbed over and, foolishly, I took that for fully healed. But a scabbed wound is merely in the *process* of healing. That scab needs time to repair the damage and knit the flesh together. To pick at it merely opens the wound again, sometimes worse than before.

At the closing festival of that last dreadful year I learned as much, to my peril.

I was so overjoyed to have my golden prince back that I did not look closely enough. I had ignored that shadow in his eyes, despite a lifetime of watching for such things, focused solely on what affected me directly. I saw my gleaming Hercules, who was beloved of Rome, and I was so grateful that he was loved, and that he smiled at me, and that he slept in my bed, and that we were together once more, that I continued to ignore that something.

Foolish.

How many times in our lives had I watched him pull on a mask to cover his hollow pain? It had happened every time I had not been there to help repair his melancholia, every time he had dealt with his pain on his own. When I had been there to pick him up, shoulder his burden and lift his spirits into the light, I had managed to bring him back. When I had not, he had suffered long and hard through his pain, donning a visage of calm and contentment while churning like a dark sea within.

For much of a year he had been playing that old masked role without me realising, for we had been so separated by distrust and sadness. So intent was I in healing the rift that I had not noticed what was happening on the far side of it. And then, when I thought it healed, I was so beside myself with relief that I continued blindly failing to realise the danger.

Commodus was in the darkest of places.

I realised only when it was too late. It was the eve of the festival of Janus that would usher in the new year and the whole city – the whole *empire* – was preparing to celebrate one of the most important festivals of the calendar. I myself, a smile plastered across my unseeing face, was contemplating what joys were to come and whether the banquet that loomed on the morrow could be engineered to somehow repair relations with the senate. See how already I was thinking of how to push for change, so blind was I to the danger of the still-healing wound.

I stood in my room, looking back and forth between two stola and palla combinations that lay stretched out on the bed, trying to decide which would look best for the next morning.

The door opened and the emperor walked in. He was unaccompanied, the guards remaining at the outer door of the apartments, all slaves and functionaries busy elsewhere. I turned, smiling, happy, and my heart skipped a beat at what I saw.

Commodus had been crying. Of that I was sure. And because of those red-rimmed eyes, the mask he had been wearing all year had slipped. I could see the chaotic darkness behind it in his tortured eyes. That shadow had consumed his blue gaze altogether.

'Oh, my love,' I breathed and rushed over, holding him.

He stood still, wrapped in my embrace.

'I cannot die, Marcia.'

It seemed such an odd thing to say that I let out a tiny chuckle and released him, stepping back. 'Everyone dies eventually.'

He shook his head. 'As a boy I slammed my head against the wall, trying to dash out my brains. Did you know that?'

Had he? I had seen his torn, clumped scalp, but never something like that. I felt sick as he went on.

'I rode into battle against the Marcomanni. Father forbade me from taking an active part, but I did. I fought like a lion. I was in the midst of a hundred men who wanted nothing more than to separate my head from my shoulders, yet it was I who came home with a king's skull on my saddle.'

I shivered as he grasped me by the shoulders.

'I have lived amid a plague that killed two thousand a day. A plague that killed my uncle. That probably weakened or even killed my father in the end. Nothing. At the villa of the Quintilii I fought with sharp blades against trained killers. I gave the order not to hold back, and I don't believe they did. But I walked away untouched.'

Horror and realisation settled into me.

'The Plebeian Games . . .' I whispered.

He nodded. 'I fought men and beasts, and I never once told them to give less than their all. I dared the gods to take me, but they will not. I cannot die.'

I stared. 'You *want* to?'

'Sometimes,' he admitted quietly, then sat on the edge of the bed amid my neatly laid out clothes. 'Sometimes it seems the only answer. Everyone I love is dead.'

Everyone? That should have warned me if nothing else, but I was focused on the immediate problem now. I needed to pull him out of this, and fast. This was dangerous ground.

'Put aside such thoughts, my love. It is festival time. A time for joy and feasts. Tomorrow will be the great banquet in honour of the new consuls. Help me choose my outfit. Or would you rather I came as Minerva? Or an Amazon?'

He shook his head, unwavering from his darkness. 'I will not be here tonight. I am going away for the evening.'

I frowned, worry settling into me. 'Going where?'

'To the barracks of my gladiators. I will sleep among their number.'

'Gladiators? Why?'

'Because I have need of them on the morrow. I shall leave my lictors in the palace. There is no place for them in what I must do. This will be achieved through blood rather than law.'

A chill ran through me. 'What must you do? What do you plan?'

'I shall attend the banquet for the two new consuls.'

'Of course. And my outfit—'

He shook his head, cutting me off. 'I will not be going there from the palace as an emperor or as a god. I shall be going there from the gladiator barracks as a killer. And I shall bring my fellow killers with me. I have one last show to put on during the banquet.'

I felt an odd tinge of relief. 'The consuls will like that. You do Clarus and Falco unexpected honour by selecting them for the consulate, and to put on a show for them . . .' Clarus and Falco had, after all, been two of his most outspoken critics. The fact that he had made them consul at all had surprised me.

'You misunderstand, Marcia. They are *part* of the show. The show is for the other senators present.'

Another shiver. 'I don't understand.'

'Clarus and Falco have to die, Marcia.'

'What?'

'Clarus has been openly speaking against me. He accuses me of bleeding the senate dry and lavishing everything on the plebs. He attacks my reputation. He sullies my name.'

In fact, everything Clarus had said was little more than plain truth, though he had certainly taken the bit between his teeth and made sport with it all.

'He can be punished in other ways,' I tried.

'No. Clarus must die. I have built a new world, a new Rome, and Commodus Hercules is glorious. Beloved by the people. I cannot have that endangered by one bitter old rich man who is too spoiled to see how I have been lenient with his class thus far.'

'No. You can't.'

His eyes hardened. 'Think hard before you attempt to impose commands upon me, Marcia. Falco is behind the destruction of my statues. The frumentarii have been at work and they have unpicked the web of my opponents. Falco is even the man behind the defacing of the colossus. Falco must die too. That is why I offered he and Clarus the consulate.'

'I just don't understand,' I stuttered.

'I wanted them on a pedestal, because there they are most visible and have the furthest to fall. And I want it in public. In front of the senators. It needs to be open and clear. They will die for treachery against their emperor, and the message will be clear to the senate. They need to understand. A knife in the dark for the pair would remove them, but it would not prevent others taking up their treasonous standard and rallying to it. I need the senate to understand what it means to oppose their emperor. I will start the first year of my new empire with a sacrifice for Janus. Two heads for the two-faced god.'

I shuddered. I had known for months that the situation with the senate was going to explode. I had been grateful that Commodus was no longer under the influence of Cleander and that he could perhaps be persuaded to handling the situation carefully. But I had forgotten that I could no longer be that influence, and Eclectus, trusted though he was, did not have enough of a voice to change an emperor's mind. I had not counted on the fact that, unseen by me, Commodus had slipped into the darkest of moods. The combination was appalling, given the timing. An angry, tortured man, seemingly beset by suicidal thoughts, dealing with men who had openly challenged and insulted him? What chance did they stand?

'You can't kill them,' I said desperately.

'Watch me. They have had leniency for too long. Now they take advantage. Cleander once advocated butchering the whole lot of them. Clearing out the senate and disbanding them. I almost let him – perhaps I should have done – but I will not be the man to kill Rome's government entire. I shall, however, take my two most bitter opponents and make an example of them to send out my message.'

I shook my head. 'It will only provoke more reaction. It will not heal the problem. It will make it worse.'

He flashed that look at me again, hard-eyed. 'I warned you not to command me, Marcia. I will not have it.'

Lord, but I had to do something. If he marched out into the banquet tomorrow with blades in hand and gladiators at his back and butchered two of Rome's highest nobles in cold blood in front of a horrified banquet of people? Even Commodus' great reputation could not withstand what that would do.

'Forget the senate,' I urged him. 'You have the army. The people love you. Even the Christians praise you and they have never approved of an emperor before. What does the senate matter? They are just bureaucrats. Please, Commodus. Don't do this.'

His hard eyes narrowed. 'I *will* have my golden age, Marcia, and I will not allow its sheen to be dulled by the tarnish of the senate. They have to live in my new world, yet they resist. How can I have a new age when bitter men cling to the old? Be grateful I plan to do this with just two deaths. Remember that Cleander would have had the lot.'

I shivered again.

'You *can't*,' I pleaded. 'This won't knock the senate into

line. It will just turn them further from you. And your beloved people will see you killing men for nothing more than speaking against you. You cannot do this. You *must* not do this.'

He slapped me.

I staggered back in shock. I had been hit by no man since Quadratus. And I would never have expected it from Commodus. His slap left a sting on my cheek and a throbbing in the flesh. I stared in horror, even as I realised what I had done.

I had torn off that scab and the wound had begun to bleed once more. Half a year of careful behaviour, reconstructing his trust, all lost in one encounter, for I had tried to change his decision. I shook my head, unwilling to believe what I had done.

'I did not mean to . . . I didn't . . . I just . . .'

He looked at me, and I recoiled from what I now saw in those eyes. 'You play me like a piece in a game, woman. I had begun to believe my mistrust unfounded. That perhaps I was being unfair. That Bruttia and Cleander had got you wrong. But no, they were absolutely correct about you. And I was fooling myself that you had changed. You will never change.'

'My love—'

Desperate. And I sounded it.

'Silence,' he snapped. 'You and Eclectus. Always trying to push me. To direct me. He's nearly as bad, but you . . . After all this time I come to you in a moment of need, and instead of helping me, supporting me, healing me, you refuse me. You push me. You *command* me.'

'I didn't mean to . . .' I reached up, imploringly with both arms. I had opened that wound and now it bled worse than ever, a torrent of dark life.

'No,' he said in a voice cold as ice. 'No. You will never control me again. *Nobody* will. And when I have made an example of those two vile hypocrites tomorrow, I shall need to make a few more examples, I think. Rome will have its new age, even if I have to construct it on the bodies of the old.'

He threw one last furious look at me, spun on his heel and stormed out of my room.

What had I done?

After everything I had worked for, I had ruined it all for the sake of two men I didn't even like. I had denied Commodus, and he had pulled down that mask once more over a soul no longer black with sorrow, but crimson with rage.

God help the world on the morrow.

XXVI

THE GLORIOUS HERCULES

Rome, 31 December AD *192*

Commodus had stormed from my room, but he did not go straight to the gladiator barracks as he had planned. Instead, enraged and bellowing threats, he retreated to his own apartments in the palace. I was beside myself. I had no idea what to do. I had clearly killed off whatever remained between us. I could not see Commodus ever coming to me again, ever trusting me. Perhaps he was right not to. But equally, what I had seen in him just then showed me how much he had changed in those months of wearing his mask and playing to the crowd. This was not the Commodus I had nurtured. This was a different Commodus entirely, transformed from my childhood friend, given to melancholia, into Cleander's monster of manic danger and heights of extravagance. A creature of violence and raw, unchecked emotion. I was not sure I would even want that man.

My Commodus had gone.

Still, even if it was almost certainly over, I did not want there to remain such a gulf between us, and despite the danger, I still had it in mind to try once more, carefully, to persuade him from the course of his murderous plan. I went to his rooms, only to find that even inside the apartment he was guarded by his gladiators, as though perhaps I might come after him with a blade in his own room.

I discovered that he had only briefly visited his apartment before heading to the private baths. I could picture him there, seething in his rage and drinking more than was good for him. I enquired as to whether he had taken wine and water with him. Yes, a single jug of wine, but he had sent to the kitchens for another.

I shivered. He was currently sober and angry, and look what he had planned. What might he decide upon when *drunk* and angry?

Resolved that I would withstand his anger and even a beating if need be, I went to the baths to reason with him, only to find my way barred. Narcissus stood at the door and refused me access. The emperor wished to be alone. Briefly I considered trying to persuade Narcissus to admit me – he had known me as long as he had known Commodus, after all – but I knew it to be a futile notion. For Narcissus I had ever been a peripheral figure, while the emperor had been his patron, his student, even his friend.

I fumed impotently. If Commodus went on unchecked, the new consuls would die in the morning in a most unpleasant and very public manner, and with them would die the reputation of Commodus the golden. He would be seen as a tyrant, at best. I had to stop him, for them and for himself. For Rome, in fact. But how could I persuade him from his path if that hulking wrestler would not let me see him?

It irked me further when a slave boy appeared, carrying a tray of small snacks, and Narcissus permitted him access. I tried to follow the boy, but my way was barred again. I retreated to the outer corridor to think. I should go and see Eclectus. Commodus had spoken of the chamberlain in the same breath and the same tone as myself. He was an ally of mine and clearly still so. Perhaps he would have a better idea of what to do, though it had sounded during the emperor's rant as though Eclectus had made himself unpopular in the same way as I. Perhaps together we might stand a chance?

Still I dithered out there in the corridor.

With a huff of irritation, I turned to have a last go at passing the gladiator on the door, but as I made to leave the vestibule and enter the bathhouse area once more, I walked straight into that slave boy on his return journey. He bounced from me and fell, his burden clattering away across the floor. I felt sorry for the lad. None of this was his fault. As he rubbed the bump on his head he had received from the marble floor, I collected up the item he had dropped.

It was a wax writing tablet of a very common sort in the palace, made of linden wood and tied with a leather thong. Such a mundane thing. When it hit the ground, the tie had come undone and I picked it up, turning it over, ready to close it once more.

I stopped. Quite by chance, I had automatically read the top line.

My heart fluttered.

The top line was my name, inscribed in Commodus' own handwriting that I knew so well.

My name!

The boy struggled up, dazed, shaking his head, apologising profusely for his clumsiness. I barely heard him. My name topped a list. Below it was Eclectus'. Warnings began to sound in my mind.

Marcia
Eclectus
Laetus
Pompeianus

The list went on, and my shrewd brain formed the link instantly with each new name. They were all those who argued with Commodus, who tried to steer him, even down to Pompeianus, who had been his father's confidante and who had tried to persuade

442

the young emperor against abandoning the Danubius war. And Laetus who, though I knew not of any argument he'd had with the emperor, had been made Praetorian prefect purely on the advice of Eclectus, with whom he was close friends.

We were all opponents of one sort or another. Even me.

I hardly dared believe what this meant. But in truth I knew even before I had the confirmation. There were few reasons for such a list, and only one blatant one.

'Who are you to deliver this to?' I asked, closing the tablet and clutching it tight.

'Centurion Adrastus, Domina.'

My already chilled blood froze at the confirmation I had dreaded. That particular centurion of the Praetorians had a name that was synonymous with death. Adrastus was the man in charge of the execution of those proscribed by imperial order. He and his soldiers were the men who took the blade to the neck of traitors and enemies of the state. They were the men who would cast a body down the Gemonian Stairs to be torn to pieces by the public.

It was a list of proscriptions.

A death list.

And my name topped it.

Oddly, it was not panic that gripped me. I was past panic. It was a sad mixture of disappointment and resolve. I would not die. I might not be able to save the consuls from the emperor's blades, but I would damn well make sure this list did not become a reality. I contemplated simply erasing the list and discarding the tablet. Perhaps that would be enough? Maybe in the morning the emperor's anger would have abated and he would have second thoughts about his proscriptions. It was possible.

But it was a dreadful gamble. If he did not change his mind and it came to light that I had waylaid his list . . . well, in Antonine Rome there are worse fates than the edge of a blade.

Cleander had made that clear with all his proscriptions, some of which had resulted in ten days of blood-curdling screams from the Palatine's cellars before a man was allowed the blessing of death.

No. I would not die. I had to find Eclectus. He might have an answer, and at the very least he deserved to know that he too was on the list.

'I will deliver this to the centurion,' I told the slave. He looked uncertain for a moment, but he had no idea what the thing was. He was only young and almost certainly could not read, and slaves did not generally refuse someone in my position. He bowed and left me with the tablet.

The chamberlain was easy to find. As I entered his office and he turned to look up at me from his desk, I noticed for the first time the darkness around his eyes. Eclectus looked nervous and tired. He had not been sleeping – I knew the signs well enough. I thought back on Commodus' words. Yes, Eclectus *had* been arguing with him. I should have seen the direction the man was headed that day by the colossus when I first lost Commodus. That day Eclectus had confided in me his opinion that the emperor was going too far.

We had both been trying to steer him and, instead, we had both steered ourselves onto that list.

'Marcia?'

Without a word, I walked over and slapped the tablet down on his desk, open and with the text visible. I stepped back as Eclectus frowned at the list. Then his eyes widened and he looked up at me again.

'Is this . . . ?'

I nodded.

'How did you come by it?'

'Through chance entirely. It was bound for Adrastus.'

He shook his head. 'I knew he was angry with me, but I had never dreamed of this.'

I tapped my name on the list. 'I fear he has been teetering on the edge for some time, but an hour or so ago I may have pushed him over it.'

'What do we do?'

I shrugged. 'I was hoping you would have an answer to that. I considered just losing the list and hoping.'

Eclectus shook his head again. 'No. That is no solution. If we wish to see another sunset we need to stop these proscriptions.'

'I cannot persuade him. I know that now. Nor, I doubt, can you.'

'No one on this list can. That's why they are on the list,' he noted, rather astutely. 'But we are just courtiers. I am not used to encountering such problems. Last time I was in danger, from Cleander, I retired and removed myself before I ended up on such a list. This time it's too late for that. Laetus will know what to do. Come on.'

And so we hurried off through the palace, Eclectus clutching the tablet tight. The Praetorian prefect divided his time roughly evenly between his headquarters at the Praetorian fortress on the Esquiline Hill and his office in the palace. With all the upcoming events of the new year, Laetus would be on the Palatine, and it was at his office that we arrived, breathless, a short while later.

Laetus greeted the news with a lot more stoic calmness than either I or Eclectus had. I admit that I had not got to know Laetus as well as I could have. Though we had become acquainted during the dark days of Cleander's zenith, once he had become commander of the Praetorians we had had little to do with one another. Peril makes strange bedfellows, though. Here we were now, a mistress, a soldier and a bureaucrat, huddled together and facing death.

'There comes a time in any confrontation,' the prefect said in a quiet, oddly menacing tone, 'when it comes down to a simple choice.'

Eclectus nodded bleakly, but I, despite being bright, had not yet grasped his meaning.

'What choice?'

'Them or us,' replied Laetus. 'Every soldier is familiar with it. You can talk about grand strategies and ambushes, pincer movements and deployments, but every man of arms knows that in the end, when death looms, it always comes down to them or you. A simple choice.'

Now I suddenly realised what he was saying. *God, no!*

'Not that!'

Laetus nodded. 'The emperor has made known his displeasure with me increasingly these past few months. I have been half expecting this, and I have been as loyal to Commodus as any man could. But I am no martyr. I have no intention of kneeling and waiting for the blade just through loyalty to a man who has cast me aside because he does not like to be argued with.'

'Agreed,' Eclectus added.

'No.' This was ridiculous. Two hours ago I had been trying to decide what outfit to wear for a feast tomorrow, knowing that my love would be with me. Now I was in the office of the Praetorian prefect calmly discussing the murder of the legitimate emperor of Rome, a man I had loved since childhood and had nurtured, guided and protected all his life, even when he turned away from me.

'It has to be,' Laetus said flatly. 'Can you not see? You said you could find no solution and neither could Eclectus. That is why you came to me, and I present you with a solution. The *only* solution.'

The chamberlain shuddered. 'But even if we contemplate such a thing, and I am loath to do so even if my own life hangs in the balance, how could we achieve it? Lucilla plotted for a year with a group of powerful and well-placed conspirators, and all it took was one mistake and an alert Praetorian and the whole thing failed.'

'We do not make the same mistake,' the prefect replied. 'The best plans are simple and small. A good strategy does not require an extended army of conspirators and a carefully constructed timeline. A good plan is basic and focused, with as few people involved as possible.'

I shivered. 'You speak as though you've done this before?'

He fixed me with a withering look. 'Was it not you, Marcia, who came to me when I was a centurion in the Guard and enlisted me in a conspiracy against Cleander? Men went to the sword for the failure of one plan. Not I, though. I stayed careful and hidden. I will not make mistakes. And I have, in truth, given thought as to how it could be done, given the likelihood of just such a list as this appearing with my name on it.'

God, but he was prepared.

'Tell us,' breathed Eclectus.

'It has to be quick. If he lasts until morning then we die. For the best results it should be subtle and hard to discern cause and origin of death. I had thought myself poorly placed for carrying out such an act in private, though there are occasional times when I am with him alone. I could slip in a knife when the opportunity next arises, but we do not have time for that. He plans to sleep in the gladiator barracks tonight, I understand, and gladiators guard him now. I would be dead before I had a chance to be alone with him. Eclectus, you have almost unparalleled access to him?'

The chamberlain shook his head. 'Not any more. He is not interested in my views. I am on the list, remember. I doubt I will get past the guards on his door. Marcia?'

I stared back and forth between the two of them. 'No.'

'Marcia, harden yourself,' Eclectus whispered. 'Us or him, remember? We do not contemplate this on a whim. If we do not act, then tomorrow we all die.'

I shivered. I could not admit the truth of that. I shook my head. I could not do such a thing. Would not. 'I cannot get to him, anyway,' I said. 'I already tried. The wrestler Narcissus guards his door. He will not admit anyone. Except the slaves, of course.'

'We cannot trust a slave to do it,' Laetus said. 'Perhaps we could do something when he leaves his baths?'

'Surrounded by gladiators?' Eclectus sighed.

'No,' Laetus answered, chewing on his lip.

I shivered still. 'I cannot be a part of it. I am a Christian.' What a pathetic excuse. Had I been such a Christian when I engineered Cleander's downfall? When I fed silphium to the empress? And the way the two men shot knowing looks at me suggested that neither of them were buying that idea.

'Would you die for him?' Laetus said bluntly. 'For that is plainly the price of refusal.'

Hesitantly, I nodded, but found that even as I tried to nod, my head was shaking. Was I not willing to die for him? That came as something of a revelation to me. But the fact was that the more I thought about it, the more I knew that the Commodus for whom I'd have died, who I lifted from dreadful misery and who I'd loved even as a girl, was gone. How long had it been now since I had seen that innocent golden prince? A year? Two years? Five? Even when I thought we had healed and become close, the signs had been there that he was not the same man. In our early days when we had made love, his fingers had traced designs on my skin. He had put me at ease and whispered of love. But now? The last time he had come to me, he had lain atop me and promised to show me something about power. I shivered now, thinking back on it. He had been lost to me the moment Bruttia poured her poison into his ear.

'Poison,' I repeated, this time out loud, and then clamped my mouth closed in shock.

'Go on,' urged Laetus, leaning forward and steepling his fingers.

I shook my head, but my mind was already working, despite my shock. I had once managed to poison the empress in these very halls with silphium, had I not? It was surprisingly easy for someone who knew the ways of the palace kitchen. At banquets and meals there were tasters to overcome, but when Commodus was alone in the baths . . .

'Wine.' God, but why did I say *that* out loud?

'What?'

Let me show you something about power.

'He's on a wine-drinking spree. He is in a rage and a foul mood, and he is drinking. He sent for a jug of wine from the kitchens and when I arrived at the baths I saw a discarded jar near the door.' My mouth and mind seemed to have decided on a course without consulting my heart first.

'But the wine will already have left the kitchens and be with him.'

'*That* jar, but the jars of wine that he gets are small ones, since they're carried through the palace by the slave boys. If he is truly engaged in drinking as I think he is, then there will be more. He will call for more wine. Poison in the jar will get past Narcissus and into the emperor unnoticed.'

God, forgive me, but try as I might to fight the facts, the simple, selfish truth was that I did not want to die.

'How do we get the poison in the jar?' Laetus mused.

'The jars are taken from stores cold, stacked in a small area of the kitchens where they are opened as required and warmed if needed. From there, they are distributed. Commodus favours Caecuban if possible, and the jars of that wine in the corner of the kitchens will be bound for him. Deal with the first open jug and it will be in the emperor in less than an hour.'

I shuddered again. What was I saying? Was I really considering this? But I could not rid myself of images of that executioner's blade falling. The quick death of the Aegyptian governor. The much, much slower and more agonising one of

Quadratus. How sharp would the blade be for me? No. I did not want to die.

'You sound as though you know the system and the kitchens,' the prefect said. 'If I get you the poison, can you get it into the wine?'

'No,' I replied decisively. There had to be limits. Even if I settled on the fact that I was willing to lose Commodus to save my own neck, I could not be the one to do it.

Laetus' eyes narrowed. 'I did not ask if you *would*. I asked if you *could*.'

Though I was shaking my head, I said, 'It would be *possible*, yes.'

'Then you must do it.'

'No.'

Eclectus suddenly grasped my arms and gripped them tight. 'Listen, Marcia. Tomorrow we all die. And Pompeianus. And Pertinax. And Falco. And Clarus. And half a tablet full of other names, none of whom deserve a blade simply for having an opinion. You cannot condemn us all for the life of a man who would execute you on a whim.'

I was still shaking my head. I did not want to die. But I had never killed. I might be corrupt and dark, but I had never taken a life myself. 'He is my love. My prince.'

'He will be your *murderer*, Marcia. Can you not see? He does not love you. Maybe he once did, but something in him has soured. He has gone too far and now he would kill everyone who might stop him going further.' He shook me. 'He ... does ... *not* ... love ... you.'

I pulled away, trying to tear myself from his grip, and stopped in shock as Laetus slapped me. I had a sudden memory of Commodus doing the same mere hours ago. *Let me show you something about power.* They were right: he did not love me. In fact, quite possibly he hated me now. And I would never be with him again, even if I lived. Commodus was gone, and only

Hercules remained now. I had an odd, cancerous knot forming deep inside. An old, familiar feeling. One that had already led me to do dreadful things in my time.

'What poison would we use?'

I could see the relief wash over the two men like a wave.

'You don't need to know that. Meet me in the Griffin room as soon as you can. Now go.'

Eclectus and I left. Neither of us spoke. We had committed to the most appalling plan, and I felt torn and ruined by the knowledge that I hated the very idea of what I proposed, and yet knew that it must happen, lest we all die.

A quarter of an hour later I was in that very room, close to the kitchens, waiting. Eclectus had gone but would meet me near the baths shortly. Laetus appeared silently, with a dour expression. He passed me a small phial of something. I made to uncork and sniff it, but he put his hand over the top and shook his head. 'It has a distinctive smell. It should go unnoticed in a kitchen full of food smells, but here it would linger dangerously. Find the jug, add the phial, and we are done.'

I took it, feeling the tremendous weight of such a small thing, for this tiny vessel carried death for a man, and damnation for me. I held it as though it were a blade.

'Meet me in the vestibule near the baths,' he said. 'I will wait with Eclectus.'

I nodded and watched him go. Uncharitably, I mused that they were distancing themselves from me should anything go wrong and I get caught. Sensible, really.

The job was ever so easily done. I had not been here in years, since my days of silphium and noon meals, but I knew the kitchens, and I knew what I was about. Holding my breath and pausing as I entered, I cast up to Heaven a plea. 'God, if this is wrong, stop me. Stay my hand somehow.' But either God sought the emperor's death in his ineffable plan, or my god is no more real than that gilded Greek the emperor emulated, for nothing happened to stop me. It took only moments to find the wine that would next be taken to the emperor and to tip the phial in and give it a swift shake to mix it all up. Laetus had been correct. The smell was acrid, but soon lost, dissipated among the heady odour of spices and wines.

I replaced the jug and stoppered the bottle, dropping it into a box of used jars and jugs awaiting disposal. I turned to leave and found a kitchen slave standing in the doorway. She was perhaps seven or eight years old, pretty in a bland way, pale and reedy, and she was inscrutable. Slaves often are. In order to prevent themselves drawing the ire of their masters, they cultivate a permanent, safe blank expression.

Had she seen? What did she know? What did she think?

My heart thundered and my mind raced. I had just committed to killing a man I had loved. Perhaps in an odd way still did. What price a slave girl, then? I was no wilting flower, stronger than I looked by far. It would not be beyond my ability to silence her, and quickly. But there are depths to which even I will not stoop. I took a deep breath and walked away. I glanced for a moment over my shoulder to see her approaching the wine jugs.

I would not kill a slave girl. I had done what I could, and now it was in God's hands. Quaking with fear and horror at what I had done, I joined my two fellow conspirators in the hallway swiftly.

'It is done?'

'It is.' *Unless God had other ideas and the slave girl threw the wine away.*

'Then we wait.'

I still could not truly believe I was part of this. As we stood in conspiratorial silence, alone, waiting for the fatal wine to be delivered, I was battered by unwanted images. That golden boy I had first known. The wooden sword fight in the garden. The horror at Fulvus' death. The melancholia I had discovered, and

452

my joy at finding a way to counter it. Distress at the appearance of Bruttia, and my joy at her departure – that in itself carried acrid self-loathing. I had wondered briefly how I could now find myself part of such a despicable plan, but other images were scattered among those of my golden prince that told a darker tale. A curse tablet. A bowl of silphium. A web of conspiracy. I was a ghastly creature, in truth. A harbinger of death. I had always liked to think my motives good, even when my actions were evil. But there was no denying it. Perhaps this was what I was really born for. To kill.

I was pondering such awful things as that slave girl scurried past, apologising to us, the tainted wine jug in hand. Had she not known? Or had she known and yet said nothing?

I realised I was holding my breath. What had I done?

I started to follow the girl, fully meaning to stop her, and Eclectus and Laetus were at my shoulders, but as I burst into the antechamber outside the baths, the slave was already disappearing inside with the jug.

My heart raced, pumping cold self-loathing around me.

It was done. To try and stop it now would require persuading Narcissus on the door, and he would need to know why. That way lay all our deaths anyway, I was sure.

We came to a halt, me shivering and sick to the stomach. Narcissus gave us a passing glance. He was not the most imaginative of men and it probably did not occur to him to wonder why three so disparate people might be found together here of all places.

We stood in the weirdest uncomfortable silence for perhaps half an hour. The slave girl had not emerged. I was beginning to feel panic clawing at me. What had happened? Was he dead?

Then suddenly a voice called out from the baths.

'Come quick. The emperor is ill.'

Narcissus gave us one quick look. 'Stay here,' he said firmly, turned and ran inside the baths, letting the door close. I was there before it shut, thrusting in my hand to stop it.

I pushed open the portal and could see only the *apody-terium* – the changing room. Exchanging glances with the other two, I hurried inside, followed by the prefect and the chamberlain. Shouts and the most appalling noises were coming from the warm bath room. We made our way over to it, with me in the lead. I stopped at the corner and we peered inside.

Commodus was naked, on his knees, vomiting copiously. The floor was already covered in his mess, and he was wracked with spasms as he gagged and coughed up more and more. Most of what emerged was a deep purple liquid, coated with froth, indicative that he'd eaten very little but drunk a lot of wine.

'It is done,' whispered Eclectus at my shoulder in a hoarse tone. I felt hollow. Dead inside. I watched as Commodus retched up more and more, but Laetus cleared his throat.

'He lives,' he whispered in reply.

'What?'

'The poison should not make him vomit. He should by now be shaking and twitching as his limbs lose feeling. He should be dying fast from the inside out. This is not the poison.'

'But he has drunk from the jug,' Eclectus pointed. I shivered, realising what had happened.

'He drank the wine, but he is ill from overindulgence. He has vomited it all up.'

'And the poison with it,' hissed Laetus.

I felt the oddest thing. Relief flooded through me. I had not poisoned the emperor after all. Commodus would live. God's plan had not called for murder. Perhaps I had even saved him by poisoning him, in an odd way. He would live.

And I would die.

Selfish voices began to beg me from within once more, eroding my thankfulness, shattering my sudden peace. I would die. These men would die. The consuls would die. Noble old Pompeianus would die. So many people would die.

The slave girl was attending the emperor, and Commodus, irritable, waved his wrestler away. 'Go. I'm only sick, you idiot.'

Narcissus turned and made for the door at a slow pace. I had already backed out, pushing the other two ahead of me. We were in the changing room once more, but while I made to leave altogether, Eclectus grabbed my arm. 'We still have to do something.'

'No.' I was vehement now. 'I tried. I cannot do it again.'

And I couldn't. I had been wicked and vicious and had challenged God to stop it. He had done so. Divine providence had thwarted my attempt. I would not defy both God and my feelings and try again.

'We *have* to,' hissed Eclectus, and I spun to him, but my eyes fell on Laetus as I did so and I stared.

Before Narcissus ambled back in, and while Eclectus and I struggled, the Praetorian commander had produced the wax tablet from somewhere and was scratching something into the list hurriedly. He snapped it shut just as the wrestler reappeared.

'I told you to wait outside,' the big man rumbled.

'Do you know who I am?' Laetus demanded.

Narcissus' brow creased as I stopped struggling in the chamberlain's grip. What was happening now? 'You are the Praetorian prefect,' the big wrestler answered.

'And do you know what *this* is?' Laetus pressed, holding up the tablet, open so that the man could see it.

'I cannot read.'

'But I know that you recognise your name, for it is on your cell door in the barracks, is it not?'

The big man's brow folded further as he peered at the wax. I shivered, confused. Narcissus' name was not on there. I had

455

seen the whole list. And why *would* it be on there anyway? I realised with cold horror what Laetus had been doing. He had added the wrestler's name to the list.

Narcissus nodded. 'That is me.'

'And this is me,' Laetus replied. 'This is the general Pompeianus. This is the lady Marcia. This is the imperial chamberlain. Do you know what this list is for?'

It took a moment, but I saw stark realisation dawn on Narcissus and his eyes widened.

'Killing. A proscription list.'

'Yes,' Laetus replied. 'The emperor will welcome his new world tomorrow by making a bloodbath of the old.'

'But why me?'

Laetus nodded, and suddenly Eclectus let go of me and stepped forward. 'It surprises you to find your name on it? Then think how we all feel. We who are the leading men of the Roman state. The emperor means to kill us all, man. This is only one list. There are many.'

What an astounding and easily delivered lie. But it made the list of names more convincing, for sure. Other lists might possibly mean more gladiators.

'But me? I am his trainer.'

'The emperor killed a Syrian prince for beating him to a lion,' snarled Laetus. God, but that was a lie and a half. The lies, though, were like arrows, thudding into the wrestler's resolve. 'Two senators, nay consuls, are to die in the morning for disagreeing with him.'

'He has to go, Narcissus,' Eclectus breathed. Still the big man looked unconvinced.

'A thousand sesterces and your freedom,' Laetus said suddenly, changing tack so fast I almost lost the trail. But Laetus knew what he was doing. The wrestler was struggling with the idea of appearing on the list. He was a fighting slave of the emperor's but had sworn loyalty to him. He was conflicted and uncertain. But gold and freedom talk to a slave on a level a free man will never understand.

There was only a moment's pause, and the hulking wrestler nodded.

I stared, wide-eyed.

'No!'

'Marcia, it has to be done.'

Eclectus was holding me again now. I kicked him in the shin and tried to break free, but Laetus was there in front of me, shaking his head. 'Him or us all, Marcia. You know that. You're not in your right mind, but you'll thank us later. You'll understand then, when the panic and confusion are gone.'

'No.' I struggled still. I was strong, and managed to slip from the chamberlain's grip, but there was still Laetus, and he was a soldier, hard and tough. Between them they held me.

'Commodus!' I wailed, hoping somehow to warn him. I could see nothing. 'Commodus! Lucius! Marcus! *Hercules!*' I was beside myself now, screaming and struggling.

Laetus and Eclectus held me tight, but dragged me forward, through the door and into the warm bath room. My heart sank and my stomach lurched. Commodus was in the water of the bath, with Narcissus struggling to hold him. They were a close match, physically, but Commodus was frail right now. Drunk on too much wine and weakened by the vomiting, he would not manage to hold off Narcissus for long.

'Commodus,' I bellowed, tears streaming down my face.

He looked at me then, distracted by my call, and suddenly, despite everything, he was my golden prince again. He was that lost little boy who had seen his family torn away by disease and disaster. The first emperor born to the purple. The god-emperor of Rome. The last Antonine. He was my Commodus, just in that one look, and I knew then that he would never have carried out that list. It had been a moment of rage and he would have

457

changed his mind in the cold light of day. The consuls would still die, but not me.

Not me.

His one look at me sealed his doom, though. I had distracted him and now Narcissus gained the upper hand. He plunged beneath the surface with the emperor and for a moment they were gone, just a churning surface of warm water to show where they had been.

I felt hollow. Lost. I shook uncontrollably.

He burst free again for a moment, above the surface, spluttering and gasping for breath. His hand reached out desperately.

'Em, help me!'

The great brute shape of Narcissus burst upwards then, a bent elbow slamming down onto the emperor's neck and shoulder, snapping the collarbone like a dry stick. Commodus shrieked and disappeared once more, the great wrestler on him.

I threw up, my stomach contents joining those left behind by the emperor close to the pool. I realised suddenly that the slave girl was cowering in the corner in panic, staring at her emperor's murder.

For that was what this was. Men may aggrandise and claim it as saving Rome. As an execution at best, an assassination at the worst. But there was nothing political or noble about this. This was a legitimate emperor being murdered by four conspirators for their own good, and nothing more.

I was sick again.

As I looked up, I saw Commodus for the last time. He emerged from the water, choking, wide-eyed, looking at me. Then he was gone again. I watched that golden hair vanish beneath the water, then the elbow, the forearm, and finally one desperate, pleading hand. And then just ripples.

Eclectus and Laetus let go of me and I fell to my knees weeping, wracked with horror, self-loathing and guilt. I watched Narcissus reappear with a splash and clamber from the bath at the far side, and I hated him then, almost as much as I hated these two, though nowhere near as much as I hated myself.

Commodus appeared then once more, bobbing to the surface, face down, arms and legs outspread as he floated, partially submerged.

I remembered bodies like that from so many years ago, washing up and down the street of the Forum Boarium.

Water.

It is the most unforgiving element, and it has plagued me all my life.

DIS MANIBUS –
TO THE SPIRITS OF THE DEPARTED

Rome, the Palatine, AD 193

I rolled up the letter and slipped it into the scroll case, melting a little wax and sealing the lid with the imperial seal, a last reminder of who I might have been, and one that would see the letter delivered untouched no matter what. Lucius Eclectus, saviour of Rome and killer of emperors, was waiting for me. All he would get was my letter, but that was for the best.

The emperor Lucius Aelius Aurelius Commodus lived for thirty-one years and reigned for twelve of them. He lost his entire family and most of those he loved. And I played my part in his downfall, for my sins. I shall not attempt to be part of this new regime, for my heart died with the emperor. Eclectus has pledged to look after me – he and Laetus both. But I don't really care. Let death come for me. The new emperor, that great general Pertinax who had saved Dacia, is said to be a good man who will carry the empire well.

I do not believe so. Rome had been ravaged by war and disease and conflagration. Commodus had rebuilt it. He had seen the plague off, repaired the city of its fire damage and put an end to war. He had begun a golden age, and while he may have taken it too far, we shall never know whether he could have saved Rome from a decline that I and others can already see coming. For the statues of Hercules are gone. The legions

460

reverted to their old names. The months are back as they were, and corrupt old Rome is corrupt old Rome once more.

They say that Commodus was an enemy of the state. There is a move afoot in the senate to have him damned, and they say Pertinax will back it. My love's name will be erased from the whole empire. His coins will be defaced. His statues will be smashed and melted down.

But there is discontent. The senate may want to erase all signs that my love lived and ruled, but the people adored their golden Hercules, and the army loved him, and neither will be content under any man who replaces him. Now a warmonger general sits on the throne. Peace will not hold for long. There will be more war. More death. More taxes to pay for it all.

They think they have saved Rome from Commodus, those fools in the senate, but what they have done is *damn* Rome. What *we* have done is damn Rome.

What *I* have done is damn Rome.

Our history now descends from an empire of gold to one of iron and rust.

The golden emperor is dead.

The golden age has gone, and shortly so will I when Praetorian blades seek me out. For I am a reminder the world cannot afford, I and those others who knew the real Commodus. I pray that my letter reaches Eclectus in time.

*L*ucius, my dearest man, I beg leave of you now. I have known you for so many years, and you, despite our closeness in many ways, both kind and cruel, have never really known me. That we might be together has only ever been a fiction based upon mutual survival, for you know that in my heart I only ever loved one man, and despite your goodness, it was never you.

Our world has collapsed through our own devices and the chaos to which we gave birth comes to consume us. You know my faith as I know yours. I must away to my confession with a priest and pursue some kind of absolution for all that I have done, and you must seek peace in your own way before they come for us. Please consider this tale my confession to you, and my explanation for how we come to this dreadful place.

I pray that my leaving you will save you the blade's edge. You were the best of us, and you do not deserve what is coming.

Dearest heart, go peacefully into the next world and pray that I can still be saved.

Marcia

*I*t began with a rush of water; terrifying and murderous. It also ended with a rush of water. A choking, deadly torrent, cloying and dreadful. In my life I witnessed a conflagration that tore through the dry kindling houses of Rome, destroying all we held dear and presaging an age of death and destruction. I endured a plague that made dry husks of strong men, ravaged the army more than any barbarian horde, and robbed Rome of the beating heart of its populace. But, for me, nothing matches those killing waves at both beginning and end.

I am Marcia, daughter of Marcia Aurelia Sabinianus, freedwoman seamstress of the emperor Lucius Verus.

I was a bad Christian, but I could have been a great empress.

HISTORICAL NOTE

When I came to write *Caligula*, the first book in this loosely connected series, I attempted to explode the myths surrounding that infamous emperor. What remained for Caligula was mostly tales told by his successors and surviving enemies and is therefore clearly biased, to say the least. In fact, when it comes to such tales as his incest and debauchery and gathering of seashells and the like, there is actually no archaeological or epigraphic evidence to clarify the situation, and so I set about to build an image of a realistic, if changeable, man rather than a monster.

Commodus has led me to face an entirely different challenge. That which is generally attributed to the 'madness' or 'megalomania' of Commodus has left us actual remains to confirm the truth. His identification with Hercules is clearly depicted on coins and statuary of the time. His changing the names of months, legions, etc., has left epigraphic evidence. Therefore what I needed to do with Commodus was not sweep aside the tales entirely (though some are still hard to credit and rather outlandish) but to analyse what the man clearly did do, and try to understand *why* he did it. And in doing so, I formed an impression that was the basis for this book.

Firstly, let us deal with 'madness'. This is a dangerous subject, since it is all too easy to label anyone suffering with mental issues of any kind as 'mad', and in antiquity this is doubly true.

So, looking at Commodus, I wondered first what 'madness' it was that led a golden prince to heights of seeming megalomania and periodic withdrawal from public life and relying upon his freedmen. Odd behaviour. And the first thing I discovered in my research is that megalomania is not an illness. It is a symptom. In fact, many of the terms used throughout history to describe sufferers of such problems are actually symptoms and not causes. The simple fact, you see, is that even in the modern world we are still largely ignorant of the mind and how it works. We still do not understand the causes of problems with it.

With *Commodus*, I researched mental illnesses and conditions to try and identify something that would explain what I saw in him. He was an intelligent man. His father said so, and Aurelius was no fool. He was loved, strong, careful and generally peaceful. He was tolerant of Christians and no lover of warfare. Yet he was given to sudden excesses, such as the almost delusional desire to fight as a gladiator, or the idea of changing the months to reflect his own names. Other times, he was withdrawn from public life, leaving men like Perennis and Cleander to administer the empire, allowing them the kind of power that no other emperor had since the time of Sejanus.

One illness seemed to fit. And the more I read about it, the more it explained Commodus. What used to be called 'manic depression', and is currently 'bipolar disorder' – and there is now a lobby to change to 'multipolar disorder' – seemed to fit. There are, of course, many types of this illness and it affects people to many different degrees, but the root fits. Periods – sometimes days, sometimes many months – of black depression, occasionally even plunging to the depths of suicidal thoughts. Something that makes sufferers withdraw from the world. And other times mania strikes, for some people lightly and just leading them to try new things, for others to the level of all-consuming delusion, leading them to believe they could fly or climb a cloud. Was this not what we were seeing reflected in

Commodus' somewhat erratic behaviour? And between these periodic ups and downs, times of stability that led a person to act completely normally. Often ups and downs are rare, and for most of their life a bipolar person is indistinguishable from anyone else. Once I saw this man as bipolar, it changed everything I read.

As I said above, the cause of mental illness is hard to determine, and bipolar is no exception. One of the suspected causes, though, is trauma. 'But what trauma had Commodus ever suffered?' thought I at the start of my journey. Born to the purple, groomed for power, no wars, no struggle for succession. Then I began to look. In reverse chronological order, from his most stable point, he had lost a close friend (some sources suggest lover), his sister had betrayed him, his father had passed on, his mother had died unexpectedly and, in unfortunate circumstances, his younger brother had died on the operating table, his uncle died, possibly of the plague, and his twin died of unknown causes, though some sort of illness is generally assumed. If the trauma of losing a loved one in bad circumstances might be a trigger for bipolar disorder, then Commodus was at risk even from early childhood.

Once I had my angle, I could start to relate it to the people and events in his life, and things began to fall into place. Commodus was no dangerous lunatic. In fact, Cassius Dio, who is generally disparaging, says of Commodus, 'This man was not naturally wicked, but, on the contrary, as guileless as any man that ever lived' (wording taken from the 1927 Loeb edition). He was a man who spent his reign being encouraged and influenced continually by one character or another, from Perennis to Cleander to Marcia. What Commodus seems to have been was a young man who suffered repeated tragedy that left him, in my opinion, with an illness that manifested itself to the crude witnesses of the time as madness and megalomania.

Many of his deeds appear quite pragmatic and realistic when

placed in context, and if they seem too outlandish, perhaps this is the effect of mania pushing a good idea into the stratosphere. I will come back to these. In the meantime, before I move on to the subject of my narrator and supporting cast, a word about sources.

We have three sources from the ancient world for Commodus. One is the above-mentioned Cassius Dio. His *History* is my second-best go-to source for research. Dio was a member of a distinguished Bithynian family, who likely knew Commodus personally, for he served in the senate during his reign. What must be remembered, when reading his work, is that Commodus and the senate were divided by something of a rift: the emperor's reliance upon freedmen in spite of the nobles of Rome not popular with the senatorial class. At the time of Commodus' death there can have been little love lost between them, and it surprises me that Dio, writing his account much later (it seems to have been finished around 230AD), even lowers himself to being as complimentary about Commodus as he was. He was looking back to events decades earlier in light of subsequent regimes, at a man who had been publicly damned.

Herodian, who is my favoured of the three accounts, wrote his history in the years leading up to 240AD. Similarly, he was witness to Commodus' reign. He was young at the time of Commodus' accession, perhaps ten years old, which means he was only maybe twenty-two when the emperor died. Again, his account was penned decades later through the influence of later regimes. We do not know much about Herodian. He may have been a senator, with the inherent bias that would bring. Or he may have been a freedman. If he was, then he was not one of any serious note, or his name would likely have appeared in texts somewhere. Herodian is not particularly forgiving of Commodus, though he does occasionally favour him with a sparse compliment. Also worth noting is the distinct possibility that Herodian was a citizen of Antioch, the city that had revolted under Cassius and suffered punishment by the Antonines. Bias comes from many directions.

The third source, and by far the least convincing, is the infamous *Historia Augusta*. Penned probably in the fourth or fifth centuries, this account is clearly written looking far back into history. Its author, or authors, repeatedly reference the now lost work of Marius Maximus. So what we are likely dealing with is a reworking of a previous biography. And the *Historia Augusta* can be rather outlandish from time to time; it feels a little as though it was written to shock or impress. As M.C. Bishop says in his book on Lucius Verus, '"fake news" (of which the *Historia Augusta* was a pioneer)'. Maximus himself was a contemporary of Commodus, so probably was a witness to much of what he wrote. But guess what? He was a senator and served in official positions under Commodus. So, once more we hit that same issue of bias.

Sometimes the sources are blatantly opposed to one another, too. On the death of Aurelius, and Commodus' plans for northern peace, Cassius Dio tells us that he imposed his father's terms on them, also demanding the return of captives and deserters and that they make an annual reparation in grain. Herodian tells us, conversely, that he 'sold peace at a huge price' and 'gave them everything they demanded'. This is a prime example of just how untrustworthy primary sources can be. Sometimes the sources are clearly simply trying to shock and poke fun, with precious little grounding in reality. Thus we have the *Historia Augusta* telling us of Commodus having 'a conspicuous growth on his groin that the people of Rome could see the swelling through his silken robes'. I chose for fairly obvious reasons not to make my emperor a 'hunchgroin'.

There are other lesser works that touch on Commodus, but nothing on a biographical scale beyond these three main texts. Quite simply, there is not one entirely trustworthy biographical source on Commodus, yet they are all we have. I have generally built this tale upon events that are either attested in inscription or numismatics, or evidenced by archaeology in some other way, or I have taken stories from the sources where they either agree across the board or at least do not blatantly contradict each other. I shall regale you with some examples here of material I discarded from the *Historia Augusta* and some reasons why.

The *Historia Augusta* notes in the days post-177 that Commodus had a brothel of beauties in the palace, pretended to be a market trader, driving chariots and living with gladiators. Since the latter are seen in other accounts at the end of his reign, it seems likely that this is just filler slotted in the wrong place deliberately to shock. The *Historia Augusta* also tells a different tale of the end of Cleander to our other sources, making its credibility strained.

In fact, the *HA* goes as far as to claim that Commodus worshipped Isis, shaved his head and carried around a statue of Anubis with which he bashed people on the head. Quite apart from the fact that this is not mentioned in any other source, every image that survives from his reign shows him with thick curled hair and a curly beard.

But my favourite from the *Historia Augusta* is, 'For example, he put a starling on the head of one man who, as he noticed, had a few white hairs, resembling worms, among the black, and caused his head to fester through the continual pecking of the bird's beak – the bird, of course, imagining that it was pursuing worms' (1921 Loeb edition). Quite apart from the almost cartoon bizarreness of this image, I cannot picture anyone managing to make a starling stay on someone's head, let alone the bird be stupid enough to mistake worms and hair. Since this is some of the quality we're looking at in that great source, I hope you can forgive me for skipping some of its material.

One scene I did keep from the *Historia Augusta*, and which

is almost certainly as much bilge as the previous paragraph, is the episode in the bathhouse of Centum Cellae, though I have twisted the original account and made it much the fault of Quadratus rather than the emperor himself. Simply, I was looking for a way to introduce Saoterus, who appears about this time and about whose background we know nothing.

Characters, then. I had much trouble with *Caligula* in selecting a narrator who could tell the emperor's tale, who had been there throughout his life as a witness, and who outlived him to tell of the end. There was no such issue with *Commodus*. The answer almost leapt off the page. Marcia was the daughter of one of Verus' freedwoman, therefore she would have been present in court life from an early age. She was the mistress of one of Commodus' cousins, then of the man himself. She had enough influence with him to be instrumental in the death of Cleander and to have the emperor free the Sardinian Christians. Indeed, the Loeb (1921) translation of the *Historia Augusta* tells us directly 'the city of Rome should be renamed Colonia Commodiana. This mad idea, it is said, was inspired in him while listening to the blandishments of Marcia.' Best of all, not only did she outlive him, but she was intimately involved in his death. The opportunity for great sorrow and pathos here was almost too much. She has to have been an interesting, strong, conflicted character. And just as Cleander rose from nothing to become the second most powerful man in Rome, so Marcia, a pleb, was at one point empress in all but name.

Add to this the fact that she appears to have been a Christian, and she becomes truly fascinating. Christianity is still in its relatively early days at this time. It is surviving as an outlandish cult among the traditional gods of Rome. Previous emperors, even good ones, had been cruel to the Christian faith, and it is worth noting that not only was Commodus not cruel, but he seems to have actively been lenient with them. That this could be anything other than Marcia's influence, especially given the Sardinia scene, is too hard to credit.

I should note here that, in Commodus' speech after his father's death I refer to Heaven. Given the nature of this book, with both Christian and pagan viewpoints, this coming from a pagan I thought needed some clarification, since there will be purist readers who will point out that Heaven is a Judaic invention and not part of Roman theology, whose equivalent would be Elysium. I have used the term Heaven as a nebulous term for the good afterlife based on translations of ancient text and for the readers' familiarity. Herodian refers to Heaven in both his explanation of Apotheosis and in his version of that very same Commodian speech. While this is partially down to the translator, I see no reason not to promulgate that term.

Marcia is not noted as having been the one behind Bruttia Crispina's fall, and she may well not have had anything to do with the lack of an heir. That is my own creation. However, to give it some credence, you must note that Bruttia had to have been an obstacle, since the moment she was out of the way Marcia was Commodus'. And there is some suggestion that rather than being infertile, Bruttia miscarried more than once. I simply built on this and linked them together.

Our sources do not note with whom Bruttia was accused of adultery, and the story of Julius Alexander in the sources is a little different. I took only the bones of it. In the source, Alexander kills a lion back in his home of Emesa and Commodus is so jealous that he sends killers to Syria, where Alexander only falls because he stops to help his companion. But even the most jealous of men would surely think twice before sending assassins over half the empire to kill a man for being better at hunting. It did not fit for me, so I brought Alexander close, where we could see his action and, though Commodus feels

474

jealousy over the lion, it is over Bruttia that he sends killers after the man.

I have had Marcia feel deep affection and then love for Commodus from youth, and this being reciprocated. Again, this is my creation, though there is no reason this could not be the case and, in fact, it is certainly more credible than some of the things one comes across in the sources. So I had my emperor and my protagonist together in their youth in the palace. Everything fell into place with a line from Herodian (Echols, 1961): 'As a slave in the imperial household, Cleander grew up with Commodus'. There we had it. We had a villain, too, from the start. Because regardless of how any source treats Commodus, they are universally damning of Cleander. Even Perennis, who gets a bad knock from the *Historia Augusta* and Herodian, gets from Cassius Dio (Loeb, 1927): 'he never strove in the least for either fame or wealth, but lived a most incorruptible and temperate life'. But not Cleander. He was a villain, and about this there can be little doubt.

Cleander, of course, comes off as the main villain, and not Commodus. And, to some smaller extent, Perennis does too. The simple fact is that the sources blame Commodus for the death of many, many, *many* people. They even name quite a lot of them. And yet the sources also generally claim that Commodus liked to live the life of a hedonist, leaving the true running of the state to his equestrian prefects and freedmen. This strikes me as self-contradictory. If you claim that Cleander ran Rome for Commodus, then those men who died in droves almost certainly did so at the behest of the chamberlain. Cleander is easy to villainise. And in making him Marcia's nemesis from the very start, it makes her part in his downfall that bit more realistic and credible. And the fact that his parting words (and those of Bruttia Crispina, her other enemy) essentially sour Commodus towards her at the end seems to fit.

I have, in the course of the first part of the book, also perhaps restored the reputation of Lucius Verus, to whom history has not been universally kind. I had the good fortune, after finishing the manuscript, to acquire a copy of M.C. Bishop's new work, *Lucius Verus and the Roman Defence of the East* (2018), which not only supported my portrayal but in fact provided me with whole new angles to add to the plot during the editing phase. Therefore, I am tremendously grateful to Mike Bishop and his excellent book, and if you have any interest in Verus, I heartily recommend reading it. Incidentally, Bishop does not necessarily accept the plague as being responsible for Verus' death, favouring perhaps a stroke as the culprit. The truth of the matter will almost certainly never be known, but I have gone with the plague, largely because it was simply the biggest killer in the world for these decades and it seems to me unlikely that none of the main cast or extended imperial family fell foul of it at all when so many thousand were carted off each day.

My apologies to Statius Priscus, who happened to be the man whose task it was to oversee the Tiber in the year of the great flood. Perhaps he was effective and useful. Certainly, he had quite an illustrious career, including war with Verus in the east and the governorship of Britain. I deliberately made a pointless patsy of him during the flood. *Mea Culpa*. Incidentally, as an aside, I was astounded to discover how often and how severely the Tiber sometimes flooded. A series of maps I came across indicated that during the worst times, much of the beating heart of ancient Rome – the fora and Subura and Campus Martius – would have been underwater.

Other characters are largely glossed over in this work. Men like Salvius Julianus who appear in the sources numerous times, but only ever in fairly unlikely tales that are generally peripheral, and even with the best will in the world would have added nothing by their inclusion. Such, for instance, is the fate of Motilenus, a Praetorian prefect who somehow appears in

190 with no other reference made to him throughout history other than that he is suddenly there and then isn't because of poisoned figs. A spurious story at best. The Commodus the sources attempt to tell us thought nothing of executing officers and nobility by the swathe sits rather at odds with the same Commodus we are told poisons a prefect he doesn't like with figs. Such is the world of trying to piece together the truth from the tabloid headlines of the day. The emperor's sister, Fadilla, is noted in Herodian as being the one to draw Commodus' attention to Cleander's treachery on the Palatine. Dio has this revelation at a suburban villa, and Marcia being the one. I went with this for clear reasons and thus was Fadilla largely rendered pointless despite being the emperor's eldest surviving sister and having a speaking part in sources. Herodes Atticus' history with the emperor and the brothers Quintilii is fairly fascinating and would make a good scene, but there is little chance of it having happened in front of Commodus, let alone Marcia, and so it has been omitted entirely.

I promised at the start of this note to come back to the more manic side of Commodus, and so here we are. While I have explained his general withdrawal from public life at times as the 'down' of his bipolar, I have made the more glittering and exciting ideas of his an aspect of his occasional mania. This is because, while on the surface the actions of the emperor in his last years might seem megalomaniacal, when one looks at them in the light of bipolar and with a more critical eye, they become a lot more explicable.

It seems crazy to think of changing so many names and identifying with a demigod. But as I've noted time and again in the story, each of these moves has many, many precedents. Nothing he did in that year or two of supposed megalomania was new or outlandish in itself. Each change was something that had been done before. The reason, I think, for the fact that it seems insane is that these many changes all happened at the same time, rather than as occasional individual shifts. It is this sudden move of a grand plan that makes it so noticeable. Again, I have alluded to this in the text, having Marcia trying to slow the process. This is indicative of exactly what I came across in my research into bipolar. With strong bouts of mania, it is not uncommon for a sufferer to grasp an exciting idea and then run with it so far and so fast that they make a good notion entirely unworkable. That is what it seems to me happens here.

The simple fact is that the changes themselves seem to have been quite acceptable at the time. An altar found at Dura Europos set up by one Aelius Tittianus labels his unit as '*II Ulpia Commodiana*'. In his list of the emperor's titles, he includes 'the Roman Hercules'. He uses the date the kalends of Pius – one of Commodus' new month names. If even a minor officer in a distant frontier garrison was clearly comfortable with these new names then that is fairly indicative of a general trend. This altar, which is the only prime piece of epigraphic evidence for this, is the subject of an excellent article called 'Commodus the God-Emperor and the Army' by M. P. Speidel in the *JRA*, 1993. And it is this one piece of evidence that suggests to me there is nothing insane or megalomaniacal about Commodus' new world.

On that same subject, isn't it interesting how the idea of Commodus changing the name of Rome to Colonia Commodiana is considered the height of megalomania and madness, while we accept Constantine renaming Byzantium after himself as a glorious and clever move? The damnation of an emperor casts a shadow over everything he achieved in his life, whether good or bad. The damning of Commodus, in particular, was so brutal that even a panel on his father's triumphal arch (opposite) was reworked to remove the son who was at the reins of the chariot, leaving his father alone in the vehicle with no driver.

I suspect there will be readers who view the Colosseum scene towards the end of this tale as ridiculously overdone and fanciful. Yes, it is. It is also lifted from primary sources and simply retold. In fact, my version of Commodus' exploits in the arena is a shortened version of the ones in the sources, and very much toned down! I have him killing four beasts with javelins, including a bear, and numerous other predators with a bow. Just as an example of how staid my version is by comparison, I will give you examples from the sources of what they say happened:

Cassius Dio: 'On the first day he killed a hundred bears all by himself.'

Herodian: 'when a hundred lions appeared in one group as if from beneath the earth, he killed the entire hundred with exactly one hundred javelins.'

Historia Augusta: 'he once transfixed an elephant with a pole, pierced a gazelle's horn with a spear, and on a thousand occasions dispatched a mighty beast with a single blow.'

Now contemplate the relative realism of my account! And

bear in mind (pun intended) that Commodus' prowess as a hunter is about the only thing that all three sources agree upon.

I will make one last admission. I am also the author of a series of Roman military thrillers by the title of Praetorian. These books also take place during Commodus' reign and in fact intersect at some points with this narrative. I have kept the two separate enough that I've not actually introduced their protagonist, the guardsman Rufinus, into this story. I did nod towards him briefly when Marcia was building her net of allies and included Rufinus, the prefect of the Misenum Fleet. I have endeavoured to make the two stories correlate rather than contradict, such that reading Praetorian will give you a different angle on the same events. Rufinus, for instance, is one of the Praetorians at the theatre when Perennis is first denounced. He is at Lucilla's villa, and the attempt on Commodus' life in the Colosseum. He is also one of the men engineering the downfall of Cleander. The only part where the two accounts truly diverge is at the start, at the death of Marcus Aurelius in Vindobona. This account follows a more recognised direction than that one. Still, I hope that perhaps if you've enjoyed this and are in the mood for a little rollicking action, Praetorian might prove interesting further reading.

As a last note, any mistakes in this book are either deliberate or my own, or both. Hopefully, you leave with a new view of Commodus not quite so informed by the portrayals of Christopher Plummer and Joaquin Phoenix.

Am I not merciful?

Simon Turney
February 2018

ACKNOWLEDGEMENTS

Commodus would still, even after two years, be little more than a disjointed pile of scribblings were it not for several people whose influence have turned it into the novel it is today. People who deserve *more* than just acknowledgement, really.

First as always comes my superb agent Sallyanne Sweeney at MMB Creative, who remains my rock in the literary world, supporting and helping me grow. Without her, and the other amazing men and women at MMB (Zaria, Adrienn, Ivan, Max and Samar in particular) I would not be able to share works such as this with you.

Thanks must go to my amazing editor Craig Lye at Orion, who took the rough first draft of Commodus and went to work like a cosmetic surgeon, cutting and stitching the coarse text and turning it into a thing of beauty. Until I met Craig, I had not appreciated the value and ability of a really good editor. Others at Orion are also deserving of note for their help in this project, including Amber Bates and Jennifer McMenemy.

I must thank all those in the writing and historical community who have supported me in the production of this novel, or whose comments and work have, in fact, helped shape it. One of the prime candidates for this is Mike (M.C.) Bishop, one of the leading authorities on the Roman military and author of many works including a biography of Lucius Verus that helped form the story. In addition to the above mentioned book, I would thank and laud the following: *Dans le Rome des Césars* by Chaillet, Saunders & Owen's *Bipolar Disorder: The ultimate guide* as well as Fiona Cooper at BipolarUK, who steered me to that book, Speidel's *Commodus the God-Emperor and the Army*, the Empire series by Anthony Riches, which covers the same era and people and does so in such style that I had to be careful not to emulate him, and Ridley Scott for making Commodus known to the world in the form of Joaquin Phoenix. Additionally, I have called upon the minds of the members of several online fora, including the excellent Facebook groups 'Friends who like the Romans' and 'Roman Army Talk'. A shout-out is also clearly due to some of my oldest friends and fellow authors in the business whose encouragement makes a vast difference, particularly Gordon Doherty, Prue Batten, Christian Cameron, Kate Quinn and Stephanie Dray.

Finally, there is my wonderful wife Tracey, without whom I would long since have been living like a blubbering hobo, my children Callie and Marcus who keep trying to read the racier parts of the manuscript until I shoo them away, my parents Tony and Jenny and my in-laws, Ken and Sheila, all of whom have been there with love and support throughout.

Thank you. *Commodus* is only a novel because of you.